Location of Love

Location of Love
Copyright   2018/2019
Calvin L Himel

First Printing   September   2018
Second Printing (re-edit)   August   2019

ISBN: 978-0-692-18957-3
ISBN: 978-0-578-55711-3

Location of Love

To all the good and wonderful people on our small planet called earth.

Introduction:

I started out to tell a story, partly from my own life experiences, and part fantasy. I think that I have encompassed some very basic human feeling in this work that may be beneficial to all who read it. I have included some bondage and submissiveness in the characters as they portray and show there human and emotional sides.

I would like to thank my wife, without whom this book would have never come to light, along with several other endeavors in my life as an artist.

I just hope all who read this enjoy it and are enlightened by it. I hope it is as much a delight to you, as it was to me in producing this volume.

Thank You: Calvin L Himel

One

Friday: Day One.

I was sitting in my office reading over the latest listing for clients one Friday evening, when I received a phone call. It was from a woman who wanted to list a couple properties for sale. Oh, pardon me, let me introduce myself. I am Charlie Harcourt, age forty-seven, six foot two, about 190lbs and average in appearance and of mixed parentage and a real-estate broker. I own Harcourt Realty, one of the best real-estate offices in town in my own opinion. I took the call since it came in real late close to five in the evening near my office closing time and all my agents were out on deals or off. Mrs. Bradley my office supervisor was away from her desk as I listened to the woman on the phone. I agreed to see her that evening even though I really wanted to go home and relax, but she seemed a little insistent for some reason. But in this business you don't turn down a listing, no matter when or how it comes, because this is a real competitive business, and since it was only about ten minutes away, I agreed to see her by six that evening. That's how I had grown my office to be one of the best in town. I spent another ten minutes taking care of some paperwork and clearing my desk before heading out. I grabbed my briefcase and placed my laptop inside, and informed Mrs. Bradley I was heading out to a new listing that had just came in. I went to my auto and headed to the location. Before leaving, I did a quick search of the property address to see what area it was in, so then I would have a better idea of what might lie ahead. I would soon find myself being in for a real surprise.

I shortly arrived at the property location and it was a condo. Older, but modern, and the design was quite unusual. I had passed it several times before since it was on a highly traveled main thoroughfare and was seven stories tall above the large enclosed parking area on the ground floor. Circular in its shape, with twin elevators, and was very well maintained. I approached the entrance and entered the hallway after parking on the street in front of the building and easily found my new client's bell, Kashia. I pressed the bell and a woman's voice answered. I announced myself and was promptly bussed in. When she called the office she insisted that I come today. I just couldn't let one slip through my hands especially after she said she had two units she wanted to sell. I pressed the button for the elevator and took it up to the sixth floor. As I exited the elevator I was amazed at how clean and neat the lay out was. There were only five doors, one was marked exit and that I assumed was a stairway. I also assumed there were only four units per floor but it could be different on the other floors as I looked around at 6A, B, C and D. I proceeded to 6B, and knocked on the door. A voice asked who was there. I stated it was Charles Harcourt of Harcourt Realty. The door opened and I was greeted by a very beautiful and stunning woman in her early fifties, very graceful, slim, nice chest, and butt, light brunette hair and she wore it in a bun, light brown eyes, fair skin with an slight olive completion, and about five foot eight in height, she wore a dress that accented her shapely figure, and stopped just above the knee, hi-heels, no stockings, small necklace with teardrop earrings. I could tell she wore no bra by the way her dress fitted with its open v neck that came together just above her stomach and accented her flawless and smooth skin and she also wore a very pleasant fragrant perfume. Her name was Mrs. Sofia Kashia. She welcomed me inside her apartment and asked me to have a seat on her sofa. The apartment was well appointed; the decor was modern, conservative and exceptionally clean. She spoke with a soft sweet voice as she briefly explained to me how she had become a widow about eleven months earlier. She stated this was one of three units in the building she owned with her late husband. He had been killed in a tragic auto accident along with his nephew while coming home after work and after they had stopped and decided on spending the early part of the evening drinking with a few friends. The nephew was driving and thought he could beat the Metro commuter train through the crossing. It didn't end well for either of them as they died instantly. Anyway she felt it was time to relieve herself of the stress and hassle of renting the other two units. Her husband had always taken care of that along with any maintenance that needed to be performed.

She stated that her husband had left her a considerable amount of life insurance and her desire to sell wasn't financially motivated. She just didn't want to be bothered, and had recently purchased a new auto; since her husband and nephew had been killed in their old one. One of the units had been rented to the nephew and his wife, and since his demise it was not producing any positive income. The other one was, but she had decided to sell it also. The third unit was to be vacated at the end of the month, and since this was the middle of the month there wouldn't be any problems. The tenants were starting to move already, they were a young couple and had just purchased a new home. However the second was occupied by the nephew's wife, she worked part time, and was barely earning enough to take care of the utilities. The unit was 6C and was a one bedroom; the second was a two bedroom, one bath and was 5B just one floor down, and was the same size and layout as the unit we were in. She stated that the nephew's wife had no lease and would just have to move. She didn't think much of her and didn't care if she ended up homeless. She had been a subservient to her husband and felt she was nothing but a little tramp and a slut. If I could get her out without any problems she would make it well worth my while. In my mind I wondered what that meant, but it wasn't an issue I was going to press right now and would wait and see what developed.

The units were much larger than I had expected based on the one we were in. She said, we could go next door and I could look around. I said that would be very good, and then I could then take some measurements and that would help me compare it to others in the area. I opened my briefcase and took out my sonic measuring device with laser and a small note pad. I left my brief case and laptop behind, and accompanied her to the unit. Mrs. Kashia removed some keys from the drawer of a beautiful cabinet near the front door, and we then entered the hallway. She was very graceful, a size slightly larger than petite. We went to 6C and she knocked on the door, and just before she was going to place the key in the lock, the door opened. There stood a woman in her mid-forties. I based this on her beautiful features and figure, which was very shapely. She had a nice round posterior, her breast weren't overly large but in proportion to her overall very shapely figure. Her hair was dark brown, almost black hair, loosely combed and wavy, and not to short, and brown eyes, very smooth slightly brownish completion, she wore no jewelry, wearing just a short skirt that just covered her very round ass and a pair of sheer pantyhose and a blouse that tied in front. She stood about five foot ten and she wore a pair of very short heel shoes. She had a really beautiful and pleasant face, a sweet soft voice and had a really beautiful smile. The body language between the two told me they were not especially fond of one another. She was introduced to me as Mrs. Victoria Cook. Mrs. Kashia and I entered the unit. I introduced myself to Mrs. Cook and briefly explained the purpose of my visit. Mrs. Cook immediately acknowledged that she was sorry for the condition the apartment was in, as she stepped to one side. I looked around the apartment and it was exceptionally clean, but very sparsely furnished. Her face seemed really very familiar for some unknown reason and tried to remember where I had seen her before, but concentrated more on what was happening right now as I began looking around. In the living room was a well-worn sofa and matching chair, a rectangular cocktail table and a combination television and video cassette recorder sat on a small end table near the end of the large room. There was a large floor to ceiling picture window and a sliding glass door next to it that led to a nice size balcony. The building was steel and concrete and all the units had a balcony. Then I proceeded to the bed room, it was larger than most I have seen in other one bedroom units, the furnishings were sparse here also. In it was a double bed, and old chest with a small photo of her and a man. I assumed it was her deceased husband. Nearby was an old sturdy wooden chair that showed signs of extreme wear and as I looked there weren't hardly any clothes in the extra-large closet, just a couple of dresses and a pair of worn gym shoes. It was spacious taking up one entire side of the bedroom. Then I checked the bathroom and it was larger than most and exceptionally clean, with only two towel racks, a wide vanity, bathtub and a separate walk-in shower, there was only one face cloth, towel and a toothbrush visible. I then proceeded to the kitchen area, it was very spacious also and very clean; it had a large window and was a combination dining room and kitchen, the cabinets were real wood, and very well maintained and had recently been polished. I looked inside the kitchen cabinets to check the condition and found they were almost completely empty; barren would be a better term. I took my measurements as I went from room to room and did my inspection and writing down the measurements. I was soon asked by Mrs. Cook if I could find her a place. I stated that once I had finished my discussions with Mrs. Kashia, I would come back and speak with her before I left today. I spoke to Mrs. Kashia and said that I had finished looking and taking the necessary measurements and would need to run some comparisons before I gave her a reasonable selling price.

I thanked Mrs. Cook for the opportunity to look around her unit. Then Mrs. Kashia and I returned to her unit. Again I sat on the couch and this time Mrs. Kashia decided to sit next to me. I took out a listing form and began to filling it out. I explained to her that I would check with the RELS (Real Estate Listing Service) to compare all the properties that were very similar to hers in the surrounding area. I also stated; that I would not be able to give her a price, until I could do some comparisons for similar properties and also it would be better not to list the units until Mrs. Cook had moved out and then we could get both units painted, the carpets cleaned, and an overall sprucing up and this would help in selling them so much faster. Explained I had a service that would take care of all that was needed for a minimum amount. I would return with the necessary paper work tomorrow for her to sign and with an asking price based on the current market. I asked if she could arrange for me to see the other unit she wanted to sell. She agreed and said that would be fine, and maybe we could have both units cleaned together. Stated that she wanted me to sell both, and was very happy that I had come on such short notice. I thanked her, and stated I would see her early tomorrow. She asked that I keep in close contact with her about the status of both units. I said that I would indeed as I stood and thanked her again and said that I was going next door and see what could be done for Mrs. Cook. She stated that she hopped I could soon get her to move and said again that it would be very rewarding if I did so. I picked up my briefcase and laptop as she walked me to the door and thanked me. I thanked her for having considered doing business with my office.

I knocked on the door of 6C and Mrs. Cook immediately opened it. I walked in a few feet and turned around in her direction and watched her as she closed the door. She asked me to have a seat on the sofa, as she sat in the large worn out chair. I told her that finding apartments was not my main business, but I had a leasing agent in my office and I would check with him and see what was available. She had a very anguished look on her face and was looking very despondent, almost desperate. I asked if everything was all right, and what seemed to be of concern to her. She went on to explain that she was working nearby at the discount store about a block away for little more than minimum wage. That she had no living relatives to depend on, and after her husband had died in the car crash, she was really scared that she would not be able to have a normal life and faced a very uncertain future and had nowhere to go and probably would end up being homeless or in a shelter. I explained that I would look tomorrow for studio and one bedroom apartments, and I knew some of my previous clients that had purchased income properties and would check with them also. She said that if they were more than $400 dollars a month she would not be able to pay the rent. I asked if her husband had left her any life insurance. She said no, he had told her that he wasn't leaving her anything because she wasn't worth the trouble or expense and made the remark several times he wouldn't leave a tramp bitch like her a dime. I asked why he would say such horrible words to such a beautiful woman. She tried smiling at me and thanked me and started to cry before wiping her face as she began telling me she grew up on the Seminole Indian reservation in Florida. That her family was dirt poor, her mother was of Indian heritage and worked as a maid, her father had Hispanic and black blood and worked now and then and was an alcoholic, and he was abusive to her and her siblings. She finished high school and

worked at a large discount store nearby until they closed and
moved further away, then she worked other various jobs. Then a
strip club for a very short period of time and that's where she met
her husband. After a short while they were married and soon after
he also started to become somewhat abusive. He was very different
in his abuse than her father. He liked bondage, tied her up at times
and treated her like he owned her. He worked full time as a
construction worker, and after several years he decided to move
here after his uncle offered him a full time job where he was part
owner.

She stood and came over and knelt on the floor in front of me
and stated she would do anything, anything; I wanted if I just took
her with me. She asked if I was married. I told her I had been a
widow for several years and was not really looking for a wife, or a
girlfriend. Jokingly I said, the only thing she could do for me was
to be a slave; and I don't think that would be acceptable to you or
anyone. To my surprise, she said that would be ok with her. She
said that her husband had tied and whipped her on several
occasions and practiced bondage and discipline on her, and even
had made several amateur videos of her submitting to him. Then it
struck me why she seemed so familiar to me, the amateur videos I
had at home and they were some of my favorite porno films were
of her. Now I recognized her, even though the videos were a few
years old, she still appeared as beautiful as ever. She said I could
do anything I wanted to her as long as I didn't hurt her. With that
said, she untied the wrap around blouse she wore that tied in front
to expose her very perky smooth round breast. I watched as she
became highly aroused and her very long large nipples began to
get hard and protrude. I was surprised as she reached for my hand
and placed it on her warm breast. Being a man and not having
touched a woman since the passing of my wife, it caused me to
become highly aroused and have a sudden massive hard on. I
withdrew my hand and sat back and listened to her as I tried to
calm my carnal thoughts. Said the last time she had sex, was with
her deceased husband and that I excited her very much. Said she
could be my housekeeper, and would be very obedient, would

clean, and cook, and do whatever, I needed. She started to cry as she reached for my now bulging crotch and begged me to please take her. I removed her hand, looked in her moist eyes and told her it would not be right for me to take advantage of her because of her dire situation. I was a professional, and it would also be very unethical.

After a few minutes, I asked to use her washroom, and rose to go urinate, which took a while as my hard on slowly dissipated. When I returned, explained that I would see what I could do to find her an apartment. But I would first give her the opportunity to see how well she would work out as being my temporary housekeeper. Stated it was only going to be temporary until she could find other employment and a place to live. A big smile came to her face. I told her that she would have to pack her personal things, such as her clothes but not any of the furniture, but she could bring her television. I asked her if that was acceptable to her and she said yes sir. Fine I said, but remember this is only going to be a temporary offer, and only on a trial basis. I would come back for her the following day when I returned to see Mrs. Kashia and that she should be ready to move and be packed up. I asked if she needed any boxes. She said no sir, and came closer and hugged me tight, and said I would not be sorry. As she held me I again became excited by her touch, it had been such a long time since I had any very close physical contact with a woman and needed to leave. I told her not to worry as I grabbed my briefcase and laptop and headed for the door. I turned as she followed me, and was crying. I asked what the matter was. Said her prayers had been answered now and felt better because she had somewhere to go, and that someone wanted her. I gave her a hug said that everything would be alright and we would see how this would all work out. I turned, opened the door, stepped out into the hallway and headed for the elevator.

As I waited for the elevator, she stood in her doorway watching until the elevator dinged, before she closed her door. I entered and pressed the button for the lobby, as I rode down I wondered how this would all play out. I couldn't wait to get home and take a shower, eat and have a stiff drink, for this had been one of the longest work days I had experienced in quite a long while. I did not know then that my new adventure was just about to begin. I arrived in the lobby and on my way out to my car, was thinking I still had to run the comps and get my seller to sign my exclusive listing agreement tomorrow.

When I arrived home, I checked the house alarm and camera systems before I undressed, showered, and fixed a sandwich because it was getting late. I fixed myself a strong drink and went to look through my porno collection; there was something very familiar with both Mrs. Cook and Kashia. Their faces, it just seemed I had seen them both before. Quite a few of my best movies were still on VHS, and they were in my home office, and I still had a combo VCR/DVD player. I went looking through the cabinet where they were kept. I enjoyed some good porno and the ones with stories were the best to me and were some of my favorites, and several of the amateur ones were exceptionally good. I had ordered several videos from a place in Florida that only dealt with amateurs from around the country; some were really hot and dealt with the subject of bondage and discipline and suspected I may have seen some with Mrs. Cook. I fast forward through several, but before finding the one I was looking for, I saw Mrs. Kashia, it was her and an older fat bellied man and she was preforming oral sex on him. Oh she was very good as she sucked and performed oral sex. The subject ejaculated on a plate, and then she slowly licked it all up, then he told her he was going to have his friends over to fuck her in her pussy and ass. He asked her if she would like that, and she replied yes. I didn't expect that, but after seeing it again, I soon remembered it. She had a very sexy body, small firm almost flat breast with large long nipples that were very firm and a really pleasant face. I continued to fast forward, until I then found the one I was really looking for. There was Mrs. Cook with the man in the picture I had seen in her bed room. I saw the two of them, it was light bondage on this tape, you could tell there was a third party taking the video, the shots and the cinematography was very good. She was lead around with a collar on her neck and a leash attached, and made to crawl as she was whipped before being bent over a chair as he pulled up the skimpy skirt she had on, he went on to spank her using, a paddle, riding crop and then a whip on her butt as it turned red. Then led her to a couch where he had her legs spread wide open as he played with her vagina, using a small whip on her clit as he inserted a dildo inside her vagina until she soon climaxed. The impression I got, was since there seemed to be several different video scenarios of them, she really enjoyed it and was into it with a very submissive look in her eyes. Several were an hour or so long and even one where he shaved her vagina. Ok, I saw enough for now and it was time for me to relax. I wondered if it was smart to bring her here or to just put her in a studio somewhere and find her a job or hire her to work elsewhere. I rewound the tapes and replaced them back where I kept them. Sat back and turned on the television, watched the news, finished my drink and before I knew it was asleep in the chair. I awoke shortly after, turned everything off, and went upstairs to my bedroom, and went to bed.

Two
Saturday: Day Two.

Well the day started as a normal day as usual, even though I now know that it would have a surprise ending. I had awakened at six, my usual time for starting my workday and did my usual morning bathroom ritual before looking through my closet for something to wear. Found the suit that I would be wearing and put it aside. I put on my bath robe and headed downstairs to the kitchen as usual. I made my morning coffee as I took the last sweet roll from the box and thought oh well I would have to get some more later as I sat down and drank my first cup of coffee for the day and devoured the sweet roll. I sat at the kitchen counter after retrieving my laptop from my home office and turned it on and brought up, first my e-mails before looking briefly around the internet and then logging on to the RELS. I noticed that several of my competitors had condos near my future listings in the same general area and some of their listings were close by along with several other properties, some homes, a church and one store. I had several more listings, eight homes, a five store strip mall that included a laundry mat, and two condos besides the two I would be listing very shortly before the end of the week. After finishing my coffee and cleaning the kitchen I went upstairs to my closet and took out the suit I had set aside along with a knit shirt, and a pair of comfortable loafers. I was intending to only spend a very short time at the office today, and began preparing to have a house guess. The place was orderly but not as tidy as it could be and I would like it to be less dusty and much cleaner, and besides maybe my laundry would be done much sooner. I had thrown myself into my work after my wife died and didn't really have the time to keep the house as clean as I would like and some things just weren't as important anymore for some reason as before. Sex had not been on my mind either or even a consideration much less a priority; it had been money, and only money. I had made $13,000,000.00 dollars over the past fourteen months and it seemed to be just rolling in now, finally after all the long days and hours and some anguish. I was ready now to spend it on expanding my office and enhancing my business when the opportunity arose and now felt it was time and long overdue and thought I was soon going to find a suitable location very soon. With my current earnings I felt it was time to come out of the shadows. I had hidden mostly all of my real-estate holdings under other names and operated them as separate companies and operated as low key as possible.

It was a little after nine when after checking the thermostat and all the windows in my large four bedroom home, locked up and went to the garage. I got in my work car and pulled out, and after closing the garage door behind me, decided to stop at Martha's restaurant for breakfast. I was a regular and Martha knew what I liked most of the time and besides she was located down the street from my office. I went inside and headed for a booth as Sue the waitress came over and took my order, two eggs over easy, ham and toast, grapefruit juice and coffee. After eating I felt refreshed and ready to tackle the day's events that lie ahead of me. I knew that a new adventure was about to begin, and could just feel it coming. I paid and left a tip, the service was always superb at Martha's.

Since I arrived at the office a little after nine, my office manager Mrs. Joanne Bradley had opened up and was on the phone already. I went and sat at my desk before I started going through my rolodex and pulled out Hector's business card and dialed his number. Mr. Hector Martinez was my person for paint and plaster and a few other jobs. His father had come here sixty years earlier from México and started a painting service. It was a family operation and over the years had grown. The whole family was involved, his four sons and three daughters and wife also worked in the business, plus some of their cousins and other relatives, and they were exceptional workers. If I had a rush job with a one day turn around, they completed it, and there work was always superb. They did it all from plaster, dry wall, tile, paint and carpentry. One son was an electrician; another one a plumber and one was a general contractor and two sisters operated a cleaning company. They also did carpets from instillation to carpet cleaning and were really a one stop service provider, and they had an exceptionally good reputation in town for all their work. I dialed his number and Mrs. Martinez answered. I spoke with her and after greeting and some small talk explained, I had a couple of jobs for the coming week and with this being a Saturday, I wanted to make sure I was on their work list for the coming week. I wanted to have things covered, especially with the two condos. Mrs. Martinez took the information and I explained that one would be available Monday for sure. Said I would call back later so we could set a date, and possibly have both done at the same time. She thanked me and stated they would be ready whenever I called back, and only had a couple jobs lined up for next week and it should not be a problem.

I hung up, and called Mrs. Kashia and asked what time would be convenient to view the second unit. And to my surprise, she said today at noon would be fine. She informed me that her tenants were moving out today, and she was going to do the inspection and return their security deposit. I said that sounds great and noon would be fine, and I would be there and thanked her. It was five after eleven as I grabbed my briefcase, placed my laptop inside along with the listing agreements for both units. I informed Mrs. Bradley that I was gone for the day, and would not be back until Monday and hoped she would have a great weekend. Besides having a broker's license, she ran the office for me which gave me more free time and was my best friend and had been with me almost from the start after I struck out on my own. She also supervised Mr. Fitz, he was Irish and in his late forties, tall and lanky, average in appearance, and had a great personality, and really was my head leasing agent. He handled leases for all the several strip malls, office buildings, and multi-units apartment buildings and supervised the leasing agents that stayed on the premises of the various apartment complexes owned under various management company names, but were really owned by me and kept track of all the rental payments. I was The Harcourt Company Inc. and an employee of said company for tax purposes. Joanne was also an employee of The Harcourt Company along with Fitz and this was beneficial for all of us and as a company made it possible to have great health insurance coverage at the corporate

rate which was much less than the rate charged to individuals. Mrs. Bradley ran the office and was my first assistant and was Mr. Fitz supervisor. Yes I lied to Mrs. Cook because I knew she could never afford any of the units I owned and especially after she said more than four hundred was too much. I avoided renting to people who appeared to be bad tenants, especially if they financially couldn't pay or it would be a strain on them trying to pay otherwise, besides her credit probably wasn't going to qualify her anyway and I didn't have anything remotely in the $400 dollar range or even close. All my properties were very well maintained and bordered on the middle to high end.

I headed out and told Joanne to have a great day, because I knew I was going to have one every time I took a new listing. I left the office and headed out and a short drive later I arrived and parked in front of Mrs. Kashia's building. I gathered my briefcase and stepped out of the car, checked my appearance and felt I was ready. As I had pulled up and parked, noticed a moving van at the buildings rear entrance. I entered the front entrance door and pressed Mrs. Kashia bell, and was promptly buzzed inside and walked to the elevators, good thing there were two elevators in the building because as the first one came down and the door opened, it was full of furniture, and with a couple men. One I recognized as a former client of mine who I had just helped find and close on the sale of a new home for him and his wife. We recognized each other and shook hands, he and his wife were very happy to be moving because they had a one year old son and were planning to have more children. They felt that a house would be a better environment for raising children, and I whole heartily agreed with them. He said that he was sorry that Mrs. Kashia had lost her husband since they had gotten along so very well. Stated I was here to list the unit he was moving from and would be present for the final inspection and would see him upstairs shortly. He said he knew because Mrs. Kashia had informed him she was going to sell the unit and was one of the reasons they had looked for a house, he stated they only had a few more things to move and would be finished very soon.

The second elevator came down and I took it up and exited on the 6th floor, and Mrs. Kashia was standing in her doorway waiting for me to come up. I greeted her and she smiled, and acted as if she wanted to hug me. I said to her good afternoon and informed her that I had run into her tenant Mr. Jones, and explained he was a former client of mine. Mrs. Kashia was dressed more casual than yesterday but still appeared as beautiful as ever, she wore a well-fitting two piece suit with the jacket that was only buttoned at the bottom and had a very sheer blouse underneath and a pair of sandals with two inch heels, her nails and toes had matching red polish and her hair was down and not in the bun she wore the previous day but in a long braided ponytail. She asked if I would come in for a moment before we headed down to the fifth floor. I was more than happy to and informed her that I would be taking Mrs. Cook with me when I left and had made arrangements to have the units cleaned, the cost was going to be no more than $500.00 per unit and asked if that was acceptable to her. I stated the people who were going to do the work were highly recommended and known for their exceptional work and any repairs, electrical or plumbing would be taken care of and carpet cleaning was also included. Also the washrooms would be scrubbed, including the tile and in the kitchens also. And she had my personal guarantee it would be done correctly. I stated since her tenant was moving a few days before their lease was up that both units could and would be done before the end of the coming week, and would be listed as soon as the work was completed. She said that was great news. I said she would not have to pay until the work was done to her satisfaction. I would need a set of keys for each unit so that way she would not be disturbed when my people came to clean, paint and prepare them for sale. And my agents wouldn't have to disturb her for any showings. I had the listing agreements with me; and after we inspected the units she could sign the exclusive agreements. I also presented her with a list of comparable properties. I recommended a price of $175,000.00 for the one bed room, and $205,000.00 for the two bed room. I had listed them based on the current market, and it was a sellers' market, and there weren't very many nice condos for sale at the present time. She said that was very acceptable to her and looked forward to our doing business together.

There was a knock at the door and she went to answer, it was Mr. Jones. He was ready for her to inspect the unit for any damage. I stood and we all took the elevator down to the 5th floor and entered the now vacant unit. It was in great shape. I took my measurements and made notations on my pad as to what needed to be done, it wasn't going to be difficult at all to clean up, the carpet was only two years old, a few of the electrical outlets needed to be changed so they would have a ground, but otherwise it was in great shape, and you could tell Mrs. Jones was a very tidy housekeeper since the unit was clean. Mrs. Kashia asked Mr. Jones if he would come up so she could give him his deposit check. We exited the unit, and he handed her two sets of keys and they thanked each other as we entered the elevator to go back up to the 6th floor. We entered her unit and she quickly retrieved and handed him his security deposit check and wished him well, we all shook hands and he departed. Ms. Kashia and I returned to sit on the sofa to conclude our business as she sat very close to me and I could smell her very faint and expensive perfume. I did have to admit to myself she was very attractive and sexy, comments I kept to myself as she undid the bottom button of her jacket allowing it to open fully as she leaned over to sign the listing agreements and being sure I had a good look at her firm breast. She signed both listings agreements, one for each unit; and handed me a set of keys for 5B. I placed the laptop inside my briefcase and thanked her. I asked if she would come with me next door as I retrieved Mrs. Cook from the unit so she could inspect it, and explained that any furniture that was left would be disposed of by the people who were going to do the work cleaning up and she wouldn't have to do anything until I had a buyer. She said she was very happy and pleased with the arraignment. She stood and faced me as she straightened her jacket making sure I had a good look before she refastened the bottom button of her jacket.

I stood after placing the listing agreements into my briefcase, and we walked to the door. Mrs. Kashia suddenly turned and faced me before opening the door and asked me if I was married. I said I once was and was a widower like her. Said she was sorry for my loss and suggested that we might go to diner one day soon. Said I didn't mix business with pleasure or believe in having personal relations with anyone I did business with and if I did a considerable amount of time would have to pass first. She then said oh, maybe after all our business arrangements were completed. Said I was attractive and she liked me very much and would like to get to know me much better. She turned around and we then entered the hall way as we approached the door of 6C and I knocked on the door and very shortly after Mrs. Cook answered the door and let us inside. She had completely packed up all she owned and was prepared to leave and had two well-worn suit cases and a duffel bag; her purse and the television were sitting by the front door. It was more than obvious she was ready to leave. Mrs. Kashia and I walked through the unit and inspected and everything seemed to be in order as we returned to the front door where Mrs. Cook was still standing wearing a pair of worn jeans and an old worn t-shirt with a thin sweater and gym shoes as she handed Mrs. Kashia two sets of keys which she accepted. Mrs. Kashia turned and handed me a set which I tagged along with the ones from 5B and placed both sets in a side pocket of my briefcase and zipped it up. Mrs. Cook thanked her for being so understanding with her and wished her well before giving her a big hug. I asked Mrs. Cook if that was all she was taking, she said yes it was. I gave her a hand with her suit cases and set them by the elevator door. Mrs. Kashia locked the door to the unit as Mrs. Cook and I waited for the elevator. I said goodbye to her and thanked her and said I would be in touch as she stood and watched us depart. Just then the elevator dinged, the doors opened, we entered and placed her bags and television inside. As soon as the elevator doors closed Mrs. Cook hugged and kissed me and said that I would not be sorry.

We exited the building and I placed Mrs. Cook's belongings in the trunk of my car and opened the door for her. I got behind the wheel and we were soon off. As we pulled away she asked that I call her Vicky or Victoria and there was no need to be so formal with her. I said ok and she could call me Charles or Charlie which ever suited her. I asked if she was hungry, she said yes. I decided to take her to Martha's for lunch; we soon arrived and entered. I led her to an empty booth since it was early afternoon and not very many people were having lunch. Most had eaten and left so it wasn't crowed as Martha's waitress Sue came over and we placed our orders. I had a corn beef sandwich with coleslaw on the side and a soda, and Vicky had the fried chicken dinner with three pieces, mashed potatoes and mixed vegetables including a salad. Our food arrived and the girl was truly famished, for there wasn't a crumb left on her plate when she finished. I asked her when the last time she had eaten was. Said she only had tuna and crackers and some peanut butter yesterday and had not been eating really very regular. And hadn't had a hot meal in over a week because she had to stretch her money. I said that was not healthy or good and that needed to change. I then asked about her job. She stated that she was unsure of how that was going to work out now if she was going to work for me also. I made her a proposition just then. Suggested that she should resign and I would employ her as my full time housekeeper and I would pay her more than her current job was paying her and we would see how things worked out, she said ok. I said after we finished our food, I would take her to the job where she could then resign.

We finished eating, I paid and we left the restaurant and headed to her now current job. I went in with her so I could pick up a few things; it took her about thirty minutes for her to take care of her business as I waited for her and they paid her what wages were due her in full, which came to about $300.00 dollars. I asked if there was anything she needed. She didn't answer and was very reluctant, as she began biting her lip and just stood looking at me and not saying anything. I said ok then as I grabbed a shopping cart and her hand and we went to the ladies section, where I asked for her size. I looked at her sternly and told her what I wanted her to get and all she had to do was make sure they fit and were the right size, panties, pantyhose, t- shirts, jeans and another pair of athletic shoes, some dress sandals and several other item of badly needed clothing. The shoes she had on were badly worn and had holes in them. I also purchased some feminine products and a toothbrush. She was very upset as we checked out since it was slightly more than $350.00 dollars. As we arrived back at the car, tears started to well up in her eyes. She started crying and I asked what was wrong. She said never in her life had anyone did anything nice for her and felt very ashamed of what was happening to her now as we placed the bags inside the car.

I told her not to worry, that everything was going to be ok. I started the engine and we headed to my house. She was at a loss when we arrived. It appeared to her to be a castle, my home is two stories with four bedrooms, five and a half baths, and a very large kitchen and a three car attached garage. We pulled up; I hit the button for the garage door to open, then turned around and backed inside. I opened the trunk and pointed to the back door and for her to place her newly purchased items by as I retrieved her suit cases. I unlocked the door and I asked her when the last time she had washed her clothes, she said it had been a couple weeks since she needed money for the coin operated washer and dryer at the condo. I told her I wanted her to wash all of her clothes and pointed her to the laundry room, which she did after retrieving her bags. I took her new stuff and placed it at the base of the staircase, and returned to the laundry room where she was unpacking her clothes from her suit cases and placing her papers and other items into another smaller bag. I showed her how to operate the washers and told her to put all her clothes in, and pointed to where the detergent was located. I turned to her and told her to put the shoes she had on in the trash can in the corner, and asked her to pick up her bags and follow me. I grabbed her television and led her to the stairs and then picked up some of the bags with the newly purchased clothing and led her upstairs, and into the bed room across the hall from mine. After dropping the large bags on the floor and placing her television on the dresser, I turned to her and asked her to take a bath and clean herself up, showed her the bathroom and said to her, make yourself at home. There was a bath tub and a standalone walk-in shower. I asked her to trim her nails and whatever she needed or wanted to do, that there were some body washes and body oils she could use before putting on her new clothes. I asked her to wear the new t-shirt and sandals I had just purchased. The bathroom was fully stocked with feminine accouchements and even some perfume. There were towels and wash clothes. Told her to take her time and there was also a robe in the bedroom closet if she needed it. As I turned to leave her eyes were filled with tears and she began crying profusely. I departed the bedroom closing the door behind me.

I went to my bedroom and undressed, removing my suit and hanging it up before putting on some shorts and a t-shirt. I went downstairs and to the garage to retrieve my briefcase. Took my phone out and hit the speed dial for Hector, he picked up on the second ring and we joked around, before I told him about the two units I wanted him to clean and paint as we agreed to meet at the location on Monday, around noon and then he would give me a price and put everything in writing. I said ok, that would be great, I thanked him and hung up. Well so far the day was going very smoothly. I was going to have a beer since I had breakfast and lunch and only ate on average two meals a day.

The easiest thing for me to do now was to make Victoria Cook and employee, that way she would have medical and dental and would be completely covered, and would pay much less for it. She would then have to get the standard employee medical and dental checkups. I went back upstairs to the bedroom she was in and knocked on the bathroom door. I asked Victoria to bring all her paper work down with her when she finished, she answered through the door, and said yes sir. I returned downstairs and went to my home office and set my briefcase down and went and opened the file cabinet that I kept all of my blank forms in, and withdrew an application for employment with my company. She came downstairs about an hour and a half later, and came into the office. She was looking so much better as she stood in the door way. She was holding an old beat up manila envelope and a small wallet as her skin seemed to glow more now than before. The t shirt was large enough to fit loosely, and came down below her butt and her legs were very shapely. Her hair was combed and lightly oiled, she wore some stud earrings and I could smell the faint odor of perfume.

She stood in the door way a moment looking around, before I came around the desk and asked her to step inside, as I took a good look at her. The room was filled with sun light from the large windows and I could see she had cleaned up very well. She wore no makeup and I could see that she had taken care of her skin. I complemented her on her looks and asked her if she had all her documents. She answered yes sir as I asked her to have a seat in the padded leather chair in front of my desk as I walked back around to my chair, explaining to her that I was going to hire her as my housekeeper. That she would be paid biweekly, and the following week we would go to the bank, and she would have to open a checking account so she could be paid automatically by direct deposit. She would have health insurance and was required to get a physical and a dental examination, which I would arrange for her. I took her envelope and went through all her papers, social security, marriage license, birth certificate, diplomas, and death certificate. I asked if she had a driver's license, she reached into her small purse and pulled one out handing it to me; it was up to date and had more than a year to go. I went through her papers carefully asking question as I handed her a clipboard with the employment application. I made hard copies of all her documents and created and up loaded them to an electronic employee file before returning them to her. I waited for her to finish the employment application, as I sat and watched her, before I excused myself and went to the laundry room to check on her clothes and placing them in the dryer, some of her clothes were out of date and all were well-worn and some were almost thread bare. I finished and placed some dryer sheets inside with them and set the dials and turned the dryer on before I returned to the office. As I entered she had just finished the application and was looking around the spacious room. She handed me the finished application as I returned. I took it and looked it over, her penmanship was neat and tidy, easy to read, and it was completely filled out and signed. I placed all her papers neatly inside a new manila envelope and returned them to her, and took my new file on her and put it in a folder and placed it into my briefcase.

We were finished for now as I stood up and asked her to come with me back upstairs so I could show her where she would be sleeping. We went upstairs and showed her all the rooms and bathrooms and where the vacuum cleaner and the other cleaning supplies were located. Showed the room that was to be hers, it was one with its own bath, the one she had just bathed in, fully furnished with bed and dressers, mirror, large walk-in closet with a shoe rack, a large window with blinds and curtains and the only bedroom besides mine with any furniture inside besides one I kept as a guest room. And then I lead her back downstairs, showed her around the ground floor, living room, dining room, kitchen with breakfast nook, office, the half bath, laundry room, and explained that I wanted things kept clean and orderly. Then took her down to the basement and showed her the recreation room with the pool table, large flat screen television, and wet bar, large bath and a sauna. I also showed her the other half of the basement that wasn't finished but was walled off. I then asked her to have a seat at the bar as I went behind. I asked Victoria if she felt humiliated when I asked her to bathe, she said no sir. I explained what I wanted from her as an employee. I said you are to keep the house clean at all times, that I didn't expect no more or less of her and she was to keep her appearance presentable at all times, for when I had visitors she would be expected to wait on us as needed. I asked if that was acceptable to her, she said whatever I wanted her to do would be a pleasure after all of her previous jobs.

And then I asked her if she would like a drink, she didn't know what and said yes sir. I suggested we have a glass of red wine. I took a chilled bottle of Shiraz from the fridge and set two glasses on the bar and poured us both a glass. I came around to the other side of the bar and suggested she sit on the couch with me. She sat at one end of the couch and I sat opposite so I could get a good look at her as we sipped our wine and said I hoped that this would be a positive experience for her. She soon finished the wine and asked if she could have another. I said of course, as I stood and returned to the bar to retrieve the bottle and returned to refill her glass. I sat back where I had been sitting and looked at her for she was truly a picture of female perfection. Then she placed her glass on the end table and came and knelt down before me, looked me in the eyes, and she said master, then again, and continued until, I said I am not your master, she replied that she was here to serve her master, that she needed to be punished for having dirty thoughts. I told her, I don't hit women. Said she couldn't be a good slave unless I spanked and punished her. Told her you aren't my slave, you are my housekeeper, or at least that is the reason why you are here. Said she was here to serve me no matter what and it's what she wanted and needed. I asked her what kind of thoughts she was having. She said of me spanking and taking her bent over the back of the couch and that she needed it very much.

Suddenly she pulled her shirt off and pulled her panties down. She asked if master would please spank and take her, she was his worthless slave and was here to serve. I finished my wine and placed my glass on the end table and I told her to stand looking at her beautiful naked body now standing before me, begging to be punished. This was the same body I had jerked off to as I watched her being submissive to her deceased husband, I couldn't resist the temptation as it now presented itself to me in all its glory. I stood and went to the bathroom and retrieved a bottle of massaging lotion and returned and stood in front of her, my dick was standing at attention in my shorts. She saw the bulge; and I couldn't hide it this time and she knew she excited me. I opened the lotion and liberally applied it to my hands, and she looked at me with the most submissive look I had ever seen. I moved my lips to hers and kissed her as I reached for her arms and held them to her sides, when I pulled my face away her nipples were hard as I bent over and flicked them with my tongue and she began moaning. I released her arms and told her to go to the other side of the couch and bend over. She walked around the end of the couch, came and

stood behind it and bent over the back. I walked around behind her
and rubbed her back and down to her ass with the lotion and
caressed the firm round lobes of her ass as I slowly placed my right
hand between her thighs and told her to spread them open and felt
her growing wetness as I moved my hand to her clit and gently
began rubbing and squeezing it before I slowly withdrew my hand.
I placed my left hand firmly on her back, and brought my right
hand down hard on her left ass cheek, as she rose up slightly and
back down, and then, struck the right cheek, repeating ten times
and alternating cheeks with each strike, and then rubbed her ass
with the lotion as it became reddish in color. Again placing my
hand between her spread legs and rubbed her pussy and parting the
plump lips and squeezed her clit as it began to protrude from its
hiding place as I caused her to have a very explosive orgasm as I
held her in place. I held her around the neck, holding her down and
spanked her again hard several more times, before pulling her up
by the hair to a standing position, reaching around with both hands
and holding her breast and squeezing and pulling her hard erect
nipples and twisting and squeezing them as she moaned. I told her
to turn around as I looked into her beautiful lust filled eyes, kissing
her puckered lips and putting my hand again between her thighs
and placing my index finger deep inside her moist vagina, then two
fingers as I rubbed my thumb against her protruding clit as she
climaxed hard again and I slowly removed my fingers from inside
of her before taking them and placing them in her open and waiting
mouth. I told her to suck them as she moved her tongue all around
them before I withdrew my hand and told her to get down on her
knees. I instructed her to gently remove my shorts, and suck my
hard dick which was standing fully at attention. She didn't hesitate
loosening my shorts and letting them fall to the floor before
expertly placing me in her eager mouth. I watched as her head
moved back and forth until my large penis disappeared completely
as she swallowed the whole thing, and I soon exploded inside her
warm mouth. She swallowed every drop I had to give, and then
slowly sucked as she reluctantly let it go and rubbed her face
against me. She grabbed hold of me and hugged me tight,

squeezing my legs as I stroked her head. I then told her to stand, and gently took hold of her nipples and squeezed and asked her if she was going to be good now, or did she need more punishment. She said with the little girl look in her eyes that she would be good but wanted master to fuck her now anyway he wanted and said she wanted very much to please me.

I then pulled and led her to the large walk-in shower, turned the water on, and waited for it to get hot as she clung to me like a child; as soon as it was warm; we entered and began to bath one another all the while continuing to feel all over one another. I bent her over, lathered her body up with shower gel and fingered her ass inserting several fingers inside her as I shoved my large hard dick inside her vagina as she was bent over and I held her arms behind her, working back and forth until I came again, afterwards I had her to kneel and open her mouth as I gave her a golden shower. We then showered and kissed and after thirty minutes or so, I finally turned off the water and retrieved some large bath towels and we dried each other off. I had robes and plenty of towels because of the sauna and handed her one. I took one for myself and we went back to the bar and drank more wine and finished the first bottle. We sat and looked at each other, as I opened another bottle and poured us even more wine and we just sat there looking at one another. I told her how great that was since I couldn't remember when I had sex with a woman last, she said that had been the most enjoyable sex she ever had, said it played into her submissiveness and she wanted very much to please me. I asked if she was hungry and what she might be hungry for, and if she had any suggestions, she said a pizza would be great. I picked up the phone a dialed Milan's for a 24 inch deluxe pizza with everything, they said an hour, and they knew the address, since I had ordered from them in the past. By the time it arrived we had rubbed each other down with body oils and were starving. I went to get the pizza at the front door and then returned to the basement bar. Vicky and I dug in, consuming the entire pizza and drinking more wine and enjoying each other's company very much, it had been a long time since I had spent any time alone with a woman and a long time since I had sex, this was really good. We finished eating and brought our garbage upstairs where we disposed of it in the kitchen waste can. I had automated the house and most of the lights were on timers, then we went up to the bedrooms. Vicky said she really wanted to sleep with me tonight, and asked me please master. I said ok. This was the first time since my wife had passed that a woman had been in my bed, and it wasn't long before we both fell asleep but not before we hugged, kissed and felt on one another for quite a long while.

Three
Sunday: Day Three.

I awoke at my usual time of around six and found and arm on me, and then I remembered, I wasn't alone anymore. It seemed like forever since I had awakened with a woman in the bed with me as I slowly lifted the arm and removed myself from the bed and gently placed it back down and pulled the covers back up over the warm body next to me. I extricated myself and headed to the bathroom to relieve myself and wash my face, rinse my mouth, and about fifteen minutes later returned and got back in bed. As I did Victoria slowly awoke and appeared groggy as she said good morning love. Then she proceeded to get out of bed and headed to the bathroom as well where after ten or so minutes she returned looking refreshed as she climbed back in bed on top of me. The covers were only covering my feet when she returned as she climbed on top and straddled me and reached down and grabbed my half hard dick and placing the head in the now open lips of her warm moist pussy. Soon I was hard as a rock and then she laid her soft sexy body on top of me with her firm breast on my chest and began to move her butt back and forth until I was fully inside of her as she licked and kissed my face and neck. After about ten minutes of kissing and rubbing we came together. We laid there as I held her and rubbed her back as she moaned and I felt her body relax. I then said in a ragged voice; it was time for us to get up. She didn't move but began again kissing me all over and was holding me like she didn't want to let go. I grabbed her by her hair and pulled her head back and looked into her beautiful face, and told her it was time to get up because we had a few things to do today, she asked what. I told her she would see soon enough as I pushed her up and she climbed out of bed. I got up and grabbed her by the hand and led her to the bathroom where we showered. After we finished bathing ourselves, we put on our bath robes and we went downstairs to the kitchen.

I started to get out the makings for breakfast, eggs, bacon, bread and then as I started to make the coffee, Victoria grabbed the frying pan and started cooking the bacon, and then the eggs and we also made toast with cheese in the oven, when it was all complete, we sat in the kitchen nook and ate. We hardly spoke a word. My mind was going around in circles trying to process all that had happened in the last twenty-four hours. I went from a pussy free life, to seemingly having what every man dreamed of, but I didn't want any more pussy right now. I felt swell and felt I would be good for the rest of the year. While we were eating, I asked Victoria about birth control. She said due to unfortunate circumstances she was unable to conceive due to an accident when she was in her teens, and had learned to live with the thought of probably never having children. That now she only had one goal in life, and that was to be faithful and loyal to me, for she had been lonely and depressed only a few days earlier, and hoped that I would come to love and appreciate her. And if I didn't it wouldn't matter because she would serve me anyway because she loved me. We finished eating before I told her we were going out to get her some work uniforms. And her clothes were in the dryer and that she should get them out and take them to her bedroom, and then we would get ready and go. I told her to take her time as we cleaned up the kitchen together and then she went to the laundry room and folded her clothes, as she removed them from the dryer before going upstairs to get dressed.

I dressed in my usual attire, jeans, t shirt, and athletic shoes and socks with a sports jacket, brushed my hair and went down stairs, as it was very close to ten o'clock. When Vicky came down she looked stunning, wearing the new sandals, leggings, and blue jean skirt with belt, blouse and the sweater, all I had just purchased yesterday for her. Her hair was combed to the side with a slight part in the middle and she wore the same stud earrings with a light colored lip gloss. I complement her on how well she looked. She had her small purse with a long strap over her shoulder. I asked her if she was ready, and she replied yes sir.

We headed for the garage. Since it was Sunday, I was going to use my Sunday car, one I always wanted since high school auto shop but it had eluded me until I was able to make my first small fortune. It was a BGT; I had found one and the dealer had it in stock. You know a funny thing about material objects is the anticipation of getting them, and once you do it seems the excitement goes away slightly, but was happy I had one and could afford it.

What had made my life the happiest of all beyond anything was the love I and my deceased wife had for one another. Nothing would probably ever compare to that, and was glad that at least once in my life I was able to experience it, but that was yesterday, and just like the song, yesterday's gone. I guess now was no better time than any to start over and release the grief that I had kept inside of me and away from the things in life that count the most and begin again with someone new. Not that I had any plans other than employing Victoria as my housekeeper, but I could see now it was going to lead somewhere, and had no idea where. I had looked at her videos for a long time and they had always excited me, but could never imagine hitting a woman. This was very different, in the sense that she wanted it and my own perversion that I was suppressing was being called upon to come to the surface. It was still difficult in a way, but then again it wasn't, but her beauty also drew me to her along with her docile demeanor. I knew inside my being, I wanted her and would find it very difficult to suppress my feelings. Funny how some pussy can change your whole perspective on life, but not only that I was very lonely inside and knew it. I just had to face the reality of just how much. Now with Mrs. Cook in my home and life I felt a change coming over me that was propelling me even more of having the most successful real estate business in town. Times change, people change and life goes on. As we entered the garage I walked past my work car and went to the side of the BGT and opened the door for Vicky, closing it after she was seated. Went to the driver's side, got in opened the garage door and started the car, we buckled our seat belts and I pulled out and stopped and hit the remote to close the garage door behind us before pulling away.

I headed to the Work Forms store, and shortly after we pulled up in front. We exited the car, went inside where we were greeted by Mr. Bill the salesman. Told him what I was looking for and wanted and he led us to the section for women's uniforms. I saw what I was looking for, a simple off white button up the front smock with blue stripe trimming the collar and sleeves similar to hotel workers uniforms with pockets. I purchased four and had Victoria try one on, it fit her very well. I asked Mr. Bill to wrap them, he folded them and placed them in a large bag, and then we were off.

As Vicky and I reentered the car, I told her that since she was an employee of my company and would on occasion have to dress formally for business occasions, or when I entertained she would need something presentable to wear. I told her I hadn't seen that any of her present clothing was suitable and so we headed to the Sweet Wood Mall where we parked and exited the auto and headed inside. I knew where to go after being married for nine years. We went to the big department store, and headed to the women's section. I knew how I wanted her to dress. We entered the dress section where we were greeted by a sales assistant. I described to her that I wanted, a black strap or strapless evening dress for Mrs. Cook. She led us to a rack as I looked through them and asked Vicky for her dress size. I informed the assistant, she wore a size ten, the assistant took one from the rack and I instructed Victoria to go to the fitting room and try it on which she promptly did, the assistant and I picked several other dresses that I wanted her to try, when she came out the dressing room she looked stunning, it was black, had spaghetti straps that crossed in back and just stopped above the small of her back and the front came down to a narrow v several inches between her breast, it looked very sexy on her. As I looked at her I though, perfect the first time as she turned around in front of the wall mirror they have in stores. I asked her how it felt, she replied that it was very comfortable, it wasn't too tight and looked really good on her as I handed her three more dresses in different colors and styles to try, she went back to the dressing room and each time she came out she was really stunning, after trying on the last dress and coming out. I said to the sales lady we would be taking all of them.

Afterwards we went upstairs to the shoe section and informed Victoria of the shoes that I wanted her to have, but if she saw something she liked that would be ok also. I sat down and watched and waited for her to find the shoes I wanted, or something close, she returned with several pairs as she sat next to me and the shoe man approached, she showed him the shoes she had picked out and informed him of her size which was a size nine and a half. He returned with several boxes, pulled up a stool and began to fit the shoes on her very sexy feet. I noticed how straight her toes were and how smooth her feet were and so did the salesman, complimenting her on them. She first tried the shoe I wanted which was an open toe three inch high heel with a strap in back in black, she tried on both and stood and walked around, returned and stated they were very comfortable, then tried a sandal with a small heel, it fitted well also, then another high heel with a closed toe and heel in black, she said they were too tight on her toes and she was satisfied with the first two pair. I told the salesman we would take the first two pair. I paid and carried the shoes for her as she carried the dresses. I lead her to the escalator as we headed to the perfume and cologne department where I asked her to sample, and find something that she really liked, she found the one she liked and said she would also like to have some lipstick and eye shadow. I said ok, and was the next counter over. She picked two lipsticks, a gloss and one shadow for your eyes and some matching nail polish. She asked if we were done, and said she was getting hungry. I said ok, and we went back the way we came and headed for the car. I placed the purchases in the trunk, and opened the door for her as she got in. I looked at her very beautiful legs, everything about her was becoming more beautiful the more I looked at her. As I turned to look at her before pulling away; I noticed the hint off tears beginning to well up in her big beautiful eyes,

I started the car and asked if she liked Chinese, she said yes sir that sounds good she said in a halting voice. Vicky had not spoken a word since leaving the mall, as we pulled into the restaurant parking lot. I parked, got out and walked to her side of the car and opened the door for her, and as she stood, she broke down and

cried profusely. I held her shoulders and asked what the matter
was. Like I didn't know as she looked at me and wrapped her arms
around me sobbing, I held her and patted her back. I loved the way
she felt in my arms as I took a handkerchief from my pocket and
dabbed her very moist eyes, then took her by the hand and led her
into the restaurant.

This was one of my favorite spots to eat and Mr. and Mrs.
Wong were the owners. I owned the strip mall. We entered and
Mrs. Wong greeted us as I asked for a booth. She could sense and
see Victoria had been crying and led us to a more private booth in
the back as we were seated. She placed the menus on the table, and
I said we would have the green tea, and it would only be a moment
before deciding what we wanted. About five minutes later Mrs.
Wong came back and took our order, it was unusual for Mrs.
Wong to be taking orders, she usually left that to her employees, so
I inquired and she said, I was special person. I thanked her for that,
and she left to place our orders with the chef. I had the Hunan
chicken and shrimp combo with noodles and seaweed salad on the
side. Victoria had a fried rice dish with chicken and mixed
vegetables. Our food arrived and we ate slowly as we savored the
meal, we finished our food, and Mrs. Wong brought the check and
our fortune cookies. I opened mine and ate the cookie as I read the
fortune inside, it said (man wasn't meant to live alone), Vicky
didn't read hers but placed it in her purse. I paid the check, then we
departed, it was almost five, and on our way home, I decided we
should stop at Sexy, a lingerie store that carries various sexual
items as I said to Victoria this was the last stop. We entered and
looked around, I took three pair of stockings with the attached
garters and a couple of the open crotch pantyhose from a rack, and
a sheer black lingerie set, a couple of fish net body suits size ten
and a sexy maid outfit and some massage oil, glass dildo, small
leather paddle, a couple pairs of padded cuffs and a collar with and
a leash, I paid then we left for home.

We arrived home soon after and I backed into the garage, we
retrieved the purchases from the trunk, and then we headed inside.
I helped Vicky to her room with her new clothing as she proceeded

to hang them in the walk-in closet and place the others in drawers.
I went to my room to undressed and put on a pair of shorts and a t
shirt then placed in my closet several of the items I purchased from
sexy.

Then I went downstairs to the recreation room and fixed myself
a gin and tonic before I went and sat on the couch and turned on
the flat screen and watched the end of a soccer game until it
finished before turning to an action movie. What a weekend this
turned out to be as I mentally began planning out in my head the
coming week. After a while I heard Victoria coming downstairs
and then she walked in front of the television, she was dressed in
the sexy maid outfit with the high heels on, and had charged her
hair style and was wearing the collar with the leash and earrings,
the new perfume, red lipstick, and eye shadow and her nails were
done. I sat up and took all of her in. I grabbed my phone off the
end table and took several photos, and she appeared lovelier than
ever. I got up and refreshed my drink and she came over and sat at
the bar and asked if she could have one also. I asked what she
would care to have, whatever I was having she replied and I fixed
one for her. After I had poured her drink I came around and sat
next to her and took her all in again, what a sight for sore eyes. I
complimented her on her looks and she said it was all for me, there
wasn't anything else that mattered to her in the world but to make
me happy and for me to be satisfied with her.

I told her that she started work officially tomorrow, and would
leave a list for her to go by on the kitchen counter; she said ok, as
she sipped her drink. I told her I didn't want any sex tonight
because I had a lot to do tomorrow and needed my rest.
Surprisingly she agreed and we both had another drink. Said I
would be making her doctor's appointments tomorrow, and for her
to fix whatever she wanted to eat, but only enough for herself,
because I had no idea how my day was going to go or when I
would return home. I also instructed her not to answer the phone
because I had a machine for that, but to monitor the calls in case I
called. After another drink we went back upstairs, since it was
close to ten pm. After showering I intended to go to sleep as Vicky

grabbed hold of me and said that she loved me. I asked if it wasn't a little too soon for her to know. Said not to her it wasn't, as we released each other and said good night as we went into our respective bedrooms, I to mine to take a shower and go to bed.

Four
Monday: Day Four.

I woke up at six seventeen, got up and went to the bathroom. I took a nice long wake up shower and did my usual morning ritual of shaving and brushing my teeth before going to the closet to pick out what I was going to wear. I decided on a more casual dress than a suit since I was going to be out of the office most of the day. I decided on my usual daily attire of jeans and a sports jacket, shirt, socks and loafers when I soon detected the faint smell of coffee. I dressed and brushed my hair and made sure I had my wallet and keys and stepped out into the hallway and went downstairs. When I entered the kitchen I was greeted by Mrs. Cook with her new smock on as she poured a cup of coffee which she sat down in front of me. I said good morning and she returned the greeting. She asked if I wanted breakfast and asked how I wanted my eggs, she had bacon in the pan cooking already, and asked if I wanted toast also. I said yes please, over easy with two slices. I took a seat at the counter where I always sit, and sipped my coffee and shortly after she placed a plate in front of me with the two eggs over easy, toast and bacon. I thanked her as she sat down next to me and had some coffee also. I asked her if she was going to eat. She stood and came back with a slice of toast and some bacon. I asked if that was all she was going to have and she said that was all she wanted. Told her I didn't expect her to be up so early and that I had not made out the list of things I wanted done yet. Victoria said that she knew how to keep house and that I should just let her take care of things, and if there was something I didn't like to tell her. I said ok that would work fine for me. I finished breakfast and thanked her again, before going to the bathroom around the corner to brush my teeth and before going to the office to retrieve my briefcase, and checked that I had everything. I checked the home security system for the outdoor and indoor cameras. I had cameras outside and that system was separate from the indoor. I made sure they were on, the outdoor screen was on all the time, but the screen would time out and wouldn't come on until you moved the mouse. The indoor was password protected and I could monitor it from my phone. I was ready to leave as I went back to the kitchen where Mrs. Cook began cleaning up. Told her I was leaving as she was drying her hands and she came over and hugged and kissed me. I stood there with my hands full, I couldn't move my arms since hers were fully wrapped around me. I kissed her back and she let go of me and said to me, not to worry as I proceeded to the garage.

Wow, felt I was going to have another great day, as I got into my work car, opened the garage door, started the engine and soon pulled out, closing the garage door behind me as I pulled away and headed down the driveway and headed to my office. It was about eight thirty and would be there before nine when we opened. I arrived just as Mrs. Bradley was opening the office door. I said good morning as we entered together and I went to put on the office coffee pot and sat down and gave Joanne, Ms. Cooks employment application. Then I asked her if any of the agents would be good candidates to help her with her duties on a full time basis, because I was thinking of a major reorganization, primarily because of all the business we had going on and it was time to become a more efficient operation. We were busier since I had purchased several more apartment buildings and was going to purchase another complex that had went into receivership due to nonpayment by and out of state company that was having management difficulties. I was purchasing the complex as an investment, they had completed a lot of improvements and were going to sell them as condos, but wanted out when they got in over there head. They were having problems elsewhere and weren't familiar with our area. The closing date was set for a couple weeks away, but it could change as it did a lot of times. Told Joanne, I would make her first Vice President and raise her salary from the $50,000.00 I was paying now to 75,000.00 annually, as a smile came over her face, that she would oversee operations and could hire or pick from the existing staff a first assistant and possibly a second to carry on her daily duties and they would also be employees. And I would separate the operations and expand the office, leasing would be separate from the real estate operations. I asked her what she though and if she had any suggestions on how I or rather we should accomplish this new operation. She said that it was about time I did something to improve the way we operated because she wanted shorter hours, and the raise was a great incentive also and any improvement was long overdue. Then asked me what the plan was.

She stated that she thought Mr. Fitz would be the perfect person to head the leasing operations since he was the licensed leasing agent and already an employee, and since that is what he did all of the time anyway. I said that it would be a separate entity of Harcourt Reality Corp. and that she would oversee operations of both, and would assist him in determining rents for all the properties. And since she was having car problems I would provide her with a company car, and all of this would be a tax write-off. She would head the real estate side until we found someone who would be acceptable. I would also move and expand the office, but had not determined where to so far. I was going to upgrade everything, computers, the waiting area etc. and that she would have a private office. She was all smiles as we stood and she hugged me, gave me a big kiss and said it was the best news she had all year. She asked what Mrs. Cook's duties were. I said housekeeper, and she would soon meet her. She would be going for her employee medical checkups within the week, as soon as I could make the appointments. But that I had to meet with Hector on the two units I would be listing before the week was over, and I was to meet him at noon today.

It was nine forty-five and I had to get on the ball as I went to my desk and started dialing the doctor's office for Mrs. Cook's checkup. The receptionist for Doctor Martin answered and I told her it was for an employment physical, said she had an opening for Wednesday at one o'clock. I said that was fine and confirmed who it was for and hung up before I then made the dental appointment for Mrs. Cook, at the dental office. They said Thursday at eleven o'clock and it was the only opening they had this week because of a cancellation. I took it and hung up, then went and poured myself another cup of coffee, and looked around the office and saw that two of my sales assistants were in and on the phones making deals.

It was ten thirty as I pulled up the RELS, and looked over available office spaces, especially the ones for sale and there were only two available. The current office was large, but not large enough for what I had in mind. I was on the verge of diversifying my company. I sat down and looked them over, and went through the photos, and then I thought about a small shopping center that was up for sale, it had a good location, but several of the stores were closed. It had ample parking, but had been milked for all it was worth by the owners, it was worth looking at. I dialed the listing agent Ms. Thomas, and spoke to her and during the conversation she stated the price had been reduced to try for a quick sale. I asked if I could look at it tomorrow, and she replied yes. Eleven would be a good time and she would call back later to confirm, and offered to drop off more information on the property. I said that would be great and she could leave it with Mrs. Bradley if I wasn't in. I hung up and looked at the clock and it was time for me to head out, it was almost eleven and I didn't want to be late. But before I left, pulled out my phone and brought up the app for my indoor home cameras to see what my new housekeeper was doing. I went through the different cameras and found her busy stripping down the beds and making them up, ok I saw enough for now. I informed Mrs. Bradley about the package. Then she asked when was her new pay was going to take effect. I said the first of the month, which was almost a week from away, and would sit down with her before the end of the week and work it all out, but I had to meet Hector and would soon return. She said ok then.

I proceeded to leave, got in my car and headed to the condo location. It wasn't long before I pulled up and saw Hector was already here. I greeted him with a hug and a handshake as we headed inside; we were both early as we went upstairs. I told him there was some furniture that had to be removed as we went up to 5B. I placed the key in the lock and we entered. I showed him a couple of the outdated outlets and he made a note of those as we walked around, then he said two days, but would be completed by Thursday. We left and went up to 6C, entered and he stated after walking around, both would be done by Thursday and $450.00 for

6C and $500.00 for 5B. I said that was acceptable, then we left. Told Hector that I was getting ready to expand and would need his services, and asked would he be interested in some major reconstruction. He said, Amigo anything for you. I told him I was going to move and expand my office also and would really love to give him first shot at whatever work was needed, and that I would also like for him to come with me when I looked over the mall tomorrow. He said he would be there, if I didn't see him when I arrived to call his cell because he would probably be walking around looking. I said ok, we shook hands and left.

I returned to the office and found Mrs. Bradley in what was our lunch room, and then it struck me. I really needed to improve the office a whole lot. I brought the burger I had picked up cn the way back, and went and sat with Joanne and as we ate together, I talked so more about the expansion. Told her about the mall I would be looking at tomorrow. And that Mr. Martinez would be going with me. After lunch I was going to go over the paper work on the apartment complex that I was going to close on. She gave me some good information about the mall, saying that it was a good location and an opportunity to help the community, and keep it from having a blighted property and was certain that it would go up in value. There was a shortage of space for startups and small business in the area. I agreed with her assessment. We finished our lunch and cleaned up. I was going to step out for a few and would be right back. Decided to drive to the mall, it was only two blocks away, at the intersection of two of the busiest thoroughfares in town and wondered why it was being sold at a reduced price. I soon saw why, its façade was outdated and needed repair. The empty stores weren't helping and there was only one business open and it had a going out of business sign in the front window. The parking lot was in disrepair and there were only a few cars in the lot, but it had space for about two hundred cars, those were the pluses along with the location, and access. There was ample access in the rear for deliveries, and it was of steel and concrete construction. I saw enough and went back to my car and drove around the neighborhood and looked to see how well the area was doing, and found a vibrant business community and newer building more conducive to business before heading back to the office.

When I returned found Mrs. Bradley speaking with a beautiful young woman. She was smartly dressed, tall, fair skin, very pretty and slim; she was very professional and business like. Mrs. Bradley stopped me, and introduced me to Ms. Thomas. I asked her to have a seat at my desk. I asked if she would like some coffee and she declined. We discussed the mall property and she told me that it was owned by her uncle and that he had been sick for several years, and had lost interest in it and had raised the rents to the point that all the tenants had moved out, the taxes and insurance were going up and because it lacked the needed improvements and needed to be modernize he didn't want to make any more repairs, or invest any more money in it. The taxes were currently up to date and the price had been reduced as a last ditch effort to get something out of it. She handed me a large envelope full of all the pertinent information on the property. I asked if she was in a rush while I looked over the documents. She crossed her long shapely legs and I asked her what the final price would be. Said her uncle would accept $3,000,000.00 cash since the taxes were soon due. I said give me a moment to think about it, then said I would meet her at the property tomorrow to take a closer look. And asked if she had any other offers on the table, and she said no. She hadn't received any calls in over a week. I asked if she would take a deposit until I looked at it, and a smile came to her face. I asked Mrs. Bradley to make a check out to; as I looked for the owner of record in the documents and handed it to Mrs. Bradley. Then asked Ms. Thomas how much she required, she stated $50,000.00, would be a good retainer. Mrs. Bradley heard the amount and went to make out the check. I asked her if we were still on for eleven and she said based on my interest ten would be even better for her. I said ok as Mrs. Bradley returned and handed me the check to sign. I gave it to Ms. Thomas along with an envelope. She said the number I had called earlier was her cell, and to call when I arrived there tomorrow. I said ok as we stood and shook hands. I walked her to the door and watched her get into her car and leave. I returned to my desk and called Hector, he answered shortly and I told him the time had moved up to ten, he said ok and we hung up.

Well it was two thirty and I continued to look over the documents and found the main part of the original mall was over forty-five years old and had been added two several times as the surrounding area expanded and there were numerous city violations, but they were mostly minor. I was thinking based on the structure, a total rehab was the only way to make this work, and that would mean an investment of more than twice the sales price. Then thought what if I tore the entire thing down and started from scratch, one advantage to that would be a big property tax reduction and a tax write-off. I could then let it sit and wait for an offer from a developer, or eventually develop it myself, or even break up the large acreage into smaller parcels, there were endless options available. I would first look and see if the structure was sound and would be worth a rehab, the price was more than right for the location. I looked again at the two office buildings that were listed for sale. I ruled them out as I researched them more thoroughly then thought about the closed furniture store that was a block away, and was a smart looking building, it was set back from the street with more than ample parking on three sides and it was two stories tall had an entrance with a large open ocular atrium type entrance area. It had been an upscale furniture store before they consolidated locations, had two elevators and was only five years old, had fire suppression and the electrical that was more than suited for our needs and was considered a green building and also had solar panels on the roof and other energy saving features. The other was to faraway and had been a medical center, was single story, and the parking was limited. The other choice was off the beaten path, and wasn't conducive to being exposed to the public. I eliminated both of them and placed a call to the agent handling the furniture store, as a matter of fact I had just been in there when they had their moving sale, and now the property was empty.

I called the listing agent and spoke with Mr. Samuelsson, said he was very glad I had called because the store owners wanted a quick sale, and were going to dump him after his listing agreement ran out in two weeks. Told him I would like to see it as soon as possible and asked what the asking price was, he said it was $890,000.00. I asked if one o'clock tomorrow afternoon was doable. He said he would gladly meet me there. I said ok and thank you very much, and hung up. It was going on near five and decided to go through my calendar and all I had set up for the coming week to make sure I hadn't overlapped any of my obligations. I was set as I viewed my up and coming schedule. I would wait till closing and leave with Mrs. Bradley since we closed late on Mondays at six pm, and the same for Wednesdays and Fridays, and on Tuesdays and Thursdays and Saturday, nine to five pm, closed Sundays. I pulled out my phone and dialed up the home app and peeped on my housekeeper, found her cleaning the basement area. I watched for several minutes before the office phone rang and it was someone looking for a home. I asked them to hold, as I transferred it to one of the sales associates who were sitting at his desk reading the local daily newspaper. Sales associates are independent contractors and only get paid when they make a sale or list a property when it sells.

That is how I started and then I started by buying my first apartment building, and then another, and another and before I knew it I had several and there is something to be said about economies of scale. I started with one twelve unit, then two more, and before I knew it I was into rehabbing older buildings and putting in individual heating with central air and bingo, I could really make a tidy sum on the rents and had eliminated the cost of energy and water. Then I ran into a neighborhood that had older brick buildings near eighty to ninety years old, you know the ones that had very large rooms and servant quarters for the maid to stay in; these turned out to be great for condo conversions. And turned out really special especially after a gut rehab, that's when I went from being a broker, who had just left someone else's office and struck out on my own. That was nine years ago, and shortly after met Mrs. Bradley, she was my first associate, and then she soon became a broker after my insistence. We have been together for eight and a half years now and it wasn't long before it really started to jump off for me. I took some of my earnings and put some on a small startup company's stock. I invested $10,000.00, and was really doubting myself, then thought I could see it going somewhere, and then it shot up and because I was one of the first thousand investors, was given a guaranteed for two years that I could buy more stock for the original price I paid. I took a giant leap and invested almost my first million. I was real hesitant because of how hard I had worked to earn it, well anyway. I made the purchase and a month before my option expired the stock exploded and my $950,000.00 at $5.00 dollars a share went to $870.00 a share, I cashed out all but my original investment which was 50,000 shares, and I still receive a hell of a good dividend.

That was around the time shortly after I had been married almost ten years when my wife died from a massive stroke that brought on a sudden massive heart attack. She had just arrived at work and was alone sitting in her car outside the beauty shop where she worked as a stylist when it happened. Luckily she was able to park her car before it happened or probably other people would have been injured in an accident. She was a small woman, very pretty and cute and had a very good personality, but loved all the bad things you shouldn't eat, like fried chicken and ice-cream. She didn't go to the doctor, and it was the high cholesterol that did her in. That was the most devastating thing that ever happened to me and that all happened just as I had set out on my own. It was the most devastating thing that happened to me since my mother passed, and then my dad. I am on my own now, and feel I am finally doing well now. My wife passed before I started really making it and ever since I have been sort of grieving and just decided to fill the void in my life by accumulating as much wealth and money as I could. And my sex life, well that was down to masturbating to porno videos. But there has been a real void in my life that money can't buy and it isn't everything, it is one of the reasons I try to help the people around me. My dad used to say, he never saw an armored money truck at a funeral yet. How true, you can't take it with you. Mrs. Bradley came over and woke me from my thoughts, and said it was time for us to start locking up. Well so far it had been a very productive day as I went and washed out the coffee pot before we locked up and walked out. Said she hoped we would have some time to talk more tomorrow. And said I would make some time, we said goodnight and got into our cars and headed home.

I wasn't quite ready to go home, even though Mrs. Cook was there, she wasn't my wife and she wasn't an obligation and I had not said when I would get home. I went down and parked across from the furniture store I would be inspecting tomorrow and imagined how it would look as our new offices. After sitting and looking for almost a half hour, decided to get some dinner and headed to Wong's to have a light supper. I loved Chinese food and was a regular customer. When I arrived it wasn't crowded since it was around seven pm, and ordered a Hunan dish of broccoli & shrimp. Fawn my waitress also brought me a pot of green tea as I waited for my order. Mrs. Wong came and asked if she could sit with me. I said yes of course, she went on to say that they would like to expand and asked if the store next door would be available. Said I would have to check because I had a lot going on and with so many different locations to manage I wasn't up on the specific's right then. I asked if it wasn't going to be available, in the near future would a change of location be acceptable. And said it would depend on how large of a space, she said the store next door was going to move, and I said Oh. But they would prefer to stay where they were. I pulled out a small note book I kept with me and made a note to check and get back to her. Then she asked me about the young lady I had come in with the last time I was there. I said she was my new housekeeper. A smile came over her face, and said, she no housekeeper, she loves you very much. I smiled back. She said Mrs. Wong know. I said how. She say, how you say English, body language, she love you, you should keep, you much too busy since wife die, you need love. I thanked Mrs. Wong for her intuitive insight as my food arrived, she excused herself and reassured her I would get back to her very soon. I finished my meal and left a tip for Fawn and exited. Then walked next door to Wong's to see what was there. And saw it was a clothing store; they had a sign in the window advertising a moving sale for the next two months. I guessed Mrs. Wong's insights were on the money and you couldn't miss a sign that big. I pulled out my notes and made additional comments before getting in my car and heading home, again passing the mall I was also going to see tomorrow.

When I arrived home several more lights were on than usual, as I backed into the garage. I got out closed the garage door and entered my home, it was quiet inside as I went to the washroom across from the laundry room and washed my hands, brushed my teeth, rinsing my mouth before taking my briefcase to the office and sitting down. It was getting close to ten as I turned on the television for a few minutes before the news came on and looked around and everything was the same but was different. Then I realized it was clean, the small specks of dust were gone and the room smelled fresh, such a pleasant and delightful atmosphere, and then remembered I now had a housekeeper. I finished looking at the news more concerned about the weather because I was going to be out most of the day, then I opened my briefcase to leave a note for Mrs. Cook or rather Victoria about her appointments, and wrote them on a large post-it-note and I closed up, turning off the lights and headed to my bed room. When I entered my bedroom I found everything in order, the bed had been made, the dirty cloths had been removed and it smelled fresh. I was pleasantly surprised, and after disrobing and entering a fresh and clean bathroom, with fresh towels. I took a long hot shower, put on the clean bathrobe that was hanging on the back of the bathroom door, and then decided to check on Victoria. I knocked on her door lightly, there was no answer, and I softly opened the door and could hear her sleeping hard. I assumed she had a full and busy day. I closed the door and went to my room and got in bed and soon fell asleep.

Five

Tuesday: Day Five.

I started my day as usual shortly after six o'clock and did my usual morning routine before dressing. I decided to wear a suit with and a knit instead of a shirt and tie. Dressed and went downstairs and found Victoria looking fresh. She had just woken up, and was making the coffee. I said good morning to her. I reached over took her by the hand and told her what a magnificent job she had done cleaning the house, she kissed me and I pointed to the note on the fridge with the times for her medical and dental appointments. She asked if I was going to take her. I replied that she might have to take herself, but would know more as my day progressed. She asked if I wanted breakfast. I replied yes please. She then proceeded to fix it as I poured myself some coffee. She asked about the empty bed rooms upstairs, and how I would like them, one was completely empty and the other had a complete bed room set in it and could be used as a guess room if I ever had any. Told her to just leave them, they didn't need much attention, except cleaning and vacuuming every now and then, the rest of the house was of more importance. She asked what time would I be home. Said I didn't know because I was getting ready to enlarge my office. Said she would like to see it someday. I said in due time, as she placed my breakfast before me. I finished eating and said thank you, and hope you have a wonderful day. We embraced, she kissed me passionately, and then I went to retrieve my briefcase before heading out. As I was leaving, thought I heard her say in a muffled voice, I love you as I entered the garage.

I drove to the office; it was early, eight fifteen as I looked at my watch. I parked and was one of only three cars in the parking lot, and was able to park right in front for once. I though at the new office we could have reserved parking, with the employees on one side of the building. I opened the door and entered, turned on the lights but locked the door behind me, when Mrs. Bradley came in we would open. I fired up my office computer and went through our computerized records; I was keen to have all my business computerized, with paper backup of course. I called my attorney and left a message for him to get back to me as soon as possible. Mr. Harold Hippies, was on retainer, and older Irish guy, jovial and was much fun to be around, he did just about all my legal work, was single and did real estate law because it wasn't as demanding as corporate or criminal. He had done both in the past and said he liked the slower pace and had his office in a store front he shared with six other attorneys. I was going to make him an offer to become my full time company lawyer and move him to our office and offer him a salary. I looked up the leases on the strip mall where Wong's was located. Found that the clothing store had one month left on their lease, but had extended an additional month. I guess Mrs. Wong had inside info, but it should make her happy. I made a note of it and left one for Fitz, and would get back to her as soon as possible, she was the person to see, she kept the books and Mr. Wong cooked and told me she kept a foot up his ass, they were a happy and funny couple.

I heard the front door open and Mrs. Bradley came in and locked the door behind her, we greeted each other. She was very beautiful in her own right, pretty brown skin, tall, five foot eleven, well built, nice figure, ample butt and breast and with a stern look most of the time, but a very beautiful face, she gave you the impression of the teacher or mother you loved but respected. She put on the coffeepot I had completely forgotten about, and came over to my desk and we began to discuss the changes that were going to occur very soon. I stated she could go to Hicks Auto City and pick out the auto she wanted, color and everything and we would add it to the lease agreement I had with them. She said ok great. I said she could go any time after work, preferably Thursday when we closed at five, and asked if that was convenient for her, she said yes it was.

I also told her that I decided to buy the big mall, and demolish it soon after the purchase and hold on to the land. Also the furniture store down the street that closed and was a newer building, I had made up my mind, and it would be our new office location. Also I was going to offer Mr. Hippies a position inside our office, because I felt the time had come for full time counsel. I thought that we should also have a receptionist/secretary. I ended my speech and asked for her opinion or approval. Joanne looked at me as I could see her turning things over in her mind. Just then the phone rang and it was Mr. Hippies, I explained to him my proposition and he said he would welcome the change of location also, the only thing we would have to discuss would be his hours, and pay. I said ok, and would call back later to let him know when I would be available, and we could come to an arrangement, he said ok and looked forward to the discussion. I hung up and Mrs. Bradley smiled and said to the best of her knowledge that she felt it was a good move and needed, and was very much long overdue. She asked about the secretary position and said her daughter was graduating from City College and had expressed interest in getting a full time job. Said she wanted to help her mother out more and asked what it would pay. I said based on her qualifications about $10.00 an hour for starters and said we would have to work on a new budget. I also said the mall, and office would both be cash deals. One other thing, since Mr. Hippies was also our tax man; it should work to our advantage. I was also a silent partner in a mortgage originating company and owned half the business, it was very profitable, and we could also rent them space in our new office, one stop shopping in the real estate business.

She said that all sounded great, and said it was time to unlock the door; I reminded her that I had to be at the mall at ten. Joanne said one of the associates had brought in a listing, and she was in the process of looking it over. Oh, I said before leaving, I gave her the info on the Wong's inquiry about expanding and what I saw on file, and asked her to give Mrs. Wong a call, tell her that next door would be available very soon and ask when she would like to talk about it. She said ok, and hoped I was wrong about tearing down the mall. I said you know we could always start from scratch. Jokingly she said, please get out, as I smiled at her and then headed for my car and drove the short distance up the street to the mall. After pulling into the lot, I recognized Hectors truck and I pulled up and parked next to him, got out and headed towards the main part of the old building. It wasn't long before I soon found Hector walking around and looking up and checking the structural integrity of the building. We greeted one another and he began to point at some of the deteriorating features on the inside of some of the load bearing supports. Hector had gone to City College and had a degree in building maintenance and engineering and knew what he was looking at. I had taken architecture in high school and two semesters in college and a year of structural engineering and we both agreed, this might not be salvageable, and was only worth the land it was on. I asked Hector if he could meet me at one o'clock and gave him the address to the closed furniture store. And stated it would not be as bad as this. Said he hoped not. Just then my phone rang, it was Ms. Thomas, and she was in the parking lot and wanted to know where we were. Hector and I headed to where she was standing, on the side walk very near the last open store. We greeted one another, and I introduced Mr. Martinez, and said I would purchase the property from her, and asked if she would come to the office to seal the deal. Said she was ready, and had the written approval to act on her uncles behalf. I said great and thanked Hector. And said see you later as we all departed.

We returned to the office, and Ms. Thomas sat at my desk. As we were conducting our business, Mr. Hippies entered the front door, he came to my desk after greeting Mrs. Bradley, pulled up a chair and I said what a coincidence. I introduced him to Ms. Thomas, and explained that I was making the purchase from her of the mall up the street and handed him the papers from the previous day as he looked them over. I offered to get them both a cup of coffee, she declined and so did he. I went to get some for myself. I returned and Hippies said all was in order, as he signed off on them. Since this was a large direct cash purchase I called the bank and made and electronic payment to her uncle's account, he had signed all the papers prior and she had brought more legal documentation with her in anticipation of the sale. Once she received confirmation of the wire transfer, she stood and thanked me. I wished her and her uncle well, she stated he had taken a turn for the worse, and was glad she was able to sell the property now. I asked her, what were her qualifications, in real-estate. She was a

broker also, but because of her uncles health was only involved
with his properties for now. I asked if there were any others
available. She replied yes, there was a small two hundred fifty unit
apartment complex which was going to be available, when he
passed, which she would inherit. Stated she didn't want to be
bothered, managing and had decided she would sell it and move to
a much warmer climate. I asked her for the location, and told her I
wished to be the first to know when and if she followed through on
her plans. And she said based on the way I handled this business
deal she would definitely make sure I would be the first to know. I
thanked her and walked with her to the car. I thanked her again and
said it had been a pleasure doing business with her and looked
forward to seeing her again one day. She smiled and thanked me
before she left. One thing for sure, she had her uncle on her mind,
you could tell by her demeanor.

I went back inside, and talked to Mr. Hippies about my offer, an
about moving him into the same office with us. He said the office
where he was now located was too small and the other lawyers had
asked him if he would open his own office. They wanted more
space and were more involved with criminal and civil actions, like
divorces and felt he wasn't what they wanted their office to be
involve in and could use the space he occupied. I said you know
what's funny about this situation. I own the building they are in. I
asked him how soon before he would have before he had to move,
and he said they had asked him if he could possibly move by the
end of the following week, or end of the month. We discussed and
I asked if he was full time here what hours did he want to work,
and he stated that ten to four five days and maybe some Saturdays.
And then I asked how much, he replied $85,000.00, to start. I
asked if a company car would help and he said hell yes. I said you
can accompany Mrs. Bradley on Thursday evening, and pick the
one you want; she was going to have one also. Said he was getting
tired of having to run to the municipal building to file documents
in his old car and that would be considered company business. I
said he will have a secretary and she would be available to him. I
said if everything this evening went as planned we should be

moving in very soon. He asked where and I gave him the new location down the street. He lived within walking distance of the new office and old. He stood, I gave him a larger envelope for the mall documents, and he said he would return with them tomorrow, and would try and have everything filed by this evening; I thanked him as he stood to leave.

It was getting close to noon and I asked Mrs. Bradley if she would go to lunch now so I wouldn't miss my appointment down the street. She said yes, great and headed out the door and down the street to Martha's. I sat back and pulled up my home camera app and looked to see what my new housekeeper was doing, she was busy washing windows in the kitchen, and when she finished, washed her hands and went to the living room and laid-back on the couch in the living room and took a nap. I turned off and was approached by an associate, and answered several of his questions before he returned to his desk. Two associates were in the office so I didn't have to answer any phones, looked over the comps for the new office and was more than satisfied with the features and price. I called up the local demolition company and asked them to give me a price on demolishing the mall. They said they would look it over before giving me a cost estimate. I asked that they include the parking lot also and wanted the property completely cleared. They said ok, and would be in touch before the week was over. I thanked them and hung up just as Mrs. Bradley returned from lunch. I had about twenty minutes before I was to meet Mr. Samuelsson, and informed Mrs. Bradley that I was going to walk down the street to the appointment, she said ok, as I stood and headed for the door before walking out.

Looking at all the shops as I walked, noticed all the local businesses were doing well along this stretch and when I arrived at the corner and crossed, I recognized Hectors truck, but no Hector. He was walking around back and finally appeared, we shook hands and then shortly after Mr. Samuelsson pulled into the parking lot. He parked and came over to where Hector and I were standing and introduced himself. We shook as he retrieved a set of keys from his briefcase. We walked to the main entrance, tinted glass double doors, he unlocked and opened them and we entered and immediately went and entered a code in a box by the door. The front entrance space had a large oval opening overhead and you could see the ceiling above the second floor, and straight ahead approximately forty-five feet was an elevator with a stair case that rapped around it to the upper level. The lighting was the latest energy saving type, the elevators were hydraulic, the main entrance was completely tiled from wall to wall and all the way to and around the elevator, I walked around the main floor and was very satisfied with the large open and sun light filled space, then we went up to the second floor, the elevator was operable, so Hector took it up. Samuelsson and I walked up the wide marble staircase. We reached the top floor, which seamed even more spacious and filled with natural light. The large oval opening in front of the elevator which allowed you to look downstairs enhanced the large space. Because of the high ceiling and windows the view downstairs was beautiful with its steel railing and glass panels, it didn't need very much work, some fresh paint and some cubicles and a few walls and it would be more than ready. Samuelsson said he had spoken to the sellers and they were willing to drop the price another $50,000.00 if I bought today and that would make the final sales price $840,000.00. I told him he had a deal, and asked how soon we could close, he pulled out his phone, stepped away for a few minutes, before coming back, and said Monday, and his office would be getting the paper work together along with the seller, he said the property was unencumbered and we should be able to close Monday. I said great as we shook hands. He said he had a few calls to make and stepped away, as Hector and I circled around, and I said, get ready you have this job, give me a price, but first I wanted it painted all white, the ceiling seemed ok, they were white downstairs and also upstairs. I was going to contact an architect for the lay out I had in mind. And would have him get the necessary permits if any were needed, and then he could start, but first I had to close. Samuelsson came back smiling and said my offer had been accepted, and we went downstairs and outside as he retrieved the contracts from his car. I signed the contract to purchase and we exchange business cards. Well I thought here we go as Hector said he had estimated about how much paint and suggested painting all the walls white primer first before choosing any colors. It sounds like a plan I told him before I decided to walk back to the office but first I walked around the outside of the entire building. The lot was very large, there was more than ample parking, with such a deep lot, and it was also wide, I estimated it might be larger than half an acer. The parking lot was on three sides, there was a double entrance drive with a ground level lighted sign which was on a small island section between the two. In the rear, there was a freight elevator and a loading dock, the façade was very modern, clean and smooth and the windows were the height of the building in front and wrapped around the top floor one forth the length of the building and ended where the elevator was located on both sides which would give the atrium and entrance plenty of natural light from above, the side windows on the upper and lower floors after that were located up high giving you natural light as well as having a wall and ran three quarters the length of the structure . This was definitely a plus, I was happy all had gone so smoothly, knowing in this business there could be plenty of glitches. I wondered why they were selling at such a low price, and headed back to my office.

When I finally returned to my desk, I pulled up the selling company on my computer that owned the property, found out after checking their corporate site they had over extended and were consolidating stores locations across the country and had taken a write off. Where they had two or more they went to having one. They sold really well made and expensive furniture and the market had really slowed down for that end of the furniture spectrum. I remembered how nice their furniture was when I had came and looked around when they were open. I told Mrs. Bradley that it went very well and was a done deal, and hoped to close on Monday. Before I cleared my desk, I call Louis Brown an architect, and told him I had a small but profitable job for him and asked him to call me back by next Tuesday and described what the job was, he said there was only one permit that would be needed and that I could call anytime and he would meet me, and I could tell him what I wanted. I gave him the property address so he could pull the blueprints and then he would be set. I needed to call Mrs. Kashia and dialed her number and informed her all would be completed by Thursday. I would call back and let her know when the work was done and we could look at it, I thanked her again and hung up. While I cleared my desk, as an associate came in and we spoke briefly. I informed Joanne I was gone for the day and would see her around noon the next day. I said good night and headed for my car, put my briefcase inside and exited the parking lot. I was tired and intended to go home and get some rest.

When I arrived home, turned around, and backed into the garage, went inside and all was quiet, found Vicky asleep on the couch. I headed upstairs to undressed and take a quick warm shower. I hadn't eaten since breakfast and decided to fix a pizza from the freezer. I put on a pair of shorts and a t-shirt, my bed had been made up and the room cleaned. I headed downstairs and went to the kitchen an fired up the oven, removed my pizza pan, diced up a onion and a jalapeno and placed the pizza on the pan spread out the vegies on top added some olive oil, seasoning and added some shredded cheese and popped it in the oven and set the timer. I went to my office and reviewed the in-house surveillance, put it on multi-screen and fast forwarded from when I left this morning, watching Vicky go about her cleaning task up until she fell asleep on the couch. As soon as I was finished with that, closed the program and went back to the kitchen and grabbed a beer, then the oven dinged and shut off, and took an oven glove and placed the pizza on top of the stove, grabbed the pizza wheel out of the drawer and sliced the pizza, before putting the wheel in the dish water. Just about then, Victoria walked in wiping sleep from her soft eyes and she came and hugged me. I hugged her back, we sat in the nook and ate the pizza, and she asked how my day went. I replied it was great. We sat and ate pizza with glasses of red wine until I was satisfied.

We went to the living room and I turned on the big screen television, sat on the couch and I stretched out and relaxed, as I flicked through the channels she sat down in the chair next to the couch, an end table separating the two. I found an interesting program on the Public Information Service channel, laid back and I don't remember when, but fell asleep. I awoke about an hour later and decided to go to bed. Victoria was still sitting in the chair as I got up. I told her good night and headed upstairs. She turned off the television and lights and we went upstairs to our bedrooms as she followed. Said she was going to take a shower, it was supposed to rain overnight and that was good, it hadn't rained in a couple weeks and the grass was starting to show it in the spots where there wasn't a sprinkler. I told her good night before going to my room and climbing into bed under the covers and going to asleep again, it was two am when I woke and heard the rain coming down very hard, saw the lighting flash outside my window and heard the loud claps of thunder. The storm was very close. Suddenly my bedroom door flew open and a tearful and frighten Victoria entered and climbed into bed with me crying and grabbed onto me, holding me tight. I held her trembling and tearful body in my arms and pulled the cover over us; she was really scared. I said it was going to be alright as I held and caressed her warm body as she slowly calmed down. Soon she was rubbing me back and she soon fell asleep. It wasn't long before I fell asleep again, this time I wasn't alone. We sleep all through the rest of the storm only to awaken and start a new day.

Six
Wednesday: Day Six

I woke a little after seven. Vicky and I hugged and felt on one another, she held me very tight and said she would be good. It was time to get up, and get cleaned up because her physical examination for employment was today. I would take her and told her it was at nine forty-five but we should leave at around nine. She said ok and went to her room to bathe. I took a shower and decided to wear my grey suit, silver tie, black shirt and shoes and socks and some cologne. I went downstairs and put on the coffee pot, and took some donuts out. Soon the coffee was ready as I poured a cup and ate a donut and just as Victoria came downstairs and joined me. She wore one of the black dresses with high heels, stockings, earrings, bracelet, and a small necklace, some cologne and had her small purse. I said good morning. She said the same and kissed me. I looked at the clock and it was about eight thirty and I said we had some time, she asked if I wanted anything else to eat. I said no we would get something after her physical. We could have lunch, she said ok because she wasn't really hungry yet. We finished our coffee and I was sitting on the kitchen stool and asked her to come here which she did. I reached around and pulled her near and pulled her dress up, and saw that she was wearing the stocking with the attached garter I had bought with a pair of black panties; she asked if master was satisfied. I stood and felt her breast through her dress and said I was. I asked her to go to the living room and have a seat as I went to the office to retrieve my SLR digital camera. Then as she sat on the couch, I asked her to give me some sexy poses, which she did. I spent about a half hour photographing her before I said it was time for us to go. She followed me around as I checked the house, then we went to the garage, got into the auto, and headed to the doctor's office, she asked if I was satisfied with her appearance. I told her yes she pleased me very much.

When we reached the doctor's office, we went inside and checked in. I informed the receptionist that it was an employment exam; she said yes, she had all the information and informed me that blood would be taken because there was a new pre-employment exam that checked for STDs and other contagions and was much more thorough than the previous employment exams. Told her to bill the office and said she had all of that information also. I thanked her and had a seat next to Victoria. The wait wasn't long before they called her in early, about ten minutes before her actual appointment. I sat and read the magazines they had in the waiting room, while I sat and thought about Vicky and having her in my home. I know she said she loved me, and I was starting to feel that way to, but I wasn't going to tell her or say anything yet because it had only been five days since she has been with me. I felt it was too soon and wanted be sure all that was happening was real. I didn't want my dick thinking for me. I had enjoyed watching the bondage videos, but the other day was my first time actually doing it. I have to be honest with myself. I enjoyed it, and when I had looked at the videos of her and her ex, I was turned on, and it's like she then just materialized, and now was standing in front of me, begging for me to spank her. The other problem was the old saying, don't look a gift horse in the mouth. I guess I should be thankful but cautious and see how this all plays out. I found myself naturally attracted to her and just like before we left home today I was treating her like she was my wife, pulling up her dress, looking to see what she was wearing, she allowed me to do to her whatever I wanted to do to her. I was excited just thinking about her. I needed someone in my life and was sure acting like I wanted it very much. We were there a little more than an hour when Victoria came out and over to me and said, they would call her if there were any problems and we could go. We exited the clinic and headed to the parking lot. I said we would have lunch at Wong's and have the box lunch, she asked what that was. I replied, you will see, and besides I had some business to take care of while we were there. We talked and I asked her what turned her on the most, she said just being with me. I said besides that, like what really was the hottest thing that drove her out of her mind. She said, it hadn't happened to her yet but being tied up and hanging, spread eagle, whipped and stimulated, maybe blindfold at the same time

with clamps on her various body parts. I asked her if that's what
she wanted. She said yes, if only I did it to her.

We reached Wong's and entered as Mrs. Wong greeted and
seated us, this time up front, she complemented Victoria on her
appearance as I introduced her. Mrs. Wong gave us the lunch
menu; I said to her that she had great insight in reference to the
store closing next door. And said we would set a day to discuss
how much space she wanted to add to her restaurant. She said
Mondays were best because they were closed. Mondays, I said ok,
but please give me a week or two. She said that was fine because it
was a little too soon but didn't want it to slip away and the space
get rented again before they had a chance to expand. We placed
out orders and drank some tea. I said to Vicky, you know that I had
never struck a woman before spanking you the other day. And that
you seemed to revel in being ordered around, and asked if this was
the way she wanted to be treated. She replied that she was in very
much in love with me and would do anything I wanted, and wanted
me to want and love her also and she was here to serve me anyway
I saw fit and knew deep inside I was kind hearted. I replied that it
hadn't been a week since we met, and how did she know that she
would be happy, or that I would love her back and would not abuse
her. She replied that she had dreamed about me before I even came
into her life. That I was the one for her, that I had already made her
very happy, beyond anything she had ever dreamed about. I said
what if I met someone else. To which she replied, she just wanted
to serve me and that it didn't matter if I had a girlfriend, she would
always be there for me. I asked if she had ever been with another
woman. She said no, but that one time Mr. Kashia and her husband
had discussed having the two of them preform a lesbian sex act and
they would video tape it. I asked if she had ever seen Mrs.
Kashia's videos, no she replied. She thought Mr. and Mrs. Kashia
had done some but had never seen any. She asked why I had asked.
And said I would have to show her. I asked how her relationship
with Sophia was. She felt that Sophia was warm towards her at
times, but at others not so much and felt she was more difficult
after her husband died. Felt that since her husband was driving

when they met their demise it was her fault. I asked how so. Said that her husband was really very upset with her and didn't know why, except that his uncle mentioned he could do much better referring to him having a wife. He had called her very unpleasant and demeaning names, tied her up and made her sit in the wooden chair in the closet for several hours before he untied her, spit in her face and slapped her and said when he got back home he was really going to teach her a real lesson and he was feed up with her and after he beat her ass he was going to throw her out on the street, except the day he did and said all that he didn't never get back and said she felt relief that he never did return. He had become unconcerned and even mean when they moved here after being around his uncle, but she didn't miss him as he was becoming more unbearable every day and had even thought of leaving him. She didn't know what was might happen to her, so she went and applied for the job at the discount store so she wouldn't have to be home as much when he was there and she would have some money of her own, and lucky for her they hired her. And since she had never gone any further than high school felt lucky she was able to make more than the minimum wage, and was for a while doing ok. Mrs. Kashia came and told her she would eventually have to move since she was unable to pay her the $700.00 dollars a month rent that her deceased husband had paid, and the insurance he had was just enough to have him cremated, she basically had nothing, and was trying to save by not eating as much and not spending on anything that wasn't necessary. When Mrs. Kashia told her she was going to sell the unit and she would evict her if she didn't leave and also said she was an undesirable slut and didn't care if she was homeless and also told her she was a worthless piece of shit and a tramp. I asked her why she hugged her when she left. Vicky said she didn't hate her, it wouldn't do any good and she did truly wish her well and she forgave her and hating her would only make her life miserable. Said god sent me to her and that was all that mattered to her now and knew I cared very much about her, and this morning when I lifted her dress was proof to her I cared about her.

Just then Fawn came with our food. I thanked her and Vicky opened up more for we really hadn't talked as much until now as much as we had sex. I asked if she had any dreams or aspirations and what she wanted out of life. Stated that she just wanted to have a simple and normal life, to be able to love someone and they love and cherish her, and not have to live on the streets homeless, or to be abused. I asked if her penance for bondage wasn't a form of abuse. To which she replied it turned her on as long as it wasn't for real, meaning she knew people in her life that had been really abused to the point that they had mental and physical problems. Said she had a need to feel submissive and serve and that was a needed turn on for her to be happy. As we ate, said that I felt very much attracted to her and really hoped I could come to truly love and appreciate her as a woman. We continued to eat and drink our tea, when we finished Fawn came and removed our empty dishes and asked if we wanted any desert, to which we both replied no thanks, then she brought the bill with the two customary fortune cookies. I ate mine after I broke it open, and read the fortune, it said (love will find you don't waste too much time) I ate the rest and drank more tea as Vicky opened hers and ate half and read the small slip of paper, then she looked at me and smiled, and passed it to me, I read it (your dreams are coming true, don't let go) I passed her mine, then we smiled at each other. I placed the money in the folder with a tip and stood as we stood and headed for the door as Mrs. Wong bid us good bye.

We walked to the car and I opened the door for Victoria and before she got in I grabbed hold of her, turned her around so she faced me as I hugged her tight and kissed her. Giving her a very passionate kiss as we stood and held each other a good minute. I told her that she was growing on me fast. I released her as she got into the car. I closed the door and walked to the other side and got in. I turned to her and she was crying as I reached over and took her hand in mine and kissed it, she leaned over to kiss me again, and said she loved me very much. I said let's play a game, she asked what kind of game. I said take your panties off, she slowly pulled the hem of her dress up exposing her very sexy and smooth

thighs and raised her butt and pulled her panties down and handed
them to me. I brought them to my nose and I could smell her
sweetness and perfume, she looked at me and smiled as I parted
her legs and felt her getting aroused, then I said buckle up, started
the engine as she asked where were we going. And I said that
maybe we should go to the mall, to which she replied she didn't
have any panties on and that would make her very hot and want to
make love to me. I said not until we first picked up some items,
and I wanted to get her something special. She asked what, and I
said it would be a surprise. I drove to the Sweet Wood Mall, it was
all upscale stores and she was dressed for it, we exited the car and
entered, we held each other's hand until we reached Howards
jewelry store, we looked around and I saw a pearl necklace with
matching earrings and bracelet and asked to see them, they were
cultured pearls and it was a very lovely set. I asked if she could try
them on and they said of course. Vicky removed the small gold
necklace, earrings and bracelet she was wearing and placed them
inside her purse, she put the pearl set on; it was gorgeous on her
and told the salesman I would take the set, and asked Vicky to
leave them on, he rung up the sale and placed in a bag the case that
it came in. I grabbed Victoria by her hand and we went to a store
nearby that sold purses and shoes. I asked her to look around. I
said you need a better purse; she was reluctant because they were
expensive. I said to her that she had to dress the part for me, and a
big beautiful smile came over her face with tears and I put my arm
around her and said don't worry, and whispered in her ear that she
deserved it. She found two purses, one black with a handle and
shoulder strap, and a light brown medium sized bag with double
straps that matched a pair of shoes, she sat down and tried on the
shoes and she said they were tight and the sales lady returned with
the right size, she put them on and was happy with the fit. I told the
sales lady we would take the purses and shoes, she wrapped them
and placed everything in a bag. I told Victoria we were going
home, and she whispered in my ear that she was so hot she was
ready to explode if I touched her womanhood. We walked toward
the doors leading to the parking lot and returned to the car, after

Vicky got in and I entered, I pulled her dress up and touched her, and as I felt her moisture she exploded and screamed with pleasure, as she was breathing with shorten breaths, I reached over her and buckled her seat belt as she grabbed my head and pulled me to her and she kissed me, her tongue went down my throat, I sat back and drove out the lot and we headed home.

Victoria sat back and looked at me the whole time on the way home and, I asked what she was thinking about. She replied how she was going to make love to me like never before and any plans I had for the rest of the day I could forget about as I pulled into the drive way and opened the garage door, pulled inside and we got out. We grabbed the bags and headed inside and got as far as the stairway when she grabbed me around the neck pulled me to her and licked my ear and started to unbuckle my belt. I grabbed her and said lets go upstairs and take off out clothes. I had to pee; she then relented as we headed upstairs. I told her to put her stuff away and I would see her in a minute. I undressed and went to the bath room to freshen up and about ten minutes later she walked in wearing nothing as I came out of the bathroom naked and she ran to me and pushed me onto the bed and climbed on top and asked, what I had meant in the car about playing the part. I said that if she wanted to be seen with me she had to look like she belonged to me. That she was to be the most feminine in appearance even if she was my housekeeper. I didn't want to tell her yet, but I was falling madly in love with her as she rubbed my head and moved her face to mine and kissed me passionately as I held her in my arms. I felt her breast, back, butt, thighs, as she reached and placed me inside of her and laid on top of me and continued to kiss me as I held her tight. I know it was early evening when we left the mall and I don't know what time it was when after several hours of pure unadulterated sex, we decided to take a shower, and get something to eat, it was fortunate that I didn't have any obligations until tomorrow and she only had a dental appointment. When I looked at the clock it was seven pm, I didn't know what I wanted and asked Vicky to think of something, she said don't even think of going out, said she wasn't finished with me. I said we had a life time, she said did I know what that implied. I told her that it was her that said as long as she could be with me she would be happy, she smiled and hugged me and began crying as she said please don't ever let her go. I reassured her everything was going to be alright.

We decided to order out, and we agreed on some Italian, a pizza and a couple of beef sandwiches, fries and a pasta salad. I retrieved a bottle of red wine from the basement fridge and we sat on the couch and we held each other. I could not help myself now as I whispered in her ear that I really loved her. I was tired of fighting how I really felt inside. And had in the few days we had been together felt less up tight and very much relaxed. I just had to complete the plans for my new operations so I could be with her more often. I had more reason to live that ever before now that Vicky was in my life. The bell rang and I checked the security cameras, it was our food order. I grabbed the cash I had taken out and went to the front door and retrieved our order, brought it into the kitchen and Vicky joined me, we unwrapped our food, made our plates, set them on the table with the wine, blessed our food and we dug in, one thing good sex will do for you is, make you very hungry. After eating we cleaned up and went back to the living room, looked at a movie and when it went off Vicky asked me to show her Mrs. Kashia. I went to my book case and pulled out the tape. I popped it in the VCR and fast forwarded to where she was, and hit play, she watched intensely as we watched Sophia Kashia's oral performance. Turns out Vicky said that was Mr. Kashia in the video with her, and she wasn't surprised, but based on some of the humiliating things she had said to her and tried to make her feel bad about herself that she should be ashamed of herself also. We watched it to the very end, then I rewound the tape and put it back in its case, putting it away, and she stood and said lets go to bed. We were worn out and would sleep very well. We turned everything off and headed upstairs. I took her to my room and told her she was sleeping with me tonight as we climbed into the bed and held each other as we talked about different things until we fell asleep in each other's arms.

Seven

Thursday: Day Seven.

We both woke up late, around seven instead of my usual six. I rolled over and started to caress Victoria and felt her smooth soft body. She was so smooth, soft and without blemishes anywhere. I was truly amazed by her completion. I then reached down and rubbed her smooth soft feet and sexy legs as I slowly moved up her body as she slowly awakened. I lay back down next to her as she slowly opened her eyes and smiled at me and reached out pulling me to her as we hugged and you know, I didn't want to let her go but my body said it was time to get up. I rose and went to the bathroom. I was very surprised when she entered the bathroom while I was sitting on the toilet taking my morning dump. I looked up at her in a very surprised state and she said that we were close enough now for her to be here with me. I relented and said ok, since it was too late and finished. I flushed the toilet, stood and washed my hands and she said she loved me and was going to her bathroom to wash. I reminded her that her dental wasn't till eleven, and we would have time to have breakfast. Said she would take care of it after she had bathed, then she would only have to get dressed to be ready. I said that sounded great as I turned on the shower waiting for the water to get warm. As I showered, I took my time, and when I finished went and applied some lotion and oil to myself before going back to the bedroom, putting my bathrobe on and heading downstairs to put the coffee on. After taking out the donuts I then sat on the kitchen stool waiting for the coffee to finish perking.

I had to meet Hector sometime this evening and inspect the two condo units that belonged to Mrs. Kashia. Then I would head to the office and go with Mrs. Bradley, Mr. Hippies and Fitz to the car dealership. I was going to be busy today as I got up and poured myself some coffee. Victoria came down in her work smock and joined me. I informed her that after her appointment I would have to bring her home so I could take care of the business I had scheduled for the remainder of the day. I didn't know when I would be back home, and not to cook anything for me. Said she had a wonderful day yesterday, and I agreed that I did also. She began to prepare breakfast and soon we were eating. It was a few minutes before ten when we finished and Vicky asked me what she should wear. I said some jeans, blouse, and maybe some heels.

We cleaned up the kitchen together before we went upstairs to dress. About twenty minutes later we were ready and met downstairs. We went to the garage and entered the car and left, twenty minutes later we were at the dental office. Vicky was stunning in her jeans and heels and it wasn't long before they called her. I pulled out my phone and called the office and spoke to Mrs. Bradley as she brought me up to date. I informed her that I would be there soon after lunch, and would be going with her and Hippies to the automobile dealership, but first had to check on my last two listing with Hector. Joanne said he was waiting for me to call, and said they would be finishing in the early afternoon. I said ok and hung up. I called Mrs. Kashia and informed her that I didn't know what time yet, but I would be by this afternoon, for her to inspect the units for the completed work. She thanked me, and said she would be home and to just knock. I said ok and hung up. I called Hector and he said they would be finished with everything at around three. I said ok and would see him then and ended the call.

I looked up and there was Victoria, with a big beautiful smile on her face, as I stood, DR.DDS Bosco came over and said she only needed a cleaning and that he would send a copy of her exam results to the office. I thanked him and we left. Vicky and I got in the car for the ride home and she said her mouth felt good and I said great. I dropped her at home and went inside the front door, and checked around before hugging her as she kissed me and I headed to the office. When I reached the office and spoke to Joanne, I reminded her to ask Mr. Fitz to be here when we closed. I wanted him to accompany us to the dealership also, she said ok as I went to my desk. I called Hector and he stated he was at the condo and his crew was finishing up and he was just about to call me. I said ok and was about to leave the office and would be on my way.

I checked my desk and told Joanne where I would be, and would
be back very soon as I left and headed to the condo.

I arrived and went inside with a set of keys I had made since
Hector had a set, I checked 5B, and he was there and they were just
finishing with the carpet cleaning, everything was fresh, the
windows were cleaned, tile scrubbed, cabinets washed and waxed,
floor cleaned. I asked Hector if they were finished upstairs and he
replied, see Senor. I said I would be back with Ms. Kashia and
would check the other unit before we came back down and he said
fine. I proceeded to the elevator and went up and knocked on 6B,
and Ms. Kashia answered and let me inside. I said that the units
were ready and needed her to inspect them before listing them this
evening and she said ok.

She looked as lovely as ever wearing a pants suit with a jacket
and a pair of low heel shoes, she smelled good, and her skin
sparkled and she had this lovely smile on her face. It wasn't hard to
imagine her lips wrapped around a hard dick like in the video, and
had to tell myself to stop thinking about her having sex. I asked if
she was ready and she said yes as she took her keys and we went
next door to 6C, the door was unlocked as we entered, she looked
at the unit, it was immaculate, the same as I had seen downstairs,
the walls were freshly painted white, the carpet cleaned and
smelling fresh. The tiles were clean and sparkling, the windows,
and the cabinets were clean inside and out and highly polished, and
said she was more than satisfied. I said wonderful, as we left
locking the door behind us. We rode the elevator down to the fifth
floor, and I opened the door just as Hectors crew was getting ready
to take their carpet cleaning equipment out. She briefly looked
around and said she was more than satisfied. She thanked Hector
for the fine job he had performed. We all left and went upstairs
where after entering her apartment she reached in the drawer of the
cabinet by the door and put Hectors name on a check, and handed
it to him, thanked him again as he departed. I sat with her a few
minutes and noticed she wore no bra or blouse and had acted like
she was going to remove her jacket as she unbuttoned several of
the top buttons. She asked about Mrs. Cook, and wanted to know if

I had found her somewhere to live. I replied that I had indeed and
she was doing very well now and seemed to be very happy with
her new residence. And with that said, told her I had to go and it
was time for me to enter the units into the RELS, and explained
that I had other business to attend to today. But I reassured her that
she would be hearing from me very soon as we were sure it
wouldn't be long before we had a qualified buyer. I stood and she
walked me to the door and said she liked me very much. I thanked
her again as I turned and headed for the elevator. As I waited for
the elevator to arrive, turned around and noticed her standing in her
doorway watching me, she had unbuttoned her jacket completely
and had a hand inside her pants as the elevator arrived and I
entered.

I got in my car and headed to the office and listed both condo
units right away, placing the keys in the key box after placing tags
on the original sets and the ones I had made. Well I had one other
thing to do and that was going to the dealership with my crew. It
was about two forty-five when Mr. Hippies came in and he sat
down at my desk, and we began our conversation and explained to
him about how I wanted to reorganize. He took out his legal tablet
and started making notes. I wanted his input, how I could make
this all work and be more efficient. I wanted to roll all the
properties into several different trusts, as wholly owned
subsidiaries, with the commercial separate from the residential. All
the other investments into another and the real estate operations
separate, with the parent company on top. He said he would look at
the best way to set everything up, and he would work on it right
away, so by the time we moved to the new location it would be all
in place. I said thankyou and then Mr. Fitz came in and said hello
to everyone then he addressed me and said boss, what did I want to
see him about. I said pull up a chair, and since it was a slow day I
asked Joanne to join, and she swiveled around in her chair since
her desk was directly in front of mine. I addressed everyone and
went over the reorganization; everyone was on board, because
everyone was to get a raise, and a car to go along with their

expanded duties, and their own private office space. I said we were all going to the dealership as soon as we closed.

It was about a quarter to five when I finished describing what I had in mind. We then started to get ready to leave. I decided to lock the doors since my sales assistants had keys if they wanted to work late. I had everyone get into my car and off we went to Hicks Auto City. As we pulled in front, we got out and were met by Mr. Fabian. I had called earlier and asked for him, he had taken care of the lease agreement on the vehicle I was driving, and had informed him I wanted a fleet lease agreement for four vehicles and was going to turn mine in also. It's been a year and told him I wanted my people to choose the ones they felt comfortable with, he said no problem. Joanne and Hippies went around looking as Fitz stood and talked with us, he knew which one he wanted and the color. I told Fabian I would keep the same model I was currently driving. Except I wanted navigation and a few more options, and a change of color, he explained if we took the top models with all the options on a two year lease with unlimited mileage we would be able to save more money. I said very well. Fitz showed him the one he wanted, Hippies asked to take a test drive, and Joanne came over and said she found the one she wanted. Fabian went through the inventory and found he had all the autos in stock. We were waiting on Hippies to return and he soon did, and said he liked the model he had just driven, which was a demo. Fabian looked up to see if he had one, yes he did. Fabian had the paper work ready. Hippies looked over the agreements and gave his ok, since it was a corporate lease agreement. Fabian said everyone could pick up there vehicles tomorrow and that was fine with us. He handed Hippies the agreements as we stood and shook hands and prepared to leave, I would turn mine in tomorrow also. Mr. Fabian said all would be ready and waiting for us. I thanked him as we all piled back into my car and headed back to the office to retrieve their vehicles.

I dropped Mr. Hippies at home since he had walked to the office and we had a nice long talk. He had lost his wife six years earlier and had great insight into life alone; he was fifty nine and was in good health. I told him as we sat in front of his home about Mrs. Cook and asked him if I had been too hasty in moving her in. He told me that he thought I might have acted a little too hasty, but then again it had been a long while since my wife had passed and noticed also it had brought about a positive change in my demeanor over the past week. And he said that was good because life was to short and it wasn't meant for man to live alone. I said what about you; he said he had a friend. I told him when we opened the new office we might have a grand opening for the staff and our best clients and if he wanted he could bring her, if not you may meet someone. Said he would look forward to the occasion if I decided to have one. I said good night as he stepped out and approached his house. I thought it would be nice if he met someone like Mrs. Kashia; he looked good and got around better than men half his age.

I headed home and it was close to eight. I was starving and decided to stop by the local Mississippi Chicken Coup and picked up a couple of three piece fried chicken dinners. I had a great day and I liked it when things didn't get complicated and went smoothly. I arrived home and backed into the garage, closed the door and went inside, and put the food on the counter, washed my hands as Victoria came into the kitchen. She hugged and kissed me a long time as I held her. Said I brought us some fried chicken. She said very good because she had last ate around two and was waiting for me to come home and was very happy to see me. I pulled out some paper plates I had stashed from a cabinet and we went to the nook to eat. I watched her as I bit into a chicken breast, she looked up at me and smiled, we hardly said a word as we devoured the fried chicken and I watched her eat. We soon finished and deposited our trash in the garbage, washed our greasy hands and cleaned off the table. She asked how my day was, and I replied that everything went as planned.

I was going upstairs to shower and she asked if she could come with me. I replied sure, as she ran into the living room and turned off the television returning as I was walking up the stairs and ran to catch up with me. She took my hand, looked me in my eyes and asked, if she could please move into my bedroom with me. Said she wanted to be with me as often as possible. I hesitated, she noticed, and said please master. I looked into her pleading eyes and then I thought, well she is here and we are having sex. This kind of caught me off guard, but it really wouldn't make much of a difference. Said she didn't want to sleep alone any longer; she wanted to be with me all the time. I looked into her eyes and said ok fine. But you can't have more than half the closet; she smiled and hugged me tightly. I had to tell her to let go and when I looked into her eyes, tears were coming down like rain. I held her and asked, why you are crying. Replied she was fearful that I would tire of her and put her out. I quoted what she had said, as long as you continue to be a good girl and do as I ask. She replied and said no matter what. I told her to put her clothes in the closet. She didn't have much, most of what she had, I had bought for her.

On my way to the bathroom I decided to take a shower, the water felt good running down my face. I lathered myself up and rinsed off, and sat on the shower bench and just let the warm water run over me and relaxed and closed my eyes for several long minutes, and when I opened them, Vicky was standing in front of me naked, bathing herself with the body wash before rinsing herself off and then knelt down in front of me, taking me in her soft hands and stroking me until I was hard and put her head down and sucked me off. Wow, with the shower in the rain position it felt wonderful as I just sat there, she stood, moved close and I placed my hand between her legs and she bent over and kissed my neck, she was hot as I massaged her vagina, fingering her and pinching her clit and a minute or two later I had to hold her as she was elevated with a massive orgasm. I stood and held her. I told her to kneel, as I gave her a golden shower, as I said to her that she had been christened by her master. I pulled her up and lathered her up with the body wash, and felt her ass and smacked her pussy with my hand and told her she had been bad, and that's why she was getting her pussy spanked and after six smacks she climaxed again as I placed my leg between hers and she was elevated with another orgasm, we let the warm water pour down over us until she calmed down and the soap was gone. I lead her out as I turned the water off. Then I grabbed a large towel and wrapped her in it, and retrieved one for myself.

We dried off and went to the bedroom as we spread our towels out on top of the bed after drying off, and told her to lie down. I took the massage oil from the headboard and began massaging her body, starting with her feet. I felt her toes and then I massaged the balls of her feet as she moaned, and slowly moved to her ankles, working my way to her calves, then thighs as I parted her legs and placed a leg on my shoulder, rubbing her thighs, one then the other, then her abdomen and between her legs oiling up her sweet hot pussy and then up to her chest feeling her firm breast as her nipples became erect, and up to her shoulders, then to her neck kissing her before telling her to roll over and started again with the back of her calves and thighs and moved to the smooth round soft butt, parting her cheeks rubbing her rectum, then moved to her back and arms as she laid there moaning the whole time, I told her to roll over again, and I parted her legs, and lay between them and put my face against her hot pussy, holding her ankles and began licking her clit, then started sucking and squeezing it between my lips, as she screamed and her body stiffened as she was rocked with multiple orgasms, I then climbed on top of her, kissed her open lips and we tonged each other, she finally calmed down, catching her breath as she told me to lay on my stomach.

She grabbed the massage oil and started with my feet slowly working her way up my legs to my ass and feeling my butt hole, oiled it then reaching my back massaged it like a masseuse, then my neck, she rolled off and told me to turn over and she again started at my feet as I watched her, she slowly moved up my body and reaching my abdomen massaged me to a semi erection before moving to my chest, arms, and neck and then gently rubbed my face before sliding down between my legs and massaging my penis until it was fully erect and then she sat on it, guiding it up into her well-oiled vagina. Then she laid down on top of me as I put my arms around her, she licked my ear and I could feel her slowly moving her hips as she continued this before I rolled her on her back and began to pump her sweet pussy with my hard dick causing her to climax again, and again until I came and filled her pussy with my hot sperm. Then I just lay there waiting to get my breath back as I rolled off of her and she turned to me and held me and we just looked at each other. We picked ourselves up and went to the bathroom and cleaned up before returning to bed, pulling the covers back and getting in and holding each other. It wasn't long before we fell into a deep sleep having sweet dreams.

Eight
Friday: Day Eight.

I woke up and lay in the bed; this had been one wild week as I looked over at the person who dropped from out of nowhere and into my bed, and life. I've have had as much sex in the past few days as I had with my wife in my last six months of her life. I wondered if my dick was going to just fall off, then realized I was really in love. I was doing things that I had only dreamed of doing. I had masturbated to the bondage and discipline movies and watched the submissive women pleasing men and some enjoying being abused, but had never in my wildest dreams imagined me, myself being in this situation. I looked over at Victoria and touched her as she slowly rolled over and opened her eyes and reached out for me, we held each other. I had heard of people connecting in a short span of time but I think we just broke the record; we both were lonely, horny, and in need for a wonderful, warm and caring companionship. I was just going to go with the flow. I pulled myself up and went to the bathroom and washed, and took a quick shower before going back and putting on my bathrobe. I sat on the bed as Vicky crawled over and I caressed her head and ran my fingers through her hair. She stood and went to the bathroom as I sat and gathered my thoughts. When she returned, she put on her bathrobe and stood in front of me and pulled me up. And said besides having the best sex ever in her life, she loved me no matter what I thought, and even though it had been only a couple days since we came into each other's lives, she didn't want to lose me and would do anything, anything I wanted. I just reached out and held her tight and said let's eat breakfast because, at the rate we were having sex, I figured I had lost at least six or seven pounds, she looked at me and laughed, and it was the first time she had really laughed since coming into my life as we went downstairs and fixed breakfast together.

Together we fixed a large breakfast, we used the last of the sliced ham and the bacon, as we prepared the eggs, and toast, jelly, and coffee, then we sat down and ate our fill, for we were truly famished. I took my vitamins and also gave Vicky some. We cleaned up the kitchen, washed the dishes, before we headed back upstairs. I brushed my teeth while Vicky showered. I was looking to see what I was going to wear. And decided on some jeans with a blue t shirt and would wear my grey sports jacket and some athletic shoes. Vicky came out wrapped in a towel as I said there were a few things I needed to take care of and would return and then we would go shopping for some food as the cupboards were bare. Said she would strip the other bed down and make it up, and was going to do both beds and change the sheets and pillow cases and start a load of clothes in the washing machine. It was nine and I had to go, as I prepared to leave we hugged and kissed.

I went downstairs and got into my car and headed to the office. When I arrived, I saw Mrs. Bradley pouring some coffee and said good morning, and she had a big smile on her face as she came over and hugged me. Said that in the past week she didn't know what had happened to me, but there was a change in the way I was acting and she hoped it stayed that way, said she loved me like a son and looked forward to the new office plans. I asked how she was going to get to the dealer. Replied that she let her daughter use her car and was going to get an associate to drop her off. I said when one of the associates comes in I would have them take her to the dealership. I would stay here and take care of things. She said ok just as Jack Phillips came in. I called him over, he said good morning to the both of us. I asked if he would do me a favor and take Mrs. Bradley to the dealership to pick up her auto, he said of course he would. As she prepared to leave, asked if there had been anything I should know about, she said no, as they departed. I sat down and shortly after Ms. Caren Brown my third associate came in, we spoke and exchanged greetings as she sat down at my desk and asked about the condo listings. I answered her questions and said the keys were in the key box, and make sure to fill out the sign out sheet if she used them. She said for sure, the sign out was also a safety and would let other agents know who had them last. I got a cup of coffee and then dialed home. I knew the answering machine would pick up and I waited for the greeting to end and called Victoria's name, she had listened to the calls, but had never answered as per my instructions. She picked up and said yes sir master. I said to make a list for the groceries and any cleaning supplies that we needed and she said yes sir. I will call when I am on my way home to pick you up, and then she said, I love you and I hung up.

The phone rang, and Ms. Brown took the call and told the caller, just a minute, and said it was for me. I picked up and it was Mr. Samuelsson, we spoke, he said the closing would be Tuesday at eleven and gave me the address of the title company. I said great and would see him there; we thanked each other before hanging up. It had been a little after nine when I arrived and it was ten thirty when Mrs. Bradley returned. I asked what happened to J, referring to Mr. Phillips the young agent I had asked to take her to the dealer and she replied he stayed until he received a phone call. He was off to see a client, well that sounds good. Told her we would be closing on the new office Tuesday just as the phone rang and I answered, it was Louis Brown, said he had procured copies of the blue prints and gave me some specifics as far as the building was concerned. I told him we were closing at eleven Tuesday, and sometime after that I would like for him to meet me there. I told him that I wanted the washrooms enlarged, and separate men's and women's and the present locations were fine, just make them larger. I wanted the same on both floors. I said since you have the prints you can draw up some layouts. I wanted a conference room and private offices, at least six on level two with a lunch room, the ground floor was for the agents and I would like low walled cubes to include work stations and a leasing area with a comfortable waiting area, and if there was enough room another conference room, lunch room and two offices. He said he would work up several floor plans and I could choose one. I told him great and would call him as soon as I had possession. I thanked him and hung up just as Joanne turned around and said call on line three. It was the demolition company. I spoke to their representative and he said it would be $30,000.00 for tear down and to haul away all the debris and have the utilities disconnected. I asked them to fax everything, and I would let them know when the property was vacant, he thanked me and I made a note of it. I asked Joanne if she had her replacement person picked out yet and said she had yet to decide between the two people she was considering. I said just make sure they are competent, and she replied for sure. I will be gone for the day and might be in tomorrow, but didn't know for sure. She told me to have a great day. You too I replied. I asked when she went to the dealer was everything ready, yes she replied, they just had to wash her car before she was able to leave. Told her I hope you enjoy it.

I said have a great day as I left and headed to the dealership. I arrived at the dealer and Mr. Fabian came out and directed me where to park. I pulled into the designated spot and looked around the vehicle to make sure I didn't leave any personal belongings, and popped the trunk and checked it also. Told him I was ready as he directed me to my new vehicle. I had chosen a silver one this time instead of black, it looked really good. He said I only had to sign a receipt and would be on my merry way. I went inside and signed, and then he walked out with me, showing me some of the new features and made sure I had synced my phone. He thanked me, and I pulled away. Called home, and after the message, said Victoria pickup please, and repeated my message. She answered, yes sir master. Told her to get ready I was on my way home and it should only be about fifteen minutes, she replied, yes sir master, and I hung up.

I pulled up, got out and went in the front door, and found Victoria dressed in jeans, blouse and athletic shoes, she had some cute earrings with her small necklace, her face was vibrant as she greeted me with a hug and a kiss and said she was ready and had checked the house already. We went out the front door and she immediately noticed the car, and said wow it was beautiful, we got in and pulled off. I said we were going to see how well she could drive so she could go shopping on her own. Said that wasn't as much of a thrill as going with me. We got in the car and headed to Osmo one of the bulk wholesale stores. We arrived and asked if she had the list, she had made one out and it was in her purse. We entered and retrieved a cart and showed my membership at the door as we entered. We walked just about every isle and had mostly cleaning supplies, some large bags of frozen meats, fish, eggs and other items before checking out and placing everything in the trunk of the car. We need some fresh vegetables, and headed to Roscoe's. After we had taken a cart and walked around the store and finding all the items on the list and more we checked out. Loaded it in the car and headed home. I backed into the garage and we brought everything inside and put it away, after we were finished I was tired and it was almost three thirty.

We both went upstairs to undress and shower as Victoria followed and then we both got in bed, hugged and soon fell asleep. When I awoke it was seven thirty. I was hungry and felt like I wanted to cook. I looked over and Vicky was still knocked out. I got up and put on my shorts and t shirt and quietly pulled the bedroom door close and headed downstairs. Went to the kitchen and took out all the vegies needed to make some spaghetti sauce. I cut up the veggies, while my meat thawed, retrieved my big sauce pan from the cabinet, placed some olive oil into it, took out my seasoning and started to boil some water for pasta and opened a can of diced tomatoes and mushrooms placed them in a bowl and mixed them together. After finishing and everything was ready, I poured myself some vino and started to cook, it took about forty-five minutes. I popped a loaf of garlic bread that came in a foil bag into the oven after having read the instructions and set the oven temperature and waited before setting the timer, as my sauce was simmering, my water boiled and placed the pasta in. Soon it was time to take it out, grabbed the strainer and poured my pasta in and rinsed. I like angel hair and after rinsing and draining returned it to the pot and covered it. Sat down and waited a few more minutes before stirring the sauce and turning it out.

I poured another glass of wine before sitting it on the table and heading upstairs. I entered the bed room. It was dimly lit, turned on the bathroom light and went over and sat on the side of the bed, looked at Victoria as she slowly rolled over and felt for me, she sat straight up, she had a frighten look on her face until she realized I was sitting there. She got up on her knees and hugged me and said she thought I had left her. She had a bad dream and held me and sobbed. I reached around and held her; she soon calmed down and asked her if she was hungry. Yes I am famished she replied. Told her to get herself together and come downstairs. I released her and headed back downstairs. When I entered, the kitchen, grabbed a head of lettuce and the cutting board. Cleaned and chopped it up and made a salad, adding a cucumber, radishes, and tomatoes. I set the table, took out our plates, as she came downstairs dressed in the short blue jean skirt and the tie around in front blouse she wore the first day I met her. I asked her to have a seat, and I fixed our plates. We sat and said grace before we ate; she said it wasn't just good but great. I only gave her a small portion and before I knew it she asked for more. I said help yourself, and when she got up, noticed she wasn't wearing any panties. I wondered what was going to happen after dinner, we drank more wine until the bottle was empty; she cleaned her plate and ate like the first time I had taken her to lunch. Said she would wash the dishes and clean up. I said ok, as we cleared the table. I placed the sauce and pasta in containers, and afterwards I sat on the kitchen bar stool and watched her wash the dishes. After she finished with the dishes she cleaned the stove, then the table. I asked for a bottle of water which she promptly retrieved from the fridge and placed in front of me as she returned to wiping down the counters and after she finished, came and sat next to me.

Victoria started talking; said she knew that I liked bondage. Had seen the videos I kept in the cabinet while cleaning and said she was in several of them and that I knew it was her in them. She hoped that it aroused me and that everything she said to me was true. That she truly wanted to be my 24/7 slave and she felt loved, really loved just by and how I had treated her. Said she was true to her word, and was sorry she cried, but life had been at times really scary for her, and was happy now that Mrs. Kashia had decided to sell, or she wouldn't have met me, and was sorry that she tried to seduce me when we first meet. She felt very cheap later that day and that she was very, very sorry. I said you know you never know in life where you may end up, who with or maybe even alone. But you have to gather yourself and press on. Told her that she may feel bad about herself, but it didn't diminish the real person she was, the one who has hopes and dreams. You are not tainted by your pass, but a much stronger person. I said if you decide you don't want to be here, it would be all right, I wouldn't feel hurt. I would see to it that you have a regular job and start a new and very fruitful and fulfilling life. And I would see to it that you have an apartment and a good job. You can be whoever you want to be. I will pay for you to go to school if you want, and you can take all I bought for you. You don't have to be here, you don't have to serve me. I don't look on myself as being anyone's master or savior. I won't lie to you and say that it hasn't been great. I have truly enjoyed having sex with you, but you have to decide the life you want to live and to be happy, it's all up to you. I will help you because of the pleasure and happiness you have given me over these few days. I owe you that much, and don't you feel guilty about anything.

I love you, and know that after being alone for so long my focus has changed, and you caused it to change. I've been told just this past week that I seem to be a much happier person, sometimes you have to overlook the way things happen and look further down the road. You know what happened? You came into my life and I am thankful for that. I take my blessings whenever and wherever they come; you aren't a slut, tramp or undesirable. You are a very good and loving person, and that is the person I love. But I think you need to decide what you really want or need to do, and the person you want to be. We then went to the living room and I continued talking to Victoria about her future, as she followed closely behind me as we sat on the sofa together. I told her, think about it sweetheart let me know what you decide, sit here and think about it, if you reach no decision I will understand, just let me know whatever you decide. I finished talking and turned on the television, as I sat on the sofa and leaned back and made myself comfortable as Victoria just sat there quietly.

After about thirty minutes without saying a word, Victoria stood and went upstairs. Thought I had said all the right things to her, but as much as she made me happy she needed to make a decision about where her life was headed. I had enough knowledge of the bondage world to know that there were many women who were voluntary slaves, some were married, and it was there forte. Was very surprised I had run into someone like her and was thankful for the experience, but if she wanted to leave I would keep my word and help her. She made me very happy and was thankful for that. It had been a little over a week and I figured she needed to make a decision before we went any further with where I saw this relationship seemed to be headed. I wondered if she wasn't upstairs crying, or packing her bags, after about fifteen minutes she came down and entered the living room. She was dressed in the high heels, the one piece stocking-garter, with the sexy maid outfit, without panties, the black leather collar with leash, cuffs on both wrist and ankles, several whips, some things that I had and hadn't purchased, she must have brought them with her.

She walked and stood in front of the television. I sat up and turned it off. I asked her if she had reached a decision. Said she had. I asked what have you decided. I looked up at her as she came over and knelt in front of me and stated. That she meant every word she had said to me as tears came to her eyes, said that if I didn't love or care for her, I wouldn't have said I would help her and that I owed her anything. That I made her feel like a real person, that she truly enjoyed being with me, and wanted to be my submissive, my slave and that she was turned on by it and wanted to have a man that loved her, that she was offering herself completely to me. To be my slave or whatever I wanted her to become. I asked what she had in her hands. Said these are the toys that she liked, that I should use them on her whenever I wanted. I said what if I didn't, would you still be happy, she replied yes. Because I love you and you make me happy, but that she wanted me to use them on her and told me that if I loved her, I would have to because it was what made her happy. I asked her, there was verbal abuse and humiliation and if these were a turn on?, she said yes sir, then I said to her, your kneeling here means that you want to serve me and you love me correct?. She said yes sir master, and that is all she wanted in the world as she broke down and cried.

I told her I accepted her offer of submission and servitude and said from this moment forward I would try to make her happy and told her to place the whips and others items on the floor and stand. I stood in front of her and looked her in her eyes and told her she was my bitch now and forever. I told her to turn around and put her arms behind her back as I reached and hooked her wrist cuffs together. Then told her to turn back around as I looked in her the face and slapped her lightly on both sides of her face and said, you belong to me now bitch. There was a blind fold along with the whips and other items. I picked it up and walked behind her and placing it over her eyes. I told her to spread her legs and stand there. I sat back down and just looked at her. I looked down at the items she brought downstairs with her, a small leather whip, and a leather cat of nine tails, a ridding crop, leather paddle, the glass dildo, and two made of latex, one short about eight inches long and about four and a half inches around. The other was about two and a half by ten inches, some nipple clamps with a chain and some clamps for hooking the cuffs together along with a large butt plug. I stood and felt her breast through the flimsy material and her nipples were standing at attention. I placed them between my fingers. I gently twisted them as she moaned. I placed my left hand under her chin as I moved closer to her face. I could see she was getting very excited. I felt her face with my right hand as she jumped not knowing what was to happen next. I asked her, who did she belong to now, she answered. I belong to you master Charlie. I asked what her purpose was, she answered, and to serve you master Charlie. I rubbed the side of her face again and said to her, you are my bitch now and forever, she replied yes sir master Charlie, and this really excited her. I removed the maid outfit and she was standing there with only the stocking, shoes, collar, cuffs and blindfold on. I picked up the nipple clamps and slowly attached one to each nipple as she moaned; her pussy was soaking wet. I placed my hand between her legs; the anticipation of not knowing what I was going to do next was exciting her. She said, master please, several times as she begged to be fucked. I told her, that it was up to me as to when, where and how she was going to get fucked. I picked up the riding crop and rubbed her all over with its flat end, up her calves to her thighs and butt to her back, across her breast and down between her legs and to her clit. I told her not to come, for I sensed she couldn't hold out much longer, then she asked again, please master, please master, please master. I said what is it slave. Please master may I come. I said when I say so slave, and not until, as I continued to caress her all over and as I gently touch her nipples. She exploded with a massive orgasm, rocking back and forth. I said, did I give you permission to come bitch, she said no sir master. I told her she had to be punished for being disobedient, and watched as the moisture from her wet pussy slowly trickled down her inner thigh, her breathing was short and ragged as perspiration started to appear all over her shapely body. I picked up the butt plug and slowly rubbed it around the outside of her very moist pussy and when it was wet enough. I instructed her to bend over as she moaned and I slowly worked it up and into her ass until it was fully inserted. It was about two inches round and four inches long as I told her to stand up straight. Then had her knell as I fastened the two ankle cuffs together and had her spread her knees apart. I had an idea; there was a wooden beam across the entrance between the living room and short hall leading to the foyer.

I decided to go and get some of the rope I kept in the garage, and soon found what I was looking for. I had several different kinds. Decided on the kind you would use for a clothes line, soft and smooth, the package was unopened. I returned and stopped in the kitchen to retrieve a pair of scissors, opening the package, and taking out and cutting several lengths off. I returned to the foyer and threw it over the beam; the two ends came down past my waist to the floor, perfect for what I had in mind. I went over and unhooked her feet. Told her to stand and helped her to her feet, then led her to the place where the ropes hung down. I unhooked her hands from behind her to in front, and tied one end of the rope to the clamp holding the cuffs together, checking that the cuffs were secure on her wrist. Then slowly pulled the rope up causing her arms to be raised above her head and then looped the long end back over the beam again and between the two cuffs and threw it over the beam again and I was able to reach it and tie them all together. I stood back and looked at my handy work. I whispered in her ear that her punishment was about to begin and removed the nipple clamps and put them in my pocket.

I went to the kitchen and brought back a small bottle of olive oil and applied some to my hands, then rubbed my hands all over her body as the oil and sweat mixed and made her body glisten as she moaned and I felt her between her legs. I pulled my hand back and gave her ass several nice firm smacks, then again, and again as she began having several repetitious climaxes. As she did I rubbed her pussy and sucked on her swollen nipples, then I stopped and let her hang there several minutes as she trembled. I went and picked up the large dildo she brought down, it was the softest and most pliable, I cut a six foot piece of rope and laid it on the floor, picked up the dildo and slid it into her wet vagina as she squirmed and left it inserted then picked up the rope, doubled it, placing it around her waist and ran the loose ends into the looped end in front and pulled it snug, and ran the loose ends down between her legs, looping each piece once around the end of the dildo before reaching behind and pulling it snuggly between her ass cheeks and attaching it to itself at the small of her back. I tightened it up so it held the dildo in place, and made sure her clit was between the two pieces of rope in front, as I brushed it with my hand, then I clamped both ankle cuffs together. I cut another short piece of rope about three feet long and used it to tie her legs together just above the knee wrapping it around several times, there she hung in all her glory.

I retrieved my digital SLR from the office and took multiple pictures of her hanging in all her womanly perfection. I walked over and whispered in her ear that I was pleased with my new bitch. I removed the blindfold from her face and looked in her eyes and gave her a big wet kissed as she tonged me back. I asked how it felt hanging helpless; she said if it pleased her master she was happy. I went and picked up the cat-o-nine tails and stood back and

whipped her lightly across her entire body, after about twenty
swats, I dropped the whip and went back and felt her all over
driving her into frenzied state causing her to have multiple
explosive climaxes again as her body was racked with pleasure. I
waited several minutes as I watched her. I then spanked her ass
with the leather paddle, and told her she was my dirty little bitch
before I unclamped her ankles and untied her knees, and then
untied her hands and let them down but remained cuffed together,
the dildo and butt plug remained inserted. I attached the leash to
her collar and slowly lead her around the room as she squirmed
with pleasure as I whipped her all over. Then I told her to spread
her legs as she stood quivering and I untied the rope holding the
dildo, and then slowly worked it back and forth before removing it
as she squirmed and came multiple times again. Then I slowly
removed the butt plug, taking my time, playing with it in her ass. I
removed the clamp holding her hands together and grabbed the
leash and walked her around and told her to kneel as I dropped my
shorts. I had a hard on that would not quit and placed it in her face
and she opened her warm mouth and took it all in as I held her
head on it and shortly removed it. I told her to bend over with her
head on the floor arms spread and with her ass up which she did. I
kneeled behind and entered her hot sloppy with moisture pussy and
I fucked her hard as she moaned and I reached around and played
roughly with her clit and she came several more times as I rode
her, I pounded her pussy, as I played roughly with her clit, as I felt
myself about to come I pulled out and pushed it hard into her
quivering ass, shoving it in deep and pumping her ass until I came
hard, filling her ass with sperm. I held her bent over and slapped
her ass before I slowly stood up. I left her like that for several long
minutes as I looked at her. I told her to stand, as I grabbed the
leash pulling her up, she stood and turned to face me and she had
tears and a smile on her face at the same time.

We held each other for a long time before regaining our
composure. We gathered everything and brought it upstairs with
us, putting the dildos in the sink to be cleaned. We showered a
long while, washing each other, then drying and laying on the bed

and oiling one another. It was almost midnight, but I wanted a
drink. We put on our bathrobes and went downstairs, and we had a
gin and tonic, and then had a several more before returning upstairs
to the bedroom. As we got into the bed, she said to me that she was
mine now and loved me and I was all she wanted in the world. I
held her tight and wasn't letting her go, and told her that she was
mine now forever as we fell asleep in each other's arms.

Nine
Saturday: Day Nine.

When I awoke it was eight, way past my usual wakeup time, that would all be changing soon when I opened the new office. I looked over at Victoria, and eased out of bed, went and rinsed my mouth and went through my morning routine, and was about to exit the bath when, Vicky entered and we briefly kissed and I returned to bed and laid back down. Shortly she returned and we both laid there looking into each other's eyes as we rubbed and felt on one another and I hugged and I caressed her smooth body and found there were certain areas on her that just sent chills and shivers through her as she held onto me and moaned, she said don't stop as I ran my hand from behind her knee upwards and along her inner thigh and toward her vagina and soon my hand brushed against her very sensitive and protruding clit as she exploded having a massive climax as I held her tightly not allowing her to move as she shook and was totally consumed with sexual pleasure. After regaining her composure said that she had never had that may orgasms ever as she had last evening and loved me so much that it hurt. I gave her a long wet kiss and said to her that she made me very, very happy, and felt it was making me a much better person. I said maybe we should restrain ourselves some because we were losing weight. After weighing myself I had lost almost five lbs. I said we need to eat, she asked if I had to go to the office today, no I told her.

She said great as we put our robes on and went downstairs to the kitchen to fix something to eat. I wanted a bacon sandwich, some coffee and a donut, and she wanted a full breakfast and started to fix it. I asked her to fix me some eggs also and shortly we were sitting down eating together. I took my vitamins, and gave her some also, before we cleaned up the kitchen and said since the weather was nice we should get out. We went upstairs and I put on a pair of my dress shorts a short sleeve shirt and my dress sandals, she picked a pair of dress shorts with a colorful blouse and some short heeled brown open toe shoes. Her face was beautiful and she

wore the pearl earrings and no other jewelry. I said you know you
will have to open your bank account soon. Said she hadn't given it
any thought, but that sounded good and looked forward to it. I
asked if those shoes were comfortable to drive in, and she replied
yes they were.

I said lets go as she grabbed her small purse, we went
downstairs to the garage and I said to her, she was going to drive.
We got in, I opened the door and gave her some time to get
familiar with the controls, we buckled up, she started the car and
carefully pulled out, she stopped and I showed her the button for
the garage door as she closed it. I told her to relax as she pulled
down the driveway and stopped before entering the street, we
headed to where I didn't know yet. She was a good driver, not
overly careful, said that she had learned to drive when in high
school she had taken the driver's education course, and had driven
her father's pickup truck. I gave her directions and we headed to
the Sweet Wood mall. I directed her toward one of the entrances
and said find a space and showed her a spot not to close to the
entrance, then showed her how to lock the car using the key fob.
She had never driven anything this new before.

As we walked toward the entrance she held my hand tightly, I
looked at her walk, her legs were very shapely, her ass was a nice
size, not too small or large and her waist was moderate, no belly,
her chest was nice, that made her look really beautiful. What do
they say, beauty is in the eye of the beholder, and well I was
smitten with her and in love also. Her body was in perfect
proportion and you know you see more in the sun light. I thought
how cute she would look with some sunglasses and a wide
brimmed hat laying on a lounge chair. We went in and walked to
the mezzanine, and I stopped her, turned her around to me, and
said to her; tell me what it is you have always wanted. She didn't
hesitate as she said me; I only want you as she looked me in the
eyes. I asked if there was anything you wanted and couldn't afford,
she hesitated and said no, she had what she wanted. I said let me
guess, me, yes she replied as she pulled me to her. I said ok but

you got to let me go because you'll get me too excited as we separated slightly.

I took her hand and told her soon you will be meeting the people that I work with and she was going to have to look, as I looked into her eyes, like you belong to me. I said the black dress I picked out, yes she replied. I would like for you to pick out an evening dress that is something you picked, your personality, she said ok. And we went into and exclusive store to the women's section, as we both began shopping. I browsed with her, she circled one rack twice, picked two dresses as a sales assistant came over and offered to help, she wanted to try the dresses on, then we were directed toward the dressing rooms where they had a couple of chairs outside. I sat and crossed my legs and waited for her to come out, and when she did, it was a stunning dress on her, a strap that came across one shoulder, it was tapered, not tight, accentuated her hips and was cut across on an angle exposing one knee, all in black, with silver trim around the entire hem, collar and sleeves and they were open. She was so stunning in it that several other patrons stopped to gawk. I watched as she modeled the dress for me, she said there was one more she wanted to try on. Ok I said as she left and reentered the dressing room and I watched as other women started to look for the same dress. Victoria soon reappeared and this dress was a tube style dress, very form fitting if you have the form, few women can wear this with the elegance as she did. It was a dark blue, trimmed in gold at the hem and collar and around the very short sleeves, it fit her very well, she asked what I thought. My reply was, fantastic. I suggested she get both, she smiled and return to put on her shorts and blouse, when she came out, I gave them to the sales lady, to ring up and gave her my credit card, she wrapped and bagged them and handed the bag to Vicky as I signed the receipt.

We then went to the shoe department and I had a seat while she looked at shoes, and came back with one black and one red hi- heel and a sandal, the shoe man came over as he said to me, back again. I looked and it was the same salesman from earlier in the week. I said yes and thank you, he took the shoes Vicky picked and returned the samples to the display table as she sat and held my hand. He soon returned with several boxes, she tried the black pumps and walked around, good she said as she tried on the open toe heels in red, then a pair in black, she walked around and liked them also, then the sandals, a pair like the ones she was wearing only they were black. She asked me if she could get all four to which I replied yes. The salesman said ok and he went and checked to make sure that they were all mated. I paid and he boxed them up and then we walked around a little more before I decided to take her to a hair styling salon. The one in the mall had a good reputation and we stopped by. I asked if a chair was available. The receptionist took her name and soon a stylist appeared and asked Victoria to come with her. Victoria asked me how I wanted her hair. I said you decide but a cut and trim wouldn't hurt, you don't need a wash, something cute. I waited about an hour before she was finished and came back with her hair looking most presentable, really sexy and cute. She became more and more beautiful every time I did something for her. Said she was hungry now, and could we go to the Chinese restaurant we went to before. I said sure and glad you asked, as we leisurely walked out to the car, placing her purchases in the trunk. I asked if she wanted to drive and she said no, that I should.

I got behind the wheel after opening the door for her, and we left the mall and headed for Wong's. Victoria said as we drove she liked their food very much, it was fresh like when she was a kid. She was sitting sideways looking at me and just sat that way until we arrived. I was about to get out when she grabbed my hand and squeezed it and just held it as her eyes started to moisten. I said its ok baby, and I'm hungry also, we got out and walked inside. And Mrs. Wong greeted us and led us to a window booth, placed the menus on the table, she said green tea yes. I replied yes, she left, returning shortly with two cups and a pot of tea, she poured and asked if we were ready to order. I said yes we were. I ordered shrimp and scallops Hunan style with broccoli and mushrooms. Vicky had shrimp with lobster sauce, with mixed vegetables, we both had brown rice, and Mrs. Wong left to place our orders. We sat looking at each other, as she reached out and held my hand, and said please don't ever let her go, I replied, I wouldn't ok. It wasn't crowded when we entered but soon after the restaurant filled up, and soon there were people waiting at the door. Our food came sooner than usual, and I said to Mrs. Wong that was quick, she replied, you special, ok. I thanked her as she left. It was unusual for Mrs. Wong to seat someone, which was usually done by the waitress. We casually ate and it wasn't long before we were finished. Mrs. Wong had Fawn take our empty dishes away and brought the folder with the bill and two fortune cookies. I opened mine and ate it and drank more tea, and read my fortune, (don't let love go when it comes to you) ok, I thought to myself how poetic. Vicky read hers, she didn't eat the cookie, hers read (good things only come once in a lifetime) I opened the folder and there was a note and not a bill, it was a note from Mrs. Wong, she said our meal was on the house and asked me to call her at the number she wrote down, on Monday. I asked Vicky if she was ready and said yes, and we rose to leave, Victoria was so stunning in appearance both men and women watched us as we left. I left the folder at the front entrance with Mrs. Wong and acknowledged I had her note, and thanked her as we left.

I asked Vicky to drive, that way she would watch something else besides me, we got in and she pulled away and I asked her if she knew the way home. She thought so as she drove and I asked her if she was ready to go home and she replied she didn't really want to leave home but was glad we did and now all she wanted to do was climb all over me. She found her way home and when we were away the lawn care people came and had cut the grass and it was looking much better. She opened the garage door and slowly backed inside and turned the car off. We exited the auto as I removed her packages and closed the garage door as we went inside. I said that I would be having a busy week and that she might not see very much of me. She said as long as I came home, she would be fine. We kissed and proceeded to take her new clothes upstairs and she hung her dresses up and put her shoes away. I asked her to put on the dress she just purchased today with the shoes she would wear. I wanted to see her dressed up. She put the black dress on that I had just purchased, it was beautiful and was very elegant. I asked her to put on the pearl necklace and when she turned around I asked her to look at herself in the mirror, she was stunning and appeared graceful and elegant, as she stood in front of the floor length mirror and started to cry profusely. I got up to hold her and she held me tight crying like a baby, I just let her cry it out, as she started to sniffle. I rocked her and started to slow dance with her and she continued to hold me tight until it hurt. I patted her back and told her. I was here for her and she slowly calmed down, I said ok you can take everything off and she did and hung the dresses up and put on her bathrobe. It was evening and I undressed and put on my shorts and a t- shirt what I wear around the house and suggested she wear a t-shirt and some panties. She put on this extra-long t-shirt and we went downstairs to the living room and snuggled up on the couch as I held her and we looked at television. Later we went upstairs and showered and went to bed touching and felling on each other until we fell asleep.

Ten
Sunday: Day Ten.

I awoke and felt more rested than I had yesterday since we had abstained from sexual activities. I think the both of us needed a rest, not that the thrill was gone. Thrill just needed a rest. And I was determined that I was going to have a restful day. I looked over at Victoria, she was fast asleep. I got up and went to the bathroom and when I finished and returned, I put on my shorts and t-shirt and went downstairs and started the coffee. I didn't want breakfast but would probably go for brunch instead. I walked around the house and checked the temperature outside and it was sixty nine degrees and the time was nine thirty five as I decided to open some windows later as I went and retrieved the Sunday paper from the front door. I returned and poured a cup of coffee and went out and sat on the deck adjacent to the kitchen and soaked up some sun before it got to hot. I sipped my coffee and looked out at the grass and trees, and thought about the coming week. Left my coffee and went to the office and took out a legal pad and returned. I opened the umbrella and started writing down my schedule for the coming week. I had to take Victoria to the bank and have her open an account. Then when I went to the office I would call Kenny, my IT guy and have him build and design a new network for the new office and hook him up with L. Brown, my architect and then the both of them with Hector, and have them all coordinate with one another to get this done right. I knew expanding the washrooms would be the biggest single cost and take the most amount of time. Then for Tuesday there was the actual closing, and I would take Hippies with me so there wouldn't be any legal problems on my end. Then the rest of the week would follow and I would play it by ear. I put down my pad and finished my coffee and went back for more, but first I went around and opened several windows all over the house and let it air out after turning off the climate control. After doing that, poured myself more coffee and went back outside and relaxed. I thought about Hippies and the reorganized office. I hoped everything went as smoothly as I imagined.

Almost an hour had passed when I heard Victoria calling my name, seems she couldn't find me and her voice sounded desperate, and then she came out bare foot with only the bathrobe on, she knelt down and put her head in my lap and I stroked her head. After a few minutes, I told her to get some coffee and come back and get some sun, she went and poured herself a cup and came back and pulled up a chair, she opened her robe and let the sun shine on her beautiful nude body with her olive brown complexion she looked good, after a few minutes she closed her robe and said to me too much sun wasn't good. I know, and told her to go in the kitchen and get the olive oil and rub herself down, which she did, my deck is private and up high, my closest neighbors are hidden behind trees and shrubs, she returned removed her robe and rubbed herself all over as I admired her body and then asked me to do her back which I did. She lay on the lounge chair and after five minutes she rolled over and was tanning her back, then she arose and put her robe on and sat in the chair next to me out of the sun. I asked if she would cook dinner. She replied, what would I like? Breakfast was really on my mind now, but I asked her to just make me a sandwich, and I would wait until dinner.

I was finished with my notes and drifted off asleep and ending up taking a short nap for about an hour. I woke and walked inside to the kitchen and Vicky was preparing a couple of ham sandwiches on rye bread. I grabbed a soda from the fridge; Vicky had toasted the rye bread, added lettuce and mustard with a pickle on the side. I was hungry and it tasted great as we sat down and ate the sandwiches. She mentioned that we would have chicken and potatoes for dinner and a tossed salad. That sounds good I replied as I walked over and grabbed her from behind and caressed her smooth soft body. Surely my feelings for her are beginning to become overwhelming. I felt like I had died and went to heaven. This couldn't be a dream; happiness was all over my face and saw the same in hers. This is what I call true love, as I caressed her, she turned around and felt her in my arms, her nipples, and butt were all being aroused by my gentle touching as I caressed her touching her in a way that made her highly aroused. She was wearing the long t-shirt as I reached and pulled it up in back and caressed and rubbed her butt cheeks, she had her panties on, as she melted in my arms she wrapped her arms around me as I felt between her legs and felt her warmth growing, then rubbed my hands over her breast and pinched her nipples as they started to harden, she was now fully aroused as I reached back down and felt between her legs again, moving her panties to the side out of the way and pushing my left index finger inside of her vagina as I held her with my other arm pinning one of her arms, and then she climaxed as I continued to massage her. Her eyes closed as her head went back and her body stiffened and shook again with sexual fulfillment. I wouldn't let her go as I told her that I was her master wanted to see her climax. I continued for about another five minutes before I removed my hand away and stuck the fingers I had inside of her into her waiting mouth as she sucked them with pleasure. I released her after she slowly calmed down. She just looked at me and in a weak voice, said thank you master.

I left the kitchen and went to my office. I worked in my office for several hours and could smell food cooking and had just finished up my project when Victoria entered and said, master dinner is ready. I entered and the table was set, the hot food was on the table. I sat down and we said grace together, then we ate some extremely tasty chicken, potatoes, and a salad. I was glad she didn't serve me any large amounts and thanked her for that, and complimented her on such a tasty meal. She had opened a chilled bottle of red wine to go along with dinner and we really enjoyed it. Said to her, that before I meet her I was cooking myself, I am good but sometimes it just seemed like a chore, especially when you don't feel like it. I finished and asked if she needed any help cleaning up, and she said no. Stated I had done enough and that was what she was here for. I thanked her and asked her if she didn't mind me keeping her company. And replied she welcomed it very much. I sat and watched her as she put the food away and cleaned up. When she finished, came over and stood behind me and rubbed my back. I turned and kissed her, we kissed and then I said we should go for a short walk. She asked where. I said we could just walk around the outside of the house a few times, I said you can wear what you have on and that's just what we did, before we came back and fixed some drinks and sat on the deck. When the insects came out we went inside, we went around and closed the windows before getting involved and made sure everything was secure, it was getting late and said I wanted to get an early start and that I was taking her to open her new account tomorrow. Vicky asked how much she would need since she only had about three hundred dollars in cash. I told her don't worry and to just keep it. It was time to turn in and we went upstairs and showered together and enjoyed each other sexually once again. We bathed, and went to bed hugging and kissing one another.

Eleven

Monday: Day Eleven.

I awoke early, before six; looked over at Victoria waking the sleeping beauty and said, time to get up as I proceeded to the bathroom to start my day. When I came out, she kissed me as I went to the closet and picked out a suit, it was Monday and I didn't know what surprises would occur. I dressed as she was coming out and told her I was taking her to the bank today and to wear something presentable. I was going to get her a business suit one day soon, just for occasions like these, and had decided to take her to breakfast before we went to the bank. We would go to Martha's. When she came downstairs, her hair was combed and she wore a flower print dress and some high heels. I told her that she had to do her nails since she wasn't wearing any polish. Clear polish would be fine and suggested to her to get it and do them we had time. She promptly went back upstairs and soon came back with her polish and started to do them. I said you can do your toes later if you want as I told her that whenever you are going out with me it was a must, she said yes sir master, as she continued applying the polish.

We left about seven fifteen and headed to Martha's for breakfast. I parked the car and we entered Martha's. Martha gave us her usual warm greeting and Sue promptly came to our table and took our orders. I had scrambled eggs with toast and sausage, and Vicky had two eggs poached, ham, and rye toast with jelly, we both had coffee, we ate and enjoyed the great breakfast. Sue came with the bill when we finished, and I left her a tip. As we left, Martha replied, do come again. I replied yes we will, as we headed back to the car.

It was about nine when we arrived at the bank, as I helped Vicky out of the car and we went inside. I filled out the sign in sheet and we took a seat and waited for a representative. I complimented Victoria on how well she looked, she replied that it was just for me, and said thank you master. She whispered so no one else would hear her. Just then, a representative, called our names and we followed him to his desk. I explained what I wanted for my beautiful employee and he started getting it together, a few minutes later he asked Victoria for some identification, she handed him her driver's license, he took the information, and made a copy. He asked if that was her current address, she said no and asked me what it was. I handed him my driver's license. Then he explained to her that a second person was needed on the account and who might that be. She told him it was to be me, since he had my ID he entered the information, made copies before handing them back to us. Then reached in the drawer and pulled out some check books of different colors and designs and asked her to choose the one she might like along with some temporary checks, she chose one in green leather.

He said the minimum deposit was a $1000.00. I reached in my pocket and gave him my bank card and told him to do a transfer. I accompanied him to one of the teller windows, and left Victoria seated in the cube type office. He had the cashier to do the transfer and we returned shortly afterwards. He explained to Victoria her checking was free as long as she retained the minimum balance and that she would receive by mail a debit card and to follow the instruction to create a pin number, said she understood, and then said we were finished. As we stood we shook hands, and thanked each other. He complimented Victoria on her appearance and she was elated. We exited the bank. I opened the car door for her as she gracefully got in, and I drove back her home. I went inside to brush my teeth before I left for work and she was standing there waiting for me. Vicky came to me and asked me to hold her before I left. Said I was too good to her and was teary eyed. I said, remember the other night what I said, she replied yes, and what you said, yes she replied. I said it's done and that we are going to move forward from here. I said if it makes you feel any better. I am ordering you to clean up this house, and you had better be looking like a lady when I come back. She started crying. Does that make you feel any better? And she said yes as we hugged and kissed. I turned and left.

I arrived at the office shortly after ten, said good morning to Joanne and sat at my desk. She asked if I wanted any coffee, I replied no thank you. When she sat down, I asked her how her weekend was. She turned and said wonderful. I told her there's something I wanted her to do. I pulled one of Victoria's checks from my pocket and handed it to her. I had voided it out and wrote her name across it, set the direct deposit up please. No problem she replied. I asked if her daughter had found a job, she said not yet. May I ask you, as her mother, would you like for her to work here? She seemed a little hesitant. Stated she had hoped that she would have found a job on her own. I asked what courses had she taken in college. Joanne said, business and law, but wasn't sure what other subjects. I asked would you mind if I interviewed her for a job. Joanne said she wound be so grateful. Will you give her a call? I have a feeling we may need her for something very soon, I just didn't know what yet. She asked when? Today I replied, the sooner the better. She turned and placed the call, just then the phone rang, Joanne answered, and she turned and said to me, line two.

I picked up, it was Mr. Hippies, and he went on to explain that his soon to be former associates had asked him to please move by the end of the week if possible. Ok I replied, that we would have it done, and asked him if he was there now, he said yes, and I asked about his files. He had two file cabinets, mostly of real estate transactions, the others were other business he had handled in the past. He needed some boxes. I mentioned not to do anything until I could send him some help. Ok he replied. We would look to Wednesday to move him here. I would clear a desk for him. Asked if he was going to be there all day today? He said yes. Ok I will get back to you shortly. Joanne turned and said her daughter was on her way. I said that feeling I had, just manifested, and went on to tell her about Harold's situation and the solution. We were going to be one big happy family. Our office was a very good size with ample space, besides Joanne and my desk, there was Mr. Fitz's and seven unassigned. I got up grabbed a piece of paper and a marker and wrote reserved in large letters and taped it to the desk across from mine. Good thing there was more space on that side. Knew Hippies had his files. I just remembered, picked up the phone and dialed Kenny Watson who was my IT guy. He answered right away and recognizing my voice, and asked what the problem was.

I said no problem, and went on to explain about the new office. I wanted it hard wired, wanted a new server and desk tops and some redundancy in the system. I gave him Louis Browns number and to coordinate with him since he was doing the redesign, I wanted them together along with Hector after I closed. And I would then be able to have an estimate of the cost and a time frame. He said that would call and do that right now. If all goes according to plan, he would only have until Wednesday. He said ok and we hung up. Then Joanne turned and said her daughter was on her way, they didn't live very far away from the office.

I poured a cup of coffee, looked at the clock, it was ten after eleven, as I sat back down, just then in walked a pretty young lady, slim, graceful, brown skin and wearing a skirt that fell below the knees, a blouse with ruffles around the sleeves and collar, she was wearing pumps, her hair was a soft brown and curly, she walked with confidence towards us. Joanne stood and they hugged before she turned to me. I stood and she introduced me to her daughter Patricia. I said nice to meet you as I pulled up a seat and asked her to sit down. Said to her, I see the family resemblance, as beautiful as your mom. I said let's get down to business, and asked what courses she had taken in college and if she was still attending. She said a couple semesters of business and law courses for the entire two years. She was close to becoming a legal aid, and had a part time schedule now. It was as intense as going to law school, but would soon be completing all the requirements. I asked if she would want to work in the same office as her mother, and if she had a problem with that. She said oh no. I asked why she hadn't found a job as of yet. And she stated that she had found one, and then went on to describe the environment, it didn't sound good for a good looking smart young woman. I asked if she was ready to start today. She gave me a big smile and said yes sir, and thank you.

She was Joanne's only child and you could tell she wasn't spoiled. I knew from what her mother had told me when we talked a very long time ago when her husband had just passed when Patricia was about eleven or twelve that she was very close to her dad. It affected them both but they eventually had gotten through it. I said you are hired right now, but I have a special job just for you, and you can fill out your application later but this may help you in your field of law. I went on to explain about Mr. Hippies and what I needed her to do. I asked if she was driving and she said yes. I asked Joanne to start her employment papers and make her appointments for her medical and dental. She said ok, and then I gave her the corporate card for the bulk store and to purchase four to six bundles of the collapsible banker's boxes to start, then go to Mr. Hippie's office and to assist him in packing his files. I want you to return here at five thirty, a half hour before we closed. I placed the corporate card and two one hundred dollar bills in and envelope and wrote Hippies office address on the outside. Said she could buy herself lunch as long as she returned with the receipts. We stood and she shook my hand and thanked me for the opportunity. Then she turned to her mother who was standing and hugged her, and walked out on her mission. I picked up the phone and dialed Hippies office, and informed him a nice young lady was coming to assist him in packing and keeping his files organized. She would be bringing boxes with her, and if he needed any other assistance not to hesitate and call me back and then I hung up.

Joanne came around my desk and I stood up, she hugged me and there were tears in her eyes, she said thank you very much. I said make her salary $45,000.00 a year as she dabbed her eyes. Besides being happy for her daughter, she was happy for me, and said god bless. I almost started to cry. I asked Joanne to go to lunch. Funny no associates had come in yet, well it was Monday and shortly Mr. Fitz came in. We spoke and he went for a cup of coffee and sat at my desk. Asked were there going to be any major changes with rentals. Told him I was going to separate the commercial from the residential. And he would be in charge of both. The way we had operated the complexes would stay the same with the complex agents staying on premises and doing credit reports and such. He was glad that wouldn't change. I said he would be sharing a secretary with Hippies. That Hippie would be moving into the office before the end of the week. Wow, he said they really wanted him out bad, and Hippies had told him about it when they were at the dealership last week. Told him you know we hold their lease. Yes he knew, with a smirk on his face. He said at least we wouldn't have to drive to Hippies office anymore. Yes I said, as he went to his desk. He then turned and said, should we raise their rent, I laughed and said it was something I had thought about, but in the end its all for the better.

I had almost forgotten, and dialed the number Mrs. Wong had given me, it rang a couple of times before Mr. Wong picked up. I spoke with him briefly before his wife came to the phone, she greeted me and said she and her husband had discussed expanding the restaurant, they had a son and daughter who were involved in the business and they had discussed opening a second location. But were all in agreement on expanding the current location was better instead, and asked how much more would I charge. Said I would have to look at the rate I was charging now, and was glad they wanted to stay. I would give them a lower per square foot price depending on how much space and the length of a new lease and would cancel the old upon negotiating a new one. She said that was welcome news and would call me back soon and I should keep this number because it was there home number. I said ok, she told me the young lady is very much in love with you. You keep, you nice man, you need good woman, I thanked her and said good bye. Joanne returned, she thanked me for the long lunch. Said I was going to get something to eat and I would return.

I went to Lucky Lobster, and tried their lunch menu. I had the boiled shrimp lunch, with coleslaw and a coke. While I waited for my food I brought up the home camera app to see what was going on, and went, room to room and found Vicky eating lunch, she had just finished and washed her hands, then went and started cleaning the downstairs wash room. My food came and I dug in.

Afterwards, on the way back as I passed the mall, noticed that, the last store had a moving sign and would be closed by the weekend. I passed our new location on the way back and it smiled at me or was it the other way around. I parked and went in and headed to my desk as Harold Green came over and shook my hand,

and said he had a couple who wanted to look at both condo units. I said that sounds very good, asked about the price. I said it was firm and get an offer in writing first; he said he would. I returned to my desk and Johanne had placed a note on my desk, and it was from the manager at the last store in the mall, they were closing Friday and moving their stock to another store Saturday. I called the number on the note. They answered and I asked to speak to the manager, it was him and he stated we could do a walk around. I informed him that wouldn't be necessary and told him he could have Sunday as well, because the mall would be demolished after they moved. He said sorry to see it go. I thanked him and we hung up.

I called the demolition company and spoke to Mr. Rogers, he owned the company and said he had visited the location and checked and the price was the same. He told me, $30,000.00, for a complete tear down and hauling away all the debris. And would arrange for the utilities to be disconnected, and it would also include the parking lot. I asked how much of a deposit, he stated, half now and the other when he finished. Said he would pull all the permits. I told him he had a deal, and where and when after Tuesday we could meet, he said his office or mine would be fine. I accepted his price and said I would call tomorrow to set a time and day. He thanked me and we hung up. Time sure flies as Patricia and Hippies walked in. They both had a box in hand and I directed them to the designated desk. They left the boxes on the desk as I stood and shook Hippies hand; he turned to Joanne and said he didn't know she had such a delightful daughter. Jokingly saying if he was a younger man he would offer to marry her, she looked at him and scowled. She told him he was a dirty old man, to which he said; maybe I should ask you out, we all laughed. It seems they had a good time, he stated that she was efficient, smart and comprehended all the legal lingo, and he turned to me and said, thanks for lunch. I said I know now you are a dirty old man; he took her to one of the best restaurants in town for lunch on my dime and told me she had the receipts. I had to laugh, she gave me the envelope and I handed it to Joanne. I am so glad everyone is here, Fitz was still here and Caren Brown hadn't come in today, J Phillips had briefly came and went and Green had left just before Hippies walked in. It was about fifteen minutes to closing when I asked Fitz to lock the door. I asked everyone to gather around, I asked Patricia to take a seat behind the others.

I said welcome to our first all office conference, and informed them as to what was going to happen in the coming week as I removed my tie, and got comfortable. I introduced Mr. Fitz and Mr. Hippies to your new secretary/assistant her name is Ms. Patricia Bradley, Joanne's daughter; Fitz stood and shook her hand and told her welcome to the inner circle. You are all employees of Harcourt Reality Corporation, everyone clapped. Welcome everyone to our first corporate meeting. I asked Joanne to take notes. I went on to say that we were the inner circle and thanked them for their loyalty and support and that was the reason for the pay increases and perks and informed them since they had my back I had theirs's. We were on the cusp of a new era in the business. I said that Hippies and I had worked out a chain of let's say command. I was president and CEO, Mrs. Bradley, was vice-president and CFO, Mr. Hippies was head of our legal Department and second vice president, Mr. Fitz was third vice and headed out assets, or rental department, which consisted of commercial and residential holdings which were going to be separate in the future. Does anyone have any questions or suggestions, so I assume everyone is satisfied? I looked at Hippies and said is that pretty much the outline, he said yes, it was. I said if everything goes as planned the building down the street will be our new headquarters, and each of you will have a private office. Ms. Patricia since she will be working exclusively with Fitz and Hippies will have her own office to ensure that everything goes smoothly as planned. I said to Pat you will be filing documents with the court and may have to go with Fitz on occasion. I asked any questions so far, ok none. We will have a conference room top and bottom with lunch rooms and enlarged washrooms, there will be new filling cabinets, desk, phones and work stations, new and improved. This is a bold step that I am taking, I am asking for your support and continued loyalty as we, embark to the next level. Ms. Patricia is our newest employee, the second employee this week, with my housekeeper being the first. I asked if there were any questions.

I stated the mall down the street was dilapidated, and we had just purchased it and is going to be demolished. Any questions, ok none, I said you are such an exciting group to talk to, ok class dismissed. They all clapped. Patricia came to me and asked what about tomorrow. I said you work with Hippies until he moves in here and then you'll be working for him and Fitz. Check with your mom for your appointments and to set up your direct deposit. I called Fitz over and told him about the Wong's and he said he understood. I wanted in on the final details, and he said ok. I told Hippies that Pat would be with him until he was moved out and gave him a number to call to have his stuff moved. We all prepared to depart, and head home. Joanne and I locked up. She thanked me again, hugged and thanked me for hiring her daughter. It was a pleasure and looked forward to a long association with both. I walked her to her car and opened the door for her and said it was a pleasure for me to do something for her after all the long hours and hard work. Said she was glad I appreciated her. I said good night because this was going to be a busy week, I could feel it in my bones. She told me that she wanted to meet this housekeeper who she knew changed me for the better. I said in due time, as I closed her door. She looked good in the new car.

I turned and got into mine and headed home, even though it was almost six I felt tired, pulled into the garage, closed the door and went in. Victoria was coming downstairs, she ran and hugged me. She asked how it went and I said busy and that I was going to have a drink and go to bed. She asked if I wanted a rub down. Said I would welcome that very much. I went up and undressed, and placed my dirty clothes in the hamper and went to relax in the bathroom taking a long and very warm shower. When I came out she had a drink prepared and waiting, and asked me to lie down. She began to massage me with warm oil. I took a sip and drank half before I laid back down on my stomach, she stripped down to her panties and began to give me one of the best massages I ever had, when she finished with my back I had almost went to sleep. She woke me and told me to turn over, I turned over and she started again, I don't remember when she finished. I had fallen asleep again. I was completely exhausted.

Twelve

Tuesday: Day Twelve.

I woke up excited; this was the big day as far as I was concerned. I got up and went to the washroom and really felt good about today. When I returned looked over at Victoria. She woke, kissed me, and then went to the bathroom. When she returned, found me getting dressed. I wore my black suit black shirt and silver tie. I went downstairs and started the coffee and she followed. She could tell I was excited and asked why. I said a plan was coming together. I hadn't discussed any of my business with her, all she knew was I worked in a real estate office. I was eating a donut, when she offered to make me breakfast. She began fixing the sausage and eggs and said I should really eat something. I told her what I wanted as she began preparing our breakfast. We ate together and I reminded her to go to the DMV and have her license updated. Said she could go by herself and get it done but first I would have to call and put her on my insurance today or tomorrow. She said ok. While you are out I would like for you to get a business suit. She asked me why I wouldn't be going with her. I told her you are a big girl. Said she would rather I go with her to the store, but she would go to the DMV. I said fine and finished eating breakfast. Then asked if there was anything she needed for the house. No she replied. I brushed my teeth and, said I was on my way. She dried her hands and came over and hugged and kissed me. Please be safe, she said as I gave her a passionate kiss, turned and departed.

I drove directly to the office; it was eight when I entered. I locked the doors behind me and went to the lunchroom to make a pot of coffee, returned and sat at my desk. Then opened the file cabinet and pulled Victoria's file before I called the insurance company. I noticed Joanne had did a credit report and pulled a work history. I glanced over them; they were what Victoria had told me, a discount store after high school, then the strip club, and finally her last job, at another discount retailer. I wanted her driver's license number. I had made a copy, found it and returned to my desk and called my insurance man. And he answered on the second ring, informed him my reason for calling. And I gave him the information, and we were done. I thanked him and hung up. The coffee was ready and I needed a cup. I wanted to clear all the small things, getting them out of the way, the mission I had set for myself was about to begin.

At five to nine Joanne Bradley unlocked the door, I said good morning. She responded, good morning. She asked what brought me in so early. I was excited about closing on our new office. She understood. Said I was getting the small stuff out the way first because I was going to be totally involved with this project. I know you Charlie and you're not going to be satisfied until it's done. Sure your right, I responded. She replied, we have been together long enough for me to know you. I know you and Patricia talked, and asked if she had anything to say about the job. Joanne said she hadn't seen her daughter this excited in quite a long time. They talked a long time, thought that you were handsome, and Hippies was funny, and she was happy to be working here with me. She thanked me again. I was glad to help because we were going to need someone we could trust. I replaced Victoria's file, sat down when Ms. Caren Brown walked in. Good morning she said and also complimented Joanne on her dress. Told me that she was happy I was in; she had a contract on the two bedroom condo at the asking price. I asked her are they qualified, she replied yes, handing me there file. I looked it over, and told her to call the seller and let her know you had a contract, at the full price. If she accepts, make an appointment to have her sign the offer. Said since I had brought it in I might want it. I said no honey. You found the buyer it's your sale. Thank you and went to her desk. It was ten or fifteen minutes later when Hippies came in, good morning he boomed. He knew I was excited about today, he spoke to Joanne and said Patricia was at his office packing files. He turned to me and asked if I was ready. I said yes. Joanne handed me the cashier's check drawn on the corporate account for the purchase. I asked Joanne to stand, and then gave her a hug and kissed her on her cheek, she stood back and said that's real happy. Hippies and I left for the closing.

We arrived at the title company. Waited and then were taken to the room where the closing was going to be held in. Shortly after the sellers arrived and we all shook hands, then the closing began, it was over very quickly considering I had gone to some that lasted an hour or longer. That happened mostly with residential but this went pretty fast, since it was a cash deal, and the property was unencumbered. When it was over I was handed the keys. We all shook hands again and I was happy it was finally over. Hippies and I left and stopped by the property. I had been given a ring of keys with a tag with a four digit code. I unlocked the doors and walked inside and punched in the numbers in the key pad, and watched as the system lite turned from red to green. I turned to Hippies just as he said wow, what a great location. We took the elevator upstairs after I turned it on. We rode up and got off, told him this is where our offices will be, he said great. I had people working on the layout and the electrical already. I asked where would you want to sit, he said he would wait for the finished product. I said ok, we went into the fairly large washroom, and I explained that there would be men's and women's instead of this unisex setup. We went back downstairs to the lower level and we walked around some more before I asked what he though. He thought I had made a wise move and the price was exceptional considering the location, size, parking, and the ample sun light and the energy saving lighting. He said he had read the specks on the property.

It was about quarter after twelve when we returned to the office. I told Joanne that she could go to lunch now. She replied saying she was at lunch, since she knew I would be gone. She had brought her lunch with her. Hippies put his briefcase down and said he was heading over to the old office to check on Patricia. I said wait and wrote down the phone number of the people he could call to bring everything over when they were finished packing his files. He turned and left. I went and sat at my desk to make the calls for making the new location into our office. The first call was to Louis Brown. Called him and after the greeting, asked about the layouts. Said he was just finishing up and Kenny Watson was going to meet him and they would both come see me because he knew I was anxious to get this project started. Asked what time were they considering? He said three at my office. I told him I would be waiting for them. I called Hector, I didn't have to wait long before he picked up and told him to meet me here at three, and he said ok he would be there. I asked Joanne if she would call, gas, light, and water, she said alright and I could consider it done before the end of the day. Ok I was off to a great start, it was one o'clock and I left to get a bite to eat. I went to the local burger joint and bought a deluxe burger with fries and a drink and returned shortly.

I decided to bring up the home camera app. I scanned the outside then the inside, no Vicky. I pulled up the bedroom cam, it was password protected, and entered it and there she was, sitting on the bedroom couch, on a towel nude, she had a towel around her head and was painting her toe nails, it appeared she was finishing as she got up and put on her bathrobe, then laid down on the bed. I turned off the app and just sat there thinking about our new office. I had tried to keep this one up to date and comfortable, but we have truly out grown it, it was a very large office. But it had drawbacks as our business increased and grew.

Before I knew, it was a quarter to three. In walked Brown and Watson and then Hector. I introduced everyone and directed them to drive down the street. Everyone left and we regrouped at the new location. Hector had been here before so he knew. We entered and Brown brought the blueprints with him and some layouts. Kenny walked around and looked for the utility room. Louis rolled out the preliminary layout choices. I looked them over. The downstairs had half way between the entrance and elevator a receptionist desk on a raised platform completely surrounded with entry on the sides. As you walked in there was a waiting area that looked like a comfortable lounge area to one side, behind that was a section where there would be low walled cubicles. Besides the freight elevator at the rear of the building where the present washrooms were, would be the new expanded washrooms. He explained I was lucky the current washrooms were laid out the way they were because it would make expanding them easier, less expensive and the same held true also for the second floor. He pointed out choices for the lunch room and conference room on the ground floor. Also there was far more space than he imagined. He laid out the plans for the upper floor, said there was more than ample space, he increased the private office sizes and there would be the six I wanted and added an extra one and a large storage room just to use all the available space, and did the same for the washrooms, only they were much larger. The conference room would be very large and the lunch room would have a complete kitchen. He had two layouts for the upper floor. I chose the first layout for the upper floor. Asked, if you and Kenny have discussed what I want, the hard wired internet connections. And he said yes. I told him he was to supervise as onsite manager. He said ok. I looked again at the lower level layout, and asked him to include two offices on the lower floor along one side. Oh, before I forget, where are the supply rooms and rooms for the servers, maintenance and clean up? He pointed to locations on the diagram for both the lower and upper levels for maintenance and supplies. On the upper as he penciled in their purpose, Kenny had found all the junction boxes. I asked Hector if he had spoken to his son, the electrician. Said he called him when we arrived, said he should be here shortly. Hectors son Juan tapped on the glass doors. I went to let him in, we shook hands, since Hector and I did a lot of business, I introduced him to Louis Brown and they began walking around discussing their approach. Hector approached and we talked, said he called Rhesus his son the plumber and he also would be here shortly along with Jesus the contractor. Just then, he walked in, his truck was outside and he saw his brothers, they hugged and were introduced to L. Brown. They walked around discussing the changes which were to take place. It was about six when we all regrouped and Brown said Hector would arrange for a dumpster to be dropped at the loading dock and Rhesus said the rear freight elevator was a plus for bringing up materials, and he could have the greater portion of the plumbing done for sure by the end of the following week. Juan said he and Brown would be going over the electrical tomorrow. I said Brown is project manager, everyone was in agreement. Kenny said the servers would be upstairs and my old server would add redundancy. Hector said he would bring in a crew to paint and clean after the new walls were up. It was open space and unencumbered. It would take about three weeks at the most. I had the keys, and was given eight sets at closing. I kept a set and gave Hector and his sons three, Brown and Watson a set each, now I had one extra set. Brown gave me a slip of paper with an office furniture dealer whom he said, the prices were better than most and had a very good selection, and they would deliver and install. I gave him the code for the alarm system along with his keys. He suggested that I should go and choose the furniture I wanted soon. I said ok. Everyone walked out and Hector patted me on the back and said he was glad I was moving to a better office instead of the current one and told me I deserved it.

I thanked him as we all got in our cars and drove off. I passed the office and I saw it was still open and had to unlock the door. Caren Brown and Howard Green were on the phones. I grabbed my brief case as Howard hung up and said yes. I said a sale and he said yes sir, the seller had accepted the buyers offer. I asked which one, he said the house that had been on the market for the past six weeks. I said oh that one, good and you all make sure you lock up. For sure he said. I said good night and left locking the door behind me. I drove home, it was late but it was a good day and couldn't wait to get out of these clothes. I removed my tie as I sat at a red light. I pulled in my driveway and decided to leave the car outside and went in the front door for a change. I unlocked the large oak door and went in locking it behind me and found the house quiet and headed upstairs and started to undress.

I had left my briefcase downstairs at the base of the stairs; I wouldn't need it until tomorrow. I undressed and went to the bathroom and relaxed and then took my shower, put on my bathrobe and walked out to see Victoria walking into the room and she came over and hugged me. She was wearing a large cotton t-shirt and wouldn't stop kissing me. When she did let go I looked and noticed her nails and toes, she used the red nail polish, and I complimented her and asked where you were. Said she was in the basement cleaning up, and was glad I was home. Hoped I wouldn't just go to sleep right away. Said I would like something light to eat. She responded that she had made a tuna salad and that wouldn't be very heavy. I said great, just let me put on my shorts and shirt. She had washed them and I would have to get a fresh pair. Ok I said as I reached for her and asked have you been good today. She looked at me and said no. I asked her what she had done.   Said she had felt on herself and hadn't asked my permission. Oh I said you need a spanking, but later after I eat. I put on some clean shorts and a t-shirt and we went downstairs and she ate some also. It was delicious and had some red wine as we ate. I asked her what she did around the house. And she explained all the different things she had accomplished. Afterwards we went to the living room and we watched the news before I said it was time to go to bed. We turned everything off and went up and undressed and I took Vicky and hugged her and said I think you need a spanking. I held her with my left hand and spanked her with my right and gave her eight whacks on her butt cheeks. Turned her around and looked at her and told her not to do that again, and she replied yes sir master. I said get in the bed and we both got in and we hugged and said she wanted me to make love to her, we did and as usual and it was great, we came together and said she wouldn't do it again as we held each other and kissed before going to sleep.

Thirteen
Wednesday: Day Thirteen.

We awoke at six; it was turning out to be our morning routine as we both now used the bathroom together. We showered together, dried off, put on our bathrobes and went downstairs to eat. I did the coffee and Vicky did the bacon and eggs, we ate, took our vitamins and cleaned up the kitchen. I was starting to see an improvement in her appearance since she was eating regular and taking the vitamins. I had insisted she take them and she could see the change also and felt better. I said you should change the address on your driver's license today. Ok she said as we dressed. I decided on jeans and t-shirt and my sports jacket as I explained to her that she would take my work car and I would drive my other car. Vicky asked what she should wear. I suggested she wear some jeans, blouse, and sandals. She said ok, dressed and combed her hair. I said a little lip stick wouldn't hurt. When she was done she looked radiant, she thanked me and we closed up and went downstairs. I would like you to come by the office when you leave the DMV. She said ok. I went to the office and pulled a return address label off a sheet and placed it on a post-it-note and handed it to her and went to the kitchen. I wrote the DMV address down and gave her my business card. We then went to the garage; I showed her how to enter the addresses into the navigation system. She got out and hugged me again and kissed me, saying she loved me. Told her it shouldn't take her long the earlier she arrived there; it was eight when we pulled out of the garage.

I let her go first as I closed the garage doors, and then went to the office driving the BGT. I was early again, I opened up the office and left the door unlocked this time, it was only eight thirty anyway. I only had a few things to take care of when I soon received a call from Mr. Robert Washington. I had a half interest in the mortgage business he operated, he was thinking of moving his office to a more visible location because the current location wasn't conducive to his operation anymore. I had sent him more than half his business and he wanted to know if I had any rental space available. I said yes I do. I didn't own the location where he was currently located. I asked what he was paying a month for his rent, he said it was $850.00 a month and had to pay electric and internet and it was slowly turning into a dump, the owners hadn't made any improvements and the maintenance was lacking. Told him I have a great location and deal for you. I asked when his lease was up. He had been thinking about moving and had a month to go on his lease and was going to go month to month after that. I told him I was changing locations and asked how many people were working in the office with him. He said his daughter and wife. I asked if they were full time. Yes he replied, and said since I had a stake, that's why he called me besides he knew I owned several strip malls and a few office complexes. I asked if he would like to be in the same location as my operation, he said not in the same small office I was in now. I said it's been a year since you have been here and I had expanded the office, he said oh ok. I told him I had one even better that would increase his business which would mean more money for him and I. Told him I was moving and was in the process of expanding and was thinking about him. That I was soon going to have more space, than he could imagine. I was developing a one stop shopping for homes. I said about half your business comes from my office and that I would like his operation at my office location to simplify the process. I had things to do but would call back before the week was out and set up a meeting to show him the new space. He said that was the best news he had since his grandson was born and said ok, and would talk to me later and before the week was out, then we ended the call.

I called Louis Brown and he answered right away, and asked him to bring the plans with him before he went to the new location, said he was just getting ready to leave anyway, and would see me shortly. In walked Mrs. Bradley and we greeted one another. She asked if my coming in early was the new norm. I smiled and said, just till I had everything operating the way I pictured it in my mind. Being a comedian she said, can I look. I said no it was far too messy for you to look, and we laughed. After getting her coffee and sitting down at her desk, I explained the unexpected plus to our new operation, that Robert Washington wanted to change locations and called asking if I had anything available anywhere. I told him we were moving and would meet with him sometime before the week was out. Told Joanne I thought it would be perfect; one stop shopping since I had a part interest in his operation and half his business came from us anyways. I then asked her opinion; she said that sounds like a real winner. I am glad that you agreed with me since you sit on the board, thank you was her reply. I informed her that Mrs. Cook would be stopping by and I might be up the street and to give me a call on my cell when she does and ask her to wait here. Ok she replied. Just then Howard Green came in followed by J. Phillips and I said good morning gentlemen as they returned the greeting. I asked Joanne do you think we need any more agents, she replied a couple more wouldn't hurt and suggested we have one keep the office open till eight pm, because some of our customers worked during the day. I said what about Saturdays, and she replied that was probably the most important day when people were out shopping. You are so right I replied, I asked her to work on that aspect and we would discuss it later. Ok it won't be long she replied.

Just about then Louis Brown came in and greeted everyone. He came to my desk and we shook hands and thanked me for making him project coordinator. I said someone had to do it because it was too much for me. I had a few minor changes and we should go to the site, said he was on his way there. He suggested I should take Joanne with me to the office equipment show room. I said no problem, and then I remembered. What was on my mind, and asked him about those horizontal files that they have in hospitals and have a higher capacity than the old standalone ones. I said there were floor outlets since it had been a furniture store and the files were electrically operated and we seem to have more than enough space. I would like one in each of the offices on the upper level and I would like the same in the lower level offices also. We prepared to go up the street as I let Joanne know I was leaving and would soon return, and she wished me good luck as Brown and I departed. We arrived and Hectors people were already hard at work, they had the dumpster and were tearing out the old carpet and the washroom walls were gone exposing the drain and supply line pipes and electrical. I showed Brown where I would like the additional offices to be located on the lower level. I explained that one whole side was going to be the real estate operation and the other was my mortgage and my rental section, he said that wasn't a big change, he pulled out his plans and there was a foldup table in the center of the floor as he laid out the blue prints, he drew some additional lines and made some notes on the side, he looked at me and asked if there was anything else. No I was expecting a small change based on the phone conversation I had with and associate. He said don't worry it would be perfect, and if there was any excess space would let me know what I might want to do with it before they started walling things in. He stated that the offices would be very large compared to standard offices and why it was important that I pick out the office suits very soon and would send me the measurements later today. I said ok, I trust you. I walked around and my phone rang, it was Joanne, she said Mrs. Cook was in the office; thank you I said and hung up.

I took my time returning to the office and was in no rush. I wanted Joanne to get a good look at her and see what she thought of Victoria knowing she would speak her mind after meeting her, something I knew would happen. I headed back and found them having a leisurely conversation as I entered. I walked to my desk and they both turned and greeted me. Mrs. Cook I see you have met Mrs. Bradley; yes she replied and had a big smile on her face, glad you two have meet. Joanne said it was a real pleasure. I asked Victoria for her new driver's license, she had a new picture and the address was correct. I made a copy for the records and handed it back to her, and said to her it was time to go, she said good bye to Joanne as I walked her to the car. She hugged and kissed me and got in the car. I told her I would see her later, and she drove away. I went back in and Joanne looked at me and smiled, something she doesn't do often, and I asked what you think of her. She said now she understood. What I asked. She said from talking to Victoria that she is the perfect housekeeper for you. How can you tell I asked body language I replied? That young lady is very much in love with you, the kind of love that only comes if you're lucky, maybe once in a life time. And now she could understand the change that had come over me and said that before Victoria, I was driven, thoughtful and successful but lacking faith, and truly needed love in my life since my wife had passed. And it had been way too long, and was glad no matter how we had met that it was meant to be. May I ask what you all had talked about? She told me how you met, and the circumstances, and how lonely she had been and unsure of herself after her husband's death, and what she feared would happen to her and how you came along and saved her. How you have treated her since meeting her, and said she had tears in her eyes as she told me how much she loved you and said she would give her life for you. Joanne said that doesn't happen every day as she stood up with tears in her eyes and said she was glad I was in her life also, as she hugged me, and said god blessed you. Told her I love you too, and there are only a few people I really cherish and you are one of them. I thanked her for the guidance and the opinions she had given me through the years and the long hours and support. We both were crying. We have an appointment. She said where. I said we have to pick out some furniture. Brown had given me the office dimensions so we could pick out what we wanted. Phillips and Green were in the office and I called both of them over and asked who would like to supervise the office until Joanne and I returned and they both said they would both stay and hold the fort down. We said if it was super serious they could call us if they didn't know what to do. Phillips was studying for his broker's license and we said he was the number one and Green the number two. I said we might not be back before closing and they could lock up or stay. Joanne locked all the important files as we headed out to my car, but not before going to lunch at Lucky Lobster. Joanne and I went inside and after being seated we both ordered the lobster lunch special. After we ate and I paid the bill, then we both headed to the washroom. I came out first. Joanne was an elegant woman to be with and I loved being with and talking to her, as a matter of fact she has been my confidant all these years. She came out and we headed to the car, and I opened the door for her as we headed to the showroom to pick out the new office furniture.

We arrived and it wasn't a fly by night operation, it was large and well lit. We got out and entered. Mr. Kevin Kent met us at the door. I introduced Joanne, and I, he stated that he had been contacted by Mr. Brown, and said he was informed that we were interested in completely furnishing our new offices with the best and most comfortable available. Correct I told him, I had the dimensions. He said that Mr. Brown had given him the rough measurements as he asked us to follow him. He showed us some suits for offices the size of the new ones we would soon be occupying, they were gorgeous. Joanne said let me please sit down, it was far more than she expected. I asked questions as he explained the size and all the amenities and the quality of the materials, colors, and configurations, we walked and looked some more. I asked about the horizontal filing cabinets and he showed us several, they came in four, six and eight foot widths and could hold up to twenty thousand files in the smallest size. He recommended the six foot models from the information Mr. Brown had given him, there capacity was from twenty to fifty thousand depending on the thickness of the files. I asked Joanne which of the three largest suits would she like. She said it was a little overwhelming, and eventually she made up her mind and chose the one called the Savanna. I chose the Chief Executive and I picked for the remaining four offices two Bergamots and two Windsor's, with a six foot wide horizontal file cabinets for all. Mr. Kent wrote down our picks and showed us office desk chairs that were very comfortable. Joanne found one she liked, said it was so very comfortable; she didn't want to get up. I found one and took two more, for Fitz and Hippies. He led us to the cubicle area. I wanted low walled cubicles, with storage cabinets on the wall side behind the desk and he showed us some variables, once I made the choice. I took eight set ups. I would hold off on the selection for the mortgage section for now. I would probably have to come back when I finalized the move. He said ok and went to run the numbers. Before he left, I asked Joanne about the other furniture in each office. She suggested we should go to a furniture store and choose the furniture and that would be more individual and classy. I agreed with her decision. I asked Mr. Kent to give me an estimated price. He came back and said $30,000.00, for the five suits with chairs and the file cabinets and the cubicles, and stated they would install and set up per directions of Mr. Brown and delivery was included, plus everything was guaranteed. He would coordinate with Mr. Brown since he was the project manager. I said to send him an itemized bill and it would be paid through the office and Mrs. Bradley was the one he had to make happy or otherwise. He smiled and thanked us for our business and said we would soon be in touch.

Joanne and I left and once we were in the car. Said she was glad her heart hadn't given out. I said it wasn't that difficult. She said it wasn't often that she would say she needed a drink. But tonight she was because it has been a day full of surprises. As we drove back to the office Joanne said to me, that she could tell I loved Victoria even though I was trying hard to hide it. She could see it and I shouldn't deny my love for her and just be happy, the change has been a positive one, and could tell in the past week not only by the moves I had made but in my demeanor, and told me she could see I was happy inside. I told her she was right and before we returned to the office, said this was the first time the both of us weren't in the office during business hours. I asked her, do you think that we should have Phillips and Green as assistant office managers, rotating the job between them and alternating the days between them and that way it would relieve us of that responsibility and starting them out at $25,000.00 a year each, plus they could still make deals and do listings. She agreed that was an excellent idea just as we arrived back before closing. Phillips and Green were both on the phone when we entered. They both had these big shit eating grins on their face. Joanne and I looked at each other before I asked what's up. Phillips said we had just landed three more listing and they were going to split them. Green said he had just received two contracts one for a condo and one on a house. I looked at the clock and asked if one of them would lock the door before asking them to have a seat by Joanne's and my desk. I said gentlemen you two have been with us the longest. I know that Mr. Phillips is studying for his broker's license, and I asked Mr. Green if he was considering it, he said he was to take the exam in one week, very good and Phillips said he had a week also. Said I assume you know I am moving the office, and they both said they knew but wasn't sure where. I said down the street. I told them Mrs. Bradley and I had discussed having and office manager when we move, but the requirement is you had to have a broker's license, the pay was $25,000.00 a year to start, the rest of your earnings would come from your work listing and selling just as you do now, but required being in the office all day, and was the reason we were approaching the both of you. Now the idea was an every other day schedule or you could discuss it between your self's, but each would have to work the position three days a week, or on one week and off the next. What do you gentlemen think, they looked at each other and smiled, granted I said this would be on a trial basis, because a broker has more responsibility. They both said they understood and were glad for the opportunity. I told them to think about it and next week we would need an answer.

They thanked us and Joanne and I said we were leaving. They said they would lock up as we bid them good night and I walked Joanne to her car. Before she got in, she said you know you're on a roll, and told me to go home because someone was waiting for me. Good night Joanne, and don't forget that drink, as I closed her door. I got in my car and headed home.

When I reached home, I backed into the garage and closed the door. Entered, and soon Victoria came down from upstairs and ran and hugged me. I hugged her, and asked have you been good and she said yes sir. Said she liked Joanne and was glad they had met. She likes you also. Then she asked me if I wanted anything to eat. Yes, the spaghetti sauce I had prepared. It will be ready by the time you finished with your shower, she said. I went upstairs and undressed and head for the shower and relaxed and when I came out after drying off found my shorts and shirt on the bed waiting for me. I put them on and went down stairs where I found Vicky setting the table, she had made some coleslaw to go with our meal, and had chilled a bottle of red wine, which I opened and poured into the glasses on the table as she fixed our plates, then we sat down and ate dinner and she was actually smiling. I asked her why. Said she had a very good day and felt very happy that I was now home with her. We ate, she cleared the table and I sat on the kitchen stool so I could watch her clean up. When she finished, I took her by the hand and lead her downstairs to the basement. I hugged her and held her in my arms and kissed her forehead and rubbed her back and then we sat on the couch and watched some television, and when it was around ten we went upstairs and undressed and went to bed, I asked her to rub my back, then I fell asleep.

Fourteen
Thursday: Day Fourteen.

The morning started as it has the past several days. I got up and began to freshen myself before coming back to the bedroom and looking at the sleeping beauty that now graced my bed as she opened her big beautiful eyes. I got back in bed and reached over and kissed her as she smiled at me, she sat up and said please don't go anywhere yet. She stood and headed to the bathroom and when she returned we both got back in bed and hugged and rubbed on one another, as we lay for several minutes not speaking. Then we kissed and I said to Victoria, I love you very much but, I don't deserve you. She reached up and held my head with both hands and told me she didn't deserve me either. Said I guess that makes us equal in each other's eyes, as we hugged each other for a long while as I caressed her and she shook as I found those areas on her that sent shivers through her as she clung to me even tighter. I stopped my assault on her body said it's time for us to start our day as we stood up out of bed face to face and held each other tight again as she began crying. I wiped her tears away with my hand as she looked at me, and we told each other at the same time, I love you. We eventually headed downstairs together for some breakfast.

We did our usual now beginning to become a part of our day team work preparations; I made the coffee and took out the cups, as she did the pans for the food. When everything was finished we sat and ate in silence before we cleaned everything up together and headed back upstairs. After we entered the bed room I took her by the hand and hugged and kissed her. I just held her as my mind was telling me, you have been alone to long, and this is love and it didn't matter what she or I have been or done in the past, this was the here and now, accept it, and run with it, as tears came to my eyes. I finally released her and she looked at me and touched my face and said she hoped the tears were of happiness since she felt the same about me. I could only shake my head as I kissed her, and we lay on the bed holding each other. I felt her face and then her whole body, then I told her she had grown on me and I thanked her for being here, in my life, and that I had never ever felt this way about anyone. Said I will love you forever as she kissed and held me. We eventually released each other and I sat up as she knelt behind me wrapping her arms around me and licking my ear. I turn and reached around pulling her into my arms as we looked at one another that look that only happens when two people know in their hearts they never want to be apart. I let her up and said I have important things to do. I have to finish what I started, and this I must do. I told her it was for us, and she was now the motivation behind me as long as she was here.

She knew and Joanne had told her as I stood and went to the closet and tried to decide what I was going to wear. Then Vicky came over and pulled the closet door open further and pointed to my dark blue pin striped suit and a pale blue shirt with a gold tone tie, and she said her man should look like he is the boss, I thanked her for her selection, and began to dress, as she put on some panties and one of her work smocks and waited for me to finish dressing, she handed me a bottle of cologne, I applied some, then she handed me a pair of black dress socks and my shoes. After dressing, she looked at me and hugged me, looked into my eyes and said, I love you and have a great day and be safe, and come home to me lover. I kissed her good bye, saying I love you Victoria Cook, and you stay safe and I will come back to you. I kissed her again, and went downstairs and to the garage, got into my car, opened the garage door and pulled out and headed to the office.

I drove to the office and when I arrived, saw Joanne unlocking the door as I parked. I went inside; said good morning and she turned and looked at me. And said good morning boss, she said wow don't you look the part. Victoria said I should look the part also and Joanne said she agreed with her. And said Victoria is good for you as she walked up to me, looking me in the eyes and said, there was a look on my face she hadn't seen in a very, very, long time. I told her that I had come to face the fact that I was in love, and stopped trying to deny it, that it wasn't going away and I didn't want it to. She hugged me and said I am so very happy you have come to your senses son.

After looking what I had spent up till now, approximately a $3,500,000.00, and then figuring with configuring the new office, hires, and demolition of the old mall, I would have spent more than $4,000,000.00, easy. I figured it was for a good cause and I had the reserves and hadn't spent any large amounts since acquiring my last apartment complex, and that was over twelve months ago. Monthly income was more than a $1,500,000.00, and I had been banking that for quite a while, with $20,000,000.00, in treasury bills, and cash reserves above $50,000,000.00. I am glad because this could all be written off as the cost of doing business, and a tax write off. While I was thinking about the new office, Joanne answered the phone, turned and said call on line two. I picked up and it was Mr. Washington, said he and his wife had talked it over about the move and she was tired and suggested they should retire. They were both over sixty and what he was really saying was, would I buy him out, he would transfer his mortgage license to my company, and said they had talked it over with their daughter whom he had employed, and they were all in agreement. I asked if his daughter was going to retire also, he said no, but I could employ her in my operation. My name was also on the license and yes she could work for me under my banner as an employee. I asked how much for a buyout, he said $200,000.00, I replied $175,000.00, he obliged, and we went on to set a date for the transfer. I asked him to send his daughter over to see me as soon as she was available. He said it was a deal and would prepare to close up shop. Take a couple of weeks, I stated so I can set up the new space. He would package all the loan files he did for me and his daughter would bring them when she moved to my location. I wished him well.

And said I would see him when we finalized the deal. We hung up as I waited for Joanne to finish her call. After she finished, I asked her if she had a minute as she turned and said yes. I said Mr. Washington is going to retire and I am going to buy him out, and we are going to employ his daughter in our new mortgage division. Joanne said wow things are really coming together aren't they. Yes I replied, must be the power suit, she laughed. I said we have laughed and cried more this week than all the previous year's put together. And she said yes we have, and said it was a good thing. I made some notes so I wouldn't forget all that was starting to happen. When Caren Brown came in and spoke to us, she handed Joanne a signed contract on one of the units that we were selling for Mrs. Kashia, Joanne looked it over and handed it to me and it looked good, they offered $500.00 over the asking price. I told her very good and asked if she had spoken to the seller, said she wanted us to look over the contract first before she called her. I said call and if she accepts, make an appointment to see her today if possible, and update the RELS listing to pending when you return from seeing her. She said yes sir, and I like the suit. Thank you I replied, as she headed for her desk. I said Joanne its lunch time for the vice president of operations, she glanced at the clock and asked if I would be here, yes I replied, as she grabbed her stuff and said she was going down the street to Martha's.

I sat and drew a block diagram of my new company structure, now that the reorganization was taking shape as I looked at what I had drawn. Joanne and I, then Fitz, he had two boxes under him, then Hippies, now Washington. Ok as I listed all the employees, including the next three, the two office managers and mortgage department, I thought that pretty much covered it for now. I pulled out my phone and brought up the home camera app. And I checked on Victoria, found her vacuuming the living room wearing the same smock she was in when I left as I turned it off, and looked out the window just as Mr. Green entered and we spoke. I asked him what he thought about the offer and said he would wait until he and Phillips could talk it over some more. I said very well just as Joanne returned. And informed her I was going to the office furniture showroom and wasn't sure if I would return. She said ok, and stay safe, as I exited and headed for my car. I arrived at the show room and shortly Mr. Kent approached and I said I needed two more suites but not as grandiose as the others, he showed me some smaller outfits, I asked to see some slightly larger ones, and they were spacious and complete with cabinets, large desk and shelving units all in wood. I said ok adding two more to the list and mark these for the lower floor. He answered no problem, we shook hands and he thanked me and said it would be added to the invoice, and then he said I like your suit. Thank you I replied as I left the premises. I got into my auto and decided to take Victoria out to dinner and called home. I had to call twice before she answered and asked what was she doing, she said she was finished for the day. I told her that I was going to take her to dinner, I suggested that she wear something stunning, with the pearls. It was three and would pick her up at four thirty and asked if that was enough time for her. She replied it was more than enough, ok. I love you, see you later. I called the Paris restaurant and made reservations for two, they asked the name, Harcourt, and I requested a chilled bottle of Champaign. They said it would be done and I went back to the office and waited until four and told Joanne I was taking Victoria to dinner and I would see her tomorrow. She said enjoy your selves.

When I got home parked in the driveway and went in the front door as Vicky was coming down the stairs. What a beauty, she wore the black dress with the single shoulder strap with the hem cut on an angle and the silver trim, black open toe high heels with no stockings. She had oiled herself and her skin glowed, she wore the matching pearl necklace, earrings, and bracelet, with the black purse with the shoulder strap, her nails were done in red and wore red lipstick, her makeup was light and had some eye shadow on. I asked her to stand on the bottom step as I took my phone out and took several pictures. I immediately took her hand and kissed it, and told her not to cry or your makeup will run. She smiled as I kissed her cheek and we went out as I locked the front door. I opened the car door for her and she got in. I told her she was the most beautiful woman in the world as she looked at me. I said you better not cry because it would make me very sad, she said ok. It took us about forty minutes to arrive at the Paris restaurant and I used the valet parking. We walked inside as other patrons gave us admiring looks as we entered and approached the maître. I stated we had reservations, he asked the name, I said Harcourt and he said right this way as we followed him, and he seated us in a reserved private booth. As we were escorted to our booth I could see heads turn as people looked at us, me in my power suit and Victoria looking the picture of womanly perfection. I held her hand as the waiter brought the Champaign, opened and poured it for us, placing the menus before us asking if there was anything else. I said no, not until we ordered, he said very wells sir, madam and departed. I looked at Victoria as we held our glasses and I said I wanted to propose a toast. I said to the woman I love, forever; we clicked glasses and drank a very good Champaign and enjoyed its very essence. We looked at the menu, and I asked Vicky what she wanted to order, she said for me to order for both of us. I said ok as the waiter approached and asked if we were ready, I said yes we would be having the same, the rib eye steak, with baked potato mixed veggies, and the Cesar salad. He asked how do you want your steaks, medium well done I replied, and French dressing for our salads, as I handed him the menus. He left and Vicky was smiling and her eyes were moist as I poured her another glass of Champaign, I asked her how she felt. She said wonderful and very happy and had never before felt like she felt now and had never dressed like she was dressed now, it is a dream and didn't have any words for it. The waiter came and set our plates on the table along with our salads. I thanked him. We ate slowly enjoying every mouth full. I said if you can't eat it all we can get a doggie bag, she said that wouldn't be necessary, we only ate half the potato, but all the steak and veggies, we were finished and soon the waiter came and cleared the table and asked if we wanted any dessert, we declined but did have a cup of coffee, and he shortly returned with the coffee and the bill. I looked at the bill, it was seventy-five, I placed a $100.00 bill in the folder, we finished our coffee as the waiter returned and I told him to keep the change, he said thank you sir. Victoria said she would like to use the wash room. I helped her exit the booth as we went toward the wash rooms near the entrance. Stated I will be waiting, since all I had to do was pee. I washed my hands and went out and waited, she came out and we held hands and walked to the valet podium. I gave him the slip with the number on it, as we waited and watched people entering and leaving and everyone was looking at Victoria, she did wonders to the dress, and was just stunning.

I opened the car door and Victoria got in, I tipped the valet as I walked around and got in, buckled up and pulled away. Vicky said that was the most wonderful dinner she ever had as we headed home. I pulled up and turned around and backed inside. I opened the door for her and she got out and hugged and kissed me as we held hands as I unlocked the back door and we entered, going directly upstairs to the bed room. We undressed and hung up our clothes, and were standing nude as we hugged each other and went to take a shower together. We bathed each other and kissed and when we finished put on our robes and headed downstairs to the basement bar and I fixed us a martini as we drank until we were ready to go to bed. We crawled in the bed and held and kissed each other and felt each other until we fell asleep.

Fifteen
Friday: Day Fifteen.

We woke up together; I rolled over, and looked at Victoria. We both had to use the washroom and we went and freshened ourselves up so we could start another day. I took Victoria by the hand and we lay back down across the bed and we kissed each other. Victoria said that it had been such a wonderful experience for her yesterday, and felt better about herself with every passing day that we're together. She looked me in the eyes and hugged me. Cried and kissed me and said she loved me like never before. Her tears were tears of joy and happiness unlike anything she had ever experienced. She was so very happy that I was proud to be seen with her after being told she was worthless and ugly in the pass. I told her all of that is behind you now, we're going to have a new life together and be happy and cherish every day because time was precious and it was up to us to make the most of it. We should have some breakfast and start our day with some food in our stomachs, she said ok, as we slipped on our robes and went downstairs to prepare another bountiful meal, made with love to start the day.

We did our usual; Vicky always prepared a really beautiful and tasty breakfast. I could cook but breakfast was not one that I cared to do. I fixed the coffee and when completed, we sat and ate; we really needed that I said to her and she responded. Yes we did. We finished and we both cleaned up the kitchen and went back upstairs to dress. But first I brushed my teeth, and then she came in and did the same. When we were both in the bedroom, we seemed not to want to let each other go. We hugged again and I passed my hands through her hair and smelled her sweetness as I held her close and rubbed her all over. As I said you know tomorrow we're going to look for your pants suits. She looked at me, smiled, and said she looked forward to spending the day with me. I looked at my suits and said its time to put some of them in the cleaners. Removed all but two, and placed them over the chair and I would drop them off on my way to the office. Ok she said. I decided to wear jeans, a dress t-shirt and one of my sports jackets with some athletic shoes because I was planning to see how the work was progressing on the new location. As I dressed so did Vicky. She put on panties and a clean work smock and began gathering our dirty clothes, removed the towels from the bathroom, taking them downstairs and I soon followed bringing my dirty suits with me. I went to my home office and checked around, then remembered that I didn't bring anything home. Then went to the kitchen and grabbed a bottle of water from the fridge before heading to the garage, placing my suits in the car and returned to the laundry room where I took hold of Vicky after she had closed and started the washer. I hugged and squeezed her butt as I kissed her. She wanted me to have a great day and said she loved me. I released her and re-entered the garage, got into the car, opened the garage door and drove out as I closed the garage door behind me and headed to the dry cleaners before going to the office. I reached the cleaners, grabbed my suits, entered and waited as Mr. Chong greeted me. He filled out the slip as he counted the number of pieces, finished and said Wednesday. I thanked him and headed out, got back in my car and continued on to the office.

It was five after nine when I arrived and Mrs. Bradley had opened up and we greeted one another, she was printing a sign to put in the front window, saying agents wanted. I said good because we were going to soon run out, she said yes, that Mr. Phillips and Mr. Green had informed her that they would take the positions we offered them. And they would alternate the Friday Saturday schedule so they both could have a weekend off. That was acceptable to me as long as it was to her. She had no problem with it. I said ok. Just then Mr. Hippies and Ms. Patricia Bradley entered and we all greeted one another, and Hippies said he would be gone about an hour. He was going to his old office; the movers were coming to pick up the file boxes and his office chair. Ok I said, and Patricia was going to prepare the space here for his files and said they could stay in the boxes until we moved, she had done such a good job arranging them that if he needed something it would be easy to find. The phone rang and it was Ms. Samantha Washington, she wanted to speak to me. Told her I had been waiting for her call and asked her to come in, I wanted to meet her. She would be here within the hour. Great I replied, and I would be waiting. Joanne placed the signs in the window and returned to her desk. Then she informed me about the new listings and contracts, basically bringing me up to date.

I thanked her and grabbed a cup of coffee and sat down and started to drink, just as an attractive young woman with a nice figure about a size 12, five foot eleven entered. She wore a business suit with skirt and blouse that complimented her well-proportioned figure with high heels, and a pleasant face, and she looked around and approached Mrs. Bradley. Said, she was Samantha Washington. I walked around to Mrs. Bradley's desk and introduced myself. Mrs. Bradley pulled a chair over to my desk and asked her to have a seat. I said what a pleasure it was to meet her. I asked, how much her father informed her of what we agreed upon. She stated that she understood I was a silent half partner with her dad and since he wanted to retire, was going to transfer the joint mortgage license in its entirety over to me. That she would become an employee at a fixed salary, but she would probably make a percentage off of every loan. I looked at her and said how beautiful she was. She wore her makeup well, and had intelligent eyes, a nice set of teeth, and pretty legs as she sat with them crossed. I said your dad has prepared you well and you are correct in your assessment, so I said $25,000.00 a year how does that sound, she said $30,000.00 and we would have a deal. Ok, and one percent of the loans, she said ok. I told her she would have her own office and she was to adhere to the industry standards and no creative financing because she would be under the umbrella of Harcourt Corporation. She asked if I wanted to review and give final approval of the loans. I said no, if you use due diligence and follow the guidelines that wouldn't be necessary, but she would be subject to review by me and Joanne. I was told by your dad you were the conscience of the office. I don't want you to start until our new offices are completed. And told her there would be plenty of room for any records she brought with her. I retrieved an employee application form and asked her if she would sit at one of the empty desk and fill it out .I said you are very pretty and I am glad you have joined our organization. She thanked me and said it would be a pleasure and looked to a long and fruitful working relationship. I showed her to a desk and pulled the chair out for her, she thanked me. Samantha sat down and filled out the application. Joanne turned to me and said, very pretty girl. I said she is going to be an asset. Yes she is replied Joanne.

Hippies returned with two men both with hand trucks, loaded with the banker boxes and he pointed to the back wall where they placed them. I asked how many more and he said two more loads and his office chair. Ok I said. They returned and then left and returned with just Hippies chair and handed him a bill, he reached into his jacket pocket then sat down and wrote them out a check, they thanked him and left. He got up and helped Patricia arrange them so they weren't in the way. By then Ms. Washington returned to my desk and pulled up the chair that had been moved and handed me her application. I looked it over and saw she was thirty-two years old, single, no children and lived alone. I handed the slip that came with the application telling where to go for her medical and dental employment checkups for our health plan. I would call and inform her when she could start and said it would be soon. And I asked if she was helping her father organize his records. She said yes, and it would probably take another week or two. They were clearing out and destroying a lot of very old records. I asked her to wait a moment before she left. I stood and said I would like to have everyone's attention. This is Ms. Samantha Washington; she will head the mortgage origination division that her dad and I co-owned but now will be wholly owned by me. I want you all to welcome her as part of our new and expanding organization. Everyone clapped and came over to introduce themselves, and I saw her smile and thank everyone once that was done. I walked her to the door, then to her auto as I asked her some questions about how she really felt about this new venture in her life. Said it was a welcome change and was surprised that she would have a welcoming committee. I said get your checkups as soon as possible and I might have a private grand opening ceremony once everything was complete. She asked where the new office was located. Right down the street and gave her the address. You will love it. It will be conducive to business. She said good bye, and looked forward to working with everyone.

It was lunch time. I asked Joanne where she was going for lunch. She mentioned Pat and her were going down the street to Martha's for something light. I said you can go now, and they soon departed. Well that left Hippies and I in the office and I said, what about you Hippies. He said he brought his lunch, as he pulled it out and laid it on his desk. I looked at the clock, it was twelve thirty five, and I pulled out my phone and brought up the home camera app. Checked on Victoria, as I scrolled through the cameras and found her eating some tuna salad and crackers. I just liked watching her. She finished eating and drank some water, grabbed a duster and went to the living room, opened the curtains flooding the room with sun light and started to dust as I closed the app. I decided to called Kenny Watson on his cell, he picked up and asked, what can I do for you? I said and office intercom, he said don't worry, he had planned it all. Great I replied. And said some things you probably hadn't thought of also. And that I would have the most modern office available. I thanked him and hung up. I glanced over at Hippies as he ate lunch. I was beginning to get hungry and thought about what I should have. At twenty after Joanne and Pat returned. Told Joanne I was leaving and probably wouldn't return, but maybe would come in tomorrow morning just to check on things. She said ok be good. I said call, if you need me. I said goodbye to Hippies and before I got to the door Mr. Phillips entered, we spoke briefly before I left.

I went to Wong's, parked and before I went in, walked over to the clothing store next door and looked at the size of the store. Evidently Mrs. Wong saw me pull up. She walked up, and said she was glad to see me. I asked her, how much space she was considering, about half and pointed. We walked the width of the store, noticed if I moved the entrance over I would have a smaller but still a good sized space left. Mrs. Wong and I walked back together and I said it was doable. We entered and I sat at a small booth. She took my order and asked if we could talk now. Sure I said. She came back with some papers and showed me what she wanted to do. I said ok. Then she asked how much more. She handed me the lease agreement, and I saw it was at five dollars a square foot for the current location in the final year, and we were half way through it. I explained to expand will cost you money. You attract people to the shops in the strip mall. I want you to stay. And I would make it conducive to you expanding. Asked if she had a blank piece of paper, and she handed me one. I would make it two dollars a square foot for two years, and three dollars for the remaining three years of a five year lease. I said you discuss it with your husband and family. Told her as soon as the space was vacant, I would void the current lease and start the new. She had a grin on her face from ear to ear. She says why so low for her. You always bring in a nice amount of customers, and they might want to stop and shop at the other stores, and that way I won't have any empty stores, then I could charge them more. She thanked me and said my lunch was on the house. Fawn walked up and placed my order on the table. I said Mrs. Wong you let me know for sure; as I signed the paper I had made the estimates on. If I wasn't present when the new lease was signed, give my agent the paper. She said thank you very, very much as she got up to resume her duties. I ate and when I finished I thanked Mrs. Wong and departed for the new office.

I pulled up and the lot was partially blocked off and there were several trucks of various sizes and quite a few cars parked all around. I saw Hectors son's trucks and the front doors were propped open. I entered and the ceiling was being painted. I continued to walk further and saw the walls were up for the new washrooms, walked over and several men were doing the tile work, walked to the other side and they were doing the tile there also. I walked out and took the stairs up to the upper level. The joists for the walls were up for the offices and on one side they were installing the dry wall. I went further back and saw the wash room walls were up and I looked inside and it was being prepped for the tiles. Boxes of tiles were stacked neatly outside and the studs were was up for the conference and lunch rooms including the electrical. I decided I had seen enough and went down and walked out just as Hector pulled up and said, Amigo. We greeted each other, he said everything was going smoothly; I thanked him and said I wouldn't be in the way. He said he would keep me up to date. I thanked him and got in my car and headed home, it was a little after four.

I arrived home and backed inside the garage, closed the door and entered finding Vicky folding clothes, she stopped and threw her arms around me and we kissed. I kissed her all over, and told her to continue as I headed upstairs. I undressed and headed to the shower to relax, another short but full day I thought everything was going according to plan. I finished showering and wrapped a towel around myself and went into the bedroom and found some clean shorts and a t-shirt on the bed waiting for me. Hung the towel back in the bathroom and headed downstairs to the bar to have a drink. I passed Vicky heading upstairs with a basket of clothes and continued to the basement bar, turned on the radio and fixed a gin and tonic and sat at the bar. I finished my drink and lay on the couch and before I knew it, had fallen asleep.

When I looked up it was eight thirty, damn I didn't intend to sleep this long but this past week has been pretty intense compared to the pace I had before I decided on a new office location. It had morphed from a regular office move into something in the back of my mind I had always envisioned. Evidently I wanted it this way, and fortunately had the means to accomplish it, but too top it off. I ran into the woman I had fantasied about, and now by some unknown power she was in my life. I just could never have imagined that this was happening to me, but it was all happening at the same time. I am going to follow my heart and love her and treat her very well.

I finished with my thoughts and went upstairs. I went in the bedroom and could hear the shower running. I decided to sit on the sofa and wait for her to come out; she came out wrapped in a towel not expecting me to be there. Came over and kissed me and asked if I had a good nap, yes I replied. She said that when she came down and found me asleep she left me because she knew I was tired, but was happy to see me now as she removed the towel and spread it out on the bed and began to oil herself as I sat and watched. What a beautiful sight it was, she sat and did her feet and slowly moved up doing her calves and then her firm thighs, stood and applied oil to her butt and abdomen, then her chest and held her breast in both hands and massaged them, she was oiling her arms as she walked over and asked if I would do her back. And I motioned for her to sit on my lap. I took the oil and applied it to my hands and rubbed her smooth soft skin from her shoulders to her butt and rubbed around until I held both breast in my hands, then down to her open legs and felt between them as she leaned back moaning. I felt her and placed my left hand on her breast and gently played with her nipple as my right hand moved down to play with her aroused pussy and clit, then she began to tremble in my arms as I gently bit the back of her neck as she moaned and was trembling as she had an explosive orgasm. I held her and wouldn't let go, her breathing was short as I whispered in her ear that I loved her and wanted her. I removed my hand from her thigh and breast and pulled her back and held her looking into her face, kissing her for a long time, before I led her to the bed. Pulled the covers back and took off my clothes and we held each other, she bit and licked my ear and slowly kissed me and moved down my body and continued to kiss me. I turned her around and pulled one leg over my head looking up at her crotch then I pulled her down closer spreading her legs apart as she held my penis in her hand putting it in her mouth as I pulled her vagina to my face and tasted her sweetness as she swallowed me. I then ran my tongue around her pussy lips and to her ass, and back again, licking her clit, then taking it fully in my mouth and sucking it as I tickled it with my tongue. She took me deep in her throat, it wasn't long before we both came in each other's mouth and I could taste and smell her sweetness. We laid there for a moment before she turned around and lay besides me, and we kissed each other, with one another's juices on our lips. And when she reached down and placed her hand on me I became hard again, I climbed on top of her and slowly entered her, making love to her again. We came together

again, and held each other a very long time. I eventually got up and
went to the foot of the bed, bent over and took her leg and raised it
to my mouth, sucking her toes as she squirmed with pleasure as I
rubbed her leg, when I released it and knelt at the foot of the bed
with her legs between mine she sat up on her elbows and reached
with one arm out and pulled me back on top of her and held me
tight and cried, kissing me all over my face while rubbing my
head. I reached and held her head running my hands through her
hair as tears started to flow, and then I rolled over and lay next to
her and held her in my arms. I held her until she stopped crying
and kissed her more, we finally released each other as I sat up and
got out of bed and reached for her hand and pulled her towards me
placing her fingers in my mouth. She sat on the side of the bed and
then I pulled her up and hugged her pinning her arms to her side
and biting at her ear, when I let her go she could hardly stand she
was so filled with emotion.

I placed one arm under hers and lead her to the bathroom and
turned on the water in the shower waiting for it to get warm, she
hadn't spoken a word since I was on top of her and now in a very
weak voice with more tears saying, love me forever, please
Charlie, there wasn't anything I could do but hold her, the water
was warming up as we just stood there holding each other. I sat on
the bench and she sat on one of my legs holding me for dear life as
she spoke in such soft tones it was difficult to hear, she said I love
you and would do anything you asked of me. And I could have her
whenever I wanted and that she would never be a problem, would
not ask for anything, just love her and not let her go. I had heard
her say these things before, but this time, like the previous times,
were from her heart. I made her stand as I bathed her like you
would a baby and then she started to rub me with the body wash,
as we cleaned each other, eventually walking out the shower as I
wrapped a towel around her, and then myself, we dried each other
and went back to the bedroom, laid out some dry towels as we
oiled each other and finally we finished. I put the oil away and as
we sat on the side of the bed. I turned and held her head with both
hands and kissed her lips, and said I want to see you smile and

slowly one came. Her eyes were swollen from all the tears. I asked her if she would be my wife, she looked at me and started to cry again. I said if you cry anymore I won't marry you, she looked at me and tried very hard not to, and I just hugged her and asked. What was her answer? And in a weak voice, she said yes, yes, yes. I held her and stood up, pulled her to me as I rubbed my hands all over her and kissed her sticking my tongue in her mouth, as she tonged me back. I wanted something to eat, so we put on our robes and headed downstairs to the kitchen. I said have a seat. I found there was a little tuna salad left. I fixed our plates with a few slices of cheese and crackers, there was some wine open in the fridge so I grabbed a couple of glasses and we sat at the counter and ate. We finished and just rinsed the plates and glasses and left them in the sink. I took her by the hand and led her to the bedroom and removed her robe, pointed to the bed as she crawled in and we just held each other until we fell asleep.

Sixteen
Saturday: Day Sixteen.

When we awoke it was almost seven. I tried to roll over but Victoria was right behind me so I twisted around until I was facing her and stroked her head and rubbed her smooth olive skin and pulled the covers back to admire her shapely nude figure, and the shape of her hips, and thighs before pulling the covers back over her as I got up and went to the bathroom to freshen up. I returned to bed and laid next to the sleeping beauty as she slowly opened her big beautiful brown eyes. She looked up and smiled at me, she slowly arose and kissed me and placed her head on my chest as I continued to stroke her head. I said, go freshen up sweetheart, she climbed out and went to the bathroom and soon returned and lay next to me and said. I do master Charlie with all my heart, as I reached over and held her as I felt her all over again. I said we have something to do today, and it was time for us to get started. I asked her if she remembered last night and she shook her head an affirmative yes. I could see it coming and placed my finger on her lips and told her you better not. She gathered herself, and I told her she had plenty of time for that later. I told her that we will go out for breakfast, and I wanted her to dress comfortably and relaxed because we were going to get her a pants suit and she might have to try on several outfits. I wanted her to look like she was loved and cared for; she smiled one of the most beautiful smiles I had ever seen. I said if you cry I want them to be tears of joy and not sadness, she finally spoke.

And said would do whatever she had to, to make me happy. I said it has to make you happy also or it wouldn't be right. Said she understood as we prepared for our next adventure. I looked on my closet shelf and decided on jeans, a knit shirt with short sleeves, some comfortable loafers and my trusty sports jacket. I started to dress as I watched Victoria as she put on some white cotton panties, she pulled out some hi-heeled sandals, and put on some brown stretch pants and her blue jeans skirt that fell just above the knee and a beige colored knit with short sleeves and no bra, she didn't need one, she was medium and firm, and with a light sweater. After she dressed she went to the bathroom and came out later with a warm rose lipstick and her makeup was soft and she asked if I was satisfied with her appearance. I asked her to turn around and told her I was fully satisfied with her appearance, as I kissed her. Asked her if she was ready yet, as she reached for the matching purse to her shoes and took her small purse and placed it inside the larger one with some makeup. We went downstairs and I stopped and filled a small bottle with vitamins.

We left and I opened the door to the BGT for her as she got in. Walked around to the other side, got in and we buckled up, opened the garage door, started the car and pulled out, closing the garage door behind us. Of course we went to Martha's, as I pulled up, and parked. I came around and opened the door for her, and we entered the restaurant. I noticed heads turn as people admired Victoria and I, we ordered and shortly afterwards, Mary brought our orders. We had a light breakfast and ate slowly and enjoyed our food, we drank several cups of coffee. I handed Vicky some vitamins, and we took them just as Mary came with the bill and began clearing the table. I placed the money including a tip on the tray and as we started to leave, I handed it to her, she said thank you sir. I replied thank you for the great service as we left. I opened the door for Vicky and said I had to stop at the office. She asked if Mrs. Bradley would be there. I said yes, we arrived and parked and we both got out and entered. I was surprised when, I found Mrs. Bradley, J. Phillips, H. Green, and Ms. Brown all in the office, and everyone spoke as we entered. And Victoria drew admiring glances from my agents. Joanne stood up as we came in and she hugged Victoria. I asked Joanne if there was anything I needed to do. She said no, that she was going to take advantage of the remaining Saturdays she had to work and show Green and Phillips the ropes. Hippies would help them with their upcoming broker's exams. I said that is wonderful and told her you deserve a raise. She said everything was fine and she would call if it was deemed necessary. I said ok. Vicky hugged her again and we walked out and got in the car and we drove off.

I headed to the Sweet Wood Mall, and to the exclusive women's store, The Palace. I found a parking spot near the main entrance and we exited the car and held hands as we walked toward the mall entrance. Victoria stopped, looked me in the eyes and said she loved me and was ready to be my wife. I looked in her eyes and put my finger to her lips and said I know you are. And then lead her into the mall as I held her hand and we walked until we reached The Palace. We entered and I saw the suit I liked on a mannequin in the store window. I said to her that's the suit I remember seeing the last time I was walking around and it just stuck in my head. She liked it also, a dark blue with gold trim around the collar, sleeves and pockets, she found another one she liked also. We found the rack, she found her size for both suits and took them to the dressing room, and shortly she came out with the beige pants suit on. It fit her very well and said it felt good and fitted her well as she returned to try the other one on in blue. This one was even more stunning than the last, and she was a terrific model. She liked both. I said ok, she returned to put her clothes back on.

We went to the cashiers desk and I purchased both suits, after they were wrapped and bagged and had received the receipt I took my lovely by the hand and we walked thru the mall until we reached Howards Jewelry. The salesman asked what we were interested in. I said an engagement ring. He led us to cases full of beautiful rings, and asked Victoria for her hand as he measured her finger. He then retrieved a tray full of diamond engagement rings. I asked Victoria to pick one; she said no, and asked if he had them in plain gold. Said he did, he returned the diamond rings to the case and showed us his selection of solid gold rings. Victoria picked a solid gold ring with two small diamonds, she tried it on, and it was two large for her slender finger, and then tried another, it fit perfectly. I asked her why she chose this particular ring, she turned, looked me in the eyes and said, the gold represented the purity of my heart and the two diamonds were us. I kissed her and told the sales man I would take it, he asked if he could clean it for us. Victoria would be wearing it. Yes I replied. He proceeded to clean it wiping it with a soft cloth. I asked Vicky to look around; she was admiring a diamond necklace with matching earrings that were three inches long and a bracelet. Do you like, I said as I walked behind her. She thought it was beautiful, but said it wasn't her, and then found a gold chain with a pendant and matching earrings. I asked if she would like to try them, she said yes. The salesman removed the set from the case and she tried them on, they looked fabulous on her. I asked if she would like to have them. She responded oh yes please. She then turned to me and stated I had gotten her enough and all she really wanted was me. I informed the salesman we would take the gold set and to wrap them up. He wrapped the jewelry up as she admired the ring and said thank you very much for making her the happiest girl in the world. We strolled through the mall and went in several clothing shops. We purchased a few blouses and jean outfits. Vicky said that she wanted to leave and had more than enough, so we headed for the exit with all our bags and placed them in the car's trunk, it was early afternoon.

I asked if madam was hungry. Yes, and said she was starving. I asked what would you like to eat, she wasn't sure. I decided for the both of us and drove to the Paris restaurant. I parked the car and we entered and were promptly seated. A waiter came and presented us with the lunch menu, and asked if there was anything else. I requested a wine list. He said yes sir and returned with the list, I glanced and asked for two large chilled glasses of Merlot from the list and said we were ready to order. We ordered the grilled salmon with rice pilaf and a salad, the waiter commenting, very good and removed the menu and returned shortly with our wine.

Victoria stated she was a plain girl and appreciated all the clothing and jewelry, but all she wanted was my love, and said she was having a hard time comprehending in the short time we had been together and where we were as far as our relationship. She was hoping her heart didn't give out after the most wonderful sex she ever had, and that she was so very happy beyond belief, and I didn't have to buy or do anything else for her, because she had

more than she had ever had in her entire life and didn't need
anything else. Asked me to please stop showering her with gifts;
she just wanted my love as we held hands. I said to her, that I only
bought her things because it made me happy and I wanted to
express it other than telling her, or making love to her, that she was
my heart now, and besides you needed some clothes. Said I loved
her, and wanted her in my life, as our waiter came and set the table
with our meal. We ate and enjoyed our food as Victoria looked at
me and smiled. I said you will be at my side wherever I go and
your life has now changed for the better, and forever. I like my
privacy so you don't have to worry about being in the public eye
all the time, but you will be at the grand opening of my new office
if I have one. She had no idea what was instore for her. She asked
where we were going after we ate, I said why. She said she really
wanted to go home and be with me and that was all she wanted as
long as it was ok with me. I said ok you can model for me and that
brought a big smile to her face which made her very happy. We
finished our food and soon the waiter approached and asked if we
wanted dessert. I said yes we would, he handed us the dessert
menu. Vicky asked me to choose. I chose the key lime pie and
some coffee; the waiter took the menus and returned promptly with
the dessert and coffee. We ate and savored every bite and soon
finished as the waiter returned and cleared our table. We sipped
our coffee. I paid in cash including the tip as we finished our
coffee and stood to leave. We left the restaurant as Victoria held
my hand, and we walked toward the car. I opened the door for her,
she got in, and we buckled up and headed home.

I was thinking what I was going to do once we reached home. I
was going to have some fun with her and play on her emotions,
and knew that I was trying to be nice to her, but she wanted to be
used, and was happy in that capacity and I was going to fulfill her
needs. When we reached home I backed inside the garage and
removed the purchases that we bought, and took them upstairs.
After we had freshened up a bit, I watched Victoria hanging her
clothes up as I went and stripped down and remembered. I had
these leather looking jeans and a leather vest that had been left

over from a cowboy and western party. After she had undressed and was only wearing panties I asked her to remove them and put on the one piece stocking with attached garter belt. I found the jeans and put them on with no underwear along with the vest. I said to her, put on the first black dress I bought you with the spaghetti straps and the black hi-heels, she complied. I asked her to remove all her jewelry and put on the black leather collar and cuffs.

Once she was finished dressing, asked her to look at herself in the mirror. She did and I said you look wonderful. I walked up to her and turned her around to face me and I asked her if she was ready to serve her master. She said yes sir master; she now had a big smile on her face. I knew then this is what she really wanted me to do to her more than anything else. I asked her if she was happy now, she replied yes sir master. I looked in the bag for the leash and the blind fold, I found the leather paddle, it had a hook and I hung it from my pants and placed the blindfold in my pocket. I took the large glass dildo and the leash and walked over to Vicky an attached it to her collar. Then I pulled her close and kissed her and told her, you are my bitch, and you will do whatever I tell you, do you understand. She replied yes sir master Charlie. I lead her around the bed room and then downstairs and all around the house as I watched her sexy ass going downstairs to the basement. I pulled her close and placed my right hand on the side of her face and rubbed it lightly making her think I would slap her as she cringed at the thought. I said to her, fix us a drink. I unhooked the leash and she went behind the bar to complete her task, she asked what did master want. I said a rum and coke and told her which rum to use and how much which she did expertly, she was very comfortable in this situation. I wanted her to become excited. I also wanted sex badly but not until I had some fun with her.

She finished making the drinks, and I ordered her to come back around and sit on the stool next to me. Once she did I said sip your drink as I sat and watched her. She asked me what I wanted her to do next. I said you don't speak unless spoken to, do you understand slave, she replied yes sir master. I continued to gaze at her. I turned the radio on and returned and watched her slowly sip her drink, soon we finished our drinks and I then reattached the leash to her collar and led her around the basement. I had her stand in front of the couch as I removed the leash, and took a seat on the couch. I told her to place her hands behind her head, she complied and then I stood and walked over to her and felt her breast with both hands rubbing and feeling them, before pulling the dress down so they were exposed and pushed up slightly by the top of the dress, and watched as her nipples soon stiffened, she was getting hot and excited as her breathing was now getting short. I touched her nipples and rubbed them with my finger tips before taking them between two fingers and squeezing and twisting them as I watched her reaction. Then I told her to spread her legs apart, her feet were about two feet apart as I reached under the hem of her dress and felt her vaginal area, it was hot and getting wet with every passing moment. I asked her, who are you? She replied that she was my bitch. I asked her if that is what she wanted to be. And she replied yes sir master Charlie. I sat on the couch and told her to put her arms down, to pull her dress up and feel herself, but not to climax. I warned her that if she did, a very severe punishment would follow, she was already looking like she wanted to climax and told her she had to first ask for my permission. I asked if she understood. Yes sir master she replied. She started to feel herself as I sat down and watched as she became more highly aroused and shortly began begging me, master please, master please, master please, as I responded yes slave, master may I please come master. I said does the dirty tramp slave bitch want to come. Yes please master sir, please master, as she exploded with a massive orgasm before I gave my permission. Said I didn't give you permission, did I slave. She replied no sir master; as she shook and her skin became moist with perspiration all over. I said since you disobeyed me slave, you will have to be punished even more. I instructed her to remove her dress and place it neatly on the chair. She complied and I then told her to kneel. I stood over her and cuffed her hands behind her back, told her to spread her knees apart, and then removed the blindfold from my pocket and placed it over her eyes.

I left the room and returned to the bedroom and retrieved the large bag with all the bondage paraphernalia and brought it downstairs to the basement. I told her to stand, as I removed the blindfold, placed my hand on the side of her face, and slapped her lightly to her surprise. I did it again and slapped the other side as she looked at me and I could see in her eyes as she zoned out to be the submissive slave she really wanted to be. I held her face and said I was going to teach her a lesson in obedience. I took the leash and hooked it to her collar as I held it taunt and commanded her to spread her legs, and removed the soft but firm leather paddle from my belt and rubbed her breast and stomach and between her legs and looked at the intimidated look on her face. I decided to blindfold her again so she couldn't anticipate my actions. After doing so I returned to rubbing the paddle over her as I brought it down on her ass cheeks, then the back of her thighs, her breast, the front of her legs and stomach and between her legs as her knees bent slightly. She was panting as I led her to the couch making her kneel as I unhooked her hands from behind and hooking them now in front and to her collar before having her bend over and placing just her head on the couch seat cushion and making her spread her legs and push her ass out. Then I smacked her ass with my hand several times and then with the leather paddle as her ass began turning a light red color. I rubbed it as she moaned.

I brought the bag over reached in and removed a bottle of massage oil and liberally applied oil to her warm ass cheeks and thighs as I began to spread her ass cheeks and pour some of the oil in her rectal crease as it ran down to her anus. I then took my finger and rubbed it around her sphincter as it relaxed to my touch before reaching inside the large bag for the glass dildo and inserting it slowly inside of her, pushing it in and out slowly until it went in an out smoothly all the while as she moaned loudly with carnal pleasure. I then smacked her ass cheeks several times. I reached for another dildo, it was large and long as I slowly pushed it into her very moist vagina, working it in and out as I teased her vagina as the prominent ridges on it teased her swollen and protruding clitoris. I left the dildo inserted deep inside her ass for a moment before I began to work both in and out of her at the same time, and then she just suddenly exploded with a very huge and long lasting orgasm as she screamed with pleasure. I slowly removed both dildos, first from her vagina and then her rectum and then the blindfold as I began spanking her butt briskly with the leather strap as she screamed, and climaxed again as I reached down and played with and spanked her clit with a thin leather strap as I held her down. I stopped and waited a short time before I pulled her up by her hair, then made her stand as I turned her around to face me. I un-cuffed her hands from the collar but left them cuffed and pushed her back down on her knees and grabbed the long leather strap and whipped her ass as she tried holding on to my leg whimpering and crying and saying thank you master.

Then I reached down and pulled her back up and I looked in her face and kissed her and she kissed me back with an endless passion. I released the cuffs and she hugged me tight as I rubbed her body. Vicky began to beg, please fuck me master, please master fuck me. I put the leash back on her and told her to get down and crawl and when she was in the middle of the floor I knelt in front of her and pulled my pants down and before I could say anything she had me in her mouth, giving me one of the greatest blow jobs ever. I told her to turn around and put her head down, arms spread on the carpet as I slid my hard dick in her hot pussy and fucked her hard as she moaned with pleasure and climaxing before I then slammed it into her hot ass filling it with my hot come as she climaxed again. I let it stay in a very long moment and when I pulled it out she turned around and licked and sucked it clean. I grabbed the leash and pulled her up to face me and taking my fingers and rubbing the come around her lips on her face as she put her arms around me hugging and thanking me. She hugged me tight kissing my body allover as I held the back of her head and she sunk to her knees. After a while she stood and said every time we have sex it got better and better and she loved me with all her heart and would be my loyal slave forever. Said that was so unexpected and really was super arousing for her. Said her ass felt real warm and if I would please rub it. I sat on the couch and put her over my knees and rubbed her crimson ass with the oil and some cooling gel and rubbed her backside as she held on to my leg. We soon cleaned up and picked up our toys and she went to wash the dildos. She returned and we put our clothes back on and fixed another drink before returning upstairs to the bedroom, undressing and getting in the shower where we washed each other and played in the warm water fingering and feeling one another and having more sex . When we finished, we dried off and oiled each other before we pulled the covers back and climbed in bed. Vicky said to me that she was appreciative of everything, repeating that said she loved me. I told her the same and she said no one could make her as happy as I did. The only thing she wore was the ring as we held each other and fell asleep.

Seventeen
Sunday: Day Seventeen.

We woke up late, it was eight thirty. We were tired after our sexual exploits of the previous day, and I couldn't wait to use the bathroom, got out of bed and finally returned to find Victoria running to the bathroom as I was leaving out as she gave me a quick kiss on her way in. When she returned we laid back down and hugged and discussed what we wanted to do today, we both wanted to lie in bed a little longer, so we pulled the covers back over us and we felt on each other until we both dosed off again. When I awoke again it was eleven fifteen. I looked at Victoria as she yawned and opened her pretty eyes and reached for me and pulled me to her as she kissed me and felt me all over and soon I was doing the same. She felt so good to me and I loved feeling on her as I felt between her legs and she moaned, grabbing me as we played with one another.

Told her I needed to build my stamina back up, and then said we needed to get up and get ourselves together. I stood and took her hand, as we took a quick morning wakeup shower and returned to apply body lotion to one another. I said we should eat something before we even considered what we were going to do and she agreed as I put on some sweat pants and a t-shirt and she put on a long t-shirt and panties, before going downstairs. It was going to be a nice day as I began opening some windows, before putting the coffee on. I said let's have a pizza since I didn't feel like breakfast. I pulled a frozen one from the freezer and turned on the oven as she prepped it. About thirty minutes later; we were eating. I asked Victoria what she wanted to do and of course she said be with me, ok come on and we went upstairs and I told her what to put on, jeans, blouse and gym shoes, not a lot of makeup and your small purse as I put on some jeans, a colorful t-shirt, athletic shoes and my old jacket. I said you may want a sweater, she asked where we are going. I don't know yet, because I haven't made up my mind. We closed the open windows and prepared to leave, she was combing her hair, when she finished we were ready. I said you are a country girl right, she said somewhat. We went to the garage and we got in the BGT and I pulled out and closed the garage door behind us and driving to the gas station to fill up.

Once that was done, we headed to the county fair; about an hour had passed since we left home when we arrived and parked. We got out and walked to the entrance, paid the attendant, and we walked around to all the exhibits and looked at the chickens, pigs, goats, and a variety of animals. We looked at crafts; looked at all the winning cakes and pies. We talked about when we were younger, then we headed to the amusement section and I bought a roll of tickets and we rode several rides until we had used up all of the tickets. Victoria smiled and laughed, as we ate some hot dogs and had a good time. We had spent several hours there and it was getting late as dust was nearing and we headed for the car. Vicky was happy as she looked at me and held my hand, when we reached the car we were both starving. Asked her what she might want, she was undecided and said it was up to me. So I headed in the direction of home and stopped at the Red Fin Seafood restaurant.

I found a good parking spot close to the front entrance as someone was pulling out, we parked got out and went inside. The Fin as it's called by the local folks is real casual, you can't help but feel comfortable and they have a real bountiful menu. We entered and were given a number. We only waited about ten minutes which gave us the opportunity to use the restrooms before our number was called. We were seated in a booth and the waitress gave us the menus. She asked what we wanted to drink. I ordered two large glasses of beer, and said she would be right back. Vicky asked me to order for her, she was overwhelmed by the menu and couldn't make up her mind. I said ok sweetheart, the waitress came back with the beers and asked if we were ready. I said yes, we would have the big fish sampler dinner, with a rice and coleslaw; she said good choice, took the menus and departed. Vicky said she hadn't ever seen a beer glass this large, it had a handle on it and said no way she could drink all of it. I said to sip it, and since we were sitting across from each other I could see the beauty of her face and her wonderful smile, it was like one you would envision in a dream as she put her arm across the table and asked me to hold her hand. I held it and looked at her long slender fingers and I rubbed her palm, and she said I was making her hot. I said as long as you're with me, you will always be hot in my eyes. She smiled at me and I blew her a kiss as she asked me if I was going to be as busy this week like the last. I explained that I had started out looking to move my office and it had morphed into what I always felt it should be, that I had to follow through with what I started, that a lot was hanging on this expansion and now that I started couldn't stop until it was complete. I told her she would see it and would be participating with the opening, and that was why I had bought her the dresses and pant suits. I told her that she was so beautiful and that she had to look like a million dollars just for me. I would not accept anything less, but once it was completed, I would be with her much more often. She said that sounded very good and wanted to know how much longer. I said no more than a month, but probably less. She said that sounds wonderful. I would not have to go to work every day or not as early and we would have more time together.

Our food came and Vicky looked at the plate. I thanked the waitress as Vicky said wow. I told her we have to build our stamina back up, so eat up as we proceeded to partake of the feast in front of us. We ate slowly and we enjoyed every mouthful, it took us more than an hour and we didn't finish it all before we were full. The waitress came over and I asked for a doggie bag and she returned with Plastic foam containers and a poly bag. We had enough for a snack later. She asked if we wanted dessert. I said to her you must be kidding and she smiled and placed the bill on the table. I always pay cash in restaurants and the bill was close to seventy dollars and I had no small change so I placed a $100.00 bill in the folder and when she returned, told her to keep the change, she said, thank you sir. We took our final sips of beer and water and departed fully satisfied as we exited and got back into the car.

We headed home and Vicky stated she hadn't eaten like that ever in her life, and was fully satisfied. When we reached home I just pulled inside, closed the garage door, and went around and helped Vicky out. I could see she had loosened her belt as I rubbed her stomach saying, she wasn't going to be a fat girl or she wouldn't be able to get in her new dresses. We kissed and went inside placing the leftovers in the fridge and proceeded upstairs, we undressed and showered together, we dried off and oiled up and I said we should go to the basement and have a drink because it was still early and we needed to let our food digest, it was almost eight so we put on our bathrobes and headed downstairs. Once we were downstairs, I fixed us a couple of drinks, turned the radio on and there was some smooth music to dance to. I took Vicky by the hand and we danced around as we waited for the full feeling to pass, we weren't feeling as full as when we first came home so we sat at the bar and had our drinks, we soon finished and felt well enough to go back upstairs. We closed up and went upstairs and when we entered the bedroom we were really ready for bed. We got in the bed, pulled the covers over us hugged and kissed each other until we were overcome with sleep.

Eighteen
Monday: Day Eighteen.

We woke up early again, just a little before six and did our morning thing, returning to bed to hug and kiss until I decided it was time to start our day. Victoria said that she had the most wonderful weekend ever, and hoped I would still be as creative in the future as I have been so far. That Saturday when I told her to put on the black dress and stockings, it excited her so much she couldn't contain herself, and knew she would be punished and besides it made her so very excited. She still thought about it and the week before when I hung her from the beam downstairs and that she was glad I let myself go in order to please her. She knew I didn't like hurting her, and she loved me more with each passing day. I said, you have made my life complete, that part of me I had kept suppressed had freed itself and I felt better and more alive and wasn't hindered by my thoughts any longer, but only she could have made it possible. We kissed and told her I had a mission to accomplish and needed to get started.

We went downstairs and had coffee and I told her I just wanted a bacon sandwich. If you don't eat the food we brought home yesterday to throw it away. Said she might have it for lunch, and would clean up after I left, as we both went upstairs to dress. I couldn't keep my hands off of her and she welcomed it, as I rubbed and felt her all over and soon made her climax. I held her and then let her go and said I really have to go. Said she would be waiting for me, and that I was driving her mad with anticipation. I went to the closet, and only had two suits, but I didn't feel like a suit and most of the time I didn't wear them. So I pulled out a fresh pair of jeans and noticed that they were pressed. Turned and thanked her for ironing them, as she sat on the end of the bed watching me dress. I chose a colored t-shirt, put on a clean pair of socks and picked out the sports jacket I was going to wear.

I brushed my teeth and hair and did a quick shave with my electric shaver and came back and put on my jacket. I turned and looked at her as she smiled at me. I like it when you smile, as she got up and hugged me and kissed my face all over, and walked me downstairs to the back door, we hugged and kissed again.

I got in my auto and opened the garage door, pulled out and headed to the office. It was eight thirty when I entered, and turned on the lights, made the coffee and sat at my desk and read the notes left for me as I brought myself up to date. The one bed room condo that I listed for Mrs. Kashia was sold. The buyers were waiting on their closing date, I would have to go to that one, and there was an offer on the second one, except the agent wasn't able to get in contact with Mrs. Kashia over the weekend. She didn't have a cell phone and wasn't home. There were two others sales pending. I thought well Hippies will be busy, there was a note from Fitz asking when Patricia would be through helping Hippies so he could train her to do the income ledgers and take her around to the different complexes and meet the resident listing agents, and requesting when we move, to relocate the old files from the various locations, at the new office. Besides we had picked up three new property listings, and each of our agents was handling one. That's what I liked about Phillips and Green they shared with Brown. Her being the newest agent or rather the last one we hired, she had been with us nine months and was very thorough. Fitz had another note. It read that he was pretty sure a small mall with about a fifty percent occupancy rate was going to be for sale soon, he made this assumption that they were having a hard time keeping tenants since a newer one had opened across the street. The location was a prime location for something other than retail. He thought I should check it out or see if I wanted him to. I thought, another mall going down the drain. I left a voice message for Fitz asking him to come in and I would assign Patricia to him so she could get a handle on things because the leasing end was the most important and always had records to be kept up to date, if he was away someone would have to take care of it. I was trying with the expansion to ease the burden on Joanne and myself and Fitz also, which she understood. Just then Joanne unlocked the door stepping inside as we greeted one another.

I told her I read all the notes and said Patricia will be working with Fitz, because that was more important than hanging with Hippies. She agreed, as I said to her I have been trying to ease your burden. We need to discuss our budget soon, and since we will be overseeing things more and not directly involved. She agreed and asked how my weekend was. I told her about taking Victoria shopping Saturday and the county fair Sunday and dinner. She asked what are you going to do with the girl. Answered that I am going to marry her; she almost choked on her coffee, before she came over and hugged me and said that even though it has been a very short time, she felt it was a good thing for me. I asked her not to say anything about it. Ok, she said. Mr. Hippies and Mr. Fitz walked in almost together and everyone greeted one another and Patricia Bradley, saying sorry she was late. I said five minutes doesn't count, and said you will be working with Mr. Fitz. Great said Fitz, as they both went to get a cup of coffee. Then returned and went to his desk as Patricia pulled up a chair and he turned on his computer.

In walks Mr. Brown with a bright smile on his face and said good morning everyone as he approached me and asked who would be occupying the upper offices. I said everyone who is here now. Why, he pulled from his backpack several color sample brochures and stated we needed to choose the colors for our offices and would appreciate it if we could do it right now. I glanced through and picked a muted shade of gold, and he wrote the number down and he also pulled out a diagram of the layout and asked which offices were going to belong to whom. I looked and pointed at the two largest facing the atrium, Joanne and I would have those, and showed him the ones for Hippies, Fitz, and Patricia, and semi-gloss for all the offices and work spaces, and off white for the two extra offices, lunchroom and conference rooms and he made a note of that. Also plants, large plants where ever possible, said he had planned on that, Joanne picked a muted green, Hippies picked a caramel color, and I pointed to Patricia and Fitz and asked them to take a moment and pick a color, Fitz chose a pale blue, Patricia picked a light rose and then for the lower level. I looked and he suggested with all the natural light a warm color would bring it out, I asked if he had any suggestions, he said a medium green as he showed me the sample. I said ok and confirmed that there wasn't very much wall space considering the windows, he said it was a great choice. I asked about the carpeted areas and offices, he said that they would be as closely matched to the wall colors as possible, and the public areas, the same would apply. I asked about the type, he said a long wearing Berber that held up to wear and tear and was easy to clean. Would the carpet in the offices be the same? He said yes, but would not be as course and the padding would be a little thicker, but we would not need carpet protectors under the desk. I said good and I knew you would be my best choice to oversee this project, and then I asked how much progress had been made. He said Hector had pulled out all the stops, had his son Jesus the contractor bring in extra crews and they worked from six to nine and these guys were the best he had ever seen, there work habits were excellent, they cleaned up twice a day, and that is why he was here with the color charts because it was progressing well ahead of schedule. The washrooms were in and almost finished, the offices were framed and dry walled, plastered and they were doing the primer today that's why he needed the color choices today. He and Hector needed to know for the carpet and had a supplier on standby, and said don't worry about the plants, he had that all figure in also. I said, ok, as he reached in his bag and handed me several large renderings. I thanked him as he departed.

The rendering were great. I showed Joanne and she said well, you deserve the best and by the way I slipped her a note, it said increase your salary to one hundred, she turned to look at me, her mouth was open and I said its only money. She stood and came to my desk and grabbed my hand and took me to the back, to our little lunch room and hugged me, tears were in her eyes and said I had done so much already she didn't know how to thank me. She released me and I told her. I loved her and we wouldn't be in this position if it hadn't been for all your hard work and long hours since we have been together, and I looked at her and said don't you even bring any of the past up. It was after we had been together a little more than a year and she was worried about losing her home. I knew something was bothering her, but didn't know what, and then she reluctantly finally decided to tell me. I had just made my windfall with the stock I invested in and hadn't said anything about it to her. I asked how much she owed, she said $77,000.00 on the principle and was eight months behind and didn't know what else to do, and the bank was threating her with foreclosure. Told her I would be right back and went to the bank and came back and gave her a cashier's check for $80,000.00 and said to her it was a gift from God. She cried then and she was about to cry now. I said we have been through thick and thin together, and we have a good thing now, the fruit of our labors and it's time to eat some of the fruit. She hugged me and said she had to get it off of her as she cried and the tears rolled down her pretty face. Pat and Fitz took a break and I think Pat not seeing her mother came back and saw her mother and me holding each other, and her mother was crying and wanted to know what the matter was. As Joanne gathered herself and told her everything was fine. I said to Joanne I couldn't have done it without you, and I think you need to freshen up. She went to the washroom and I led Pat back to the work room reassuring her everything was ok. I am sure she will tell you one day. She looked a little bewildered but completely satisfied and returned as Fitz and her switched places at his desk.

Joanne reappeared and sat down and the phone rang, it was for Hippies and he sat back in his chair and started a conversation, it rang again, it was for me and was from the tenants of the last store in the mall down the street, the manager informed me they had completely moved out and would drop off the keys today, and they had closed all there utility accounts for the location. I thanked him and hung up. I went through my notes and found the number for Mr. Rogers, dialed his number, his secretary picked up on the second ring. I explained who I was and the reason for my call, she said he wasn't in but would have him call me right back. I thanked her and hung up. I stood and said to Joanne I would be out for a moment and was going up the street. I drove to the mall and parked and looked around, the doors were all secure in the empty stores as I drove around back and everything seemed secure, as I came back around and sat in my car. I received a call from Mr. Rogers and asked him how soon he could get started, he said two weeks, but in that time he would contact the utility companies and get the gas an electrical services disconnected, along with the city water and sewage departments and he would contact the city building department and notify them and get the demolition permits and fence off the property. He said since it was approximately sixty acres it would take a couple days just for the fence, I asked how he wanted payment, he gave me two options, electronic or cashier's check. I said I would arrange for electronic transfer and to text me the account information, and said he hoped to meet me soon. I said my office was a short distance away from the mall; he thanked me and hung up.

I returned to the office and by the time I reached my desk the text came from Rogers and I gave Joanne the information for the payment. Mr. Fitz came to my desk and said that they were going to take an early lunch so he could show her the complexes closest to the office and they would be back before closing. I said that was fine and he didn't have to check with me, just work with her and be sure she knows all the locations. I didn't expect her to learn it all in a week and take whatever time he had to in order to bring her up to speed, because she would be doing most of the work. I asked how her computer skills were and he stated they were better than his.

They soon left and I sat down and looked at the newspaper that Hippies had brought with him and looked through the business and real estate section and found an article that caught my attention, it was circled with a pencil. It was the golf course that happened to border the mall I had just purchased, it was family owned and the heirs of the woman who passed away were fighting the board of the club about control, the heirs wanted to sell but the board didn't and the problem was membership had dropped the past few years and a clause in the will made it possible for the board to take a stand, but with a declining membership it wasn't going to be long before they would soon be bankrupt. Which gave me an idea, since it bordered the back of the mall and was almost eight hundred acers, an was bordered by a busy street on the east, and the railroad tracks a half mile to the west, and cross divided by a two lane country road at about a third of its length, and mid-way, and by a six lane east west street, and across the street to the east was the county forest preserve that paralleled it for two thirds of its length, and was part of the large ridge line that this whole area was on. Decided I would put a feeler out to both parties. I had another idea, but waited for Hippies to finish his phone call, so I just put a note with the article on his desk, and asked Joanne if she wanted to go to lunch since it was eleven thirty. And she said yes since there wasn't anything going on now. She left and I sat back and thought about what information Hippies could dig up.

Mr. Hippies finally finished his call, moved some files around his desk, and said he wondered if I had seen the article. Said he would check it out right away as he picked up the phone and made several calls. After about half an hour, Hippies said we could talk to both parties. Said the town it was located in was also involved. I said let's set up a meeting. I would like to buy it if possible and wanted to know the position of all parties involved. He said there was a court date set for next week. I asked could we find out what position the town was taking. He said they wanted to preserve it and opposed any development, but didn't have the funds because they would have to hold a bond referendum and that it would probably fail as it did the last time. The heirs wanted to sell; the club board was trying to hold on based on the old lady's will. I asked what was in it, he said as long as they, the club could pay the taxes and operate, out of debt they were good to go. But had been operating in the red for the past year, so it was a tossup as to what would occur in court. I asked can we make an offer to both parties. I just wanted to secure the land and redevelop it at a later date; he said that could just be the ticket. I said the mall was coming down and with this being adjacent would be perfect for something I had in mind. He said he would get more information and if he had to, would go to the court hearing. Great I told him. Hippies said he was going to lunch, as I sat and went over the expenses, of the past few weeks again. I was well within my range of spending and could afford it, as a matter of fact, I had to spend or be taxed.

I was making the money work for me, it was a constant buy and sell situation and I loved it. Joanne's birthday was several days away and I was going to do something special for her. I didn't know what it would be but I love to see women cry because they are happy. I thought that a special dinner for her, to include Pat, Hippies, Fitz, Vicky and myself would be grand, and I would get her a gift. And knew what it was, and she would look good wearing it. It was the diamond necklace set Victoria said was too much for her, I though how perfect. I wouldn't have to worry if it fit. Soon Mr. Phillips arrived and we spoke and said he had received notice of his exam date and would be taking it Thursday and stated he felt prepared. I said his new position would start as soon as he passed and received his credentials, and he thanked me for the opportunity. He went to his desk and made some phone calls, shortly after turned and said he would be back and was going to go see Mrs. Kashia and get her signature on the contract for the condo unit and would return. I said that's good news as he prepared to leave.

Hippies returned from the back just as Joanne walked in the door. I explained to her about Phillips. Great she said, and for me to go to lunch. Hippies asked if I would be back and I said yes as I departed. I loved the action in my office and was glad; I had such good people surrounding me. I decided to go to Martha's for lunch and decided to walk, it was a block away and I liked her home cooking. I looked in the shop windows on my way to the restaurant and saw quite a diverse business community. I finally arrived and was greeted by Martha and took a seat and she came over. She was glad I had come and recommended the special for the day; it was fried cat fish, greens and corn bread with coleslaw, sounds great and said I would love to have that. She said coming right up, it shortly arrived and I dug in and enjoyed every mouthful. I finished and got up and paid. Martha said she would like to talk to me about expanding, but didn't want to incur the cost of moving and asked me about the two shops on either side of her. I pulled out my notebook and made notes. Stated she was in no rush and was only making an inquiry because she only wanted to expand the seating area if possible. I said ok, and if I didn't get back to her Joanne would. She thanked me and I headed back to the office. More people were eating out and it was a boon for restaurants, the walk did me good as I arrived back.

Philips had returned with the signed contract, and Joanne was checking it over, she also gave him some pointers he would need to know when he would be sitting at her desk. I was about finished for the day and decided to walk toward the new office which was the opposite direction of Martha's and a block away and looked at the various businesses as I walked. It seemed that all were doing well which was good. I approached the corner of the side street and looked across at my new headquarters and marveled at the beauty of the building. It was modern, energy efficient and was beautiful with its green solar glass. I crossed and walked toward the entrance, and opened the doors. As I walked in marveled at how much progress had been accomplished. Hector greeted me, Amigo, as he came from the back; we shook hands as he said he wanted to show me around. All the walls were in place, plastered and being painted with the primer base, he showed me the wash rooms, they were completely tiled and the fixtures were waiting to be installed. The ventilation fans were in and he showed me the other washroom and it was completely finished. We came out and he showed me the two lower level offices, they were spacious and the wall sections were in place and he showed me where the glass partitions would be to include the doors, and the lower level lunch room. He then lead me upstairs and we took the stairs, all the walls were in place and a small crew were plastering the drywall which was up and showed me the spacious conference room, lunch room and the washrooms, which the tile work was complete but were waiting for the fixtures which were outside in boxes. We walked around the ocular opening and he said this area would be tiled from the elevator all around and they would start tomorrow. I asked when he thought it would be complete, in two weeks, and thereafter it would take a couple days to clean and apply a coating to the tile and for it to dry, and said cleaning the windows inside and out. Cleaning up the parking lot and cutting and manicuring the grass and foliage, and said that he was happy that I had chosen him for such a large project, he also said I didn't need to pay until he was finished and knowing me he would have an itemized bill. I said that sounds like a winner. I appreciated his thoroughness, we shook hands and went downstairs and I walked back to the office.

Upon returning Hippies motioned me over and said he had more information on the golf course. I sat down as he ran down the details. Hippies said yes, about the town wanting to keep the land as a park or golf course but the last referendum to purchase the land had been defeated and the only thing they could do was stymie any development they didn't like and, the heirs wanted ten million if they could sell, and it looked like the outcome would come in a court decision. I said to contact the heirs and set up a meeting or rather, make them an offer and we would see what happened. He said he would go to the hearing. I would work on a plan I had in mind. And asked what that would be. Stated I would preserve the park like appearance and a portion of the course, and the concept would be a park like setting with condos around the perimeter and this would add to the tax base and should appease the town, he said that might work. I asked what hold did the club have in order to prevent the sale. Said he would talk to both attorneys, ok good I replied. I called Louis Brown and left a voice mail for him to give me a call. I sat back and decided to check on Vicky and brought up the home camera app, I found her cleaning the house and changing the sheets on the bed; I closed the app, and looked at the clock, it was close to four, and Mr. Green came in and spoke and sat at his desk and started to place several calls, he finished and came over to inform us that he was scheduled to take his test Thursday.

We both said oh at the same time. He asked what. And Joanne informed him that Phillips was also taking it the same day. He said great, he asked Joanne if there was anything he should know before the exam. She said I don't know if you feel prepared. We both wished him the best as he returned to his desk. Hippies said the heirs had an offer for ten million. I said offer them $14,000,000.00, call them back and put it in writing and fax it to them, he said ok. About ten minutes later I spoke to Louis Brown and said this was a new job, that I wanted some conceptual drawings, and went on to explain where it would be and what I had in mind. That I wouldn't need them for at least several weeks, and there was no rush, the office had top priority. I hung up; this would be a boon for his career being a young architect and looked at the clock, but was really waiting for Hippies to get off the phone. He finished pulled some forms from a cabinet sat down and filled them out and handed me a paper to sign; it was an offer for the course. I signed and handed it back as he filled out a cover sheet and went to fax it off. Well I got that out the way. After he finished he said he was gone for the day and I let Joanne know I was getting ready to leave as soon as Fitz and Pat returned, and they entered shortly. She seemed excited and sat with Fitz as they made entries into the system.

I said see you all tomorrow as I departed for home, and then I thought about Victoria as I drove. When I reached home I left the car outside and went in the front door and entered, and went to wash my hands and then went to the laundry room where she was folding the sheets. I helped her and she placed them in a basket. As I reached for her and pulled her to me and we hugged and kissed. I unbuttoned her smock and felt her breast and then between her legs as I pulled her panties up putting pressure on her and making her moan, as I asked her what was for dinner. She said she hadn't thought about it and hadn't taken anything out. I said when you finish we will go out and get something light. She had eaten the food from yesterday and didn't want anything heavy. I said great, I said just put on some jeans or something, ok she replied. As I went to the office and went through the mail which was mostly junk and there were only the gas and light bills. I opened them and wrote out the checks, filed them away and put stamps on the envelopes then left them until I could mail them tomorrow. Soon Victoria came down dressed in jeans and a t-shirt and athletic shoes and we went outside, got in the car and went to a nearby sports bar and had a burger and a salad. When we finished we came back home as she asked how was my day and I replied, I was busy. I parked in the garage and we entered and washed our hands and I said let's have a beer. I pulled a couple cans from the fridge and poured them in glasses and we sat and talked about our day then went to the living room to watch the evening news before going upstairs to undress and shower. We came out and spread out some towels and gave each other a rub down, even though it was before eight I just wanted to rest, so we climbed in the bed pulled the covers over us and she kissed and rubbed me to sleep.

Nineteen
Tuesday: Day Nineteen.

We woke at the same time and felt on each other until we both had to use the bathroom. When we returned we laid back down and pulled the covers over ourselves and held one another. I said to Victoria that I loved her so much and just squeezed her and felt her head. I held her tight, said her being here made me feel so wonderful inside and didn't know that I could love one person and feel like I felt for her, and asked her not to hurt me, because I didn't want to live without her. She started crying and touched my face and said she felt the same way. We kissed and just held each other for a long time, before we finally decided to get up as we put on our robes and stood and just held each other. Said to her, I would be honored to have her as my wife, and more tears came to her eyes as she crying. She said that it would be the greatest honor to have me as her husband and that she loved me so much she wouldn't want to live if we couldn't be together.

We kissed more and I said we should go downstairs and at least have something to eat. She said ok, as we went downstairs and fixed ourselves some breakfast. We ate and just looked at one another and when we finished, cleaned up the kitchen. Went back upstairs and I grabbed my cell phone, it was nine. I knew Joanne was in the office and called. She answered, and said I wouldn't be in today. She said it was all right and if something came up she would give me a call, and if I didn't answer she would leave a message. I thanked her and hung up. I turn to Victoria and said I just want to be here today with you for some reason. Couldn't explain why, I just wanted to. We took our robes off and climbed back in bed as I held her and caressed her body. I was madly in love with her, and said she was overjoyed I decided to stay home with her, as we slowly caressed one another. I felt her all over and she did the same to me, we held each other and we went to sleep again soon holding one another. When we awoke again it was almost noon, we picked up where we left off at and then decided we needed to eat again. I asked her if she wanted to go out and get something. She didn't want to leave home. Told her I would cook if she helped, she said tell her what to do. My reply was clean the shrimp after they had thawed. She said sure, but we needed to put on some clothes and get out of our robes.

But we went downstairs in our robes anyway, and removed a bag of shrimp from the freezer and placed them in the sink. Took Vicky by the hand and we went back upstairs and when we entered the bedroom and removed our robes, took her in my arms and said to her. Are you going to be a good girl today, and before she could answer, told her, I think you need a reminder, and told her to kneel in the bed at the foot. She complied, told her to spread her legs wide and put her head down with her arms stretched out in front of her, she did as she was instructed. I said get that ass up, as I rubbed it, and then spanked her ass lightly and rubbed her between her legs, I felt her getting wet as I played with her and lightly smacked her pussy and clit as she exploded with a massive climax. I rubbed her and she came again. I said turn around and stand, when she did her face was filled with tears and she grabbed me and said thank you master Charlie and said she was wondering when I was going take her. I said on your back and she climbed in the bed and I said slide up as far as you can and spread those sweet legs, she did as I laid between them and kissed her sweet pussy, I held her breast with both my hands and squeezed her erect nipples and licked and sucked her pussy and clit making her explode again, and I continued and didn't stop as she was rocked with several more orgasm's one after the other. I slowly climbed on top of her and inserted my hard penis inside of her and slowly went in and out of her as she screamed with joy as she held on to me. I continued until I felt I would shortly come and pulled out and grabbing her ankles raising them high, and slowly inserting myself in her hot rectum, and slowly sank it inside of her as she squirmed with pleasure, she was screaming fuck me master, oh fuck me as I came in her ass, and let her legs go and laid on top of her and licked her ear, as her breathing was short and labored, and so was mine. I rolled off of her and we held each other for a long time, I looked into her big brown eyes as we felt each other. I put a finger to her lips and she raised her head and took it in her mouth, I said to her, you belong to me now and forever. She cried and held me tight; kissing me as I said that was the best sex I ever had in my life. And she said it was the same for her. We slowly arose and helped each other to the bathroom, where we took a shower together, giving each other a thorough cleansing. After we came out, and had dried one another, and catching our breath, we finally dressed. I wore my shorts and a t-shirt, and she a pair of panties and a t-shirt. We kissed and I said to her that I couldn't keep my hands off of her. Said that I satisfied her to the point of madness and didn't want me to stop and told me to take her whenever I wanted.

We finally made it back downstairs. The shrimp were almost thawed, as I opened the bag and poured them into a large bowl and ran some warm water on them and added some lemon juice, setting them aside as I removed the veggies I was going to use in my dish. Removed the cutting board, and took out a bell pepper, onion, jalapenos, celery, and garlic, I asked Vicky to peel the garlic before she cleaned the shrimp and she grabbed my butt as she went to get a bowl to put them in. I finished cleaning and dicing the veggies as she finished with the garlic, and then started on the shrimp. I used my mini food processor to chop the garlic. I pulled out a sauce pan and placed some olive oil in it, as I turned a fire on underneath and let it warm up, then retrieved a pot and added a cup of rice, adding water and salt and placed it on the stove and turned on a low fire on under it. I added my veggies to the sauce pan, added my seasoning, stirred and covered, and let it simmer as my love finished cleaning the shrimp; she rinsed them and let them drain. I asked her if she would get us a bottle of wine from the fridge downstairs, she said anything I wanted and proceeded downstairs and came back with a bottle of California red. I said good choice as I placed it in the fridge, stirred the veggies and opened a can of diced tomatoes, added a spoonful of sugar and stirred, I checked the rice and turned it off and added the tomatoes to the veggies, and shortly added the shrimp and turned the fire down to a low simmer as Vicky sat and watched, she started setting the table as I stirred the mixture and covered it waiting for the shrimp to slowly cook. Vicky said we had some coleslaw. I said good and she dished it up in small bowls and placed them on the table with the wine glasses. I checked the pot and stirred, turned the fire off, opened the wine and handed her the bottle as I prepared to serve us. I took the plates, dished up the rice on both plates and then the shrimp with vegies on top. I placed the plates on the table and we both sat down, we held hands as we said grace. We were both very hungry, and she said it was the best she had ever eaten as we enjoyed the meal and each other. We savored the food and drank our wine, and when we finished Vicky said she would wash the dishes. I placed the rice in a plastic container and the shrimp mixture in a smaller pot and let it set and cool. When we finished, I took out our vitamins and we both took them.

Vicky came and hugged and kissed my neck as we went to the living room, sitting next to one another, with my arm around her shoulders as she held my hand and rubbed it. I pulled her so she was looking up at me, she laid in my lap, she felt my face as I rubbed her thigh, I said you know we need to walk around the house again, she sat up and we went out the front door and walked around the house four times before we returned and then went and sat on the deck. It was a beautiful and sunny day, and even more beautiful since we were together and very much in love. We watched the sun setting before we went back inside and fixed some dessert, we ate some ice cream. When we finished we drank the rest of the dinner wine, as I said to her it was time to prepare for bed, we went upstairs, undressed and got into bed. We left the covers off as we rolled around and felt each other. Vicky told me to lay back and she went and got the blindfold and put it on me, said for me to relax, the next thing I felt were her soft hands rubbing me with massage oil, it felt so good as she licked my ear sending shivers through me, she felt my penis and my feet, arms and chest and she sat on my face. I could smell her sweetness and I tried to lick her but she kept it out of my reach until she just slowly eased it down and I licked around her vaginal opening as I felt her tongue on me as she licked my balls and placed my penis in her mouth. I felt her licking it and arousing me even more, then it was gone and felt her turn around as she placed me inside of her as she then laid on top of me. I felt her warm breast on my chest, as she moved her butt up and down, she moved her head close to mine and licked my face before she removed the blindfold and licked my ear and gently blew in it as she rocked back and forth sending shivers through me.

I wrapped my arms around her and reached down and squeezed her butt and she said spank me. I slapped her ass as she moved her butt around on top of me as she started breathing harder before she climaxed over and over again until she just laid still with me inside of her. I rolled her over and she said give it to her, as I slowly moved in and out of her, and then I came, it wasn't much for we had worn each other out. We held each other and didn't bother to get up. We just pulled the covers up and turned the lights out and fell asleep. When we woke up several hours later, it was two in the morning as we went and spent almost an hour in the bathroom, before we came out clean but still needing rest as we crawled back in bed and held each other again and went back to sleep.

Twenty
Wednesday: Day Twenty.

I woke up at six thirty, after looking over at the clock and just laid there. I had to go to work today. Looked over at Vicky and she was fast asleep, good, man wasn't meant to live on pussy alone. Went to the bathroom to relieve myself and felt like a new man when I came out. Looked in the mirror, returned to the washroom and weighed myself. God I had lost ten pounds, returned to the bedroom and looked in the mirror a second time. I would know when I put my pants on, and looked for what I would wear, what I would have worn yesterday. I started dressing and was all ready to go downstairs when Vicky rolled over; she didn't wake up, good. I really enjoyed being with her but I had more important things to do right now and had to go. Decided not to wake her, placed my pillow where I would have been in the bed. Pulled the covers up and kissed her lightly and left. Fixed some coffee, reached for the donuts before going to the office and scanning through the security cameras, before returning and pouring myself a cup of coffee and eating a donut and then realized how hungry I really was. I really need some food as I took my vitamins and had another donut. I went back upstairs and looked in on sleeping beauty, she was knocked out and had her arm on the pillow I put in my place and she was gone to the world. Went back downstairs and dumped out the coffee pot, rinse it out and left, it was eight when I left, pulled out the garage, closed the door and headed to Martha's.

I arrived and ordered ham, poached eggs, grits and toast with coffee, when I finished, paid and left as I headed to the office. It was almost nine when I arrived and opened the door, leaving it unlocked and turned the lights on, making the coffee as I returned to my desk. There were some notes, all were about future closings. Well I didn't miss much. Joanne and Pat came in together as we greeted one another. She said it had been a quiet day yesterday, like before I started my origination project, and said that was good. I brought up the home camera app on my phone, and went straight to the bedroom camera. Vicky was still asleep and hadn't moved. I turned it off and took the renderings that Mr. Brown had left and a roll of tape and taped them to the wall, now we had some art, the office didn't look quite as dull. I said to Joanne that we needed to go to a furniture store soon and finish furnishing our offices so when we had clients in our office they would have somewhere to sit. I asked her if she wanted to go together. Said that would be most welcome. I said we will wait a couple more days before we go. She asked about the current office furniture that we were using. I hadn't thought about it. We could sell it, or donate it. She said she would ask around and see. I said ok.

Pat was at Mr. Fitz computer working on some ledger inputs, and I asked Joanne how well she seemed to adapt. Joanne said very well, and yes she was enjoying it. And with Hippies giving her pointers on her legal aid classes, she seamed much happier now. I said that's good, and happy it was working out for her. She was really excited she would have her own office. I said she will really need one with the new operational format. It was getting close to ten thirty and pulled up the home app again. I looked in on the sleeping beauty just as she turned over and realized I wasn't there, she sat up and when she looked at the clock, she knew I wasn't there and ran out of the bedroom naked, going downstairs and looking all over for me, she went and opened the door to the garage, and then ran to the office and stood at my desk looking for the phone number, before she realized it was programed into the phone. She was shaking, just then the office phone rang and Joanne answered, she turned and said it was for me. I picked up and said good morning, Charlie Harcourt speaking, before I could finish I heard her voice and she was crying. I was still watching on my cell phone as she asked why I didn't wake her. You were sleeping so well I didn't want to wake you and you needed your rest and calm down its ok. She finally got a hold of herself, and said I love you. I knew you would be ok. She calmed down and I said its ok baby. I have to go, and I love you too. She said she loved me more. She hung up and I watched her go back upstairs and then she realized she was naked and put her robe on, then she took my robe and held it in her hands and climbed in bed with it, and laid down holding it and I could see she was crying. Then she got up and went to the bathroom and came out and put her smock on and nothing else. She went to the kitchen and fixed herself some breakfast as I turned the app off. I said to myself she really loves me, not just the physical, but the emotional. I need her to be strong for us and really will have to let her know that when I get home. I asked Joanne if she wanted to go to lunch. She replied ok, and took Pat with her and they left.

Hippies came in shortly afterwards and we spoke. Said he spoke to the mayor of Evermore, and they were open to ideas that would preserve the essence of the golf course or a park like atmosphere and were waiting for the court ruling as to the disposition. He expressed interest in your idea for redeveloping the space where the mall is. He said it was going to be a lost to their tax base, and the offer the heirs had received was from out of state and he preferred working with someone local that knows the community. I said depending on how the court rules, is key. And if the heirs win in court, and accept our offer, we should meet with him and see if we can work something out to our advantage for both parties. I like that there is this large wooded area, and I think some type of development can be done. That sounds like all will rest on the court ruling. Yes said Hippies, it will. Then I received a call from Watson and he asked if I could come down to the site. I said yes when Joanne returns from lunch. I asked why. He and Brown wanted to have me approve the placement and location of the televisions in the various offices, and wanted my approval. I said ok and it shouldn't be long, and hung up, just as Joanne and Pat returned. Said I had to go up the street and would go to lunch afterwards. She said ok. As I prepared to leave Phillips and Green entered, we exchanged greetings and Joanne stood and asked them if they were ready, both said yes as they pulled up chairs to her desk and she started to explain the functions they would be performing soon, and gave them some last minute pointers before there exam tomorrow.

I got in my car, but before pulling out brought up the home app and checked on Vicky, she was busy cleaning the bedroom, changing sheets and vacuuming. I closed the app and headed to our new location. I was amazed at the progress that had been made since I was last here and entered. Brown and Watson were just coming from the back when we greeted one another. Kenny said as they showed me the waiting area, a wall section where he said that a 110inch flat screen would be mounted, it would have a cable connection, and I would be able to run presentations on it through a closed circuit. I said to him before I forget, that I wanted the individual desktop screens to be no smaller than 32inches, he made a note of that. Said he got it. We went upstairs and Brown showed me based on the office suits that Joanne and I had chosen their positions, and where the file cabinets would be and that we would be facing our office door entrance from our desk, and where the 65inch television would be mounted on the wall, the power outlet would be unseen behind them with the cable and antenna connections. Said they would be the new 4-K with DVD players which would be located on a shelf so you wouldn't have to get up, and that the offices on this level would have multi screens, meaning, we could have e-mail, on one, the RELS on another, and whatever on the third. The telephones would have intercom features. I said that will work well for us. He went on to explain that all the office suits will face their entrance doors, so you will just have to look up to see who is entering, as he showed me Joanne's office, and the location of where her desk would be located, as it was being painted, we walked around to the conference room, it would have a large flat screen, 70 inches, they would all be the latest available, and he said the ones in the offices would be all the same size. I noticed all the offices were painted except mine; Joanne's was being painted now. He explained that the file cabinets were here and would be the first to be installed, then the carpet, followed by the suits, and then they would mount and hook everything up. Kenny said he was bringing in a couple of associates to help set up the network, and was glad I mentioned the monitor size today, he said it was the only thing he hadn't ordered, he said with the multi screens 32inch might be too large. I said use your own judgement, but nothing less than 24. Brown said to me that since I hadn't chosen any conference tables or chairs, he had, and asked if that was all right with me. I said of course as he pulled out pictures of the two sets. He showed me the first one and said it was in the line I had chosen for my office, and was called the Executive, it sat twenty and had the chairs also, said it was $15,000.00, and the one for the downstairs conference room, sat twenty-four, and came complete also, was $13,500.00, both were solid wood. And finally as we walked to the atrium opening, he showed me the tile that had just been laid, and said Hector moved up the schedule for it, after the bathrooms were completed and ask if I wanted to see them. I said of course. We entered the men's, it was beautiful, the colors were a mix of white and pale blue and trimmed in dark blue, there were, two toilets, and two urinals, with partitions, and a double sink. We then went to the women's and the tile work was the same as the men's, except the colors were, dark pink, and two shades of rose, the lighting was bright but not glaring, it had three toilets and a triple sink, both were spacious, all the fixtures were white. I said this is fantastic; we turned and left. Kenny wanted to show me the server room, it was a ten by ten space in the rear of the building and all the cables were neatly arranged in cable guides. He explained the previous occupants had a complete surveillance system, the outside had twenty cameras; they were color and were exceptional because they had a zoom feature, some that were even in out of the way locations operated by motion detection. There were twenty located inside also, he said when he found where they were wired, they all came together in the server room, which was the only room that was constructed with concrete blocks and a steel door, the monitors and everything were still in place, it was the control room also for the solar panels on the roof, he and Hector power washed them so they would operate at full efficiency, and applied a coating that made the water runoff and would help keep them cleaner. He said I would be able to monitor the complete system from my office, and only I would have that ability. Said it would not be cost effective otherwise, also you could come in here and monitor the system, and that this room would be kept at 55 degrees Fahrenheit, at all times, he said only I and Joanne should have access, said he would keep a key for maintenance purposes, and asked if that was acceptable. I said yes you're my IT guy.

We went downstairs and Brown showed me where the cubes would be and he assumed that an agent would get a client and bring him to his mini office, the desk would be positioned facing out from the wall and had ordered three chairs per cube for clients, he said I had already chosen the desk chairs. He asked if that was acceptable and showed me a picture of the chairs. I said very well. We went and he showed me the washrooms, conference room, and the lunch room, said he had ordered a fridge, and two microwaves for both upstairs and downstairs, said he eliminated having a stove upstairs because it complicated things and it wasn't really necessary. He looked at Watson and asked did we cover everything, he said yes. I said the plants. Oh yes, he said that the building being environmentally friendly was conducive to plants and would aid in filtering the air and had arraigned for a botanist to give him recommendations on low maintenance plants, and they would be coming tomorrow, that he worked for a company that supplied and maintained office and building plants, he said the cost was less than $1500.00 annually. He asked if I had any more questions. I said Joanne and I wanted to finish furnishing out our offices with furniture, and if he had any suggestions. He recommended high backed chairs and sofas, and the higher end furniture stores would have more of what we wanted. I said how soon should we go to pick something up, he said we should be looking now and handed me several of his business cards. He said pick out whatever and give them his card and he would take it from there, and to put whose office it would go to on the invoice. I asked if there was anything else, they both said that was all they had for me now as they skimmed through there notes.

I thanked them and said I was getting out of their way. It was two and decided for lunch I would eat at Super Burger. I arrived and chose there double burger, decided to eat it there before I returned to the office. When I returned, saw that Joanne had Green at her desk as she sat at mine. I asked her to come back to the lunch room with me. We have to go shopping soon for our

furniture, and asked when she would like to go. She said we could go look this evening. Thought about Victoria, and being gone later than expected might worry her. I said tomorrow or Friday. She said tomorrow would be fine since we closed at five. I asked if everything was under control, she replied yes.
Think I need to go home. She replied yes, I know, as I said good night to her and Hippies. I went home and it was almost four when I backed into the garage. I entered and Vicky came running with tears in her eyes and hugged me tight for a long while and kissed me and asked me never to leave without waking her. I walked her to the living room and sat on the couch with her as she kissed me and I held her. I said you were sleeping so hard I didn't want to disturb you. She said no matter, she wanted to see my face every morning of her life and was pleading for me never to do it again. She asked me to promise as I wiped her eyes. We went upstairs and I undressed down to my shorts and used the bathroom, and when I came out, she was standing at the foot of the bed and dragged me to her and pulled me on top of her and asked me to make love to her as she opened her smock and that's all she was wearing as she pulled off my shorts and took her arms out of the smock and pulled me to her, she said lover you belong to me. I love you as she placed my hand between her legs and I felt her as she moaned and grabbed me and pulled me closer. I made love to her and was gentle as I entered her and she exploded. I continued to make love to her as she had multiple orgasms before I came. Then we just laid there, she kissed me like she hadn't seen me for months. Finally, she calmed down exhausted, and we went and showered together, finished and putting our robes on and going downstairs to eat. We ate a light meal. I said we should go to bed early so you can see me in the morning, she smiled as we held hands and sat in the living room for a couple hours watching television until our food went digested before going up to the bedroom where we rubbed and kissed and held each other before falling asleep.

Twenty-one
Thursday: Day Twenty-one.

I woke up at five forty-five and went to the bathroom, when I came out it was six. And the sleeping beauty was tossing and turning so I returned to bed and touched her. She stopped moving and slowly woke. Then she opened her eyes. She reached out for me yawning, rose and went to the bathroom. She came out several minutes later and sat next to me, leaning on me as I placed an arm around her. She looked up and smiled, as I said do you see my face now. Yes she replied, and was happy I was here. I love you, but I can't continue having sex every day. Said that it was taking a toll on her also, but couldn't explain why she was acting this way, why she was so aroused, it didn't happen until we met. Said I've lost ten pounds in two weeks and can't continue or I will have to lock you away. No you wouldn't. You don't want me to go there or maybe get you a chastity belt. Please, no she cried. I said if you feel you need sex, use your dildo. I can't and won't anymore, it doesn't mean I don't love you it's a physical strain on my body. I said we need to eat, let's go downstairs and fix something.

She said ok, and that she would fix breakfast for her man. I thanked her as we put on our bathrobes and went downstairs. I did the coffee, while she fixed some sausage and eggs with toast. I ate a donut and drank coffee until she finished cooking. We sat at the counter and ate and told her it would be a long day because Joanne and I were going to shop for some office furniture and didn't know how long it would take to find what we were looking for. I asked her if she would be all right today, and if there something that was on her mind. She was upset that I didn't wake her yesterday. I said you have to be strong for both of us, you are a grown woman and have lived long enough to be secure and especially now since you are with me. What do you have to say for yourself? Said she was sorry that she had acted that way and would not let it happen again and would be the woman I expected her to be. Told her I was proud of her, and she had to at least try to live up to the expectations I had in my mind of what I wanted for her to be, or tell me now, that you can't so I won't be disappointed. She was sorry she acted like a child, that she would be my woman, the one I fell in love with. I have to get ready to go. Said she would get control of her emotions and calm down, but had never had multiple orgasms ever before and not until she and I had made love and it's become more and more intense every day. She didn't know if it was the food or the vitamins or how I held and touch her. Said it was over whelming and just had a hard time being in control around me. Just being with me made her hot, said she was on the edge now and was having a hard time controlling herself and didn't know if there was something wrong with her. Said she wanted me to feel her right now. I said come here as she stood in front of me. I held her with one arm and felt her, I said you are a bad girl and spanked her vagina as she quickly exploded as I felt her and said that's all you're getting for now as I flicked her clit and rubbed its extended head as she shook and climaxed again. I held her till she calmed down. She said her clit had gotten much larger since we have been together and it didn't help her self-control.

I said you can clean up the kitchen later, but I want you to come upstairs with me now. We went upstairs and when we entered the bed room I said take the robe off, she complied. I told her to stand in the middle of the floor and to put her hands behind her head and spread your legs, she did. I got in her face and asked her how she felt right now. She said she wanted me to fuck her anyway I wanted, to use her, to whip her if I wanted. I squatted and looked at her shaved pussy; her clit was standing out as she started to perspire. The anticipation was starting to become overwhelming as her breathing became short and told her don't move, to just stand there. I started to dress; it was difficult for me also. My dick was rock hard just looking at her but I had to get through this. I had my briefs on and she could see I was excited, she begged me to touch her, to fuck her. I said don't you dare move; she didn't as I could see her excitement grow with each passing minute. I had my t-shirt on, then my jeans and socks. I came over in front of her and said you need to get control of yourself. She begged me to at least touch her, and then she said, please master please, repeating it over and over. I said please what. Touch me she screamed. I said put your arms down, and asked her if she wanted to feel herself. She replied yes please master. And I said ok. She touched herself and exploded with a huge climax till her knees buckled and she was kneeling as her whole body shook. I said enough; stop, as she slowly removed her hand. I asked how you feel now, do you feel relieved. She could hardly speak and said she still wanted to feel me inside of her. Sorry. When you think you have self-control I will fuck you. She begged to let her suck me off. I said no. I said put your robe on and come with me, but first I got the collar and leash and put it on her, then lead her downstairs. I stopped at the door to the garage, turned and kissed her. Told her I loved her, and she better clean the house and I didn't want to find a speck of dust anywhere and that she was my sweet bitch and had better get control of herself, or I would have a new punishment for her and she wouldn't like it. Kissed her and said I love you, she looked happy now as I released the leash and left.

I passed the old mall and observed that the fencing was up and a utility crew from the gas company was digging, to shut the gas off, just as the electric company crew pulled up, the demolition process had begun. Well, I was making progress all around, and then turned around and headed to the office. I opened up, but locked the door behind me and went and made the morning coffee before sitting at my desk. Brought up the home camera app and looked for Victoria. I had made it out of the house without having sex. Wondered how long I could keep that up. Found her with her smock on as she still wore the collar. She had just finished in the kitchen and was starting to clean the cabinets as I turned the app off. Then went through the papers on my desk and worked out an estimated budget, after the office was completed expenses would level off and things would settle down. The mall would be demolished and the price for the vacant land would increase. It was more desirable as vacant land in a busy corridor than it would be with buildings. I would set the price at $8,000,000.00 and wait and see what would happen with the golf course. The new office was going to be close to a cool $1,500,000.00 furnished, but it's what we needed and I wanted. I was a member of the realtors association and had been all along but I wasn't one of the big boys and definitely not in the click. I was a small fry and stayed out the way and out the lime light. I just built my business from the ground up, and Joanne has been here with me all along, and would do anything for her, that's why we get along so well. I have always gotten along better with women than men. I didn't hang out with any, as a matter of fact, of the men I known, my best friends have either died, and several others have moved away, I just didn't have any. I looked around the office it wasn't much, because all of my profits I reinvested, they became assets and more investments, you wouldn't think that this little hole in the wall looking real estate operation was in control of close to $500,000,000.00, in assets that's why I was changing things. I, or rather we, and had out grown the space, time to move on up.

Joanne and Patricia unlocked the door and woke me from my thoughts. I said good morning ladies. They said good morning Mr. Harcourt. I asked what was with the formal greeting. They both smiled at me as they came to my desk. They asked me to stand. I did, and saw they had tears in their eyes as they both tried to hug me at the same time. I hugged them back, and said I love you two. Patricia said Joanne had told her why she was so loyal to me, and what I had done for her years earlier. I played dumb and said what, I didn't do anything. Joanne said when she was going to lose her home. Oh the gift from God. I said God tapped me on the shoulder, and told me life is what you make of it and the people you can help, that's all, I said don't worry about it. Patricia hugged and kissed me and said she loved me for just being the person I was. And Joanne said she wouldn't have said anything except Pat insisted that something was going on, and wanted to know. I said that's all right, just you two keep it to yourselves, ok. They dried their tears and went to work. I asked Patricia if it she wanted to come with us. Said she would feel honored. I looked at Joanne and asked. Are we set for this afternoon? Yes we are, and asked if she could ask me about what happened at home yesterday. I left the sleeping beauty in bed and when she woke up and found I was

gone, the little girl kicked in and she panicked. She asked me not
do it again because she wanted to see my face every morning
before I left. Joanne said that's love, and I'm glad you are going to
marry her, and said she wouldn't leave your side for any reason,
and you aren't ever going to find that kind of love, you can't buy
that.

I know, and told her about when we went to the jewelry store.
Joanne said no she didn't, said again you would be the biggest fool
if you let her go, and said that God sent her to you, and that's why
in this short span of time it's so intense for both of you. She asked
what kind of wedding. I said the court house. I don't have any
friends, and most of my close family is dead, basically you and
Pat, Hippies, and Fitz are my family. She said that's why she was
sent to you, believe me, God placed her in your life and look at
what you have accomplished. You and I know you have been
thinking about this move for months. But after you met her it's like
you let go, and now look at what's about to happen. I am so happy
for you, I truly am. I said you know me better than I know myself
sometimes. Joanne said I had a good heart and that's why she was
happy to work with me all these years. I said it hasn't been that
long and if you hadn't been here I couldn't have done it. I got up
and hugged her, I had tears in my eyes, and we were both crying.
Patricia turn around and saw us, and said are you two ok, we
answered together, yes. By then Hippies came in and brought some
donuts, and he broke the ice, he looked at us and asked who died.
Joanne and I started to laugh. Hippies said he thought he was
coming to a wake, he could tell we had been having a moment. We
kind of explained, but not much because it was personal for both of
us. Then Caren Brown came in and greeted everyone, and poured a
cup of coffee and asks, who brought the donuts and we said
Hippies, and out of nowhere she kissed him. I said it must be love
in the air. Fitz came in and greeted everyone, and got himself a
cup, and we all looked at him, and he said what, we laughed, and
then explained what had just happened.

Hippies said he hoped Phillips and Green passed there exams
because we had three closings next week if they didn't either I or

Joanne would have to go. I said yes, and asked if she wanted to go to lunch. Said she brought hers today; and wasn't going to let Martha fatten her up. I sat back and pulled my phone out and brought up the home app and watched Victoria mopping floors, as she left the kitchen and went upstairs and cleaned the bathroom. Good she needs to stay busy as I watched for twenty minutes, and then she went to the kitchen and fixed herself some lunch and I turned off. It was close to noon and said I was going to Wong's. I drove over and had a box lunch. Mrs. Wong came over and sat down, she said the family had discussed the expansion and she wanted to do it, and then asked about the walls. I said, we would split the cost, she said that was good for them, and I would have the papers drawn up and set a date, for the work once the clothing store closed. I would partition the store first. Then remove the adjoining wall. That way there would be less disruption for you, and if you were closed for two days it could be done quickly, the other option is a plastic sheet would be erected and you could stay open. Now the cost I will split with you is for the wall only. Once you have the space the painting and décor is on you. You do understand. She said we split cost for wall, going up, and this wall coming down. Yes I said. She asked how much. Said, not that much. I have the people and it would only take a couple days at the most. My food came and Mrs. Wong said ok, we do. Thank you. She said free lunch for you today. I thanked her as she left with a smile on her face. The food was good as usual and I ate it all. I stood to go and Mrs. Wong introduced me to her son, and asked that I explain to him, what I said to her. I said no problem. Her son was born here. I asked if he could step outside for a minute and we walked next door. He said his mother was excited and started to speak in Chinese, and even though he understood, she would talk so fast sometimes he missed some of the things she would say. We walked to the adjacent store, told him that I would divide the space first and showed his roughly where it would be before removing the wall that separated the restaurant from the new space. That the Wong's and I would split the cost of erecting and removing the walls, but the décor was there baby. And the cost should be about a thousand and no more, so you're looking to pay half. He said that was a very good deal and now he fully understood. I said your mother is sweet, take care of her, he shook my hand and thanked me as I departed and returned to the office.

It was after one when I got back and everyone was in, including Hippies and Fitz. I asked them if they wanted to follow us to the furniture store or did they want us to pick out the furniture. They both said for us to choose for them, I said ok. Fitz asked to keep it simple, and so did Hippies. I said ok. They said it was my baby, and would be happy with whatever I choose. Everyone settled into their routines, and I brought up the camera app on my phone to see what Vicky was doing now, she was lying on the couch asleep, she still had the collar on as I turned off. I was going to look for some dust when I came home, just because. It was now close to closing, and sat back, when Phillips and Green came in, they were smiling, and said they both passed, and boy were they happy. We all stood and clapped and congratulated them with a well done. Said I would put them on the pay roll starting Monday. Joanne gave them the employment applications as they went to fill them out, it would be a couple days before their licenses came, but we could pull the numbers tomorrow. Joanne and I hugged each other, and I said to her, you have done a marvelous job and now we can go to the next step. She said yes, and was happy for both of us. It's almost time to go; and had about a half hour. I said to Green and Phillips that I wanted them to work with Joanne the next couple of days, until they would be officially employees. Starting Monday they would officially be in there new positions. I shook their hands again, and told them we are so proud to have such talented young men working for us. They thanked me and said they couldn't have done it without our support. They hugged Joanne and thanked Hippies for all the advice and assistance he had given them. It was five two; Hippies and Fitz said good evening and left. I asked if anyone was staying, everyone said no. Green and Phillips said they were going to have a drink together. So everyone prepared to depart. I said to Joanne and Patricia, we should just all go together in one car, they said fine.

I locked the doors after turning off the lights, we got in my car and as we got near the new office I pulled into the parking lot just to show them the building, and Hector was standing outside smoking and saw us. He walked over, and I said, we were just looking. He said come inside and look around. I said we had no intention of interrupting anything. He insisted, we all got out as he led us inside. Joanne said hold me. I held her; tears were forming in her eyes. I said you helped create this, and said you need to get it together, as she wiped her eyes. Hector led us around the ground floor, the walls had been painted, the paper and boxes had been removed, as he explained that they were going to lay the carpet tomorrow, and we walked toward the washrooms. They were completely finished, he said they would be cleaned next, showed us the section where the agents would be, said things are going faster than he had ever expected. Showed us the conference and lunch rooms, they were large spaces and would be very comfortable, and the office equipment would come after the carpet was laid. He led us to the elevator and we all went upstairs. All the offices were completely painted; each was the size of a small home. Joanne and Patricia knew there's by the color of the walls, he showed us the conference room, the lunch room, and the washrooms. He said next they would be, installing the carpet, the file cabinets were going in tomorrow, the office suits were coming and the furniture store people would assemble them, and Kenny would start with the electronics. I thanked him for such a fine and detailed job. He said my choice of Brown and Watson made it so easy, and when everything was done his sisters cleaning company would come and make sure everything was spotless. I thanked him and asked Joanne if she remembered the suite she had chosen. She said she couldn't get it out of her head. We went back downstairs and I thanked Hector again.

We went to get in the auto and Joanne took my hand and we faced each other, she smiled and was crying at the same time. I hugged her and held her and said, everything is fine, and you of all people deserve the best. I released her and she just looked at me, and said she was speechless and that this was going to be the second day she would have to go home and have a drink. Patricia was standing there the whole time, and tears were in her eyes also as she came and hugged me, and said she loved me. I started to cry. I never felt that what I did made anyone this happy. Joanne said now she understood why Victoria had called and was upset. I said we have to go, even though the store didn't close till nine, I opened the door for both as they got in.

We arrived at the Homes Furniture store. I walked around and opened the doors for my tearful co-workers, and led them inside. I turned and said ladies; I want you to look happy, and I will try my hardest not to make you cry anymore. I said give me a big smile; as they forced themselves to give me great big grins. I said ok, and we then entered. We passed up the modern furniture and came to the more traditional. Saw what I had in my mind that I was looking for just when a salesman approached, and greeted us. I explained what we were looking for, and where it would be located. He said they had a section that would probably have more of what we were looking for.

We followed him and went to the upper level. There we observed more of what would complement our offices. It didn't take long to make our selections. I chose a complete set, it was high backed and very comfortable, came with a wide sofa that could seat five, maybe six people, and a smaller couch, two chairs, two end tables and a large rectangular center table. I chose two classy lamps from another set. The color was a dark gold color with a semi stripped pattern. Joanne chose the same set, but in a dark green, we both had chosen colors that were similar to the wall and carpet colors. Patricia picked a different set, with a sofa, love seat, one chair and two end tables with lamps, in a burgundy. I picked for Hippies, the same set as Pat. Only the color was different, a dark brown, and for Fitz, the same set only in a dark blue, all with tables and lamps. The salesman led us to a desk as he wrote up the order. Told him where it was to be delivered, and gave him the names of the people based on the color and furniture as to their placement, and to address it to the project coordinator Mr. Brown. I asked the cost, he added everything up, and said there was free delivery, with tax it would be $25,000.00. I used the company charge card, and when the transaction was complete, he said that he would personally see the order through. Said he would be lucky to sell that much in six months, he thanked me, and didn't want to let go of my hand. I asked him if he needed a hug, he laughed, and said if I had any issues to give him a call and handed me another business card. Went over to where my ladies were still looking and, said my dears it's time to depart.

We all left, and I opened the car doors for them, and headed back to the office so Joanne could get her auto. I waited until they were in and pulling away before heading home. When I arrived it was a little after eight. I had a great day and looked forward to seeing Victoria. I entered and she met me at the door, hugged and kissed me and said she was glad I was home. She still had the collar on, she handed me the leash, and I attached it to the collar. I made her stand outside the washroom as I washed my hands. I came out and looked into her big beautiful eyes and pulled the leash and kissed her lips, she was highly excited. I pulled back and led her around wiping my finger in places where I might find some dust, we entered my office. I held the leash loosely as I looked around, went to window sill and wiped my finger across it. I said oops, what we have here as I looked at my finger tip and it was dark with some dust. I held it up and put it close to her face, and asked her what it was. She replied it was dust, I said do you remember what I said this morning and she said, yes sir master. What did I say, she repeated that I had better not find any dust or she would be sorry. I said that is correct. I said a disobedient slave must be made to suffer, whipped, abused, punished or locked in a cage. She was beginning to tremble, her eyes were getting watery. I said you know what your punishment is going to be as I pulled on the leash, and looked into her moist eyes. She said no sir master. I reached behind her and removed the collar and leash, letting them fall to the floor. I said your punishment is to be, and waited a few long seconds as she looked frighten and very upset, as if I was going to really punish and torture her. Your punishment is going be, and waited a few more long seconds, no punishment at all, as she began to crying profusely. As I wrapped my arms around her and she hugged me and just cried, and I whispered in her ear that I couldn't hurt the one I love, as much as I love you. She cried and kissed me, I didn't think she would ever stop. I felt her butt and she pressed herself against my leg as she climaxed in my arms, and continued to cry and climax at the same time for several long minutes, she could no longer stand so I scooped her up and laid her on the couch, she reached out and pulled me to her and wouldn't let go. I was soon able to look down at her and rubbed her face, she was so choked up with tears. I pulled her to a sitting position, and put my head in her lap, as tears came to my face, she felt my head as I rose up as she bent over and kissed me all over.

I grabbed my tearful love by the hand and led her upstairs; she undressed me and herself and led me to the bed where we made the most beautiful love to one another yet. I had never felt this way about anyone ever; it was worth more to have her than all the money in the world. When we finished, we didn't want to let go of one another, we just held each other. Victoria said to me finally speaking for the first time since I came home. That when I left and said, she would be punished that it made her so hot and frightened her at the same time, and was driving her out of her mind. And when she bumped into the stool in the kitchen she had an orgasm, and thought she was losing her mind. She was relieved and surprised when I said her punishment was no punishment, and just couldn't control herself any longer. She wanted me, said her heart ached whenever she thought of me holding her. I asked her what you are feeling right now. Said she was ok now. I said to her you aren't going to die on me, are you? She said no, but the way I touched her, and felt her made her crazy and didn't know why this was happening to her, it had never happened to her ever before, when I looked at her, or even spoke to her it seemed everything associated with me affected her. She prayed that someone would come into her life, prayed every day, asked God to forgive her for her indiscretions and begged for his forgiveness and that when her husband died, felt a burden had been lifted, but didn't know what lay ahead, and felt that she was going to be punished for her pass.

She became more humble, and when I came to sell Mrs. Kashia condo, she felt that her punishment was just about to begin, and then she did what she had never ever done before, offered herself to me not knowing who, or what would happen, and when I said that wasn't necessary, was overwhelmed with regret and grief and said after I left she cried and prayed. The next day when I came and took her with me, she was determined to be good, a better person, then things just happened. She had dreamed of me before I ever appeared to her and didn't think much of it, thought they were just dreams, but have turned out to have been premonitions, and they have come to pass, and that her prayers were answered.

She loved me no matter what and tonight said it was one of the dreams that she had. Was sorry she was so emotional, but was so overjoyed, that it would be hard for anyone else to imagine and that I couldn't fully understand her love for me. I reached over and held her; she cried and said I love you so much. I said lets go bathe, we took a long hot shower together, and came out placing our towels on the bed, and she applied oil to me first, and when she was done I did the same to her. I started with her feet and I kissed them, I sucked a toe as she squirmed with pleasure, and continued to do her whole body, when I got to her head, I rubbed her face and took my finger and slowly rubbed her lips as she reached for my hand and put my finger in her mouth. She reached out and pulled me so I was on top of her. Her body between my legs, and we kissed and I looked into those big beautiful brown eyes, and said to her. I love you with all my heart, and asked her again, will you be my wife. She pulled my face to hers and said, yes, and would be the best wife ever as we kissed and she had tears of joy in her eyes. We got up and got under the covers, turned off the lights, hugged and kissed until we fell asleep in each other's arms, again.

Twenty two
Friday: Day Twenty-two.

I woke happy and looking forward to a productive the day.
Looked over at Victoria, she was sleeping as I eased out of bed and
went to the bathroom. When I returned, lay back down next to her
and touched and felt her. I loved her and felt it in my heart, as she
slowly woke, and opened her eyes. She smiled at me as I felt and
stroked her head, rubbed her face and kissed her. Then hugged her
and felt her warm body all over. She had to pee and went to the
bathroom, returned and got back in bed and said good morning
lover, as we held each other. We have a hard time letting go of
each other. I felt and squeezed her butt and rubbed her thighs and
moved my hand up her back as she moaned and hugged me tight,
and said I was driving her crazy. I asked her, what she was going
to do today. Said she would get the dust I had found in the window
sill. I asked if that was all. Said she would just go around dusting. I
told her, she was coming with me today, and that I wanted her to
be with me, and didn't want her to be alone, felt maybe it would
help her calm down. She said it might help some, but the way she
felt about me she would probably never get over it. I said when I
felt your thighs I could tell you have lost some weight. Said eleven
pounds but she felt good. I told her we should eat before we left,
because I loved her breakfast.

We put on our bathrobes and went downstairs and began
preparing breakfast again just like almost every morning since her
arrival in my home. When we finished, we sat in the nook and ate
as we looked at one another. Victoria spoke, said she had lost all
control of herself and her pussy was twitching now as we sat and
ate and asked if there was something seriously wrong with her. I
said her being with her was having a serious effect on me also and
wondered if there wasn't something wrong with me also. We
finished eating and we started cleaning up the kitchen together as
usual. When we finished, took her in my arms, and just held her as
I kissed her forehead. I was having a serious erection as I held her.
I placed my right leg between hers as I licked her ear causing her
to shiver and shake and soon climaxed in my arms several times.

I asked her what she was doing to me, I had never felt like this before about anyone. I had lost control also, and just looking at her was driving me crazy and told her we almost forgot to take our vitamins. I held her as we went upstairs and she sat on the bed, and told her to lie down. I opened her robe and had her spread her legs as I looked closely at her vagina and clitoris. It was noticeably larger before going to the bathroom and retrieved the petroleum jelly, mixed it with a topical antiseptic cooling jell and liberally applied the two together to her vaginal area, rubbing gently as I pulled the skin back over it. Then rubbed her and she said it was feeling so much better. I said it needed tender loving care; it wasn't that it had grown; the poor thing was slightly swollen. Told her not to wear any panties for a few days, and said in a day or so you will feel much better. It is feeling better already. She asked how I knew what to do; I said you have dryness and it occurs when it isn't lubricated enough and it gets irritated. This is why you felt like you were losing control. I think if you wore a dress it would feel better, no jeans, panties or pants, let it breath and keep it lubed with the petroleum jelly or olive oil, you need to apply it three to four times a day for the swelling to dissipate, ok baby. She said yes doctor. I said you are going with me. It's time to get dressed. I looked on her side of the closet and found a dress as she stood and held it up and said, wear this, and it fell well below her knees. I put on some clean jeans, grey t-shirt, sneakers and would wear a sports jacket. I asked her to wear some comfortable heels, and if you wear stockings, wear the crotch less pantyhose or the ones with the attached garter belt; she chose the garter belt ones. I said good choice. I was ready, but gave her time to get ready and said there was no rush, and I would be in the office, she said ok from the bathroom.

I went downstairs and looked at the clock, it was after eight thirty and turned on my computer, and made a few notations, before turning it off. I sat in the living room until my baby came downstairs, and when she appeared, she looked beautiful. I said you will be spending a day with me at work, and asked her if she was ready for that. Said that whenever she was with me she would be overjoyed and happy. I said Joanne's birthday is coming and want to get her something special because I wouldn't be where I am if she hadn't been there to help me. Victoria said she understood. Told her the reason I'm telling you this now is I don't want you to be jealous. You remember the diamond necklace set you said was too much for you. Yes she remembered. I am thinking of getting it for her. She smiled and said that would be such a wonderful gift. Said she wasn't jealous because she had all she would ever want, and it wasn't material, it was me, and my love for her. I kissed her and we walked to the garage, I opened the door for her. Vicky said I love you Charlie, forever.

We got in and I pulled out, closing the garage door behind us. Stopped at the drug store and we went in and purchased two small jars of petroleum jelly and two tubes of the antiseptic cooling jell. I placed one each in the console and told her to keep the others in her purse. We headed for the office; it was about nine thirty when we arrived, and entered. Joanne and Patricia were the only ones in as Joanne stood and hugged Victoria, when she saw her. I introduced Patricia to Victoria, and said Vicky is going to be here today. Joanne told her to pull up a chair and they began talking. I turned on my computer and at ten Mr. Green came in. I introduced Vicky. Joanne asked Vicky to pull a chair over by my desk, as she let Green sit at hers and pulled a chair over and sat next to him and gave him a brief rundown of what he would be doing. I interrupted them and asked about Phillips. Mr. Green said he would be in later, and would sit here tomorrow. I said ok. It was ten when Hippies then Fitz walked in. I introduced Victoria to both. I had Victoria sit closer to me. I reached in my drawer and pulled out the folder that I kept photos of my first office in, it was me standing in front and a cardboard sign I had an artist friend make for me in the window. Harcourt Realty was all it said, that was over nine years ago, the second was the same office, but Harcourt Realty was now painted on the glass. It was Joanne and I. The third was the present location and it was Joanne, Fitz and I, they were taken several years apart, and the next one will be all of us in front of the new office location. I had them in protective sleeves and showed them

to Victoria. Asked her to pass them to Joanne and when she did
Joanne smiled and started to cry. It was a rough time for her then,
and the photo brought back memories, she handed them back and
walked to the back. Vicky stood and followed her and they were
gone for about half an hour before they both returned. I suggested
they go to lunch and take Vicky with her, and Joanne took Vicky
by the hand and Patricia followed and they walked down the street
to Martha's.

Then there were only Hippies, Fitz, Green and myself, I got
everyone's attention and told them that Joanne birthday was
tomorrow and wanted to know if they would attend a party for her,
they all said yes, I said it's on me I just need your body's there. I
said the other thing is it's a surprise. I asked Green to call Philips
and let him know I wanted him present, he said ok as he placed the
call, hung up and said ok. I thanked them and they went back to
work and I called the Paris restaurant and asked to make
reservations for one of their side rooms for ten people. I requested
a six pm to ten time frames, and Champaign and a medium size
German chocolate cake, and wanted it for this Sunday evening.
They said no problem and asked what the occasion was. I said a
birthday, did I want a sign, I said give me the works and gave them
the details. Ok thank you. I said fellows six pm Sunday at the Paris
restaurant, suits or sports jackets please. I called Ms. Brown and
told her the details, and I would like her to wear a dress and hi
heels, and not to be late, she said yes sir, I hung up.

The ladies finally returned and they had taken about two hours,
which was fine with me; Vicky came and hugged me when she
returned. I was going to get something, and Hippies said he would
go with me, Joanne suggested that Green and Fitz go also, so all us
guys got in my car and we went to Wong's. We arrived and Mrs.
Wong greeted us, she led us to a booth, I introduced her to all, and
there place in my origination. I said to her Mr. Fitz will probably
handle your new lease if I'm not available. We ordered and soon
our food came, Mrs. Wong and Fawn worked together, and I said
to Mrs. Wong, you aren't giving us special treatment, she said yes,
you special to me, I thanked her. We ate and enjoyed our food,

when we finished, I paid for all. We were gone a little over and
hour. When we returned it seemed the girls were having a good
time. They asked if we enjoyed lunch. I said yes we did. I went to
the front and asked Patricia to step outside with me while Joanne
was distracted. Explained that I wanted her to take her mother out
to dinner and handed her a small slip of paper, telling her when and
where, and it was a must do. I said lie if you have to it's a surprise.
I said it's the one most important thing she would ever do for me. I
asked can you do it, she said it shouldn't be a problem because she
had mentioned she wanted to take her out. I instructed when you
walk in give the maître your mother business card. She said ok,
and would do anything I asked of her. I thanked her and we
returned. I don't think we were missed. I sat at my desk. The phone
rang Joanne answered, said it's for you. It was Kenny Watson,
Brown had shown him the desk suits, and based on how large they
were, wanted to know if he went with the 32inch screens, would
twins monitors be enough for everyone upstairs, yes I told him,
and said the security monitor would be located inside a cabinet
with doors in my office behind my desk. I said that sounds good,
asked him if there was anything else, no he replied and he was
running cable now, before you go, I asked about Wi-Fi, we would
have it and would be password protected, and there would be one
for guest also. I said well that's good, and hung up.

It was around two and I said to Joanne we had something to do
and would have to go. She said ok and be safe. I will see you
tomorrow to just check on things. She asked that I bring Victoria
back again sometime soon. Said I would as she stood and hugged
Victoria. We prepared to leave, and I was happy they got along so
well, as we left and said good bye to everyone. I taped on Pats desk
and she gave me a thumb up. I opened the car door for Vicky and
headed to the Sweet Wood Mall, and while we were driving, I
asked what you ladies talked about, she said not much. But now
she better understood me and how much of a caring and good
person I was and not to just to her, but to everyone that ever came
into contact with me. That what she heard made her love me even
more. She said Martha even sat with them a short while, and when

Joanne told her I was your girlfriend. Martha said I know he's going to marry you. I asked how she knew, said are you living in his house. Yes she replied. He's a one woman man honey, and men like that don't come every day. Said several months after she open her restaurant and was late and short with her rent, he gave her three free months, and when she needed money to send her son to college, gave her a check for $5000.00 so he could attend. Then Joanne told about when she was going to lose her house, what you did, and Pat about giving her a job. And about how you saved me. No one knew what you had done for each of us until we all sat there and were telling our stories, you never bragged or told anyone what you had done, as tears came to her eyes how fortunate she was that I wanted to marry her. Vicky dried her eyes before we arrived. After we arrived at our destination, turned to her and said we won't be here long, not unless you want to do some shopping. Vicky was still choked up and didn't speak as I got out and walked to her side of the car and opened the door for her as she hugged and kissed me in silence.

We went inside and headed to Howards Jewelry. We entered and the set was still in the window display case. I liked the set, it hadn't sold because of the price, $18,000.00, and the salesman asked if he could help us. I said yes sir, the diamond set in the window. He asked if I would like to see it, yes I replied. He removed it from the front window, he placed it on the counter in front of us, it was white gold, it had three rows of diamonds, and each row was larger than the one below and in the center the three largest ones were mounted vertically, it came with matching tiered earrings, and a bracelet. Said I would purchase the set and to please remove the tags, and asked if it came with a case, he said it most certainly did. I requested that it be gift wrapped also. He said yes sir. I asked Vicky if she had seen anything she liked. Said that pearls were always what she had always wanted. I paid and we left and suggested we go to Himies. It was an exclusive women's store and went to the fragrance department. I asked Vicky to pick a perfume for herself, and I picked one Joanne had mentioned she liked but was just too expensive. The saleslady showed me what I was looking for, told her I would take the big bottle, she complied and Vicky found one she wanted. I made the purchase and we departed. Vicky asked me where we were going next. I asked what did my love desire. She had only eaten some chicken salad at lunch with the girls and was hungry again. What does my dear desire? Said the seafood restaurant we went to after we went to the fair. When we arrived at the car I locked our purchases in the trunk and as I was about to open the door for Victoria, when she pulled me to her, and said she had never known anyone as generous as I, kissed me and said she was swollen allover, from being loved.

We drove to the Red Fin and when we arrived found a great parking space, it wasn't crowded being a weekday, we entered and were seated in a booth and Vicky asked if they had smaller glasses of beer than before. They sure do, I said to her and we had the medium sized glasses. We ordered ale, looked over the menu and were soon ready. And Victoria saw what she wanted this time. The waitress appeared, and Vicky had the steak and lobster, baked potato with a tossed salad. I ordered the white fish platter with shrimp, rice and tossed salad. She left to place our orders. I was looking around looking at the décor when I turned back around; Vicky had her hands folded with her elbows on the table with her chin resting on her hands, just looking at me. I asked if anything was wrong. She replied no, that she had been blessed, and would be with me forever, and said she prayed every night that no harm ever came to me. Our food came, we ate and I was surprised when Vicky cleaned her plate, we finished and were completely satisfied, finished our beers and when the bill came, paid and departed for home. After we had gotten in the car Vicky said thank you Charlie, said she was very satisfied and happy as we then headed home.

We listened to some soft rock on the way home, when we arrived, I backed inside and we entered. We checked the house and I went and looked at the security footage and all was in order. I went back and retrieved her perfume from the trunk, but left the items for Joanne in the car. We went up to the bedroom and undressed, I wanted a drink. So we put on some comfortable clothes, I asked how was the little girl, she said she had kept it oiled and applied the petroleum jelly and antiseptic several times and said it felt so much better now, but she still wanted me, she pushed me onto the bed after I had put on my play clothes, laid on top of me and kissed my face and said her heart ached for me, and would for the rest of her life. Said I wanted a drink and she relented and let me get up and followed me downstairs to the basement. I fixed a drink and pulled the cover off the pool table and asked her if she had ever played. Said a long time ago when she had her first job. I set up the balls and made the first shot, it wasn't long before she was making shots that amazed me. We drank and had a swell time, before we had gotten tired and decided to return upstairs and take a shower together. We undressed and held hands as we entered and washed ourselves and each other, and then we laid down and applied the massage oil to each other, pulled the covers back, got in hugged and kissed the way we have since being together and then going to sleep in each other's arms.

Twenty-three
Saturday: Day Twenty-three.
	We woke up together again; we hugged and kissed each other as it was becoming our morning and nighttime ritual. It was truly wonderful having someone close again, only this time it seemed even more wonderful. I wondered if it was because my bed was no longer feeling cold and empty, or because I had grown older, more mature and settled. I really couldn't express in words how I really felt inside. Vicky said good morning love, and I said good morning to you as we slid back under the covers and petted one another. You know it's time we freshened up, yes she replied, as we went to the bathroom together again. When we came out we put on our play clothes before we went downstairs to fix something to eat. I decided on a grapefruit, coffee and some coffee cake. Victoria decided to have the same. We sat and looked at each other, smiled and laughed about her eating all of her food yesterday. I said to her tomorrow, I want you to wear one of your dresses, you can decide which one, but I planned a surprise birthday party for Joanne, I would like you to look ravishing. It was going to be at the Paris restaurant, the one I took you to when you wore your pearls, and please wear them again for me. Victoria would do anything I asked. I will be gone a short time today but have to pick up my suits from the cleaners and you can help me decide which one to wear. We cleaned up and returned upstairs. I prepared to see what I was going to wear, and had undressed when Vicky came behind me, she reached around me and pressed her chest into my back as she reached around and took me in her hand stroking me until I had a hard on. I had to resist because I knew when I got back we would be at it. I turned around and held her, and said to her you need a little more time for the swelling go down. She was disappointed when I said that, and told her I was sorry, and that she needed to relax. She wanted me now. I told her no, and said if she didn't stop I would spank her. She said spank her because she wasn't going to stop. I asked her if that is what she really wanted, she said yes sir master, and if I didn't fuck her to spank her. I told her to kneel in the bed, ass up, and spread your legs wide.

I thought this is what she wants, she was ready, it was a beautiful sight, but I couldn't do it. I came over and told her to stand and she did. I grabbed her wrist and held them and I said to her. Even though that is what you want, I'm not going to do it because I love you and kissed her as I held her. I let her go and started to dress. I had all my clothes on, and when I turned and looked she was kneeling, holding the whip in her hands. She said master please. I told her to stand, she did. I looked in the bag with the toys, there was a pair of hand cuffs we had never used, and the two keys were still attached. I removed them and the ankle cuffs and her collar. I turned and cuffed her hands in front of her, put the collar on her neck, then the ankle cuffs and grabbed the blindfold. I clamped her hands to the collar, put the blindfold on and hooked the leash to the collar and led her to the empty bed room and told her to lie on the floor. She did, and then I released her hands from the collar and hooked them behind her and then to the ankle cuffs. Said that I was the master and the slave does what the master wants, and makes no demands or threats, you will stay her until I return and release you. Do you understand slave? She replied yes sir master.

I left and locked the door behind me. I checked to make sure all the appliances were off including the stove. Checked all my stuff before I left and went to the garage and got in the car. I checked the home camera app and brought up the room where I left her. She laid there rolling around as I pulled out and closed the garage door. It was the last thing I wanted to do, but you have to do what you must. I stopped first at the cleaners; Mr. Chong was happy I came to pick up my suits. I paid and hung them in the car before proceeding to the office. When I arrived Mr. Green and Joanne were there along with Ms. Brown, I spoke to all. Went to my desk and found it clear, before I asked Joanne to step in back. I said we need both Green and Phillips at the same time in order for us to truly operate the way I see things developing. She asked what it was I had in mind this time. And I stated someone has to go to the closings, and someone has to be in the office, so in order for this to work the way I envision it, we will pay them $50,000.00 each, one handles closings and one handles the office, and they can still alternate. But will make it a week on and a week off. I said the whole objective was to free you and me from the daily management of the office. We have more going on than any office in town I knew of. The only thing is no one knows how large we really are because we have been in this store front office and because of the way I set up the management of the properties we own. I said take a moment and think about last year, how much did we make as a company. That's why I formed the corporation; it was the only next logical step. She said yes, she remembered. She replied about $50 million.

I or rather we have been so caught up building this into what it is and we haven't taken time to look back at what we have accomplished. I said you get those two up to speed and we will let them know Monday when there employment starts. I am willing to pay more in order to keep them here. I just want you to think about it and let me know what you think. I have two more closings to go to, the last two listing I brought in, and then I'm through with the daily routine of the past. I bought the mall and put a bid on the golf course, and closing on the complex very soon, just look at all the property under our control, we have more important duties and it's time for us to pass the ball on and grab the next one, and you know I always look out for you. You and I did this, I didn't do it all alone and you know that.

So Monday you tell me what you think, and you know I value your opinion. Like the time you said you had a bad feeling about that strip mall. I pulled our offer off the table and two weeks later the government took the owners to jail and to court. Said yes she remembered. I said that was all I had on my mind for now. Joanne agreed with me, but would think about it. I thanked her and gave her a hug, you know I love you like a sister. You have everything under control? She replied yes. Just have Green and Phillips in Monday morning. Ok she would, as I started to leave, she grabbed my hand and looked me in my eyes, and said she had never known a better person, and she prayed that God watched over me. I thanked her and we walked back up front. Said I was stopping down the street, and that's another thing, we may be moving sooner than we think, and wished them well as I departed. When I got in the car I checked on Victoria, she was doing fine, she had calmed down some, I turned off before going down the street.

I pulled in the parking lot, and it was busy. Got out and walked inside and just stood inside the front doors and looked around, and saw the bare concrete floor had been cleaned, the carpet had been laid in the new waiting area, the two lower level offices were complete as I walked over and looked, the glass partitions were up and the doors were hung, the file cabinets installed and were carpeted. I walked to the other side where the real estate agents would be located, the carpet was down, and the internet cables were coiled and tied waiting for the cubes to be installed. Then I looked in the conference room, the carpet and paint was completed and the wall mount was up and the cables were tied and hanging, the washrooms were completely done. I went to the elevator, taking it upstairs, stepped off and looked around, looked over the rail and walked around it standing above the entrance and looking back. It was a beautiful sight, bright and open. I could see Joanne's office and mine, the walls were painted as I walked toward them and the partial glass walls were up, the rest were painted, and the carpet was laid. They were still laying the carpet in the other offices. I decided to leave and walked down the stairs, as Louis Brown walked up. We shook hands and said I was just looking. He said the good news was the furniture from the office supply was coming Monday; all the file cabinets were installed and the last furniture Joanne and I had chosen would be here before the week was over, and the plants would be here also, he said everything was going ahead of schedule. I said continue as I thanked him and shook hands again before departing.

I checked on Vicky before heading home. I had sound and she was crying, she said please master, please and was whimpering. I got in my car and headed home. Backed inside and closed the garage door grabbed my suits and went inside. I hung my suits up and decided to have some fun with Victoria. I undressed and put on my leather vest and pants with no underwear, retrieved the keys for the cuffs, hung the paddle from the pants loops, put on my black cowboy boots, looked in the mirror; I was ready to play master. I walked up to the door and put my ear to it. I heard whimpering. I unlocked it and went inside; she heard me and realized I was there, and said how my little slut doing. She said please master, I will be good and released her hands from her ankles and told her to kneel. I got a hard on just looking at her. I attached the leash, and told her to stand and helped her up. I held her face with my left hand, asking her who was she. She answered that she was my dirty bitch slave. I asked her what her purpose was. She said to serve me. What does the slut wants her master to do to her. Wanted her master to fuck her any way he wanted. She was totally excited as her nipples were hard and stood erect; her clit was starting to protrude as I asked her if she had learned her lesson. She hesitated, and said yes sir master. Said I detect some hesitation, you haven't learned your lesson have you. You want me to spank your ass don't you? She said yes sir master. I let her stand there and as she started to perspire. I took the paddle from my belt and rubbed her pretty thighs; she felt the leather against her body and became even excited and started to tremble and perspire as I passed it across her breast, and across her nipples and rubbed it across her clit, she became so very excited she started biting her lip. I held her chin with my left hand as I touched the side of her face with my right and saw the anticipation even though I couldn't see her eyes. I lightly slapped her, then again, then I slapped her with the left hand, before I removed the blindfold, she was zoning out now. I held her face with both hands, I looked in her eyes, tell master what the slave wants. In a very low voice, said she wanted to do whatever master wanted. I asked what are you, she replied that she was my bitch and I could do anything to her I wanted. I said on your knees and lick my boots slut, she bent over and began to lick one, and then the other one as she complied I drug the strap across her exposed back and butt. After a short while I told her to sit up and open her mouth, as I pulled my dick out and stuck it in her sweet mouth. And then I pulled it out, slapped her face with it and told her that was all you are getting. She begged me. please master, please master, I want it please. I let her suffer. I said stand, her hands were cuffed behind her, and her breathing was short with anticipation as I asked her who loves you. She answered you do master. I felt her between her legs, you like that, as I stuck a finger inside of her, moving it around and felt her moisture growing as she tried hard not to climax. The more she did the harder it became, then I rubbed my finger across her exposed clit, and she then exploded. I had to hold her to keep her standing up as she shook intensely and said thank you master, in a voice so low it was barely audible. I told her to spread her legs, wide, wider I said as I stepped to her side and held her wrist up forcing her to bend over as I took the paddle and spanked her ass lightly, then her thighs. I stood her up, released the hand cuffs, hooked the leash to her collar, gathered up all I had brought with me and told her to get down and crawl back to the bedroom. After entering I stood her up, removed the cuffs and collar and told her to bend over the end of the bed. I undressed and walked up behind her, told her to raise her sweet ass up, and slid my hard dick into her moist and waiting pussy, as I held her clit in my left hand, causing her to have several multiple climaxes, as her knees buckled, I pulled out, pulled her up turned her around pushed her back onto the bed and entered her as I held her tight and fucked her until I came.

When I released her she just lay on the bed and she kissed me with what little strength she had. I let her lie there until she tried to sit up and I helped her as she just held me and looked into my eyes. I took her into my arms, she hung on to me and wouldn't let go. I sat holding her a long very time, rubbing her head as she looked at me and finally said, she knew I loved her and she loved me. It was early evening when our sexual escapade ended and when she had regained her strength enough for us to shower together. I said to her as we dried off, I know you are hungry. She replied that her master had tied her up and hadn't fed her today and she was going to shrivel up, and his pussy would be gone, she had to laugh at that one herself. And said she was starving. We put on our robes after applying body lotion to one another, and she grabbed me. And just held me as she felt my body under the robe and she opened it and kissed me all over. I pulled her up and opened her robe and felt her also, she moaned and looked me in the eyes and said it was so wonderful being in my arms. I asked her aren't you hungry, she shook her head, yes as we released each other and headed downstairs. We fixed some sandwiches and heated some canned soup, and then we sat and ate. One thing for sure, we weren't over eating. After finishing we went to the living room and watched television for several hours, looking at and old movie about two people in love before heading to bed. Of course we held each other until we fell asleep.

Twenty-four

Sunday: Day Twenty-four.

We awoke to another beautiful Sunday morning. The sun was shining brightly and the temperature outside was pleasant. The birds were singing and it couldn't have been a lovelier day. We woke later than usual, and Victoria was so close to me I could only get out of bed. I went to freshen up and when I returned Vicky was just opening her eyes. She sat up and looked at me as she got up and headed to the bathroom. I sat back down on the bed and when she returned flew into my arms. We laid back down and petted one another. I felt her all over as we kissed and said that she had my heart and couldn't get enough of her. She hoped I would always feel that way about her. I wanted her then, and told her so as I climbed on top of her as she pulled me to her and we made love, it was so sweet, and we climaxed together and just held one another as I rolled over, and we laid there still touching and rubbing before we fell asleep again.

It wasn't very long before we woke again. We told each other how much we loved the other. Said to her that I would not ever lock her in a room again, and that it was wrong of me to have taken that chance, and asked for her to forgive me. Said I was forgiven, and that she had driven me to do it, and was sorry that her actions caused me to act that way. We forgave each other and kissed. I said you know today is going to be Joanne's special day. Victoria said she was looking forward to it, and couldn't wait to see the look on her face when I give her the necklace. You know she is going to cry they all did when they told their stories of how I had touched each one of their lives, and said that's what took them so long when they went to lunch. They had to get themselves together before they could return. Said Martha was even crying and it was tears of joy because, I had touched each one in a special way. That she was honored to be in my presence and every day was a blessing. She held me and started crying, and said it was because she had never been this happy in her life. I held her tight and stroked her head as she raised her head and kissed her. I thanked her for making my life so fulfilling. Our embrace was long and sweet. Eventually I said don't you know we can't live on love alone as she looked up at me with those big brown eyes and smiled, and said, if she could she would be a fat girl. I said ok slim let's eat something, please. We finally dragged ourselves out of bed, putting on our robes and going downstairs.

We made brunch since it was almost noon; we ate enough to take us up to dinner, some fish fillets with pork and beans. I doctored the beans, and we were fully satisfied when we finished eating, taking our vitamins, and then relaxing. Even though we had plenty of time, I suggested on what we were going to wear. We went to the living room and looked at some television and around two-thirty we went upstairs to prepare for the party. After Victoria took off her robe she stood in front of me and I felt her body. I looked at the marvelous shape of her figure, and how she walked. Told her I was proud that she was mine, all mine and we hugged again. I took a shower, and she accompanied me. Told her when we come out, we need to exert some self-control. It would be difficult until we had our clothes on. We bathed; I know we were the cleanest people I knew because some days we had showered up to three times. Finally we came out and dried each other off before oiling up. Vicky asked me about the panties. Doctor, she said and laid back, I looked, and the swelling had disappeared. She said it felt so much better. I said it's up to you, but you still should use the doctor's formula on it. She would put her panties on last.

I asked her what suit she thought I should wear; she looked and chose the dark blue pinstripe, with a pale blue shirt, and a gold striped tie. Asked her what was she going to wear, she couldn't make up her mind and asked me, she really liked the one she wore last time. I said good and you didn't wear stocking last time. I suggested the other one; it was a blue and trimmed in gold, similar but not the same. We will have on the same colors, she said ok. When she finished dressing, she was stunning, the dress accentuated her figure, the pearl set, made her stand out, and she wore her new perfume. It was really nice, was faint and not one of those in your face fragrances, she had on the dark brown open toe hi-heels, with matching bag, and had fixed her hair in a new style that accentuated her face, her makeup was light, not heavy, since she didn't need any really, and her lipstick was a rose color that matched her fingers and toes. I said you are just too lovely to touch as I took several pictures as she modeled for me, before she took some of me. It was a warm and pleasant day, she brought a sweater along anyway that was the same color as her dress, and went along well with it.

We were ready, as it was a little after five and had requested everyone be there at six before Joanne and Patricia arrived. We checked that we didn't forget anything as we went downstairs. We would take the BGT, but I had to get the gifts from the trunk of my work auto, and did. I handed them to Victoria after she was seated. I pulled out, and close the garage door, as we drove to the restaurant. We arrived about at five forty, I used the valet parking, and the valet opened the door for Victoria, as she stood waiting for me to escort her inside. There were people waiting, it being a Sunday and she drew attention from all who saw her and it made me very proud. We entered and I gave my name and we were led to a semi private room, when we entered, only Ms. Brown and Mr., Green hadn't arrived. Fitz, Hippies and Phillips, was present, and five minutes later, Ms. Brown accompanied by Mr. Green arrived, and everyone greeted one another.

The room was tastefully decorated and there were seating card and a special one at the head of the table for the honored guest with her name on it. There were balloons and streamers, but it wasn't overdone, we had our own waiter at our disposal, and all was prepared. I thanked everyone for coming and said it was most important to me that they all were in attendance. The waiter alerted us that the honored guest had arrived. Joanne came in, followed by Patricia, we all clapped, and sang happy birthday to you. Joanne was elated and overcome by our enthusiasm; she started to cry, as I took her hand and led her to her seat. As she sat down, I asked for everyone to please have a seat. Patricia sat across from me; we were the two sitting closest to Joanne. I was still standing, as I said ladies and gentlemen, we are gathered here, those who work every day with Mrs. Joanne Bradley, one of the finest, dearest persons you will ever know, my name might be on the sign, but behind the name stands the people, each and every one of you. Harcourt Realty would be no where if I hadn't had the support, loyalty and help of Mrs. Bradley, and I know we wouldn't be here today if it wasn't for her. I know because she was the first person to come to work for me, and has been with me since the beginning of my venture. She has made all of you welcome and has made our coming expansion possible. I love her and there isn't anything I wouldn't do for her or any of you here today. It's an honor to have her by my side and to see her pretty face every day I come to work. And with that said I just want to present her with a gift from the bottom of my heart, this small token of appreciation and true loyalty. I handed her the case with the jewelry, and the box of perfume. Everyone stood and applauded. She started to cry before she even opened it, when she did she stood and hugged me. Said I didn't have to give her anything. I owe you this much, as I handed her the perfume, and asked her to sit down. She cried and was truly surprised. Patricia hugged her and consoled her mother. Hippies said three cheers for Joanne, and we all joined in, as she soon calmed down and wiped her eyes. She wanted to thank everyone for coming and thought she was going to have a quiet dinner with her daughter, and didn't have any words to express how she now felt. I waited several minutes before asking if everyone was ready to order and asked the waiter to pass out the menus. Patricia asked Joanne if she would like to try it on, she relented as Pat helped her take off her current necklace and asked me to do the honors as I removed it from its case and hooked the clasp behind her neck, everyone clapped. We took pictures and she looked stunning. I handed her a menu. Joanne said, now every time she looks at me it's going to bring tears to her eyes. I said you need to eat something and stop thinking like that, and finally she smiled. I said you deserved it and so much more. It's some of the fruit I told you about.

We placed our orders, as I excused myself and went to use the washroom, when I returned Joanne was in a deep conversation with Pat and Victoria. I stood and talked with Fitz and Hippies, they both said to me well done. I thanked them and they both said they wouldn't have missed it for anything in the world. I spoke to Mr. Phillips and Mr. Green and asked them to come in at opening; they said Joanne had informed them already. I said very well, and thanked them for coming, as I spoke to Ms. Brown and complimented her on her appearance. I asked if she was related to Mr. Louis Brown. She said that he was her brother. I assume that you know he is my project coordinator and she said yes, they shared an apartment. Small world, and asked if she had any intentions of becoming a broker. Yes, but wanted to gain some experience first before jumping into deep water. I understood, and said when you do, come see me. We were expanding and I like to keep productive and attentive people on staff, and we had other areas, like apartment management and would soon have a mortgage origination department. Everyone placed there orders, and we sat back for some small talk. Vicky moved over so I could again sit next to Joanne, as she grabbed my hand and squeezed. Told me she was happy, and had gotten past the tears, and said I was special. I said you are very special to me and have been for a very long time. Hippies asked me how I was able to pull this off in such a short time, since the restaurant was one of the best, and always had people waiting. I said by being a silent partner. Oh he responded. Told him I would explain one day. Our orders came and Joanne said grace. Everyone dug in, we had Champaign to go with our meal, when we finished and our dirty dishes were removed, the cake was brought in. I knew it was her favorite, German chocolate. It had no candles on it. The waiter cut it and served Joanne first, then the rest of us, and there was also ice cream. I said to Vicky, you're going to get some of your weight back; she looked at me and made the comment you want to bet. Everyone enjoyed themselves and had eaten very well, as we prepared to depart. Joanne thanked and hugged everyone, as our party prepared to leave; two of the chefs came in and asked how the food was. All said they enjoyed it. I shook their hands, and thanked them for being attentive to my request; they said what I had done for them they would never forget.

My party began to depart; and Victoria and I were last, as we stood our turn in the valet line. Victoria asked what the chef meant, when he said what I had done for them. Oh just a business arrangement. She asked is there anyone you haven't helped. I just helped a few people that's all, and handed the valet my ticket. He pulled our car up as I opened the door for Victoria. Handed him a tip, got in and we headed home. We were glad to be home and to get out of our clothes. I couldn't wait to brush my teeth. Then said I was going to have a drink before going to bed, and my lovely came with me, she wore her sheer night gown, looking like a sex goddess, as I said to her I am too tired to be enticed. I fixed our drinks. We toasted each other. Vicky said that was a wonderful thing I had done for Joanne and she will always remember it. We had a couple drinks before we went back upstairs and to bed. When we got in bed we held each other and kissed and said I wanted to sleep since we had such a full day. Vicky said it has been as we hugged until we fell asleep.

Twenty-five
Monday: Day Twenty-five.

Another beautiful morning was awaiting us as I awoke and felt a soft hand touching me. I turned slightly and Victoria was looking at and I turned fully to face her, she smiled and reached out touching my face. I was about to speak as she placed a finger on my lips, and snuggled up under me. I wrapped an arm around her and began rubbing her back. We were like that for several minutes, before we both got up and went to the bathroom. When we returned we lay across the bed and held each other again as we hadn't yet spoken a word. She broke the silence when I pressed my lips to hers. I love you so much Mr. Charlie, and come safely home to me. We got up together and proceeded to go downstairs to fix something to eat after putting on some clothes. I drank coffee, ate some coffee cake, while Victoria poached some eggs, along with some toast. I asked her why she was so quiet. Replied that she felt secure and a warm feeling that had come over her during the night and now felt calm and relaxed, loved that the feeling of insecurity had left her and she was savoring the moment. She knew I loved her and that I couldn't help being the loving person that I was, and happy that I shared myself with her, and she would be here for me. She was going to clean the house and wash the dirty clothes but would first come upstairs with me before coming back and cleaning everything up after I left for work.

We cleaned up a little, before going back upstairs together. Vicky hugged me and she had gained control of herself as I held her tight and close to me. Said that she understood the mission I was on and would try not to be difficult anymore, but did want me to feel on her before I left, that her desire for me hadn't waned, but had grown more intense. Only now she was learning to live with me much better. We held each other as she kissed me and opened her legs as I placed my hand on her thighs. Said she needed my touch now before I left, and asked if that was all right with me. I said whatever you need my love as I touched her and she held me tight. I felt her breast and caressed her body as I slowly moved my hand down to her thighs and felt the inside of both as she licked and sucked my neck and felt her warmth and held her vagina in my hand before slowly moving a finger around the outside before slowly feeling the inside of her, and spreading her moistening lips apart, feeling her moisture build as she moaned and held me even tighter as I pressed a finger feeling deeper inside of her, and just behind her clit and slowly touching her clit with my thumb as climatic spasms started rocking her body with an unending frequency, then taking my fingers and pressing the lips together as she moaned and felt her juice in my palm. I moved my hand and held her butt and squeezed the cheeks, she was panting as her breathing slowly returned to normal after several long minutes. I licked her ear, causing her to squirm with even more pleasure. I held her for a few more minutes, before letting her go, and she said thank you Charlie. Said she could now make it through the day until I returned to her. Decided I would wear my jeans and a shirt today; this was the week I was going to prepare for our move. I dressed as Victoria sat on the bed and watched me dress, when I finished she came over and her eyes were moist. I reached out and held her, pulled her head back with my left hand and kissed her lips, she cried and said she loved me so much. I love you to Victoria, but I must go sweetheart as I kissed her and she came downstairs with me to the garage door. I turned and kissed her again, then left.

I got in my car and opened the garage door and pulled out closing the door behind me. I was on a mission and had a goal I was trying to reach. I drove straight to the office, when I arrived it was eight thirty five. I opened up, and decided to leave the doors unlocked and put the coffee pot on and fired up my computer. I then looked at the coffee machines, hell everything else was going to be new why not the coffee machine. I made out a list, seven coffee machines and two microwaves. One extra microwave per lunch room and a coffee machine each, one coffee machine per office, and one for my mortgage person. We needed shredders also, I would get eight. At nine Joanne walked in, she was impeccably dressed, followed by Mr. Green and Phillips. I said good morning to all and welcome to Harcourt Reality. Gentlemen get a cup of coffee if you want, and good morning Mrs. Bradley, I stood and hugged her. I hoped you had a great day yesterday. Said she had. Ok they returned with their coffee. I wanted you here because there has been a slight change in plans, and it will be more beneficial to the both of you. I have confidence in you both and don't want to lose you to another outfit, you have been under our tutelage, and that's time we invested in you. To put it to you straight, I realized we had a dilemma. Sometime this week I would like you to walk down the street where the furniture store used to be, that will be our new office, the entire building. The good news is your pay starting today is $50,000.00 per year not the amount I told you last time, and you can still make sales and list properties, and I encourage you to do so. The change and the reason for the increases are. One of you will manage the office, and the other will do closings, you will however alternate, but someone will be managing the office at all times, and someone will be at the closings representing us. Do you understand? And do you have any questions. They looked at each other and smiled. It's important that you understand the seriousness of what I am throwing you into, but Mrs. Bradley and I will be overseeing the entire company. Since I don't believe in leaving my employees in the dark, the reason is, even though we are in this non-descript location, we are not really the small operation we appear to be. I couldn't offer you the money you are about to earn if this was a nickel and dime operation. I won't tell you how much, but request your discretion, its company business. Do you have any questions so far? No they said. Good, first I want you to understand that, yes we are a member of the realtors association. But I have never tried to impress anyone, just salted every penny away, took advantage of opportunities, reinvested and making some lucky and wise investments, and meant what I said yesterday. I could not have done it without Mrs. Bradley, she was here while I was out there hustling, and now we are all here, you too are younger and it's time for us to pass the ball on. I have a couple closings to go to and then I won't be dealing with the sellers and buyers of homes. The mall down the street that's being demolished, Harcourt realty just purchased it. I am moving on to another level and I am asking you to fill my shoes and Joanne's on this one. I am giving you an opportunity that Joanne and I wish we had, and I am asking you two to take our places, so we can progress even further. I know this might be a lot for you to comprehend right now, but all I can say is, we really need you both, and I am asking do you accept the challenge. Phillips responded and said that they were ready, and appreciated the confidence we had in them. I looked at Green, and said he felt they were ready. Ok until we move, you will pick up as much knowledge as you can from Joanne and me; there are some closings this week. One of you will go with me and Hippies, we will play it by ear until we move, then it will be just as I described. The other things, if you aren't sure about something, anything don't hesitate to ask, Joanne or I, or even Hippies, or Fitz. I understand we are throwing a lot at you in a small amount of time. I want you to be sure of yourselves and know experience comes over time and I personally want to thank both of you for having the balls to get ahead as I shook their hands. Do you have anything to add, Joanne? She smiled and said not after that. It's quiet now; I think we should take a quick walk down the street and will be back shortly as I turned to Joanne. She said ok just as Hippies came in and greeted everyone.

I walked down the street with my new office managers and talked about how I struggled to make it and my lucky investment, we reached the corner, and I turned and said behold the great edifice. We walked across the street and were greeted by Hector, Brown and Watson; I introduced my two new managers. Green knew Brown as we all shook hands, and said we wouldn't be in the way or here long, was just giving a pre cursor tour. We entered and I showed them around and they were impressed, taking them upstairs and they said it was beautiful. We went back downstairs and walked around and out. I asked them what they thought. Said they were impressed and would be happy to work there. I told them that the split was the same on sales, just like when they were agents. Said they understood. We walked back to the soon to be old office and I the answered any questions they had. When we came back, they took over answering the phones, something Joanne and I had done. Joanne and I talked about the move and she suggested we start packing. I said yes, and ordered some banker boxes. Mr. Fitz came in and spoke to everyone and I walked up to his desk where Patricia was making entries, asked him if all the records at the complexes were ready to be shipped. He said they would be in a few days, and it would give the leasing agents more room in their offices. He asked about the desks, and what was going to happen to them. I asked if any of the locations needed a better desk. He said some do and what he was thinking was that we would use the movers to take the desk to the locations, and then they could bring back the files on the return trip. I said that makes sense. You organize that after we move from here, he said ok. I said no records older than five years, and then we will purge the paper files once a year after everything from the past is stored electronically. I asked if they were boxed by year. He said they were and would arrange for a mobile shredding company to take them after we moved them to the new location, and the loading dock at the new building would prove to be very useful for that. He said during the rest of the week he was taking Patricia to the remaining properties. Good I told him as I returned to my desk.

Shortly two women in their late fifties came in, they asked Mr. Fitz about the sign advertising for agents and he showed them to Joanne's desk. I stood and introduced myself after Joanne had spoken to them. They were curious about our sign, looking for agents. They had seen it the other day when one of them was a couple doors down getting her hair done. They worked at Roam reality, a really large agency with offices nationwide. I knew how they operated, they charged the agents for desk and nickeled and dimed them. They wanted to know how we operated. I let Joanne explain that we didn't have any charges for using the office and they would be independent contractors and not employees, would sign an agreement with us, where any listing they brought in were ours and they in there agreement could determine how long they wanted to stay with us, and any sales we would split and it didn't matter if they were brokers, they had to be licensed and have their own access to the RELS. That they could set their own hours and that we would like to have them spend some time in the office for walk- ins. They explained that working for Roam was fee heavy and cut into their commissions. They both asked when they could start. I said now if you like. They said they would be back tomorrow so they could inform the office they were working out of that they were leaving, if they weren't here tomorrow, then the next day for sure. I asked their names, they were Mrs. Mary Newman, and Mrs. Susan Hartman. I said welcome, and when you come back you will have a full interview. They thanked Joanne and I and departed, with smiles on their faces. It was lunch time when Hippies came in.

Joanne and I went to lunch together and we walked down the street to Martha's and conversed about the move. I said you know I will have a photo taken of us standing in front of our new office. Said she expected that, to add to my collection. Yes I replied and wondered how you would guess that. She laughed as we entered the restaurant. Martha greeted us and said such a rare sight seeing the two of you together, as she placed the menus on the table. I told her it was the new change that was coming. I mean Joanne is CEO now. So what are you? I said still the boss man. She laughed and said I was full of it. I ordered the baked fish with rice and a salad. Joanne ordered, the lunch special. We talked as we waited. I guess your sign is about to pay off. Said we still need a couple more and I agreed with her. Our food came and we ate and enjoyed each other's company. I paid and we walked back, which was good for the both of us. She thanked me again for her dinner party yesterday. Oh, I said to her when we take our photos at the new building, I want you to look real special. Said she would do it for me, as I opened the door for her. She asked Green and Phillips, if they had any questions so far. They responded no, not yet. Fitz said he and Pat were going to lunch and might not be back before closing, and said he would drop her off at home if that happened. Joanne said ok, as they left. I sat at my desk and brought up the home app and looked in on Victoria, she was true to her word, she was cleaning the house. I turned off after panning the outside cameras. The phone rang, it was a call from someone who was inquiring about the agent's position, and Phillips directed the call to me. I said hello, and what would you like to know, the person said she had seen the sign, and wondered if it was just for agents only. I said it was but we were going to move and might have some other positions open, but had yet to determine the hours or pay. It was a woman and asked if she could come in anyway and talk. Stated I would welcome it. She asked if tomorrow was ok. I said yes, and asked if she was a licensed agent, she said no but had worked in the loan department of a bank and wondered if we had anything to do with loans. I said in a couple weeks we would be having our mortgage origination department at the same location. I asked her name, Mary Anne Jones, and asked if ten o'clock was ok. She said yes. And said I would be waiting to talk to her. Thanking her for the call and hung up. Joanne suggested that I could go, because she had it under control and was savoring the time she was going to spend here before we moved. I said ok, and Hippies reminded me that I had the closing on the apartment complex Thursday at one. I hadn't forgotten, and departed.

I headed home and when I arrived backed inside the garage and went inside. I surprised Vicky, since she didn't expect me so soon and was happy to see me, as we hugged and kissed. I went upstairs and put on some shorts and a t-shirt. When I returned asked what she was going to cook. Said she hadn't thought about it. Vicky was folding clothes, when I decided to take some chicken breast out the freezer and placed them in a bowl of water to thaw and took out a box of rice mix, removed the pan and started to prepare our dinner. Later after I had everything seasoned and simmering and the chicken baking, prepared a salad, and found a bottle of wine for dinner. By the time I finished cooking, she had finished the laundry and cleaning up. I called her downstairs as I set the table after I had finished cooking and dished up our food. She came down and we sat and ate. When we finished Vicky said she would help me cleanup, as we sat and talked and sipped more wine. She had a very productive day was and glad I was home with her and wanted to watch some television. We finished, washed the glasses before going to the living room and watching television for a couple hours. Before we decided to shower and go to bed. Vicky said she was tired, and I could use the rest also as we bathed each other, and asked her, you seem to be doing much better. Said she listened to her doctor and he was still treating her. I said he must be a good doctor. Yes he is, and is the hands on type. Oh, I said. Does he have the touch? He has the most wonderful hands that had ever touched her. I'm jealous. You are really funny. What is his name? She said Dr. Charles Harcourt. Oh, I said I have heard of him. She was in love with him. Loved when he placed his hands on her, made her feel warm all over, like this as I oiled her after our shower. Yes doctor, she replied. We finished and went to bed and rubbed each other to sleep.

Twenty-six

Tuesday: Day Twenty-six.

Another great day was starting as I opened my eyes and looked over at Victoria. She had turned over and had her back to me, as I touched her and felt her softness and caressed the curves of her body, she woke and turned around to me and smiled. She and pulled me to her and said good morning my love. We hugged and kissed as we felt on one another before getting up. We went to the bathroom before putting on the clothes we had on yesterday evening and went downstairs to fix something to eat. I suggested we have a pizza, it is bread, sausage and veggies, it's a meal all rolled into one, and that's just what we did. And a half hour later we were eating. I like changing up the menu every now and then. We ate the whole thing, had some coffee and were ready to start our day. We went back upstairs and Vicky asked that the doctor examine her. I said the doctor would check his patient's progress as she lay on the bed and exposed herself. I went to get her topical medication and returned to inspect her and to apply the lubricants, rubbing her gently as she moaned and came to a rousing climax. As she lay there, I climbed next to her and felt the other parts of her soft smooth body, and said the doctor has relieved his patient of her stress. She pulled my body to hers and said she was satisfied now and would be able to recover fully. We kissed before I got up to dress for the day. I decided to wear a suit, and put on the dark brown one with a blue shirt and beige tie and a pair of brown loafers. Vicky was sitting up, and said I looked sharp, and then she stood up and put on one of her smocks and said she was going to iron all of my jeans she had washed. She liked keeping the house clean for me, and was satisfied with her life, because I was in it and was the most important thing in the world to her. I kissed her as she walked me downstairs. She kissed me again and said have a great day and come home safely to her. I held and kissed her and said I loved you and that she was the most important person in my life.

I departed and drove to the office, arriving at eight thirty. Opened the door, turned on the lights, and made the coffee. At nine my crew came in, first was Joanne, and Green, and five minutes later Phillips. I said good morning to everyone as they returned the greeting. Joanne said that Kenny Watson called last evening and that, he and Brown found that the building was equipped with a backup natural gas generator; it wasn't on the blueprint copies he had obtained, but was on the originals, and was able to locate and contact the architect who designed the building and found out where it was located. He said he would call and tell you today. I said that is awesome, we won't be in the dark then. Shortly after the phone rang and Mr. Green answered, said call on line two was for me. I picked up and it was Kenny, and he gave me the specifics and how they had missed it, it was really kind of hidden, and fully secure, and operational. They tested it, and it would keep the building fully operational all the time. I said that is wonderful news. It was set to start after a five second interruption if we lost outside power. He said he just wanted to let me know, before he started work. I thanked him and hung up.

The morning seemed to be passing quickly, as it was almost ten when I looked up and a very petite woman entered. Very pretty, short hair curly hair and brown skin, about five six in height with a very nice figure and smartly dressed, with a skirt just above the knees, blouse, and suit jacket, necklace and earrings, stocking and hi-heels, as she walked towards Mr. Green, and said she was here to see Mr. Harcourt. I heard her and stood, walking to where she was standing, introduced myself, and ask her to please follow me. I pulled up a chair for her. She was Ms. Mary Anne Jones. I told her it was a pleasure and asked her to please have a seat. We talked and she was aware that we had a mortgage company, and most of our loans had come to the bank she had worked for. She had worked first as a teller and moved to the loan department before being laid off when the banks started consolidating operations and closing some locations. She asked if there were any positions available here that she could fill. I said we are primarily a real estate company, but you might be interested to know that we were in the process of moving the office to a new and larger location. Asked her how much she knew about the mortgage company that I used. She stated many of the loans had been accepted by the bank she had worked for previously. Stated I owned the mortgage company and they would be moving with us to our new location. She liked working in the field and wanted to continue. I said it would be a week or two before we moved and I had one person already in the department, and didn't know if there was going to be enough demand to justify two people. She said that if I advertised for pre qualifications and originations that would bring in more business. I asked had she attended college. She said yes, majored in finance and business, and did taxes on the side. I said to her that I liked her bold approach. I don't have room here right now, but I want to give you an opportunity with my company. A smile came to her face. I asked. Have you been out of work long? She said three months, and was desperate, said her rent was due and had another month before she wouldn't be able to pay her rent in full. She didn't want to be evicted, and liked where she lived. I asked her the address, she told me. And I asked who the management company was where she lived? She said the management company was called Riverside Management. I said just a minute. I pulled up my properties on my computer, and she lived in one of my complexes. I turned to her; she had a lovely face, and was cute. You won't have to worry about the eviction. I see you are only a month behind and would contact them on your behalf. Would you be willing to accept a job as a receptionist, this might be just temporary, before we can possibly give you a position in your field. Yes she would, and would be very grateful for the opportunity. My leasing agent is out this week with a new employee, and won't be in till next week. I am going to give you an employment application to fill out, and it will explain all you will have to do. Next question, how are your finances, do you have gas money, are you short of cash or hungry. No, not yet, and said she was using her savings and unemployment to get by for now. Ok, you will start next Monday and you will report to me, or either Mrs. Bradley, we will have something for you and I will discuss what we will pay you by the time you start. If we keep you it will be at least $40,000.00 a year. Is that acceptable, Ms. Jones. She said yes, and was thankful for the opportunity. I asked Joanne for an employment application.

I handed her the application and directed her to an open desk where she could fill it out. She seemed more aggressive than Ms. Washington, but I really hadn't sat and talked with her long enough to make such a conclusion as of yet. Joanne looked at me, and said the employee roster is starting to grow. I said think about the layout down the street, you enter, what do you see, a desk straight ahead, so you approach, and are asked, can I help you. Do you want to see if you qualify for a loan, do you want to buy a house, or sell one, or do you wish to rent an apartment. Someone has to direct you. Also we may need a sign in book, your name and reason for your visit. Or a sign directing you to sign in, and eventually someone will come. I prefer the personal contact, and then the receptionist can call whomever. Which one would you prefer if you were a customer? And besides based on her aggressiveness, she wants to get somewhere and why not with us. Joanne said we will see, wont we. Yes we will I replied. Joanne said a receptionist was a good idea, and said we would have a shakeout time and see how things worked out. I said that's the way things will be looking. Ms. Jones returned and sat down by my desk as she handed me her application. I looked it over; she had worked at a department store, and a Loan Company before the bank. Was thirty five years old, single, no children, had a masters in finance, and a bachelors in business, and was a certified public accountant. I asked her how come she hadn't mentioned the accounting. She wasn't sure about getting hired and just failed to mention it, but she had mentioned the tax preparation, figured that would have covered it. I said ok. I asked what goals she saw for herself. At the moment she was just concerned with survival. Just at that moment Mr. Hippies came in, and spoke to everyone. I introduced her to Hippies, and handed him her application, he looked it over and asked her some questions about taxes, and several what if questions, he handed her application back to me and said he could use the help in that area, and said since we were spread so thin, he would recommend hiring her. Then asked would she be working with him. I said do you need the help. He said in order to keep ahead of where we were and was headed, yes. I turned to Ms. Jones and said you will start Monday. I said to

Joanne, another desk to go in the office with Patricia. She said yes, and should we call instead of going. Yes, call Kent and add a desk to the order and we will have it installed, and call Kenny and let him know also. Joanne called Mr. Kent and I called Kenny. We informed each of the changes. That office would have a slight rearrangement. I said to Ms. Jones, thanks to Mr. Hippies you will be working for him until further notice, and welcome to Harcourt Realty Corp. I shook her hand and asked her if she had any questions. She said no, and I noticed her trying hard to maintain her composure. Hippies saw it to and shook her hand as her eyes started getting watery. I asked her if everything was all right. She said now it was, and thanked us very much for the opportunity, and asked what time Monday. I said nine o'clock. Said we wouldn't be sorry that we hired her. I thanked her and walked her to her car. I said to her, you might want to have some jeans and something to work in handy because we were due to move next week. She thanked me again as she departed.

I walked back in and said to Hippies you have an assistant, he thanked me and said he was glad that he didn't have to bring it to my attention. I said you must have prayed on it, because she just walked in the door. I asked if Joanne was ready for lunch. Said she was ready. As we left together I suggested we should go to Wong's. It had been a while since we had Chinese. We arrived and Mrs. Wong greeted us and led us to a booth, and said you special that are why I take you. I thanked her as Fawn came with the menus. I asked for some green tea, and Fawn shortly brought a pot of tea and cups. I knew what I wanted, and ordered the salmon lunch box with brown rice, and the sweet and sour soup. Joanne ordered the chicken lunch box, with fried rice, and miso soup. While we waited I pulled out my phone and checked on Victoria, she was busy vacuuming the house, and thought she was so at home. I turned the app off as our food came. We enjoyed our meal, and told Joanne about the Wong's expanding next month. She liked coming here and was happy they were staying. Said I made it real conducive to stay and they didn't want to move anyway. We finished and after I paid, read my fortune cookie, it said (you found the one to fill your life with joy), I passed it to Joanne and she read

it and laughed. She knew it and I shouldn't be surprised. Asked
her, if she was ready to return? She said lets go, as we departed and
returned to the office.

When we returned I checked that everything was going
smoothly and I headed down the street. I walked to the new office
and entered and found Brown instructing the office furniture
people on the desk placements. He saw me and came over. I know
you got the message about the office, he said yes and suggested we
go look, the furniture was still in boxes outside and said lucky I
called before they had set it up, I said we ordered another set the
same as the first one, he showed me how it would be positioned,
and there was more than enough room for a second, he called the
store and ordered the reverse set, so both would be on the same
wall with a six foot space between the two, facing the door, he
asked did I think and additional file cabinet would be needed. I
said that's a good question. I said order one and it would be on the
opposite wall, what about power to it, we walked over and he
showed me a floor plug and said no problem. Ok then. I didn't
know your sister worked for me. He said yes, and said that I was
good to my employees, and stated that she and Mr. Green were
dating. I kind of picked up on that Sunday. He wasn't sure how
serious they were. Just then Kenny walked in; he said I called just
in time for him to run a second cable. I thanked both of them for
their attention to detail. Said all the office suits should be
completed by tomorrow as far as the furniture was concerned, even
the additional desk setup. Kenny said this level would be set up
and should be up the following day, and after they set up the cubes
downstairs, he would have a crew in and everything would be
complete. Hector told them he would bring in a cleaning crew
starting tomorrow and they would work thru to Saturday and we
should be able to move in Monday at the latest and the foliage
would be here Thursday, and I should start packing up the old
office. I still had some business to take care of, but would do that.
We headed downstairs and I ran into Hector. Amigo he boomed,
he was glad to see me and said real soon. Said they were all
looking to finish everything by Sunday for sure. I said to all of
them I was impressed and satisfied that they took an interest in

doing such a fine job. Hector said I deserved it and glad I was his friend. I thanked him and all of them. I have to get back and get the troops ready. Shook all their hands and headed back.

When I returned, Joanne, Hippies, Phillips, Green, Fitz and Patricia was all there. Fitz said they only had two more complexes to cover and then he would be finished showing Patricia all the complex locations and introducing her to the managing agents. I asked for everyone's attention, Monday we will be moving, so pack up anything that you won't need till next week. Make sure there isn't anything in any of the desk, ok. And asked to speak with Patricia, I informed her that she would be sharing the office with a Ms. Jones who would be working for Hippies in regards to our taxes. She said that was great because it would be lonely by herself. I said at least you had the opportunity to choose the color and furniture. Ok that's done. I asked Joanne about the coffee pots and shredders, said the store would deliver when she called. I can't think of anything else. Any questions, and told Fitz he was in charge of clearing the old office of the desk and said he was going to send one to every location and even the one we were closing on. Also before I forget we should have two new agents tomorrow. Everybody said great. I looked at the clock it was close to four as I sat down and contemplated our move. Joanne handed me a letter from the association, what's this. She said the annual dinner. I opened the invitation, it was a month and a half away, requested a reply in three weeks. Joanne and I had attended, several times and we would this time, we could have a table, but needed eight people for a table. I asked her to canvas our employees, including the new agents, maybe we should have a show of force, we will not be on Front Street, and you know we were in the back every time we attended. She said that was because we didn't have a table. Yes that is correct, check and see, we will play it by ear. I went back to my thoughts and would leave at five with everyone else. I thought about how well I was organized and how much better things will be after the move. I had spared no expense and now I could push to new frontiers. I had my eyes on and old industrial site that was going on the block soon; it was slowly being surrounded by new development. But first I had the complex this week and sometime next week was there one of the Kasha condo closings.

Joanne woke me from my thoughts and said time to go boss. I looked at her and smiled. She said go home, Vicky is waiting on you. I said yes she is, as we all left. I said good night to everyone and turned out the lights and locked the doors. I looked back and thought how in this place I had built my company and small fortune. I would miss it, but just like and old car it was time for a trade in. Got in my car and headed home. When I arrived, I backed inside and closed the garage door and unlocked the back door and went inside. Vicky was waiting for me as she hugged and kissed me, holding me tight and said she was glad I was home. She went upstairs with me and hung my suit up after I emptied my pockets and asked if I wanted to take a shower. I welcomed it, she turned the water on and returned as I removed my underwear and socks and placed them in the hamper. She undressed and accompanied me in and bathed me as I stood under the shower head and let the warm water run down my body, held my head in her hands, and kissed me, we finished in the shower and dried off. She placed a towel on the bed and said she was going to give me a rub down. And said I looked tired. Told her I was, more mental than physical and it would be over soon. I laid on my back and fell asleep never knowing when she finished. When I woke, I was covered with a spread covering me and Victoria was right there next to me. She rubbed my head and kissed me. She had been here the whole time, and would never leave me. I reached over and wrapped my arm around and felt her as we looked at each other. She said it was time to get in the bed proper. I got up to pee and she had pulled the covers back and was in bed waiting for me. I got in and kissed her and she said go to sleep lover as she rubbed me to sleep again.

Twenty-seven

Wednesday: Day Twenty-seven.

When I awoke, Victoria was already awake; she had snuggled up behind me and was caressing my body. I slowly turned and put my arm around her, and we kissed and continued to touch and feel one another before we finally got up out of bed and went to freshen ourselves. When I came out the bathroom and looked at the clock and it was six fifteen. I liked getting up early and loved seeing the sun rising, and hear the birds singing. We put on our bathrobes, and Vicky said she wanted to fix me a decent breakfast and not a pizza. Said that she knew this week would be tiring on me, and hoped that all went well. She would be here to sooth my aching bones, and it didn't matter if we didn't make love just come home to her so she could hold me. I was the light of her life now and that's all that mattered to her. I hugged her tight and kissed her sweet lips, and told her, I love you. We went downstairs and started to prepare a wonderful breakfast for ourselves. I prepared the coffee and sat at the counter watching her, and soon she finished, fixed our plates and we sat and ate together. I said that this week was going to be busier than most. I had some interviews for today, and a closing tomorrow and we were starting to pack up to move. Told her I didn't want her to see the new office until after we moved and everything was completed. She understood and was happy for me. We finished eating and cleaned up the kitchen.

We went back upstairs and I brushed my teeth. When I came out of the bathroom, Victoria was lying on the bed and asked me to come hold her before I dressed. I laid next to her and we held each other. She began crying as she buried her head in my chest and I held her and rubbed her back under her robe. I felt her body and soon she stopped crying. She told me that they were tears of happiness, and for me to not be upset, as she kissed my face. She said the doctor had cured her and she was doing fine now, but would continue to use the lubrication. I said that's good news and I don't want you to be stressed. I said it's time for me to start getting ready, as we sat up still holding one another. I felt her breast and touched her nipple, then kissed each one, before I stood up and went to the closet. Told her, I would be wearing jeans all this week and part of next until we were finished with the move. She said that I would have a clean pair for everyday and didn't have to worry about that, and they would be pressed. I thanked her for being the most wonderful housekeeper ever; she laughed and said she was happy doing it. I said to her we would soon go to the court house and get a marriage license, because I didn't want her to get away. She came to where I was standing, threw her arms around me and said she didn't want to get away. Asked if she should be concerned because she knew, I liked women. I said not since you're in my life, you are the one I want to be with forever. I finished dressing, and wore a sports jacket; it's what I was accustomed to all these years, going from house to house, closings and all the associated things I had been involved in. I had to be comfortable. It was time to go and Vicky was waiting to walk me to the door. I went downstairs as she followed closely behind me, as I turned before opening the door, and looked at her; she was the most beautiful woman I had ever laid eyes on. I couldn't help but think how our paths crossed, but was happy beyond belief that it happened. I held her in my arms for a long moment and kissed her. She looked at me, and said I love you forever Mr. Charlie, and come back to me. I squeezed her one last time and kissed her forehead and thanked her for the breakfast. I turned and left, got in the car and opened the garage door and pulled out, closing it behind me as I drove away.

I arrived early and was the first one there. Put on the coffee pot and returned to my desk. Turned on my computer and pulled out the block diagram I had drawn the previous week. I tore the sheet of paper off the tablet, and drew a new one, this one was more detailed. Box one was I, box two was Joanne, then boxes three and four were Hippies and Fitz, under Hippies was two boxes, one was taxes, the other was legal, under Fitz's box, were all the different management companies I had created for the different complexes, there were nine. I wrote down the names of each, each contained two complexes each, with the exception of one that handled the smaller assets, such as multi-unit standalone buildings, there were forty one, if they were all together, would constitute a small complex. No leasing agents there, Fitz handled these directly. Rents from all were sent directly to banks, and they sent us via computer the payment records, and charged a nominal fee, it was simpler and more cost effective. I grew my company, bit by bit, and Joanne was here holding down the fort, she had a broker's license and a management license as well. She had some idea, how much money the company made. But she dealt mostly with the listing and closings, and managing the agents. She knew I had a few complexes, and had only really paid attention when I brought Fitz into the office for just the management side. He had a management license and was a sales associate. Hippies knew all, even the investments, because he did the taxes. Overall monthly income was about $1 million a month, then you take out for, taxes, and insurance, there were deductions for improvements and maintenance. That was one of the reasons for multiple companies. And they all came under the name of my holding company, Heaven Holdings, then that came under Harcourt Realty, so if you looked up Harcourt Realty you would only see this office and the real-estate transactions that were made. That's how we stayed a small looking outfit. And that was for the residential properties only. I was in the process of creating two new management companies for the commercial side. One would be for office space, the other for commercial, and there were several strip malls, and some were larger ones with twenty or more stores each. I was going to separate these for tax purposes, it would give me more leverage when buying more property. Ok Hippies and Fitz would each have an assistant, good. Not too big and not too small. By the time I finished with that, I shredded the old paper, folded the new and placed it in my pocket. I looked and it was a few minutes before nine. Joanne should be here soon, as I went and poured myself some coffee, came back just as Joanne, walked in followed by Patricia, Green and Phillips.

I greeted everyone. Just about everyone went and got some coffee. We sat around and talked as Joanne and Green started to put some boxes together, and started packing files along with Patricia. I took a couple boxes and was placing my personal files in the box. I placed all our blank forms in one; knew I was going to need a couple. Things had calmed down by the time Mrs. Newman and Hartman came in and I said welcome ladies, and asked them to have a seat at the desks up front. Mr. Fitz came in and spoke to everyone. He said Pat and him had two places left and would see what transpired today before deciding to go. I spoke to our new agents, asked that they fill out our forms, and when they finished I would speak to them. Hippies came in and said good morning to all, he turned to me after seeing Joanne and Green placing files in boxes, and said he was all packed up. I said you never unpacked. Shortly Mrs. Hartman and Newman had finished their informational forms, I asked them to pull up chairs, and moved back so there was more room as I looked over their applications and made copies of their licenses, including drivers and said, welcome, and asked for everyone's attention. I introduced them to all, and explained their positions, then to Mr. Green and Phillips who would be there managing brokers. They appeared to be happy with the decision to join our reality. I asked if they didn't mind taking a walk, and said they would love to. Both were in there fifties and dressed very well, and were very attractive. I said when we move you will be dealing with Mr. Phillips and Green, but my door will always be open to anyone in the origination, as I took them up the street to show them where the new office was located; I didn't want them to get lost.

When we reached the corner, we crossed the street and walked across the parking lot and entered the building as I showed them where their desk would be located. Workmen were setting up the cubes and installing the furniture, they said it was very spacious, and looked at the size of the cubes, a large desk with a comfortable chair and three chairs in front of each for clients. I showed them the washrooms, conference room and the lunch room; they said they were highly impressed. We rode up on the elevator and I showed them where everyone's office would be. We soon rode back downstairs as Hector came up and shook my hand. Then I asked the ladies to excuse me a moment as Watson and Brown approached. Brown said we could start moving in, all the furniture was installed upstairs, and the furniture people had finished the two lower offices as well, all that was left, were the cubes on the real estate side. Kenny said all the computers upstairs were in and operational. And downstairs was being installed as the installers finished with the cubes. Brown said the other furniture was here and Hector had people working on that now. Kenny asked when I got back to the old office, to shut the system down so he could remove the server. Hector said he would send a crew to move our files, and it would all be done today, and we could start occupying the new space. Said his cleaning crew had finished with upstairs, and we could move in. Brown said the plants would be here tomorrow. I said great, asked if there was anything else. Brown said after we were moved he would show me the generator and the other building equipment. I asked about the sign out front. He said today, and he was having one to place in the window down the street informing the public that we had moved and where to. I like that you have covered all the bases. I thanked them then walked over to where Newman and Hartman were standing, I said ladies when you come back after today, come here. They looked at each other and said they were impressed as we walked past the receptionist island. We walked and they asked various questions. I answered most of what they asked. When we returned they thanked me. I asked them to wait until next week to come in so we would be a little better organized, they said they would. I shook their hands and they departed.

Ms. Brown was here now. I got everyone's attention, and said we are moving today and to start packing up. A crew will arrive shortly to move everything. I turned to Hippies and said we only needed the paperwork for tomorrow. He said calm down; he had all of what we needed in his briefcase. I called Fitz over and asked him to come with us tomorrow, he said he planned to. I turned to Joanne, which leaves you in charge of everything until we get back. She said no problem and don't worry about a thing, she had it covered. Everyone packed and labeled their boxes, just as a truck pulled up and five men entered with Hector, he announced they were here move all we wanted moved. They had hand trucks and in ten minutes, there wasn't a box anywhere, just empty desks. I went back in after making sure all the computer terminals were off and powered down the server. I poured out the coffee, and turned off the machine. Joanne called the store and arraigned for the shredders and coffee pots to be delivered. Everyone was almost gone, when Louis Brown came in with the sign for the front window, followed by Watson. Said he was going to do a quick disconnect, and had two people with him and they were going to remove all the electronics. I said I had just shut down the server. He asked for our passwords so he could transfer files from the old computers and clean the hard drives, getting it all done today, and would stay until it was done. It only took a little more than half hour and there wasn't anything but empty desk. Kenny took everything, telephones, printers, and the shredders, the coffee pot also. I had seen Joanne take the coffee and sugar and other stuff. I walked through the entire office, looked around, and had shed a tear when Joanne walked up behind me, tapped me on the shoulder. I turned around and she saw I was having a moment and hugged me and said time to move on, it was a good run, but it's time to go. I turned out the lights and locked the door. I turned around and looked at the new sign in the window behind the letters painted on the glass, Harcourt Realty. She was waiting for me, took my hand gave me a hug and said we're starting a new day Mr. Charlie.

We each drove our cars down the street and there were signs, employee parking, and the on one side of the building they were labeled, with reserved signs placed in front of them, directly across the sidewalk in front of each spot, with our names on them. I parked in the first one, Joanne parked in the second, Hippies in the third and Fitz, in the fourth. Then, there were a signs that said guest on the other rows, there were three rows of parking on this side, and this was a single row and all the spaces were reserved, and behind us was the double row with a small concrete walk between us and the others. On the other side of the building was a double row, and in front parking for about twenty autos. I got out and waited for Joanne, when she got to the side walk. I took her hand and we entered together, when we entered mostly everyone had gathered at the entrance, and began to clap and cheer, it was a little overwhelming, and had to gather my composure. I looked at Joanne and she was almost in tears also, we just hugged each other as tears came to our faces. Everyone cheered us. I thanked them as we went to the elevator and the ovation died down. We went up and got off; I went with Joanne to her new office. Her desk had been set up, the computer with double 32 inch screens were to one side, and the other furniture was arraigned, and made a nice seating area, kind of like a living room with the wall mounted television. She hugged me again, and said we did it didn't we. I said yes, it wasn't easy, but it paid off. She said I want to see yours; it wasn't much difference except the wall units were larger along with the desk, same twin screens, television on the wall, and the security monitor in a wall cabinet behind my desk. We walked around and found Hippies sitting at his desk admiring it and the furniture. He looked up at us and came and hugged us both. I said let's check on Fitz, he was sitting with his face in his hands, when he looked up, he had tears in his eyes, as he stood. I had never seen him this emotional, he came and shook my hand and hugged me, then Joanne. Hippies said what about me, and Fitz hugged him also. He said that this was beyond what he had ever expected. Fitz was a man of steel, it was one reason Joanne and I had said he was the perfect person to deal with renters, he was hard core. I said it would not have been possible if we hadn't worked as a team. I thanked them and said lets unpack. Joanne said the store deliveries should be here by now and probably were on the loading dock. I said you each have a shredder coming and a coffee machine if you want. And Kenny Watson will bring your old computers; he needs you to open the systems with your passwords so he can transfer your files. I said to Fitz that Pat would be working for him so those last two complexes you can take her to next week or whenever. I need you to get organized here and then we can resume a full operation on Monday. I want you all to come with me so you will know where she is located. We all walked around the corner to where Pat and Ms. Jones will be located. Patricia was busy unpacking her stuff. There were two large desks with matching shelving units in the extra-large office. Hippies said great. Come this way as I showed them the conference room, the table was set up, there was a large screen television for presentations, and a floor cabinet, podium, and bulletin board and dry marker boards. There was a place for a coffee machine, then we went to the lunch room,

it was spacious, with large comfortable tables and chairs, another
floor cabinet, with a marble top and a double sink, two spacious
wall cabinets, with twin microwaves mounted underneath and a
place for a coffee pot and a refrigerator with ice dispenser in the
door. I said to Joanne when the coffee pots come put one down
stairs and one in the conference room and one in here and we will
place the others in storage, until someone wants one of their own.
She said that made more sense.

I had to get my files moved and would see them all later. I went
to my office and, Louis Brown was waiting and Kenny was setting
up the old computer for a file transfer. He wanted to talk about
keys. I said ok, when everything was completed, he had made
arrangements to replace all the locks, since all the upper offices
had locking doors, left one key on each desk and they were
labeled, he handed me a ring, it had a key for all the doors upstairs,
and the two offices downstairs, and including the storage rooms,
the elevator and all the interior doors, said the washrooms didn't
have locks. Friday he would have a lock smith replace all the
exterior locks, and wanted to know, how many keys for the front
door. I said ten. He said when that was complete he would give
them all to me. I asked him to show me the generator. We went
down stairs, there was a door across from the loading dock, he
unlocked it and we went down a set of stairs into the basement. I
said I didn't know there was a basement, he said at first he didn't
either and pointed out the pumps for the hydraulic elevators, then
we walked toward the rear, and he unlocked a door and we entered
a room, and there stood a natural gas powered diesel generator,
you could see where the main power for the building entered
underground and the switching gear was located here also. Wow I
said. He said it's so silent when it runs it amazing. I said for a
furniture store they had gone to extremes. He agreed with me. We
walked out, and the door locked as it closed, said it's isolated from
the rest of the building, and said when it comes on all the outside
lights come on if it's cloudy outside and makes the place look like
and island of light. We exited the basement and returned upstairs.
Said he had other things to check on. I thanked him and we parted.
I returned to my office and Kenny had finished placing my

computer files into the new computer and said he would destroy all the hard drives and dispose of the rest thru his second hand computer store. Fine I told him and he went to finish the installations in the remaining offices.

I sat in my new chair; it was more comfortable than when Joanne and I shopped for the furniture and equipment. Looking around and noticed a sliding door and went over and opened it, and it was a closet for your coats, it blended in so well you wouldn't know it was there, great. Sat back down and the computer was on, checked my files, and all had been transferred. We all had lost track of time, looked at the clock and we hadn't been to lunch, it was close to one. I shut off my computer and went to Joanne's office. She had finished and was sitting on the couch in her office looking up at the sun light as it played on the walls. I knocked and said we haven't eaten; she looked at her watch and said no we haven't. I said let's get something light. We checked on Hippies and Fitz, and then Pat. We all decided to go together. Kenny had done all our computers so we were straight. We went in my car and Hippies, and headed to Wong's. We arrived and walked in. Just in time for the end of lunch and there weren't many people, Mrs. Wong seated us all at one long table. We ordered and everyone said they had been so caught up in moving, and it having happened so suddenly, but not unexpected that they forgot they were hungry. Mrs. Wong took our orders, and said, we her special people. Our food came shortly and we all ate, we really didn't know how hungry we were. We enjoyed our food and each other and when the table was cleared and our fortune cookies came, I couldn't wait to open mine. Tore into the wrapper and ate half, it read (you will be successful in your endeavors) I passed it to Joanne; she read it and said you are. Then she asked do you print these? Why I asked. She said they all seem to suit you every time. It seems that way. Everyone was ready to go, I paid and we departed. Mrs. Wong said do come back, you know we will as we headed out.

When we returned, Joanne and I surveyed the downstairs progress, all the cubes were installed and the furniture crew was cleaning up, and some of Hector's people were vacuuming the carpets, Kenny's people were unpacking the new computers and hooking them up. Joanne and I checked out the conference room, the television was installed; the table and chairs were in place, it had been cleaned and ready as we walked to the lunch room, it was ready also, and mirrored the one upstairs, only slightly smaller. I checked the wash rooms, the only thing was, there were no towels or toilet paper, I pointed that out to Joanne, and she said there was some we brought from the old office. We are going to have to get some, she said noted, and would place and order with the bulk store and have it delivered, with soap, then I noticed the liquid soap dispensers, said to her just like when you move into a new house, yes she replied. We found the shipment of shredders and coffee pots, there was a hand truck that you could use like a cart. I readjusted it and I placed four shredders and two pots on it and took it up on the freight elevator. Joanne came with me and said you can get a car in hear can't you. Sure seems like it, I replied when the elevator stopped. We got off and I dropped a shredder at every office except mine and then helped Joanne unpack the coffee pots in the lunch room, she said she was going to get the sugar and coffee, and detergent and set up the lunch room, clean the new pots and brew us some. I said by the time I come back if you find the toilet paper I will put some in the bathrooms. I unpacked the shredders, set them in the offices and left the operators manuals on each desk. I finished, and went down to get one for myself, and low and behold, there was a door bell at the dock, it rang and I pressed the button for the overhead door, it opened and a delivery man was standing there with a delivery of paper products, ten fifty roll cases of toilet paper and ten of paper hand towel just as Mr. Brown walked up. He signed for the delivery, and there was a case of dish washing detergent and ten cases of liquid hand soap and four cases of bleach and liquid pine cleaner, two buckets with ringers, four mops and four cases of paper coffee cups. He said most would be in the storage closets, located between the wash rooms, and the rest in the main storage room. He said nothing had slipped past and suggested that I let him finish. I said yes sir, and took the hand truck with a shredder to my office. Unpacked it and collected the empty boxes on my way back to the dock and took them down on the freight elevator. Brown was still down on the dock and said he would take care of all the trash and had a truck coming tomorrow. I thanked him for being so thorough. I returned to the lunch room and Joanne was still there and had brewed a pot of coffee. I said you don't have to order any paper and soap, Mr. Brown has taken care of that also. She said well, that's a relief. We used the cups from the old office and we decided to try out the new chairs, they were very comfortable. Told Joanne I was going to get a marriage license next week. She asked where were we going to have the ceremony, I said the court house was as good a place as any. Said she was happy for me and Victoria and would like to be there for us. You will be the first to know. Hippies and Fitz came in, said they knew it wouldn't be long before we brewed some coffee, and shortly Patricia joined us, and said she was looking for everyone.

Pat said it was going to take a little while to get adjusted from the other office where you could see everyone at one time, even with the open glass walls and door. I asked if everyone found there closet, Hippies said he hadn't yet and Fitz said he was very surprised when he found it. I was going to check on the progress being made, before leaving while I have you all here. The outside door locks will be changed when all the work is complete, and everyone here will have a key and that should be no later than Friday. I went down stairs and took the stairs so I could see the beauty of the building and when the foliage comes it will really be beautiful. The furniture people were finished and had removed there tools and the cartons the cubes came in, Hectors people had finished the cleaning and Kenny's people were finishing up with the instillations and more than half the screens were on, and installing the software. I walked to the lunch room and Green and Phillips were sitting with Ms. Brown, talking, one had went to the store and bought a case of soda and placed it in the fridge. They said they liked the automatic ice dispenser in the fridge. I said my people deserve the best. They stood and said they would do their best to make me proud. I said that you need to check on the progress being made you might want to get yourselves ready and enter your credentials and create your pass words, the system is the latest. They said ok and went out. Kenny was at one of the terminals as I said these are the people that will be working down here. He said oh good and asked them to pull up a chair as he informed them of the difference from the ones they had used previous as I returned upstairs. It being a Wednesday we were used to staying to six, I looked at my watch and it was five thirty. Everyone had dispersed and was in their offices arranging there desk and furniture. I checked the phones and called Hippies and he answered, said I was just checking thing out, Kenny had typed up a list of the extensions, and he had left one on every desk. We found complimentary desk calendars on every desk, they were the largest I had ever seen and you could write on them for days. The key boards were wireless along with the mouse, and in a box I found a desk plaque with my name on it. I said Mr. Brown deserves a bonus, and Watson, and Hector also. I had great people and knew great people. Walked to Joanne's office and asked her if she found the box, said she just did and was surprised. I was also. Mr. Brown thought of everything. I asked her if she was ready to go home. She was and needed a warm bath, this had been one hell of a day, and we were looking forward to it, but will be back tomorrow. Hippies and I have the closing along with Fitz, yes she said, so let me go coordinate with them, and then I am leaving. So good evening to you and see you tomorrow, we walked to Fitz's office and said see you tomorrow at nine and we will go together, he said he was on his way out. Ok tomorrow then I checked with Hippies, he was ready to go. See you at nine, ok and good night. Kenny had my people's attention as Brown walked up. I'm leaving, he said that was good and said he would lock up, and said one other thing, besides the lock changes, there was an alarm system and we could change the code then. Said he was going to lock up and had gotten all the keys from Hectors people, and Hector still had a set and Watson and himself. Said for me to go home and get some rest. I was more than happy with the way he had handled things. We shook hands, and I prepared to leave as Joanne and Patricia exited the elevator and walked around the receptionist station. We all walked out together, as I said good night ladies, and we all headed home.

I went straight home, and when I arrived it was seven, backed inside and couldn't wait to take a shower. Vicky was in the living room and came running when she saw me drive up, and hugged me and kissed me. Said I looked tired, but happy, I said we moved today as expected it but it was still a surprise. So many people put there all into it. Said you know why, don't you, you are a good person and people don't mind going the extra mile for you. Told me to go upstairs and undress and get in the shower and she would fix my favorite drink and be right up, when I came out she would rub me down. I said thank you sweetheart, kissed her and went upstairs as she went downstairs to the basement. I undressed and took a shower, sat and relaxed as the warm water ran over me. Soon Vicky came in with me and we washed each other and rinsed off, and dried each other off, she pulled the covers back as I sat on the couch and sipped my drink. I thanked her for being so attentive, as I sipped my drink she knelt and rubbed my feet, then she stood and oiled herself and sat in my lap, and I applied oil to her back, when I finished she sat next to me and waited for me to finish my drink. After I finished she said lay on your back, which I did as she massaged my body starting with my feet and working her way to my head before having me turn over and doing my backside, rubbing me to sleep before waking me and making me get under the covers.

Twenty-eight
Thursday: Day Twenty-eight.

I woke, and just laid in bed thinking, the move was over, but didn't know if everything was set up the way I wanted. I thought that it shouldn't be difficult now. I had a really simple operational format; and besides we just changed locations, more room and a more conducive work environment with more centralized services. I really hoped the move was worth the expense and would bring in more business since we were more visible. I turned and found Victoria awoke just looking at me, she smiled and reached out and touched my face, just as she had done so many mornings. She came closer and kissed me, and said good morning my love. I kissed her and said good morning sweetie as we hugged and held each other. I caressed her body and sent spasms 'through her as she began holding me even tighter. Told her I must get started because I have a closing today. She relented and reluctantly said ok, as I climbed out of bed. She held out her hand and I pulled her up with me as we went to go freshen up. She would fix us some breakfast, because I shouldn't leave without eating first. I agreed with her, so we put on our bathrobes and went downstairs to prepare something to eat.

She began her usual morning routine, as I fixed the coffee. She prepared sausage with onions, eggs and toast with cheese melted on top. She had gained four pounds and was beginning to feel much better now. I told her you look better and your skin has a glow to it without even being oiled. She had noticed it also but wasn't going to stop caring for her skin, and said it was most important to her. I said that's what attracted me and you are naturally beautiful and now you belong to me, as she placed a plate of food on the counter before me. We sat and ate together as I thanked her for giving me the massages the past couple of nights. They had done wonders for me and I will make it up to you. She said that wasn't necessary and there wasn't anything I had to make up for because I had done so much for her. That she owed me for everything and had done all she could ever hope and dream for. She would love and care for me, and keep me healthy and happy, and be at my side and support me through thick and thin. If I lost everything I owned, as long as we were together it was all that mattered to her, loving me was more important than money or possessions, and hoped we would have a long life together as one. I had just finished eating and was drinking my coffee when she said that to me. All I could do was stand and hold her and I cried, really cried. No one had ever said words as meaningful as those to me ever. There were people who I liked, or cared for, but none could carry the love I could feel and hear in her voice. The greatest possession anyone can have is the love of another. I held her tight for several minutes, before I looked into those big beautiful brown eyes; they were wet with tears, as I kissed her sweet lips. We finally released each other, and said to her, that she gave me the greatest reason for living, and told her, I love you Victoria, and thank you for being here. We cleaned up the kitchen together in silence, and when we finished went hand in hand back upstairs.

I was preparing to dress, when Victoria lay on the bed, opened her robe, and said doctor, doctor, please doctor, will you look at me, I turned and looked, said oh, my patient needs attention as I walked over, and asked her, what seems to be the problem. She said it needed attention. I looked her all over and touched her breast, gently feeling her nipples as they stood up at attention with my gentle touch, and slowly rubbed her belly, as I moved my hand down to her open thighs. I looked at her sweet vagina; the clit was starting to protrude, as I then went to the head of the bed to retrieve the ABC jelly and returned. Saying before I administer this, I must examine it more closely as I laid between her legs and blew on it and she screamed, she started to pant as I took my fingers and parted her vaginal lips and then licked her clit and circled it with my tongue all around as it came out to it full length, and placed all of it in my mouth and clamped down with my lips and tickled it with my tongue, as I moved my hands to hers holding her down. She violently erupted screaming with pleasure as I held her hands and raised her ass up off the bed as I continued to lick and suck her clit and lick around the inside of her pussy lips. I held her for several minutes until she lay still and breathless, before stopping and crawling up next to her and wrapping my arms around her quivering body and holding her tight. I held her for several long minutes until her breathing became normal, then I sat up and liberally applied the ABC jelly, and laid back next to her with my hand still between her legs as I massaged her as she moaned and exploded again. She jerked and had wild spasms, as I removed my hand and she slowly began to calm down. I sat up and closed up her robe, as she lay there unable and willing to move.

I went and brushed my teeth, did a quick shave with my electric and came out and prepared to dress. She was still lying on the bed after I had dressed. I grabbed her extended hand and pulled her up; she stood and wrapped her arms around me, looked up into my eyes and said nothing as she buried her head into my chest. I led her to the stairs and asked if she was all right. Said in a weak voice that, she was more than all right now, we hadn't made love in several days and she needed my touch more than ever. We went downstairs, and she walked me to the garage door. I unlocked the door, turned and kissed her. She said come home to her, she would always be waiting for me. I kissed her again, turned and entered the garage and got into my car and opened the door, and pulled out, closing it behind me as I drove down the driveway.

I had awakened early and so when I reached the office it was about a quarter after eight, parked in my designated parking space. I was the first to arrive, sat a moment and looked around before getting out, decided to walk around my new building. It seemed to be so much larger than when I first looked at it. It took a good ten minutes for me to make the complete circuit around since I had stopped several times to look at the different features I hadn't noticed before, there was still a large dumpster next to the loading dock door in the rear and it was half full of empty cardboard boxes that had been flattened to allow for more waste to be placed inside along with some discarded building materials. I came back around and unlocked the front door and entered, wondered where the light switches were, and then I remembered there was a key pad just inside on the left side and Brown had given me a code to enter. I had one minute to enter it, or the alarm system would go off, he had tested it, and it was very loud, had sirens on the outside of the building that made it obvious something was wrong. He also said the fire alarm had a different sound, and had a recorded voice that said fire, please evacuate, he had sent me a video of when he tested it, along with starting the backup generator. When I entered the pin number on the key pad the lights would all come on automatically. I looked up and they did. He had also said for the size of the building with the solar panels on the roof and sun sensors inside, that I probably would spend about the same amount on electricity as I did at the old office. I checked the front door, it had locked automatically. Another thing he had mentioned to me, which was amazing, but he said was a safety, the front doors could be set to unlock and lock at a given time, suggested we program it after the outside locks had been changed. Said he would feel more secure with the locks being changed given how many people had been given sets of the original, keys and copies could have been made. I agreed with him. Thought how amazing and into the future we had just come, but with what I invested with the new computers and televisions we needed hi tech security.

I took the elevator upstairs, stepped off and stood looking down before unlocking my office and then going to put on a pot of coffee. The new coffee machine was much larger and had a larger capacity than the old one we used before and it brewed so much better. Joanne had showed me just what to do yesterday, so I knew what to do now. I checked the washrooms and the paper and soap had been installed, checked a stall and it was ready to go. Walked out and looked in the custodial closet, opened the door and found a floor sink on one side, a new mop bucket and mops mounted on the wall over the sink, shelves on the other side filled with supplies, and a note was taped to the door, stating extra supplies were in the main storage closet. It was where the office supplies were to be kept. I walked around until I soon found it, looked inside and found what had been delivered, and the boxes of blank office forms and paper we used. Closed the door and went back to the lunch room and poured myself a cup of coffee. Walked out and entered my office, turned on my computer, while I waited for it to come up, I turned around and opened the cabinet where the security monitor was located, found it, and it had a pull out shelf, with a key board and a mouse ball. When I rolled the ball, the screen came to life. With ten boxes, each representing a camera;

there was a paper in a clear protective sheet, with instructions on operating the system. I followed the instructions; it was very simple, similar to the one I had at home, only with more cameras. If I punched a number, and hit enter, that particular camera would show on the monitor, or could enter several different numbers, two at a time or four, split screen, there was a list on the back of what number for each camera and location. I played around and soon saw Joanne and Patricia as they arrived, followed them to the front door, watched as Joanne unlock the door and enter, the sheet explained how to switch to the internal cameras. I did so, and watched them in the lobby, and while they were in the elevator, and when they got off, and as they approached my office. They stepped in and we greeted one another, I said the coffee is made, and asked Patricia to come in and have a seat. I explained about Ms. Jones and her qualifications and Hippies recommendation, I don't know if you will be working with Fitz all the time but someone other than him had to know what his responsibilities were. You having some law under your belt and continuing to go to school in that area will probably have you working for Hippies sometimes also. So between the two of you both you will probably be working for Hippies and Fitz and just wanted to let you know because both positions are new and never existed before. Said that she understood, and was glad she wouldn't be in the office all by herself. I said as a matter of fact let me call her and have her come in today if possible. Patricia thanked me again for the opportunity. Joanne had arrived early, and Green and Phillips hadn't yet arrived. I picked up the phone as I reached for my new employee chart and dialed Ms. Jones at home. She picked up on the second ring. Said good morning, and asked if she was available and could she start today. Said she would be here shortly. I informed her we had moved and gave her the address and asked her to report to Joanne, thanked her and hung up. I used the phone and called Joanne and she answered, informed her that I asked Ms. Jones to start today. Mr. Green and Phillips walked in; we spoke and I directed them to Joanne's office. Hippies entered followed by Fitz, we greeted one another and Hippies said the closing was scheduled for eleven. I said ok and said they had a few things to do before we departed. Hippies said we could leave at ten thirty; it wasn't that far away, I said ok. I looked at the inside cameras and Joanne was downstairs with Green and Phillips and Ms. Brown, they were where the receptionist would be, there was a computer station there, looks like they are trying to decide where to sit, well they will get it together.

I called Ms. Washington, she picked up on the third ring and I asked if they were finished with their cleaning up the old office, she stated that all the records she was going to bring were packed and ready, said she was going to call the movers and make arrangements and was intending to call me today. Told her that we had moved, and she could have them sent over now and that there was a loading dock and they could be left there, and that she should come in also and that her office was waiting for her. And asked her to tell her dad that he should call me later today and we could complete our business arrangement. She thanked me and said she would be in before she hung up. Time seemed like it was flying as Fitz had done his walk through of the property Tuesday and Pat had been along with him, so that part was out of the way. Hippies and Fitz came in together and said time to go boss. I closed up the security cabinet, turned off my computer and we walked out together. When we went downstairs and let Joanne know we were gone, just as a person walked in, stopped us and said they were looking for a home. I asked if they had been pre-approved. They said yes, and took them over to see Ms. Brown and asked her to help them; they thanked me as I continued with Hippies and Fitz. Fitz said he would drive and we piled in the SUV he had chosen. It wasn't long before we arrived, and went inside and sat in the waiting room until the sellers party arrived. Then we all went into the room where the closer was located and documents were passed back and forth and the check given to the seller and shortly after the transaction was completed. We soon departed.

Fitz said since the complex was completed with all the upgrades to include individual heat, and we should consider selling them as condos. He spoke to the leasing agent; he didn't reside on the premises, and offered them a unit so like all our other complexes someone would be available 24/7. Said they were willing to accept our offer but he had told them they would have to wait and see what the big boss decided on doing. I said ok little boss. He laughed and said that's funny. Fitz asked how soon it would be before I came and looked around, said everything was completed and was ready to be leased or sold. I said it's the last planned purchase for this year I hope for right now as far as I can see but you know how things can change. I asked about occupancy. Fitz said the contractor had just finished the last building and was one of several he and Patricia had inspected. The contractor didn't want to be stuck with the materials when he found out they were going to sell because they were losing money. Only one building was half occupied. I said ok, you know what's to follow. He said I can only guess I know what you're going to do. Yes you do, it's a very nice area, and there is a housing shortage all around there and we were going to have a move in special. You know I will look on the weekend and check this out before making a decision. I asked Fitz what he thought about selling it as condos. He said they were condos all along, which the tax index numbers were already in place from the original builders, and we would do so much better selling them as such, because the taxes would be higher than if it was built as apartments. We would have to charge $1500.00 a month or more for the studio units alone because they were so large inside to be profitable. Said I will definitely look this week end and decide. I needed keys; he said he had the master key to the recreational building where the office was located, and the key box where all the keys were located, said they were all individually labeled. I asked him to please give me a set. Ok boss.

When we returned, Phillips was seated on the receptionist platform, and being funny said, can I help you gentlemen, and do please sign in. I like that approach, so this is what you all decided on. He said yes everything he needed was right here, computer terminal, phone, and intercom and could see everyone entering and could work from here, thanks to the network that was in place. Stated they had decided to see how well this works out and avoid having a receptionist. I said that sounds very good. Green was in the first cube, and was on the phone and Ms. Brown was talking to a young couple in the second. Good, I thought as Hippies and Fitz returned upstairs to their offices. I turned around and Louis Brown was showing several men where the foliage was to be placed and I could see several trucks near the loading dock. I proceeded to my office and a light on my phone let me know I had a call, picked up and it was Kenny. He asked if we had any problems, not so far, said he was in when I was out and had left a bill for his services and a release for the old office and computer equipment. I asked if he wanted an electronic transfer, he said that would be fine, ok then, and I will mail you a release. He said ok and we hung up. I pulled out my phone and checked on Vicky, she was putting the ironing board away, I paned through the other cameras, including the outside ones before I turned off. I did the electronic transfer to Kenny, his was probably going to be the lowest, it was $31,575.32, that included all the equipment and services, and what he was going to pay the crew he had employed. Next was the office furniture, including the other furniture. All together it came to $77,770.41, well worth it. Then Hectors bill including his sons, and he would pay them all from his account and for the carpet, paint, tile and all the other items came to $255,000.00. I had Hectors account info and paid him electronically, and the others. Mr. Brown had yet to send one. I looked up and it seemed like trees moving around. I walked out just as a person opened my door accompanied by Mr. Brown and they wheeled in a massive palm, it was beautiful and so was the pot, they placed it out of the way and it enhanced the beauty of the entire space. I followed them out and Brown said they were just finishing up; the offices were the very last. I could see it had taken four trucks to bring all the plants as he went downstairs with them on the freight elevator. I looked around and it looked like the inside of and arboretum. There was foliage everywhere, evenly spaced and there were long horizontal boxes with shorter plants between the taller ones around the atrium. Joanne came out after they left her office and said wow, how beautiful. We went downstairs and looked around and the plants gave the space a very warm and inviting feeling.

Oh she said Ms. Jones is here. I went back upstairs and to their office and Ms. Jones and Patricia; they were arranging the furniture after the plants arrived. I said ladies; they said that they were just finishing with the new arrangement. I said well, let me speak to you both, I asked Ms. Jones if it was ok to call her by her first name, she said yes of course and please call her Anne, she preferred using it. Said I had spoken to Pat earlier and this was a shake out over the way we operated before now. I said you two complement each other's talents and you might be working for our leasing agent some time also, depending where we need your talents, just wanted to let you know you won't be doing taxes all the time. She understood and was thankful to be here and have a job and would not disappoint us, said if she does something wrong do not hesitate to let her know. She shook my hand, and said she had prayed that we would keep her. After I get some things out the way I would have a staff meeting. And next week the mortgage person Ms. Washington would be here and her office would be downstairs. Anne asked if it was Samantha Washington. I said yes it is. She smiled and said she knew her well and was one of the most thorough and competent loan persons she had ever met. That her loans were so good that maybe only one in a hundred were ever rejected, she was the best, and all the people she had met since being here were the most competent group she had ever seen in one place. I thanked her for her support and said you two enjoy your office. Before I leave, do you like the washrooms? They looked at each other and tried to speak at the same time, said they found hard to leave. I thanked them and left and walked to the wash room and washed my hands, and returned to my office. I could look across and see Joanne's office now with the plants, and it was a wall of green leaves, it was wonderful.

The phone rang and I put it on speaker, it was Joanne and she asked about lunch, I said ok. Said she was going to get Pat and Anne and would meet me downstairs. I walked downstairs using the stairs as they came down on the elevator. What a cute group as they exited. Joanne said lunch was on her today. She drove and I sat in front with her, where are we going? Just sit back and see was her answer. When she parked we were at the Roman Gardens. We got out, and I opened the door for Pat who was sitting behind me. We entered and waited to be seated, and were soon shown to a comfortable booth. I was seated next to Pat, as we were handed the menus. I decided on the tomato chicken and pasta with a light cream garlic sauce, a Caesar salad, and a large glass of Pinot Noir. We waited for the waiter, he returned with water with a slice of lemon, he began taking our orders and after the ladies ordered, I gave him mine. He collected the menus and departed. Asked Joanne how things were working out downstairs. Great so far and didn't think we would need a receptionist. I said well, since we had three new employees for now. I explained about the locks and the key pad, and when the office closed, it would be closed, only the six of us would have the code. She said very well. I said we might want to think about the hours, but saw no reason for a change. She said Ms. Brown had picked up the clients, the ones who walked in as we were walking out and a couple who came in later. I said very well. Anne knows Ms. Washington, and said she is more than competent. Anne explained her contact with her and how efficient she was. Joanne said what about the complex. I would check it out over the weekend and decide if it would be a rental or sell it as condos. Fitz says it has a club house where if you are resident, you can hold parties. That sounds nice, what's the cost of rent? I said $1500, a month, to start; it has one, two, three bed room units and I think studios. And it's why I must do a look see. The area is hot and there is a shortage in the area of rentals and condos. It has individual heat and air, and you pay your own water, some units have two baths. I am leaning towards rental, but condos might work out better, since Fitz said the tax numbers have been issued. Maybe I could have you girls do some research and give me some recommendations. I asked Patricia what she thought when she went with Fitz. She said that she wasn't sure, but they were really nice, large and very modern and were more like homes and kind of thought it would be better to sell as condos, because they seemed too nice to rent and knew renters didn't take care of apartments like they should.

Our food came and the conversation ended somewhat. We ate and everyone enjoyed the food. When we finished the table was cleared, and were asked if we wanted dessert, we all declined. Joanne paid. I thanked her for the treat. We exited the restaurant and I opened the door for Pat as she sat behind me again for the trip back. Joanne said it was time someone treated me, after all I had done for everyone else. Joanne I really want to thank you. We returned and exited the auto and I again opened the door for Pat. We entered and dispersed. I walked around the lower level and looked at all the plants, Louis Brown approached and said the locksmith was here and changing the lock tumblers. They were special and he would make the keys in his truck. There were only two to be made, the lock for the loading dock door and overhead door switch would be keyed the same. The front would be different. He said we could change the entry code anytime. I asked him, you changed the code once correct, yes he said, and I should change it again, he showed me how, it was very simple. He said I would see him again once the locksmith was completed with all the locks. Ok I would be in my office.

Headed to my office and looked at my watch, it was almost three and we would close at five today, Mr. Brown came in and asked if we could sit on the couch as he handed me a thin narrow three ring note book, he placed several set of keys on the table, each set had a tag, I asked him if he could wait a moment, and I went and asked Joanne to come with me. We returned, and asked him to start over again, he had a small can on the table, that contained all the old keys and all the original sets had been accounted for, and asked us to place the originals we had in the can. Then said all accounted for, after I went and retrieved the extras I had. He covered it and set it aside. Then he laid out four rings, each had four keys, and each had the key heads covered with a colored plastic cap, he said one set was for me and the other was for Joanne and two spare sets, he said the blue cap key was the front door, the green was for the loading dock door, and the red did the basement and generator room, the purple was to the server room, and there a small key for the paper towel and toilet paper dispensers, and the spare keys for dispensers were in the custodial closets on both floors, the fifth was the office door keys. He asked that we each take a set; he opened the note book and said it was the telephone directory that Kenny has set up, and contained the instructions for programing the doors. He went on to say he took the liberty since all the work was complete to program the doors to automatically lock at the different times based on our current business hours. Said if you came in early after entering the code, the doors would lock until they were set to open automatically, which was nine, and said we could change the pin anytime, and only those with keys needed the pin. If you came in early and opened the door for someone, the door would still lock until the set time. He checked the inside cameras to make sure they weren't block by any of the plants, and gave me one extra complete set of all the keys, and eight front door keys. Was there anything we wanted to know? I asked what did I owe him, and handed me a detailed invoice for, $47,000.00, I said that's all. He said yes, and it was a real pleasure to have worked for me on this project. He said he almost forgot the plant people would come once or twice a month when we were open to check on the plants; they were all low water plants and they would remove and replace any that were sick or dying. He had also arranged with Hectors sisters company, Cassia Clean to send a person every day to clean the washrooms and vacuum while we were open and they would come at ten am. She would contact us later about a contract and schedule, and said she would call next week or probably come in person. And he said when the building was closed there were motion detectors throughout the interior, and the alarm peoples contact information was in the book, he said as he handed me a slip of paper for his electronic payment. I asked him to please wait a moment, I wanted him to show us how to change the pin before he left, but first I went to my desk and pulled out the company check book and ledger and made a check out for $10,000.00, and put his name on it, and where it said memo, wrote for a job well done, placed it in an envelope, then with him and Joanne, went downstairs, and he reset the system turned away as I entered the new pin number. It beeped twice and was set. We both shook his hand and he said don't hesitate to call if I had questions as I handed him the envelope. He walked out and I asked Joanne to wire his money. Yes sir she replied.

I went back and retrieved some key tags and wrote names on them along with the door code, Hippies, Fitz, Green, Phillips, Pat and that left three extra. I had brought the small safe from the old office and placed it in a cabinet behind my desk. I opened it and the small note book fit inside and placed the extra keys in it also. Used the phone to call Pat, Hippies and Fitz into my office and gave them each a key, and gave them the pin, and told them where it was and how much time they had, and briefly explained how the doors operated. Hippies said he really didn't need a set. I said as a member of the origination he had to have one. They left and I paged Phillips and Green, they came in and I handed them each a key, and briefly explained the same thing to them. They left and returned downstairs.

I went over and sat in Joanne's office on the sofa; she joined me and sat in a chair. She had just completed the wire transfer to Mr. Browns account. I had personally done the others earlier, and said she knew. What are you thinking? She was taking Saturdays off now, but would come in later in the day tomorrow, and when she felt they had some time under their belts would go to a five day work week. Asked me that's what you wanted for me, am I correct. Yes love; it's what I always wanted for you. I am going to check on the girls. Hippies had dropped a very large pile of files on Anne's desk, and Pat was catching up on her work from Fitz. Asked Anne about her direct deposit, she had given the info to Joanne. Ok left and had a better feeling about our new operation as I walked around the oval and could see the sign out front with my name on it. I would make arrangements for a group picture, out front for next week. Went back to my office and pulled up the home camera app. Vicky was still cleaning, the bathroom this time as she came out and went downstairs, my house was the cleanest it had ever been. I turned off and sat back. It was almost five, I gathered the papers to look at tomorrow, and would wait until next week when Ms. Washington joined our group to canvas everyone for the Association dinner, and do the group photo out front. We were close to our day ending, and decided to try out the new P.A. system, picked up the phone and hit the designated button, (this is management, your work day has ended and you are requested to leave, thank you). I soon heard cheers and clapping. I closed up and turned off my computer, and went downstairs and sat in the waiting area for everyone to depart. I watched as Fitz and Hippies came over and sat down with me, it was five exactly when Joanne, Anne and Pat came down on the elevator, Green and Phillips appeared and said they had powered down the terminals and I asked Green to go outside and let the door close and see if it would open. He did as I asked and when he tried to open it was locked. I opened the door and thanked him as everyone began to leave. I entered the pin and walked out.

Since it was the middle of spring, the sun was setting later. We wouldn't see lights on early until winter. Everyone drove away and headed for home. I arrived at home and backed inside, got out as the garage door was going down and unlocked the back door and entered.

Vicky was in the kitchen cooking, she stopped and we hugged and I planted a big kiss on her face, said don't let me stop you. She said it was almost done, and turned the fire out from under the pan, checked the oven, and said she was glad I was home. I washed my hands and came back; she said that we should eat first. Ok I replied, and placed my shoes by the stairs, came back and helped her set the table. Said she had been busy all day and was very tired, but we would eat first before we bathed. While she let the rice dish sit we hugged and she was musty and I drew in her scent. She said I smell don't I. Said a little, but if you were working all day it was to be expected. This morning she felt full of energy and hadn't stopped all day because if I was working for us she had to do her part. I held her and kissed her lips, she was tired, and I could see it in her eyes. I said it's my turn to give you a massage after we eat. I released her and she fixed our plates. I brought up a bottle of wine from the basement, opened it and filled our glasses. We said grace and ate; the food was delicious, as we ate slowly and talked about our busy day. We finished and cleaned up the kitchen before we went and sat on the sofa, watching some television for a short while as our food digested. We looked at a one hour mystery and then the early news at nine and half way through turned everything off and went upstairs, undressed and put our dirties in a pile. She would get them tomorrow, went in the bathroom and let the water run over us as we held each other and lathered up one another and rinsed off. Dried ourselves and spread out some towel after pulling

the covers back on the bed. She rubbed me first as I lay stretched
out and turned over, when she finished with me, she lay on her
back. I felt the tension leave as I rubbed her feet and legs, she
started to get more relaxed and I knew it wasn't going to be long
once I did her back that she would be asleep. She turned over and
was almost asleep before I started rubbing on her, and by the time I
had reached her neck with my massaging, she was in a deep sleep.
I woke her and she climbed into bed properly and adjusted herself
as I slid in besides her, pulled the covers up, turned off the lights
and we both fell into a deep and very relaxing sleep.

Twenty-nine
Friday: Day Twenty Nine.
       I woke a little after six as usual. I looked over at my sleeping
beauty, she was fast asleep and removed myself from bed and
headed for the bathroom and was totally refreshed when I returned.
Vicky was sleeping so peacefully that I decided to go downstairs
and make some coffee and not wake her. I put on my bathrobe and
went downstairs, made the coffee and returned before it finished
brewing. I didn't want and episode like before, she was too
precious to me now to upset. Besides I promised, as I lay back in
bed and began caressing her. She soon felt me touch her while still
in her slumbering state as I caressed her and moaned before slowly
opening her eyes and pulled herself closer to me, she yawned, and
placed her arm around me, and looked up and smiled. I kissed her
as I rubbed her head and ran my finger through her hair. She sat
up, and had to go to the bathroom returning several minutes later
and climbed back in bed. We snuggled up, as she wrapped her arm
around me. Said the coffee is ready. Great was her response, and
was glad I didn't leave her. I won't, do that again. She thanked me.
       We put on our robes and went downstairs; she asked me what I
wanted to eat. I said a couple of poached eggs and toast would be
fine, and a glass of grapefruit juice. She said coming right up, and
started to prepare our breakfast. Soon it was ready and served the
food as we sat in the nook and ate. It was a light meal and wasn't
long before we were finished eating, she would clean up later;
there wasn't very much to do today. I said well, get some rest, and
don't over work yourself like yesterday. After recovering from me
feeling on her, she had this sudden explosion of energy and just
couldn't stop until she felt satisfied everything was clean. She slept
well, and didn't have any dreams and was feeling very rested now.
She asked what about you. I feel great. Said when I rubbed her last
evening, I knocked her out, my touch was magical on her body,
and she had never felt anything like it before. I have to go as we
went back upstairs after finishing our coffee. Looked in the closet
and put on a clean pair of jeans, t-shirt and my walking shoes,
when I finished, Vicky was sitting on the couch with her arms
wrapped around her knees, I shaved, brushed my teeth and came

out and put on my sports jacket, as she stood and came to me, and we hugged and kissed. She was going downstairs with me as we walked out of the bedroom and descended the stairs. When we got to the back door, I turned and pulled her to me, held her with my left arm and held her head with my right, put my lips to hers and kissed her. Then placed her head against my shoulder and gave her a squeeze, as we said we loved each other at the same time. I turned and entered the garage, as she watched me get in the car, before she closed the backdoor.

I pulled out as usual, stopped and watched the garage door go down, before pulling away. Headed to the office and arrived early, it was eight and I was the only car in the massive parking lot. Got out and walked toward the front door, placed my key in the lock turned and opened the door, it closed as I entered the pin, the light turned from red to green. I walked out the door and let it close, when I pulled to open, it was locked, great, placed my key in the lock again and entered, looked at the key pad and it was still green. It was a beautiful sight with the plants everywhere. I mean everywhere and there placement was marvelous. The lights were on in the places they needed to be. I walked up the stairs and when I reached the second level, I walked around the oval opening looking down to the lower level. The plant placement was spectacular. Mr. Brown deserved the bonus, and was happy I had rewarded him, he really deserved it. He will definitely be my man on my next endeavor, the golf course if it plays out in my favor. After my sojourner around, I put a pot of coffee on for myself and crew.

I entered my office as some of the lights came on, sat at my desk and turned on my computer and watched the twin screens come to life. Pulled up the internet, on one, then the RELS, on the other screen, entered my pass word and entered the system. I looked for properties near the complex I had just purchased and were located nearby. I went back to the first screen and entered the address to the main office on My Maps World, when it came up did a walk around in various sections of the neighborhood. Then went back to the other screen, and looked at listings. I opened the cabinet where the security cameras monitor was, moved the mouse and the screen came to life, looked at the list and chose a camera with a view of the front door. There were even some mounted in the parking lot looking toward the building, they were mounted on some of the lamp post and I chose one where I could see the entrance and entire parking lot at the same time, and left it on that camera, there was even a zoom feature. Made me wonder why someone would build a store with all this security and backup power, wondered if this wasn't built to be some undercover setup. I will look deeper into the seller, could have been a CIA front company of unknown sorts. Anyway I went back to the RELS and scanned through the listings, the prices were up, higher than in most areas for condos and homes. The apartments were really scarce and the rents were high when you found one. I looked and found the reason why. With the homes, the lots were oversized, half acer average, or larger. I checked to see if there was public sewage, yes there was public sewage, water, gas, electric, and all of the utilities were all underground, and in a five mile radius there was only one mall, and it was pretty exclusive and then there was one other medium sized mall, with some major retailers, they weren't far apart. Looked for other factors that had the prices up, taxes were average, there were several, a couple industrial parks and one bordering the river, there was a junior college, and the schools were very highly rated. When I pulled them up on the second screen, there was something missing here. Then I saw it, several high-tech companies had research centers nearby. I checked each company, and there employee wanted listings. They were very high paying jobs, as I looked at the schools again. The grammar schools were in the top five percent for the state, the high school offered courses in computers; the junior college was one of the top five in the state also.

It was five to nine when I noticed cars entering the lot; it was Joanne and then Fitz, then Brown and Phillips, a car pulled in I didn't recognize, and it was Ms. Jones. Joanne opened the door and entered, it was nine now. Went back to my searches, there were only two rental complexes; they weren't as well located as my new property. Ours was closer to all the schools, and on one side of it was a large public park, that also included a public golf course, it was a tenth of a mile from the main arterial street, and within biking distance of most of the office complexes. I checked if any office building were for sale, along with strip malls etc. found only one office complex for sale. It was a series of eight one story building on twenty acers. I took the sellers information down. Based on the info and Fitz observations, I would continue as a rental, but was really undecided and would have to look first before making any final decision.

I picked up the phone and buzzed Fitz; he answered, asked him to come to my office, and hung up. He entered shortly and gave me the set of keys, and said they were for the complex. I asked him to have a seat, and explained I was doing research on the new location. Said I am leaning toward a high end rental, there is a shortage, our location is prime, the amenities are better than most. I see it has a park like atmosphere, need some operating cost projections, landscape, snow removal etc., and based on the room sizes, what you think the rents should be. He recommended selling it as condos. We would need to change the name, and a new management company. He said he would work on it, and asked if we were going to have any staff meetings. I said next week after I have all the cost for moving, and all the vendors have been paid and I had a chance to look over the new complex. He said ok boss and departed.

I picked up the phone and called Ms. Jones into my office; she came promptly, asked her to have a seat, and complemented her on her very professional appearance. She thanked me. Said I don't want it to be a surprise to you, since I brought you into the inner sanctum, so I will tell you myself, the complex in which you live, we own, and since I operate it as a separate entity, you will pay your rent as you have been, but will give you and employee discount equal to half a month's rent, and you will be refunded that amount on your pay check. Since you will be involved with accounting, that's why I'm telling you, so you heard it from me. And as a resident and employee, you can let us know if you feel something is amiss. I am not asking you to go looking for anything, just let us know if you feel the management isn't on the ball. Do you have anything to say regarding what I just told you?

She looked at me and said, thank you very much. Oh please don't say anything about this to anyone outside. The only people that know are your coworkers, Joanne, Fitz, Hippies, and Pat. While you're in here there is a realtor's association dinner, and I would like for you to attend. I will have more on it latter. Do you have any questions, comments or anything you want to know, this is your chance. Said that rent deduction was more than welcome because she needed to replace her savings, and figured that in a couple years she would need a new car, and she would put that away in her savings. Good I replied, and hope you meet all our expectations. I stood and she thanked me, and her eyes were watery. I needed a cup of coffee as she walked out and returned to her office.

I took my cup, and stopped over and said good morning to Joanne. Told her this isn't as close and personal like the old office. She said no, but we weren't going back. I informed her about Ms. Jones rent and she said she would make a note of it so it would become automatic. Stated I was doing some research and must finish. See you later. Joanne said she was going to check on the operations downstairs. I went back and finished my research. Reached in my pocket and pulled out my block diagram, then went to the conference room and there was one of those dry marker boards that have replaced those old messy chalk boards. I copied my diagram onto it and placed it back on the easel. I was preparing for next week, returned and called the number for the office complex for sale, spoke to the agent handling the sale. He said I should make an offer, they were asking $5,250,000.00, and said I would. Hung up and pulled it up again, there were newer building around, some had a few vacancies, I wondered about the market. Picked up the phone and called Fitz, gave him the RELS number and asked him to check vacancy rates for office spaces around the area, he said ok. I pulled out my phone and entered the new WI-FI credentials into my phone and then pulled the camera app up and checked on Vicky, she had dropped a load in the washer and then went to lie down; ok she was doing fine and closed the app. Got up and went out and looked over the rail and looked downstairs. There was and older couple at the desk as Mr. Phillips picked up the phone and Green soon appeared and led them to one of the cubes, I couldn't see, but knew where they were headed.

As I stood there in walked Ms. Samantha Washington and Phillips picked up the phone and my office phone started ringing. I answered it. He said Ms. Washington is here. Send her up please, and thank you. She entered shortly and I stood and welcomed her in my office. She said most impressive, and I asked her to have a seat. She stated the truck was on the way with the files she was bringing with her and she wanted to spend some time getting organized before her official start. I said right this way and we went downstairs on the elevator. I escorted her to her new office. We entered and she just stood frozen for a long moment. I asked if she was all right. As she looked at me and said, she couldn't have imagined anything as magnificent as this. Thought she would be stuck in some little cubby hole of and office. Out of nowhere she hugged me, and then said she was sorry. I reassured her it was quite all right with me. Walked over and picked up the phone and punched the phone for Ms. Jones, and asked her to come downstairs. She appeared promptly, and when they saw one another they hugged each other. They were all smiles. I asked Ms. Washington if it was alright to call her by her first name, she said sure and welcomed it. I explained to Samantha about office hours, and access, said she understood. I asked Anne, if you are caught up and have some spare time would you help Samantha unpack. When your truck comes as I led her to where the loading dock door was located, thru the double wide swinging doors that were already here from the previous owners, and pointed to the controls just as the bell rang. I pushed the button for the dock door, it opened and a truck was backed up to it. I opened the side door and allowed the driver to entered, he opened the trucks cargo door, and he had a hand truck inside. The loaded a stack of boxes and Ms. Jones said right this way please. There were about twenty boxes. Samantha said it looks like a lot, but in a file cabinet it wouldn't amount to much. When the driver finished unloading and had pulled away, I closed and secured the dock door. Went back and showed her the file cabinet, she said it was just fantastic. She thanked me and asked when did I wanted her to start. Monday would start our first full week and we were in shakeout mode right now. Said she would be ready. I asked Ms. Jones to please show her around. Said she would as they started unpacking. I returned and contemplated on and offer for the office complex, it had been one of the first in the area, so it was old and outdated. I took out a fax form, filled it out and gave a low ball offer of $3,750,000.00, and did the cover sheet and sent it over. I would take Victoria with me tomorrow to check out the new condo/apartment complex.

It was lunch time and I hadn't seen Hippies since he came in as I walked to his office. He was busy putting his files away in the new file cabinet. Hello Harold, he turned and said oh it's you. Yes it is, and I see you're busy. Yes he replied. I said did you inform your old associates of your new location. Said he had and it really hasn't caught on yet; they were so fast, that they were actually slow. I asked what's for lunch, said he had brought his and saw no need to leave his beautiful surrounding. Ok then as I went to Joanne's office, and asked, what's for lunch, she said lets walk down to Martha's. I said ok, and the longer walk should be even better for us. She grabbed her purse and we went downstairs and outside and walked the two blocks now to Martha's passing the old office. We arrived to a friendly greeting from Martha. Then we sat down and ordered. I decided on an Angus burger, fries and coleslaw on the side. Joanne had the special, it being Friday, fish, potatoes and mixed vegetables, with a salad.

Joanne and I finished eating, and on the way back, she asked me had I ever though that I would be where we are now. I said emphatically no, I had no idea. When I took the chance on that stock, and it exploded and it set the course of what I thought I could do if I had some money. And the idea was always there in my mind, and the looming possibility of failure had always existed. But there is a saying; a try always beats a failure. The other thing is, once you understand our monetary system, you have nothing to lose; it's all built on thin air. I know that sounds grouse, but a little cash goes a long way if you play it right, people with connections always have the advantage, but you and we had to do it the hard way. I am thankful that I have known good people like you, and the folks that are around me now, and have been in the past. They are the reason we are here now, and if I can't help someone, then there won't be any hope. Once you lose hope, there isn't much left. I have helped you and a lot of other people, it does the heart good, what is it that they say in the bible, treat people like you want to be treated, it pays off, its good karma. I believe in that, what you do in this life affects the next, and there is no reason to be mad about anything. I have learned to let it pass. If a person does something that make you mad or even upset you. You have to let it go, your being mad doesn't hurt them, it eats on you, it can consume you, that's not good at all, it can affect your health. I want to live as long, and as happy as I can, and you know why. Because there are good people in my life like you, I love you, and I am thankful every day I see your pretty face, and your lovely smile, and not just you but everyone around me, as we reached the old office and stopped. I said it wasn't given; we had to show we deserved it, we did it together, you were there with me and I will never forget that, and you have a special place in my heart and always will. I looked in her eyes, and they were filled with tears. I hugged her, and then we walked back in silence, till we almost reached the front doors. She took my hand, faced me and said that it was a privilege to have me in her life. I hugged her and kissed her cheek before we entered, and went to our respective offices. It being a Friday, it was one of our long days.

I went down to see how we had done with walk-ins so far. I approached the desk, it was slightly off set to the side, and not directly in front of the elevator, and asked Mr. Phillips how it was going, he said very well, and before I could ask, said we had as many walk-ins today, as we had in a week at the old office. I said that's good news because I had to pay for all of this. Told him to keep up the good work, as I walked back and Mr. Green was busy with a couple, and Ms. Brown was on the phone. Good thing I will have more associates next week. walked around and found Samantha placing the last of her files in the cabinets, stopped in and asked how was she doing, said things were going smoothly and asked where to leave the empty boxes, if you can flatten them there was a large box on the dock, and she could place them in there, she said ok, and told her she should come up and talk to me today if she had the time and if not, Monday, she said for sure. I went to my office and checked on Vicky. She was fixing some lunch; good the girl needed some nourishment.

It was about two thirty when, Ms. Washington asked to come in. I said have a seat on the sofa, I came and sat in one of the big chairs. I asked her what her approach was going to be to bring in business, she said to wait on walk-ins would be a slow approach. Said her dad did advertise, in church flyers, and they were inexpensive and tax write off, it had paid off along with being listed in the phone books, and now the internet. Didn't want to jump in all of a sudden, didn't know what my approach would be. I told her that had been my approach also; that I did advertise, but it was infrequently. Told her I had just hired Ms. Jones the other day and she approached me based on the knowledge that you had processed loans for me, and had expressed how to increase business. She lucked up because she is a CPA, and my attorney, Mr. Hippies recommended I hire her. She had expressed the desire to do loans. I told her I had a person, that being you. Frankly the loan process and the profit margins aren't that important as to what I want to provide. If a qualified person walks in here, someone who wants to own, instead of rent, I want to be able to provide full service, qualify them first, then show what's available, and hope they make a purchase. I want to provide beginning to end service. I am just one cog in the wheel, you are another, but all of us together will take the customer full circle. Said she fully understood. That's why you are and employee. If you need any help, let's say ten people come in, and want your services; I can have Ms. Jones assist you, but knowing how applications for loans work you will have to split with her, is that acceptable to you. Said she would agree to the terms. Or would you rather I pay you more, and you drop you taking a percentage. The advantage would be, the customer's points would be lower and the hustle is removed. She said that would be more acceptable to her, and asked what I should pay her. I said what you see as acceptable. She said $60,000.00 or more and said that a guaranteed income would better suit her. Had seen how trying to make things work, made loan originators cut corners and do unscrupulous things. The terms were very acceptable and felt better already. I thanked her for her candor and a willingness to work with me. I asked if there was any travel involved with the process. I didn't know because her father handled that end. Yes, on occasions mostly to negotiate with banks. So you would accept a company car. Yes off course. Told her to let me make a phone call and you can pick one, as an added bonus for being an employee. I heard good things about you and your agreeing to what I want to do, just makes it all the better. Your hours will be the same as all of us, and you can have Saturdays off because banks aren't opened all day on Saturdays, but you can come in if you want. She said that was most acceptable to her, and as we stood, she asked if she could give me a hug. I said of course and working for me would be like working for her dad, but better. Buy the way he will be here next week, said she knew. I was happy to have her as part of my organization. Oh by the way, before you go, I just acquired a large apartment complex, I am going to do a close up inspection over the weekend, if I change my mind and decide to sell it as a condo complex, we should be prepared to offer loans to applicants, but wait until Monday, before worrying yourself about details. This is just a heads up. Said she understood and will enjoy being part of the Harcourt team. We shook and she was all smiles as she departed and would be here until we closed, I thanked her as she walked out. The day was progressing smoothly,

Fitz walked in and sat down, he informed me he had called the manager at the new complex, told him he could take applications, but not to process them, inform them that a decision hadn't been made as to whether it would be rentals or condos. When it was built the original application was for condos, and property tax numbers were created, then before it was complete, the people who financed the project decide to make it rentals, that was four years ago and ran into serious problems, then the outfit we bought it from came in. Started to rehab and complete the unfinished units before they ran into financial problems, and that's when we came in. He said based on what we paid, and the long term outlays for ground keeping, snow removal, his recommendation still would be to sell them as condos. Said if we didn't he felt it would be a headache in the long run, plus we wouldn't have to wait on the county to issue tax id numbers because they were already in place. I agreed with him and said now we can assemble a team, we have the ability to do the loan applications, and a sales staff. He asked, I guess this is next week's agenda. Sure is, but I am still going to go look. He said I should just to make sure before making any decisions. He said great and would be in his office, and left.

I picked up the phone and called Hicks Auto City, asked for Mr. Fabian, after several minutes he came to the phone, told him I wanted to add three more to the current lease agreement, he said that wasn't even a problem, wanted to know when they were coming. I asked if today was good, he said yes, very well. I said they would be there in an hour. I used the PA this time and called for Ms. Washington, Ms. Jones and Ms. Bradley, to come to my office immediately. They were all there within four minutes, asked them to have a seat on the couch. I explained to them what was going to occur in the following weeks. My people needed reliable transport, and being females I would always be concerned with their safety and for that reason, I was going to provide them with a company car. Ms. Washington knew she was going to get one, but because I could see into the future, I was going to do it now instead of waiting, and besides it was a tax write off anyway. I called downstairs and asked Phillips who was there, he said Green and Brown. Send Green up in five minutes please, and hung up. I said Ladies, Mr. Green will take you to the new car dealership in a few minutes; you will speak to a Mr. Fabian, you will pick a car of your choice and then return here. Its two o'clock now and we close at six today so you have plenty of time. Do any of you have any questions or comments, none did. Mr. Green entered, I handed him my car keys, and asked if he would take these young ladies to Hicks Auto City, to see Mr. Fabian. And you will wait and bring them back, thank you. And the happy group departed.

I walked over to Hippies office, he was sitting on the couch going thru some papers, and informed him of what I had just did and what I planned to do with the latest purchase and the reasons why. He said it made sense to him also, and thought it was a good move. Said it should pay off also. And the additional cars would help with our taxes. Are you happy here? He looked at me and said, he was thrilled after all the years he had spent in cramped offices, he finally felt like he had made the big time. It looks like the office of a high priced attorney and would be impressive to anyone who had to see him. He thanked me for caring about the people who worked for me, and that I deserved the best boss award if there was ever one to be given. I am going back to my office if you need anything. I looked over the rail downstairs before returning to my office just as Joanne came to me and asked what was the page all about. I asked her to come sit in my office, she sat in one of the big chairs and I sat on the sofa, and ran down the plan that I was about to initiate, she said that makes logical sense, and should be profitable. Also I was going to pay for a table at the association dinner, and all our people had to do would be to attend, and asked how many to a table. Said they had two choices, one seated eight, and the other seated five. I said get us two eights, that will cover everyone, and we want them next to one another. Fitz and Hippies can bring their girl fiends if they want. Was there anything on there for parking? Yes it was extra and reserved, add that to the reservations. Joanne said you have always been low key before now and wondered why the change. I said it's time to come out of the dark closet. You know what I would like you to wear. Said let me guess. Yes you know, it's time and feeling sure of myself now. She said let me go and make the arrangements, you know it's a month away. Yes I know, oh and we are going to plan to have some advertisements when we sell those condos. Said she understood. Went to my desk, and thought about next week. It was almost four when Mr. Green returned to my office, and handed my keys back. I asked him how it went. He said it went well and I have some happy women walking around, said look out for hugs, and said they didn't expect it. Said he had some calls to make. I thanked him. He said it was no problem and left as Pat came in and asked me to stand as she hugged me. I asked her what did she pick and when would she get it. Mr. Fabian said Monday, and he would have it delivered here. Ms. Washington came in and she hugged me, said she would be sure to do her best, just for me as she was followed by Ms. Jones, she hugged me also, and thanked me an had tears in her eyes, looked at me, and just cried as I held her. I said it was all right. I wanted happy people around me, because if you're happy, your work will reflect it.

Asked them to all have seats, Ms. Jones soon composed herself, as Samantha; put an arm around her shoulder. I said you are all very special, and all I ask is for you to do your very best. And next week we will have a staff meeting. I will ask for your opinions, and I don't want you to hold back anything. There is a real-estate association dinner, and unlike most agencies. I am paying; all I ask is that you attend. You are some of the most beautiful women I have ever had the privilege to know, you all dress very well, but I want you to look your very best, Joanne is making the arrangements now. I want to just thank you for being here, get your rest over the weekend. Then asked when will you two receive your cars? Mr. Fabian told us we could pick ours up tomorrow. You are both off anyway so that isn't a problem. And he said they would be ready when they opened. Ok that's out the way, and I'm finished with you all for now.

They all departed, as I sat at my desk, all the while I had never turned the television on. Grabbed the remote out of the drawer and turned it on. Flipped through the channels, turned to a weather channel, watched for a few minutes and turned it off, well it works. I looked at the wall, and thought I would get one of those really large oversized clocks. Turned to the security system and found a camera that covered the area where my associates were, Green had a couple with a baby in a seat at his desk, and Ms. Brown was talking to three people, looked like a family, two women and a teen. I panned through and all was well. I looked at my watch; it was almost five thirty, pulled out my phone and checked on the house. Victoria was taking something out of the freezer, and was placing pots on the stove. I decided to call her, used the office phone and continued to watch on my cell, it was ringing, and watched as she left the kitchen and went to the office; she waited for the greeting to end. I said Vicky baby pick up, she did and said lover, I asked what are you doing, said she was starting dinner for us. I will be home right after we close. Said she loved me and we should be able to eat soon after I arrived, and she missed me very much. Told her I loved her, and hung up. And I closed the app.

Went to the lunch room and found Joanne cleaning up, we poured ourselves the last cups of coffee before she cleaned the pot and I sat in one of the chairs, told her I was going to try to sit in every chair one day, she laughed at me and said I was crazy, when Hippies walked in and said to me I had a closing on the Kashia condo Wednesday at eleven, said he left a note on my desk, thanked him as he sat with us, he said these were some really comfortable chairs and said good choice. Joanne sat down and sipped her coffee, asked when the cleaning crew was coming again. I said Monday. We sat and talked until it was six, then we prepared to depart. When we went downstairs everyone was sitting in the waiting area. I said go home everyone. I counted heads as we all departed and entered the pin and was the last one out the door.

Got into my car and headed straight home, and my soon to be loving wife. Traffic was average for a Friday and arrived in about forty minutes. Backed inside and closed the garage door, and entered to the smell of baked fish. Vicky was taking something out the oven, I waited until she sat it on the stove top, took off the oven gloves and we hugged and kissed each other passionately. We released each other and I went to wash my hands. Vicky said we could eat in about ten minutes and that was great as I took off my jacket and hung it on the railing to upstairs and took off my shoes and returned and looked in the fridge. Vicky had already brought up some wine and set the table. She began to serve our plates, we soon sat down to eat, and the fish was very good, along with the baked potato, veggies and salad. Afterwards we cleaned the kitchen together and I took the garbage out. We went on the deck and finished drinking the bottle of wine. There was a breeze blowing and it felt good. We sat and talked as she sat close enough to hold my hand.

We enjoyed the sun and the breeze for a long time before we went inside and washed the glasses before going upstairs. We undressed each other and went to shower together. Standing under the warm water and bathing one another was one thing we both looked forward too. After a long while we finished and dried one another. We spread the towels out onto the bed, and then we began massaging one another. Vicky said she wanted me inside of her and said it had been several days, and was going to really be bad if I didn't. That doesn't sound very good as we laid down looking at one another. I placed my left arm around her so her head rested in my shoulder, and pulled her close and place my right leg between hers, I kissed her as I rubbed her back with my right hand then slowly moving down to her butt and thighs as we were laying on our sides. I looked into her eyes as I held her, as I rubbed her upper back with my right hand, and said you want to be bad, that's not good at all. I was rubbing her butt, raised my hand and smacked her, catching her by surprise, and then smacked her several more times as she held me. She was excited now as I held her with my left arm. I moved my right knee up and rubbed it against her warm pussy, and then with my right hand gave her ass several more harder smacks, then rubbing her ass, told her bad girls have their butts spanked when they act up as I pulled my knee away smacked the lips of her now highly aroused pussy and protruding clit. She erupted in a violent climax, she was still in my grip as I place my leg back between hers, and spanked her butt again as her clit rubbed against my leg and told her you are a very bad girl and I am going to fuck you good, because you are really bad. I released my grip on her and moved on top of her as I spread her legs and penetrated her hot pussy with long strokes. She screamed fuck me master as she came again, and having multiple orgasms. I said you have been so bad you are going to get fucked in your ass bitch, as I grabbed the back of her knees pulling them up exposing her ass and sticking my throbbing penis up her waiting asshole, and as I slowly stroke her I came, filling her ass with a massive load of hot sperm as she hollered in ecstasy. I slowly eased myself out of her ass and lay next to her and holding her tight. She kissed and licked my neck and face with her tongue as I rubbed her all over. Vicky said she needed that and would be really good now, said she missed being in my arms and me inside of her because I was so tired when I came home these past few days. She rubbed her fingers through my hair, we soon got up and went to the bathroom to shower again in the warm water as we washed the love juice from ourselves, and returned and caressed and oiled one another again before we removed the towels we had placed on top of the bed, and putting them in the pile with our dirty clothes. We pulled the covers back, turn off the lights, climbed in bed, and into each other's arms, and felt each other as I caused her have several more eruptions as I felt her and kissed her, before we eventually fell asleep.

Thirty
Saturday: Day Thirty.

It was a very nice spring day when I woke up facing Victoria. When I did, she was facing me. I touched her, she was still sleeping as I slowly rose and went to the bathroom. When I returned her eyes were still closed as she felt for me. I touched her hand and lay back in bed and placed her finger in my mouth, licked it and her eyes slowly opened. She smiled as I released the finger and she pulled me to her and held me. She had to go to the bathroom, getting up and returning shortly. We picked up where we had left off before falling asleep. I felt between her legs and it wasn't long before she was panting, and I was hard as rocks and climbed on top of her as I slid into her and pinned her arms down slowly working my hardness into her. She moaned loudly as I took advantage of her, she climaxed under me as I continued and didn't stop as she screamed and whispered in her ear that bad girls have to serve there master. She was frantic as she bucked and had a massive climax. I exploded and came at the same time filling her with another full load of hot sperm. She held me tight until she couldn't any longer, and lay panting as I rolled off to the side and we both waited until our breathing returned to normal. It was a long while as we laid there looking and embracing one another.

Eventually I got out of bed, grabbed her hand and pulled her up and took her to the shower with me and we bathed, and washed off the love and funk of our passions, she cleansed herself, taking a douche before turning the water off and drying off. We returned to the bedroom and applied a light coating of oils and body lotion to ourselves. When we finished oiling, I said let's eat something and informed her that she was going with me today. We put on our robes, and could see now she was very relaxed. We fixed breakfast, sausage, poached eggs, toast, coffee and we split a grapefruit. We sat and ate in silence. Finished and cleaned up the kitchen, and after we finished I pulled her to me and rubbed my hands through her still damp hair. She hugged me tight and looked at me with her pretty eyes and smiled, said she knew I loved her, and she loved me.

We went upstairs to the bed room and I sat on the couch, she kneeled before me and placed her head on my lap as I stroked her head. Then pulled her up and had her sit on my lap as I opened her robe and felt her breast, before rubbing the side of her face and she took my finger and placed it in her mouth. Love we must get dressed and asked me what I wanted her to wear; jeans would be fine or those tights and a skirt and some athletic shoes because we will be walking quite a bit today. Take your time, and look cute and sexy for me. I put on some underwear and pulled out a pair of jeans, t-shirt and my walking shoes, and a sports coat. I dressed put my wallet and stuff in my pockets and got my keys. I would have to stop at the office, and get the keys for the complex. I shaved, brushed my teeth, and came out and put my jacket on, told Vicky I would be downstairs as I walked around the house and went to the kitchen and grabbed a bottle of water and took my vitamins. Then went to my office and turning on the computer, waited for it to come up and plugged my SLR into it and downloaded my pictures to a personal file on a secondary hard drive. Erased the cameras memory and before unplugging it, made sure the cap was on the lens. Turned off the computer, and went to the kitchen. As I waited on Victoria, took out some vitamins, took mine and placed hers on the counter. Just then she came downstairs, she wore a pair of jeans, a blouse, and athletic shoes, some loop earrings, and light colored lip stick, with her small purse with the shoulder strap. Said she was ready as I handed her the vitamins. She took them, and we went out the back door. I locked it, opening the car door for her, and before she got in pulled her to me and kissed her.

We pulled out as I closed the garage door, before leaving I looked at her and said you look so beautiful today. She smiled, and said just for you love. We headed for the office, it was ten when we arrived, and she looked after I parked and opened the door for her, took her by the hand, and said this is my new office. We entered and we were greeted by Mr. Green. I said good morning. Victoria and I took the elevator upstairs, as she asked the whole building. Yes baby, the whole thing is mine as I led her to my office and retrieved the keys I needed from my desk drawer. She said it's very beautiful, and the plants are amazing, she sat on the couch and said this is wonderful, and the couch is so comfortable. I told her to follow me, and took her hand and showed her Joanne's office. She said I know she loves it. Come on we have something to look at, as we walked down the steps and she was amazed at how beautiful it was. We left and got back in the car.

Told her that we were going to look at a property I just purchased and wanted to take a closer look at it before I decided to rent or start selling it as condos. The drive took about an hour as we pulled up outside the club house. We got out and I unlocked the club house door, then unlocked the office door and turned on the lights. I looked at a map of the complex on the wall, there were twelve building, and each had four each of studios, one, two, and three, bed room units, sixteen total per building. I went to the key box, there were only seven keys missing and those were the rentals, all located in one building. I needed to sell these fast. I took all the keys for one building, and chose number 7 to look at, closed the key box and locked the office door and the outside door. We got back in the car, and soon found building number 7, and pulled into one of its parking lots. We got out, and each unit had an individual entrance. The lot was spacious and was on both sides of the building. The units were back to back, as I found the key to a studio apartment and we entered. The room was very large, the kitchen was spacious and there was a large closet and was set aside like a separate room, and the bathroom was really oversized, with a linen closet inside, bath tub and a walk-in shower, and even had a large patio with a rail around it, and the elevation put it a more than a foot above ground level. The appliances were the latest, and the room where the water heater and central air unit was located also contained a full sized washer and dryer. We finished looking and went outside and I locked the door. Found the key for the one above, we entered and walked up the wide staircase, and found the same layout as below, only it had a porch. We left to see a one bed room unit, and opened the door and found another spacious apartment, the rooms were very much oversized, the bed room was large, and the rooms so far are oversized compared to buildings that were similar. We exited and made sure the doors were locked. Then went to a two bed room unit, same oversized rooms, only this had two baths, the baths were slightly smaller than the one bed room but still very large and spacious. We exited to a three bed room unit, the rooms still were large, there were two large baths, a good size kitchen that was larger than most and had islands in the kitchen, the upper units all had porches, we exited and locked the doors. One thing for certain, was they all had in unit laundry's extra-large and very spacious rooms and bathrooms with both bath tubs and walk in showers. I was seeing what Fitz, and even Pat had said when I had asked them both, and with the in unit laundry would be a nightmare over time.

Just then two police units rolled up. The officers got out and approached us. Asked what we were doing here and asked for some identification. I showed my driver's license, stated that I purchased the property and was looking them over before deciding if they would be condos or apartments. The officers returned our IDs and said they hoped they would be condos. I asked why? Both officers replied that apartments were more of a problem with people moving in and out constantly, and wasn't as stable as homes or condos where people owned the property. I agreed with him on that point. He also wanted to know how soon they would be for sale. Very soon I said. They asked if they could look at them. I said sure what size, and described the number of bed rooms that would be available. One officer said two, the other said three. I asked up or down. One said up, and the other said down. The keys were marked and we all looked together. They were impressed by the room sizes as we all looked at several units. They asked would there be any discounts for vets, fire or peace officers. I said it would be a major consideration. I would send a loan officer and an agent to set up shop within a week or two. They shook my hand, and said this was on their patrol and they would keep an eye out. Thanked you. They saw my vet plates and asked what branch. I said army; and they thanked me for my service.

Vicky and I got in the car and headed back to the club house so I could replace the keys. I unlocked the doors and replaced the keys to their proper place, and locking the door behind me and we started looking around the club house, just as both the officers entered and said they were curious about the building. It was very large and had a steel structure, a full kitchen, and could be used to feed a mass of people; it had washrooms you would expect to find in a stadium. Indoor gym, locker rooms for men and women with washrooms and showers, a divisible basketball court, with a separate hand ball court, and there were tennis courts inside and outside, also an indoor Olympic size swimming pool, and one outside. After looking around, I took several photos and we left with the officers locking the doors as we left. This was a definite sell. The amenities would be a problem in the long run. Vicky and I drove around, looking at the different buildings, and then we headed back to the office.

On the way back we stopped at Wong's, and Mrs. Wong seated us, and said to Vicky, you lucky woman, he special, she know, Mrs. Wong left and came back with a pot of green tea and knew just what I wanted. I ordered the Hunan shrimp with broccoli and noodles, Vicky ordered spicy chicken with pea pods and rice. We drank our tea and waited for our order. Holding hands; I looked at her delicate fingers, and rubbed her palm as she looked at me. Victoria asked what I was going to do with the complex we just looked at. I was going to sell them as condos. She asked why. Explained that there were factors whereas rentals would present problems over the long run, and problems cost money, and in my business the less problems, the better the profits. She wanted to know like what? I said the large expanse of grass. The club house was another, and with winter, there would be snowplowing. It would better function as a condo. Our food arrived; and resuming our conversation, Vicky said it was a beautiful place to live, like living in a park. I said that would be a good selling point, but another problem, leaves, water and other factors, it wouldn't be profitable in the long run and was the reason I was going to sell it, and beside it was built to be a condo. We ate and enjoyed our food. I said if we get stretched out with the staff, I may have to ask you to help out. She said that would be quite all right with her. We enjoyed our food and each other, finally we finished, and the bill came along with the fortune cookies. I opened mine, read what it said (life is too short not to have love in your life). I ate my cookie and looked at Victoria. Asked aren't you going to open yours, she opened it, pulled the little slip of paper out, and read it before handing it to me, I read it (true loves only comes once if you're lucky). I looked at her and she was looking down and was covering her eyes. I moved her hand, she was crying. I took a napkin and dried her eyes, as Fawn came and took the bill away. I took Victoria's hand as I stood and helped her up; she fell into my arms and held me, and said she loved me so much. I could see Mrs. Wong in the distance looking as I led Vicky outside, Mrs. Wong said, come again.

I led Vicky out and put her in the car. When I got in she was looking at me, she said please take her home because she wanted to hold me, and love me. I said that's where we are going baby. We arrived and I backed inside, she was out the car before me and when I opened the door and stepped out, she was standing there and grabbed me and pulled me to her. She placed her arms around my neck pulling me to her as she kissed me passionately, and said she was mine forever, and started crying again, as I wrapped my arms around her. I rubbed her head and pulled it back and kissed her, led her into the house and upstairs. We had undressed down to our underwear when Vicky pushed me onto the bed and climbed on top of me and placed her head on my chest, I wrapped my arms around her and just held her. Finally she raised her head and looked me in my eyes. She placed her finger on my lips and said, when she read the fortune, and all the others it meant to her that she was where God wanted her to be with whom she was supposed to be with. That all her life had led her here, she would do whatever I asked of her, would be loyal and faithful to me and love me forever. She was crying because her love for me was unending, and couldn't put it in words, but wanted to, had to tell me how she felt. I rolled her over on her side, held her as we laid there holding one another. I released her, got up and put my robe on. I put my hand out and pulled her up, told her I needed a drink. She put her robe on and we headed downstairs. Victoria and I fixed a couple of gin and tonics and set them on the bar. I turned the radio on. Vicky sat next to me and I looked at her. Told her that she was the love I had always dreamed of but she has to stop crying every time anything reminded her of how lucky she felt. We finished the drinks and I fixed us another. Told her to stand, I pulled her to me, looked her in her eyes, and asked her what she was thinking right now, she said how happy she was being with me. Then I asked her what she wanted me to do with her right now. She responded saying she wanted me to take her to the bedroom and play with her. I opened her robe and felt her body. I took her nipples between my fingers and asked her did she like what I was doing. Yes she replied and said she liked when I touched her that it sent shivers through her and excited her and it was a feeling she had never experienced before. I asked if she felt that way now, yes she replied, as we sat down and finished our drink. Then I went around and fixed another. After we finished the third drink I helped Vicky upstairs, and put her to bed, it wasn't long before she was soon asleep. I checked the house before returning, and got into bed with her and falling asleep myself.

Thirty-one
Sunday: Day Thirty-one.

When I woke up it was six, the sun was bright in a cloudless sky. I hadn't been paying much attention to the weather lately. I looked over at Vicky as she still slept. I put her to sleep yesterday after all her tears of happiness. I went to the bathroom and came back shortly after putting on my robe and going downstairs. I made my morning coffee and pulled out the frying pan, taking some bacon out, placed it in the pan and turning on a low fire on and placing the pan on the stove. Then some bread turned the oven on and placed several slices in and aluminum pan before placing it inside, and taking the sliced cheese from the fridge and placing several slices on a plate. The coffee was now ready as I poured myself a cup and taking several sips, before returning upstairs and checking on Victoria. She was sleeping very well and I returned downstairs. I turned my bacon over and covered it, did the same with my bread and placed the sliced cheese on top and closed the oven door. I thought about how I was going to sell the complex as condos, I hadn't done it before, selling an entire complex as individual units and decided to look at my contacts, and get some more information. Went to my home office, turned on my computer and after clearing up e-mails started looking and soon found a marketing company, wrote down there information, they specialized in real estate sales. I would contact them tomorrow, and find out if they handled such things. It would seem much easier, to contract it out. I would prefer that, over sending my people out. There wouldn't be any individual commissions, and besides I had a very small staff, much too small for the size and scale of this property. I was in this for the money and any profit was a plus weather it small or large, just as long as we came out ahead. Even with a lower profit margin it would still give us exposure and make us known. I looked through the association website and found several more, wrote them all down and would contact them tomorrow. Went to the front door and picked up the Sunday paper. It was the only one that I had delivered. I went immediately to the real estate section, and as I scanned through found an ad for a distant condo complex, about twenty seven miles away, it was being sold under a real estate company's name, but there was a marketing company handling the sales. Took the info down, and added it to my list. I checked on my bacon. It was done and took an aluminum pan and lined it with paper towels and began placing the bacon on it as I turned out the fire. Turned around and removed my cheese toast from the oven and turned it out. After finishing my first cup of coffee I decided to return upstairs. Vicky was just starting to awaken; she opened her eyes and placed my hand on her head, leaned over and kissed her. Said good morning love as I helped her sit up, she leaned against me and yawned, said she had never slept that well before. She rose and went to the bathroom, returning after a short while and looking refreshed as she hugged and kissed me. Asked what I had been doing and could smell coffee on my breath.

Told her I had been up and fixed some bacon and cheese toast and asked if she was ready to come downstairs. Yes as she grabbed her robe and we went downstairs. Asked if I wanted any eggs, I said sure why not and used the pan I had just cooked the bacon in and very shortly we had some eggs to go along with what I had prepared. We split a grapefruit as we sat in the nook and ate. As we ate, Victoria said, you put me to sleep didn't you. I had to admit to her that I did. Told her that she had such an emotional day I felt she needed the rest. That I was concerned with her state of mind sometimes and she should just accept things as they are. That she was in my life, and I in hers, and didn't think it was going to change and we loved one another and it was going to stay that way. Soon she would be Mrs. Charles Harcourt and would no longer be the housekeeper I hired. Oh you will still keep house, but you will be my loving wife, forever, till death do us part. She looked at me, and I said come here and let me hold you, because I could see it coming, and if you want to cry about it, so be it love. She fell into my arms whimpering as I held her. I looked into those big beautiful eyes, with the tears streaming down, and said to her, I love you very, very much and I am the luckiest man in the world to have you in my life. After a long and tear filled moment we started too cleaned up the kitchen as it started to get very cloudy outside. I turned on the radio to the news station and soon they gave the weather report. We were in for some heavy rain fall and it was expected to last all day, we had gone nearly a month with only the occasional shower, but now it seemed we were in for some serious weather and the grass could surly use it. When we finished, asked my love what she wanted to do, she said anything as long as she was with me.

I said let's take our shower since we hadn't last night and before the storm comes. We went upstairs and showered together, came out and oiled each other up and got back in bed and held and felt one another. I could not get over how beautiful she was her shape, color, her soft skin. We dosed off, only to be awakened by very loud claps of thunder. Vicky held me tight, and buried her head in my chest. After the storm had passed she asked me to make love to her. I felt her and rubbed her body as she felt mine, I was holding her again with my right leg between hers and she was grinding on my leg, I moved my knee to her vagina and she exploded as I held her, she cried as her juices flowed and I moved my leg and placed my hand on her and rubbed her vaginal lips and played with it and fingered her clit as she went crazy with ecstasy and moaned and said please don't stop. I continued as she felt my hardness and said put it in her please. I climbed on top of her and spread her legs and slid into her hot moist pussy, then after several minutes moved one of her legs inside of mine and she screamed as she came again, then I moved her other leg, so both hers were between both of mine and pumped her and was rubbing against her exposed clit, I held her under her shoulders, feeling her back, a spot where she was very sensitive, then she went crazy. I came and she screamed and held on to me for dear life. I slowly rolled off and lay next to her, and we waited for our breathing to return to normal. She rolled next to me, said never in her life had she ever experienced multiple orgasms like that. She began kissing my face, and feeling me, and held me in her hand, and rubbed my chest with the other. I turned and felt between her legs, and felt all of our juices and played with her as my touch sent shivers thought her. I moved my hand and placed it on her butt and placed my leg between hers again and spanked her, she moaned and she climaxed again, she begged me to please stop. I told her she was bad and needed a good spanking and cried as she climaxed again. I stopped and in a baited breath said, she would be good as I squeezed her. When I released her she laid on her back panting, her breathing returned to normal shortly. I rolled her over onto her stomach and felt her, from her feet to the back of her neck as she moaned. I got out of bed and rolled her again toward me and took her hand and sat her up. It was still raining outside when I looked out the window. I took her other hand and pulled her to a standing position, she fell back and sat on the bed and asked that I let her catch her breath, said she felt weak. I pushed her and she was again on her back, I leaned over her and said I was going to play with her all day, and if she was prepared for that. I told her you said you would do whatever I wanted whenever I wanted, as I placed my hand between her legs and felt her again and took a nipple in my mouth and pulled it and tickled it with my tongue sending shivers through her. She came again with my hand inside of her as my thumb rubbed against her clit. I stood, and her butt was at the edge of the bed, grabbed her ankles and placed them on my shoulders as I leaned forward and looked down at her, she looked up at me as I was hard again and slapped her quivering pussy with my dick. I pulled her up and she held me in her hand and slid down on the floor to her knees and placed me inside her mouth and I soon had a massive organism, as my come was dribbling out her mouth and taking my hand and rubbing it all over her face, as I held her head with the other hand, and she licked it with her lips. I pulled her to a standing position, we looked at each other, she hugged me with all the strength she could muster and we just held each other, and said at the same time, we loved each other. We went into the shower again and washed and held each other; we kissed a long time. We dried each other off, before taking some towels and spreading them on the bed, we oiled each other again, when we finished we lay down, pulled the covers over us as we held one another and fell asleep.

When we again woke it was midafternoon, I looked over at Victoria, as she yawned and opened her eyes, and we reached out and touched one another. She placed her hand on my face, and came close and kissed me; I reached over and touched hers. Soon we were in each other's arms once again, we didn't want to let go. I rubbed her back and squeezed her butt cheeks, she said don't stop, as we tongued one another. I stopped and said aren't you hungry, and she replied yes, but didn't feel like cooking and didn't want to leave home either, said she felt weak from making love. I said we have food in the freezer, and all we had to do was heat it up. I said are you prepared to get up now, she said yes. We got up and put on some house clothes which consisted of some jogging pants and tops. We went downstairs, and as we did I looked out the window and the rain was still coming down but not as hard as it had earlier. I looked in the freezer and we had several choices, I chose the spaghetti sauce I had prepared and froze. We would only have to boil water for some pasta, and make toast for some garlic bread. We worked together and about an hour later we were sitting down eating and we had garlic bread and a salad along with our spaghetti. Our bodies were starving as we sipped some chilled red wine, and placed a candle on the table with the lights dimmed as we ate and looked at one another as if it was the first time we had ever seen one another. We both knew that we were meant to be together from this day forth. When we finished eating we sat and sipped our wine, we held hands and I looked at her slim delicate fingers as she smiled at me, and then she finally spoke. Mr. Harcourt, as I looked at her, she said that I would not be disappointed with her because she was going to be the best wife any man could ever hope to have, and that she would do anything I asked of her, that she belonged to me, and she loved me very much. She asked me to hold her again, and she came over and sat in my lap and held her. Suggested we look at some television, we cleaned up the kitchen and left the dishes and pots to dry in the dish rack, and then we headed for the living room where we sat together and had the television on, but really paid more attention to one another than watching it. When the news came on, it was the only time we paid any attention, when it went off; we turned it off and went upstairs, undressed and climbed in bed. We felt on each other until we fell into a wonderful and deep sleep.

Thirty-two
Monday: Day Thirty-two.

I awoke to another fine day as I slowly opened my eyes. The rain had left the air smelling fresh as I turned over and touched Vicky; she turned over to face me, and opened her eyes. I kissed her before getting out of bed as I headed to the bathroom and she soon followed. I did my usual morning thing and soon had finished shaving and freshening up and went and put on my sweat pants and shirt, and Vicky shortly followed me as she put on her sweats also. Vicky folded the blanket that was on the bed and stripped it down before going downstairs together. I helped her with the load of dirty sheets, robes, towels and pillow cases and clothes taking them to the laundry room and leaving them on the floor. I left her loading the machines and prepared to make some coffee before she came in the kitchen and began fixing breakfast. Victoria said she was happy it had rained the day before because she so much enjoyed being with me. She was going to clean up and open the windows and freshen up the house. She finished cooking and prepared our plates; as we sat down to eat. I had another cup of coffee before returning and sitting back down to finish my food. Vicky asked if I was going to be busy today. I said that most Mondays were, and especially this one, and would not be home until after six.

She said that she would miss me and told her I felt the same way, but that was life and the way things worked. After I finished eating and rinsing my plate off before placing it in the dish water along with my coffee cup, Vicky followed me and did the same as I headed back upstairs as she followed. I started to dress and was standing nude preparing to put my underwear on when Vicky came over and rubbed her nude body against mine. We hugged and kissed and said that was all she wanted was to feel me in her arms before leaving. We released each other and she put on her smock as I dressed, deciding on my usual attire of jeans, because I had a closing this week and would wear a suit then. I finished dressing and filled my pockets with my necessities and prepared to leave. Vicky was waiting for me as we went downstairs together. We arrived at the back door, turned and faced Vicky, hugged and kissed her, told her to be good and that I loved her very much. I got in my car and then remembered the newspaper. Went back inside to my office and gathered all my notes and the real estate section of the newspaper from yesterday and folded them and placed them in my pocket and headed back out as Victoria was standing there looking coy. I grabbed her, pulled her to me placing my hand between her legs and rubbing her as I pressed her firmly against the wall, biting her neck and causing her to soon climax. I released her, pulled her head back by her hair and kissed her, turned and left as I took my notes with me.

I got into my car, pulled out and close the garage door as I drove down the driveway. I was the first to arrive at work again, entered the edifice that was now mine, and went to my office. Placed my notes on the desk, turned on the computers, then went to the lunch room and made some coffee. I waited until it finished brewing, poured a cup and then returned to my office. Pulled out my notes and started dialing, the first number was to the marketing company handling the condo sale I found in the newspaper, they answered and said sales. I asked for their corporate number and was told this was a sales office only and was directed to check the internet. After hanging up sat down and did just that and soon found their web site. I thought we needed to update our web site also; it would help with rentals and our new loan origination department. There web site said they specialized in the sales of condos, office condos and large properties to assist realtors who otherwise needed additional but only temporary staff and would also provide the advertisements, banners and a professional sales team. I dialed there phone number and asked to speak to a representative, they asked the purpose of my call, I explained why and was soon speaking to the president of the company, Mr. Peters. And explained what I wanted done, and the area where my property was located. I put our conversation on speaker, it lasted, about half an hour, he agreed to meet me at the property location later that day. Said I would call back very shortly after consulting with my staff, which let him know I was serious. I ended the call after telling him I would call again around ten and we could set a time to meet this evening. I checked their better business credentials and they were highly rated, he gave me two choices, a flat fee or a percentage, I would have to get Fitz to add up the profit vs. expenses, but anything over what the purchase price was would be a plus. I paid $15,000,000.00 and based on my sales figures I could make $44,000,000.00 off it and one percent would be $440,000.00. That would be the cost of using this company, so my profit would be $28,000,000.00. I will shoot this past my staff first. I drank my coffee and would have a meeting in the conference room, with everyone except the sales associates, Green and Phillips, Brown, Newman and Hartman. It was almost nine when I poured another cup of coffee; I was getting geared up for another action packed day. I pulled out the newspaper add, called the reality company that had hired the marketing company, and asked to speak with the president or CEO, they put me on hold, and soon I spoke to a Mrs. Foresight, said she owned the company. Explained to her who I was and the reason for my call, and asked if she was satisfied with the service from the marketing company. She said very much, that it had netted her a profit and they had done a marvelous job. And explained they covered the advertisement, provided licensed sale agents, had open houses until almost all the units were sold, and sold the units much faster than she could have done with her very small staff. She asked me about the property I would be selling. I explained briefly and the number of units and she said anything over twenty units and she would recommend using there service because you wouldn't want to be left holding the bag and would definitely want quick sales. I thanked her and asked if she would be attending the association dinner and she replied yes and was looking forward to attending. Said that I would love to meet you, and she said it would be her pleasure. I thanked her for her insight, hung up and thought this approach wouldn't hamper my operations here; well at least my employees would have no problem getting to work and no excuses.

Looked at the time, and it was quarter to nine. And began preparing my notes, called the marketing company and set up a meeting at the new complex with Mr. Peters for one o'clock this afternoon. He thanked me and would come fully prepared, after he did some research on the area. I thanked him again before hanging up. Looked at the time again and it was five to nine. Opened the cabinet where the security camera controls were and moved the mouse and the screen came to life, the security camera screen was where I had left it and watched as the reserved side of the parking lot began filling up, and everyone was here including all of my associates. I waited until ten after before I paged Joanne, Fitz, Hippies, Pat, Jones and Washington to the upstairs conference room. I waited as I saw them all pass by before I went in and stood at the podium. I greeted everyone and said good morning all. Explaining why they were all here as I wrote on the board the figures. Stated I agreed with Mr. Fitz on his suggestion to sell the complex as condos and my reason why. And explained to them about using a marketing company that I had contacted and asked if anyone have any questions? Before I let you return to work, I would like Mr. Fitz and Ms. Washington to accompany me to the meeting with the marketer, and asked Mr. Hippies if he want to go, he said yes, anyone else; Ms. Jones raised her hand. Ok, and said it's at one o'clock at the complex club house we just purchased. Said to Ms. Jones I appreciate your coming and showed Fitz my figures and asked what he thought. I said based on the police officers I met we would knock $5,000.00 off the purchase price of any loans we originate with proof of employment. That's for vets, fire and police. It should enhance our sales and be a plus for our loan department. Does anyone have anything to add, any suggestions or complaints. Ok dismissed. Hippies said what time should we leave, I said twelve. And we will have lunch on the way back.

Fitz and I drove, Hippies and Washington rode with me and Jones with Fitz, we arrived about fifteen minutes early and entered the club house and headed to the complex office and Fitz was greeted by the leasing agent. Fitz informed him of our intentions and asked if he lived in the area. He did and turned down Fitz offer of working for us as an associate. Shortly Mr. Peters arrived and entered, we all shook hands, and I introduced him to my staff as he was accompanied by his secretary and his first assistant. We walked around the club house as his secretary took notes, and then we went into the office and looked at the large map on the wall and took the keys for the second closest building within walking distance. Mr. Peters informed us before we left that his service provided the advertisements in the local newspapers for a distance of a fifty mile radius for two months, and he would have and open house for qualified buyers, and would have loan officers from various banks on site, and that his service was a flat fee or a percentage. He stated on his quick research of the area and noticed there was a shortage of affordable housing, that once he started predicted that half the units should have contracts within thirty days, we walked to the building and we viewed all of the units upstairs and down, and on both sides. He asked what our asking price was as we returned to the club house. There were several tables and some chairs that the resident agent set up while we were away that Fitz asked him to prepare for our return as we all sat down and he gave us some of his brochures from previous sales he had held for other real estate agencies. Ms. Jones had her lap top and checked these out while we were having the discussions. Ms. Washington asked him questions about the onsite loan officers. He said they worked for banks and on commission and that is why they were eager to provide there services, and his agents did the showings, and wrote up the contracts and all were all licensed. Fitz handed him our selling price list, he handed it to his secretary, and she made some computations and handed it back to Mr. Peters. He said the only thing we would have to do was providing access to the buildings, and he would handle the closings for and additional fee. He said for the sixty days service to begin, he said by the start of the coming weekend, and full service, he would charge us $700,000.00, it would be for advertisements, showings, providing the loan agents, contracts, and closings. I asked him to give us a moment. Fitz, Hippies and I walked a distance away, then asked Ms. Jones to come over then she returned and Ms. Washington walked over. We all agreed for the cost and the time frame it would be easier and most cost effective for us.

We returned to the table and I informed Mr. Peters he had a deal, said he would have a contract draw up and we could sign tomorrow and said he required ten percent up front. Stated I would give him twenty percent and wanted him to start as soon as possible. And said he would get his staff started right away. He would have the contract drawn up and I could sign tomorrow. Hippies reminded me I had a closing tomorrow, so we made it for Wednesday here and we would set a time tomorrow. We shook hands and I mentioned Mrs. Foresight. He had just completed selling condos for her, and they did particularly well. We all left the club house after returning the keys and Fitz and I talked to the onsite agent. He would stay until we no longer need his services, we thanked him and departed.

We all piled back into the cars and headed back to the office, but stopped at Red Fin Seafood for lunch. Being after the lunch crowd had departed, we were all seated promptly at one large table; we placed our orders and were soon served. Hippies and Fitz sat on either side of me as we discussed using the marketing company. Both felt it would be better than disrupting our office operations and the fee was nominal against the profits we would make. Ms. Jones added that we should have someone on site to oversee and to be sure they were compliant. I asked her if she would take on that responsibility, she said she would, and Ms. Washington said she would also. I would spot check them also and asked, so everyone is in agreement that this is the way to go then. Everyone was in full agreement. Once we have a start date we will set some kind of schedule. Everyone enjoyed their food and I paid and we all headed back to the office.

It was almost five when we returned and everyone headed to their offices to continue with their work. Pat was downstairs with several people who were filling out loan applications when we returned, and soon Ms. Jones headed downstairs to help out. I contacted Mr. Thomas, the person who had designed our web-site, and told him we needed to do an update; he said Joanne had been in contact with him already. I thanked him and hung up. I pulled out my cell, and brought up the home camera app, and found Victoria dusting and wiping the window sills and washing windows, she had the ladder for the ones up top in the living room. Panned through all the cameras inside and out, all was well, and closed it up. Hippies came in and had drawn up a non-performance document to be attached with any contract we signed with the marketing company, and said he would come with me when I met with them again. As he was leaving, Samantha entered and said, Pat and Anne were downstairs since we had this sudden flood of people who wanted loan applications and she wanted to ask me how long they could work with her. I said till you can clear things up, said she needed Anne, but when it lightened up would sent Pat back first. I said ok that was fine. About an hour later things had gotten back to normal and Pat returned, and after that Anne also. I wondered what was going on. I found Joanne and asked her, said she had contacted Mr. Thomas the day we moved in and had him update our information on the web-site, and that created a surge when everyone left. I told her what was going to occur with the condo sale and we had decided to let the marketing company handle it, she said that made more sense than us trying to sell it with our small staff.

I returned to my office and brought up our web-site, I hadn't looked at it for several weeks and saw that Joanne had covered all the bases, leasing, sales, and mortgages, and it looked inviting, ok very well done. My people were taking care of business, small but very efficient. It was almost closing time, what a day it had been, and very productive. I checked the inside camera in the downstairs area where the agents were and our two new agents were busy, one had just shook hands with a couple as they left, and the other was on the phone, Ms. Brown was on the phone also, very good. Panned over to where the mortgage origination area was and Ms. Washington was just finishing up with another couple, as she stood and shook their hands and walked them toward the door. The waiting area was clear and everyone was tiding up, it was ten minutes before closing. Soon everyone had gathered in the waiting area waiting, as Hippies, Fitz, Joanne and I entered the elevator and went downstairs, and the rest of the staff walked over and we walked out, it was six and punched in the pin and exited. We got in our cars and headed home.

When I reached home it was almost seven, backed inside the garage as usual and entered. I was greeted by my dear Vicky who came running and hugged and kissed me. I took my shoes off and carried them upstairs with me as she followed. We could shower before we eat. I said ok that sounded like a winner. I undressed and prepared to enter the bathroom when Vicky grabbed my hand and hugged me, said what I had done to her this morning was so very exciting and a real surprise. Told her I hoped she enjoyed it, said she had as we went in and showered together and had sex while we bathed and when I came out I was clean and much relieved. As we dried off, asked what was for dinner and she said tacos, and had prepared them especially for me. I put on my sweat pants and top, she did the same and we went downstairs to eat, we had beer with our food, and they were some of the best tacos ever. I believe the best food is prepared at home. We ate and I helped her clean up, and shortly we were sitting in the living room looking at television. We looked at the news before we retired to the bedroom early and I crawled under the covers in the freshly made bed and Victoria and I hugged and told me to lie on my stomach as she massaged me again as I fell asleep.

Thirty-three

Tuesday: Day Thirty-three.

Another glorious day awaited me. I felt good as I woke and
rolled over and Vicky wasn't there. I could hear her in the
bathroom as I climbed out of bed and went in and found her
washing her face. She said good morning love as we kissed and
went about our business. By the time I had finished cleaning up
and shaving, Vicky was sitting on the edge of the bed waiting for
me. We lay across the bed and hugged and rubbed each other. I
said how about some breakfast baby girl, she said sure thing baby
boy, as we put on our clean bathrobes and headed downstairs. I did
the coffee as I always do and said I would like my eggs over easy
with sausage instead of bacon, she said my wish was her
command. She did as I asked, and soon we were sitting down
eating. I thanked her for being so attentive, said she would do
anything for me. After I finished eating and poured myself another
cup of coffee, I sat and watched while Vicky cleaned the breakfast
dishes and pans. I finished drinking and started to go upstairs; and
she followed close behind. I entered the bed room and began to
dress. I had just put my underwear on when Vicky approached.
She turned me around to face her and asked me to hold her before I
dressed. She had her robe on and it was open. I held her with one
hand as I passed the other over her warm body feeling her,
squeezing her arms, breast and butt. I felt between her legs as she
held on to me, I smacked her pussy several times before feeling
her. Shortly after she climaxed as I held her tight as she rocked
back and forth with climatic pleasure. I asked her if she was alright
now, and said in a bated breath she was. I released her and began
to dress. I put on my grey suit, blue shirt and a silver grey tie and
some cologne. Put some lotion on my hands, and a pair of black
shoes. I looked in the mirror and straightened my tie and saw
Vicky's reflection in the mirror as she put on a smock and was
starting to make up the bed. I placed my wallet and other stuff in
my pockets and told her I was leaving as she stopped and went
downstairs with me. When I got to the backdoor, I turned, pinned
her up against the wall again, bit her lightly on her neck, took her
right arm and put it behind her back holding it in place with my

left, as I felt between her legs with my right hand, and told her when I returned, if she hadn't been good, I would tie her up and whip her butt till it turned red, and she wouldn't be able to sit down. She soon climaxed several times and began crying and said she would be really very good. I said in a harsh tone you better be bitch, and the house better be clean, she said yes sir master Charlie, as I placed the fingers I had inside of her into her open mouth, and told her to suck them, she did as she was told. I then kissed her and she kissed me back and said she loved me. I turned and walked out the door as she stood and watched me get into my car and pull out. I closed the garage door as I drove away, and thought to myself that should really make her day.

I arrived early as usual and opened up as I went to my office and hung my jacket in the closet, then went to the lunchroom and started the coffee before returning to my desk, looked up Mrs. Kashia's number and dialed, she answered on the second ring, said good morning to her and who I was in case she hadn't recognized my voice and reminded her of the closing. She said and associate had called and she was well aware of the closing. I asked if she wanted me to pick her up, or did she want to meet me there. Said she preferred if I would be so kind as to pick her up. I said that would not be a problem, since the closing office wasn't very far away and would pick her up around ten thirty. She said that was fine and would be very happy to see me. I wondered what that meant based on the last time I had seen her. I hung up, went to the lunch room and poured myself a cup of coffee and headed back to my office and turned on my computers and the television, tuned to the local morning news and turned down the volume. Well yesterday cleared up a lot if all goes as planned. Wondered if Pat had received her car, I will soon find out when she comes in. At least by providing a company car my people will have reliable transportation, plus I have another tax write off, and began pondering the idea of providing the associates with one, maybe Green and Phillips at least, since they were employees. Retrieved the papers for the closing, and decided to carry my briefcase. Would have Joanne make out a check to New Age Marketing for

$140,000.00 and we will have a non-performance rider, and I will do some spot checks.

I opened the cabinet and checked the security cameras and looked at the parking lot, checked the time, it was eight thirty. Joanne pulled up and got out, and entered the building; she came straight up and ducked in and said good morning, and after getting some coffee she came back and sat in my office. I asked what had her here so early. Said she was up and just decided to see if she could be here before me, I laughed. She said after we had left yesterday it slowly started becoming hectic, like there was a sale going on. I said after we all agreed to use the marketing company and when we returned it truly justified our decision. She said listen to you, we this, we that, boy you are changing. I said more heads are better than one. I am running this like a corporation now, look at the profit we are expected to make, gross should be $44,000,000.00 and the net will be $28,000,000.00, and we will have to invest that. I have the closing today for one of the last listings I took. The contract signing tomorrow with the marketing company, and I don't know about those other three days. And when the marketing company begins selling the condos, I have a couple volunteers who will monitor things. So no moss will gather here. And also plan to get the marriage license tomorrow, so things are moving along. Then we have the association dinner, and by the way did you make the reservations yet. Joanne said, there was free parking but it was reserved and said that she had reserved a space for each of us. I asked about the two new associates and how they worked out. She said it was going along very well so far. We still have to get some pictures taken of us all, and stated I wanted a large clock for in here. Would you call a photographer for our group picture, she said what day. Thursday or Friday, really prefer a Thursday. Did Pat get her car I asked? Yes she replied and is overjoyed with it? She said ok and said she hoped Hippies brought some donuts. I said send Pat when she comes in if he doesn't, she said ok.

It was nine o'clock and everyone was coming in and I punched Samantha's number and asked her to come upstairs. She appeared about five minutes later, looking very pretty. I complimented her, and she was a very beautiful full figured woman. I asked her how much money would be needed to actually move from loan origination to and actual mortgage company. She said it would take several million, and said Anne might be better able to answer that question, I picked up the phone and called Ms. Jones and asked her to come to my office. She promptly appeared and I asked them to have a seat in the sitting area as I grabbed a tablet and we all sat together. Based on both of you having worked in the financial sector, what it would take to become a mortgage company. They said of course capital, and I asked, what other things would be necessary in order to accomplish this. They listed several things. Such as the value of the property, interest rates, etc. I asked them if they had the money would they loan money for the purchase of homes. They said it was very risky and that most big banks bundled loans after a short time, and had did that, but then had lent money to people they shouldn't have. It was called creative financing and that led to the last crisis. They both said they would look for other investment options other than becoming a mortgage lender. I was exploring options, and wanted their opinion, I thanked them. Samantha said we could do what is called self-finance. I had been basically doing that all along. Anne said you can charge yourself interest on loans and it would be tax deductible, and was done all the time. I knew about that but preferred to avoid doing business that way except for my own self-financed projects. She said it was a great way to tie up assets, and avoid taxes. I thanked them, but before you leave. You know in order to keep tabs on the marketing company would require working weekends, they both said yes, but would do it for me. They felt at home and felt I had done so much for them already and they would work out a schedule and asked if it would include Pat. I said if she wanted to, and they said she had expressed an interest, and would come see me soon, and they understood everyone would take part. I said yes, too much was involved not to.

I thanked them as they departed. I was glad I had Victoria because they were very beautiful women and I didn't like mixing business with pleasure. They were loyal and one of the reasons why I had never approached Joanne. It was almost ten when I went to get another cup of coffee and Pat had just returned from Famous Donuts, with a couple dozen. I picked a cream filled and sat there in the lunch room and ate it, drinking my coffee, just as Fitz came in and poured a cup and sat and talked to me, said he wanted to spot check the marketing company during the week. I said great because the girls were going to do the weekends. He said I guessed we have that covered. I said yes, and hope this all works out well. Pat entered and said oh here you are, and that she would participate with overseeing the marketing company also, and thanked me for the auto, and that she would coordinate with Anne and Samantha. I thanked her as she turned and left. Fitz said since I had hired Pat we were more on top of things and the backlog of paper work was starting to clearing up fast as the record keeping was becoming more quickly up to date now. Looked at my watch and said I have to go, I had a closing. He thanked me for being a great boss, and wished me well. I said he made me a good boss because of his loyalty. We shook hands and I returned to my office. Put on my suit jacket and picked up my briefcase and headed out to pick up Mrs. Kashia.

I walked down the stairs and stopped by the front desk and Mr. Green was handling things today, I spoke to him briefly before walking over to where Mr. Phillips was sitting looking at listings. I asked him to grab his jacket and come to the closing with me since it was his sale. He said yes sir and told him to call Joanne and let her know, which he did. When he finished we promptly left. We arrived shortly after at Mrs. Kashia's residence and entered and were buzzed in, we rode upstairs and she was standing in the doorway, and asked us inside, as she was preparing to leave she took her purse from the living room table. She was dressed in a light brown skirt with matching jacket with a light blue sheer blouse, light blue stockings and brown short heeled shoes, her hair was in a bun, she wore a beautiful gold necklace with matching earrings; and her makeup was not overdone and had on a pink shade of lipstick. She was a very beautiful woman. Mr. Phillips and I reentered the hall way as she locked her door. We went downstairs and exited and I opened the front car door for her. We headed for the closing office and she waited until Mr. Phillips opened the door for her, he had been the selling agent for this unit. We checked in and sat in the waiting area, until we were called. In the meantime Mrs. Kashia was being very seductive as she sat opposite me, crossing her legs so I had a very revealing and tempting view of her inner thighs and observed she was wearing crotch less panty hose and unbuttoned the top buttons of her jacket, and smiled at me while complimenting me on my suit. I thanked her and was glad they soon called us inside the room where the closing was being held as we handed over our papers to the closer and a few minutes later in came the buyers and there attorney, we all shook hands then sat at the table as the closer went thru the procedures and since the property wasn't encumbered with any leans it went fairly quick, the checks were cut and handed to us and the deed was transferred and it was over in a matter of few minutes. We wished the buyers well. This was for the one bed room unit that was previously occupied by Mrs. Cook. After wards I asked Mrs. Kashia if she wanted to stop and deposit her check. She responded yes please, and I asked her at which bank. She said First Century, and we drove over, it was in walking distance of her residence.

I parked and we accompanied her inside to make her deposit, we waited as she deposited her check and after she returned handed me an envelope which I placed inside my suit pocket. Once we were in the car I looked inside and it was a check for $5000.00. I turned to her and said that this wasn't necessary. She reminded me that I had done her a favor of removing a very undesirable person and had done it promptly. Said my office had contacted her again for the closing for the two bedroom unit and it was scheduled for next week. Felt I had done her a service beyond what any other agencies would have done and had been very prompt about it. I drove to her residence, walked around and opened the door for her, she asked me to please come up for a moment.

I left Phillips in the car and went upstairs with her. Upon entering her apartment she asked me to please sit down, she sat close by and asked if I was available for dinner. Told her I had just moved my office to a new location and was in the process of getting things organized because I had such a small staff. Said I appealed to her very much and would like to know me so much better. I said that in my business I had to be prudent when it came to dealing with clients on a very personal level, and we would have to conclude all our business relationships before I even took into consideration dealing with a former client on such a personal level. I thanked her for being a very generous client as I handed her back the check, and explained I couldn't and wouldn't accept it. Said I had a legal obligation to fulfill our contract according to the terms. I appreciated her offer of friendship but couldn't until all our business was concluded and then a certain respectable amount of time would have to pass before I would even consider any type of relationship. While I was talking she had unbuttoned the top three buttons of her jacket, and I could detect in her voice a certain excitement. I stood and said I had other business to attend to and looked forward to our next closing. She hesitated before walking me to the door and after having taken her jacket off, as she began to undo the top buttons on her blouse so she could make certain I could see she wasn't wearing a bra through the sheer material. I shook her hand, and could see her nipples standing up through the very thin material, as I exited her apartment. I waited for the elevator and turned around, looking back before it rang and noticed her blouse was completely unbuttoned as the elevator door opened and I entered. I turned around to face the door looking back as she completely removed her blouse before the elevator doors closed. I exited the building and got in the car, Jack asked me, what that was about.

I explained how you had to maintain the perfect business relationship at all times and briefly told him when I had gotten this listing about a person Mrs. Kashia wanted out of her unit. That I had removed them and found them a place to stay, told him why she had handed me the check and when I went upstairs, gave her back the check, and the reason I could not and would not accept it, and how she tried very hard to seduce me. She attempted to flirt with me before I got on the elevator. He said wow. I said as a man you have to be very, very careful every time you deal with any women, no matter where you are. I told him this conversation is between me and you. When Joanne came and first started to work for me. I saw a very beautiful and sexy woman, my wife had died a few months earlier and was grieving, but I had made a fortune on a stock I took a chance on and didn't care about anything but making some money. Joanne was going thru a hard time after her husband died as well, we all were then. I helped her and she stuck by me. I considered it a business relationship and it has been a very wonderful and fruitful one. I only recently allowed a woman to be close enough to live with me. And I only need one. I look at the women who work for me and they are some of the most attractive women I have ever seen, but it's for the eyes only. Remember, women have the power to make or break you, so you have to be strong and not sell out your morals. One night stands can mean your downfall if you are not careful. When you find a good woman, it's going to be a give and take situation, just be sure she's on your side. Be honest with them, don't lie and don't cheat, they know, you can't hide, they can smell another woman on you and little do you know it, your demeanor changes, and a good woman will study you, because she loves you and wants to make you happy, it only natural. Jack said his father had told him much the same thing as I had just told him. I said Jack you've been warned and it's up to you which road to take and the honest one is always the best. He thanked me for my advice and I said its lunch time.

We stopped by Super Burger and got us something to bring back with us, then headed for the office. We got out and Jack waited for me as I grabbed my briefcase and said he enjoyed having gone with me today. I told him I enjoyed his company, we entered and parted ways. I went up on the elevator, dropped my briefcase in my office and removed my jacket, and went to the lunch room and then the washroom to wash my hands, before returning to eat my lunch. I was sitting and eating when Pat and Anne entered with their lunches. Told Pat I have heard good things about your work, and just wanted to thank you for doing a fine job. She thanked me as I finished and went to the washroom before returning to my office.

I pulled out my phone and pulled up the home camera app, and checked in on Victoria. She was vacuuming the upstairs, and the house seemed in order. I closed the app and looked at the time, it was a little after two, turned to the security system and scanned the premises, and noticed Hartman and Newman on the phones. I called Joanne and asked if she had canvassed everyone for the association dinner, and she said yes, and everyone would attend. She had contacted a photographer and he would be here Thursday at ten, and I could decide what I wanted. I thanked her and hung up. I thought about tomorrow, now that I had one of the Kashia closing out the way. Hippies went to the court hearing about the golf course, and when I passed the mall, demolition had started and it wouldn't be long before they would be finished. I would bring Vicky with me and would stop by the court house on our way back which reminded me I needed to call and set a time. I looked thought the folder and dialed Mr. Peters. I had his direct number, and he picked up on the second ring. We spoke and agreed on eleven. And that he would have an agent there everyday from eleven until seven pm in order to maximize potential sales, and would have tables set up with the lenders cards and forms on them, that he had contacted the newspapers and they would start running the adds starting this Thursday and just wanted to confirm that I was going to go thru with our agreement because he usually didn't start before receiving a payment. I had every intention of using his firm for this venture, and stood behind my word. I informed him that my staff would also be checking to make sure things would go as agreed. He said he had no problem with that, and as a matter of fact, welcomed it. Told him I would see him tomorrow, we thanked one another and he hung up.

Well that was settled. It was three when Hippies appeared and said the judge continued the case until next week and would rule then. I informed him eleven tomorrow at the club house, he said ok, before leaving for his office. I sat back and thought about what I had told Vicky this morning and thought about having a little fun with her, and I would try something new, got to keep it exciting. I soon received a call from the agent handling the office complex near the condo complex I just purchased. He said the sellers had looked at my offer and he would fax me their counter offer, I asked how much, he said $2,000,000.00, I said send it and I would get back to him as soon as I could. He thanked me and I soon received the fax. I looked it over and would look at the property when I was in the area tomorrow. I would buy it and develop it myself, but first I would look at it, the land is what I wanted most. It was after four and was close to closing, so I started to line things up for tomorrow, I had stopped taking stuff home. And just set up things for the following day here, it was so much more convenient. I looked at my watch, and it was close to five, turned on the television as I noticed it getting dark outside and the lights coming on inside, there was a severe weather alert and thunder storms and heavy rain, and all of a sudden it just started to pouring down rain, the lights flickered for a second and my computer rebooted, the television went off and I turned it back on, the weather report was still on. I walked out of my office and around the atrium and looked out the window and it appeared the power was out in the neighborhood. I could see down the street over a block away and see the intersection and the traffic signals were out. We were the only folks around who had power. I returned to my office and noticed on the security screen a flashing icon and moved the mouse ball to it and clicked and the power screen came up, it showed power output and consumption, the length of time we had been on backup and shortly the utilities were restored. I watched the screen as it said outside power restored. I turned back to an outside camera and watched as traffic slowly began clearing up as it continued to rain hard. I watched the news station and there was always something tragic going on. It was very near five and I was all set for tomorrow and put on my jacket, closed up the cabinet that I used to monitor everything and shut down my computer and decided to check the building. Going to the back and through the big doors and took the freight elevator downstairs and checked the back doors before walking up front and sitting in the waiting area, the agents had left and Hippies and Fitz waved as they left, it was five to and Phillips and Green came over and we engaged in some small talk, Samantha came and sat with us, then Joanne, Anne and Pat came downstairs.

You all can go. I got this as they exited; I punched in the code and walked out. It was still cloudy and the exterior lights were on and the inside ones went off shortly after we departed. I pulled away and headed home, evidently there were sporadic power outages and it took a little longer than usual to get home. I noticed the neighborhood was dark, except for my house. I had a backup generator. I had this house built, and had a steel frame and concrete floors where others were wood. I had a backup power, sprinklers, and fiberglass sheeting under the tile roof, sound proofing and energy monitoring system along with the security system with inside and outside cameras, alarm system, motion detectors. I specked the systems myself. I backed inside and closed the garage door. I entered and Vicky was cooking dinner. I walked over to her as she was stirring some mixed vegetables. She covered them and turned the fire out, turned and threw her arms around me and kissed me. She asked if I wanted to eat first before changing. Yes, as I took my suit coat off and hung it over the banister and took off my shoes and washed my hands as Vicky dished us up. She had set the table complete with a chilled bottle of wine. She placed the plates on the table with the food; it was baked chicken breast with mixed vegetables and a salad, with French bread. I poured our wine and the food was very good and I complimented her on her skills. We finished eating, as I sipped my wine and looked at her. We cleared the table, and I sat at the counter and continued to sip my wine as I watched her cleaning up.

When she finished I gave her my glass to wash and after she placed it in the dish rack I asked her to come stand before me. Told her to open her smock, she did, and then I asked her did she remember what I had said before I left, she said, yes sir master Charlie. Told her I know you did everything I asked, didn't you. She replied yes sir master as I watched her anxiety slowly building. I stood and smelled her, she was slightly musty. I said you are dirty, you smell, and what do you have to say about that. She said she was dirty because she was cleaning her master's house. I said we are going upstairs and when you get there you are to crawl into the bedroom, do you understand, she replied yes sir master. I picked up my shoes and grabbed my jacket and when we reached the next level she got down on her hands and knees and crawled into the bedroom, I hung up my suit and emptied the pockets as she remained on the floor. I had only my underwear on and told her to stand and remove her smock; it's all she had on. Went and removed the ropes I had used on her before, told her to put her hands behind her back as I tied them. Took another length and put around her neck tying it between her breasts and running it down between her legs and tying it to her hands. Then made sure her pussy was between the two ropes, and took another strand and wrapped around her below her breast, and another just above tying them in back, similar to the Japanese art of rope tying known as shibari, I tied the two ropes together between her breast causing them to stick out along with her nipples. I looked at her and asked her did she remember what I had said this morning. She said yes sir master, looked into her eyes and asked her did she deserve to be punished. She said yes sir master. And asked if that is what she wanted, her response was yes sir master.

She was so excited as I touched her nipples with my fingertips, she flinched and moved away slightly, causing me to pinch them between my fingers and her knees to bent slightly as I told her to spread her legs. I looked as the ropes squeezed her pussy lips and caused her clit to start protruding as I touched her clit with a fingertip as she moaned and started to perspire. I gathered a handful of her hair in my hand and pulled her head back and kissed her, I told her the reason I was doing this to her was because she was mine and asked her if that is what she wanted. She said yes sir master that she would belong to me forever. I asked her if she was enjoying be tied up, she said yes sir master. I took the short whip, and paddle and returned to where she was standing as she was about to explode. I felt her ass and gave it several smacks on both cheeks with the paddle causing her to have a violent climax as I held the rope between her breast making her stand up and putting more pressure on her pussy as she jerked back and forth. I touched her nipple with one hand and squeezed as I held her in a standing position, before picking up the whip and using it on her butt and thighs and breast as she was rocked with several more orgasms. I stopped and knelt in front of her and licked the extended clit as it came out of hiding and she screamed and her knees buckled as I stood and eased her to the floor as spasm after spasm rocked her body as she knelt on the floor. I rubbed the inside of her thighs with my hand and enjoyed playing with her as I began to untie the ropes in the reverse order I had tied them. Then the only ones holding her were on her hands, as I played with her pussy and her whole body was covered with sweat. I laid her down and rolled her over and untied her hands as she lay on the carpet and begged me to take her and do what I wanted. I told her to get on her knees and bend over with her head on the floor. I smack her butt with my hand several times on both cheeks before I removed my underwear and entered her hot wet pussy, and placing a hand around her and rubbing her clit as she climaxed over and over again. I pulled out, and laid her on her back and climbed on top of her entering her again as I bit her nipples and told her she was my bitch as she exploded again. I pulled out and climbed up climaxing in her mouth and she then rubbed my come all over her face and said how sweet it was, we laid on the floor and held each other, after a while I pulled her up to sitting position, she said that was so exciting, and helped her up and we headed to the shower, where we felt on each other more, we were both exhausted after we came out and after drying each other off, we applied the massage oil to one another before we pulled the covers back and climbed in bed and continued to feel on each other, until we could no longer could stay awake. It was early evening still as we fell asleep.

Thirty-four

Wednesday: Day Thirty-four.

We woke again before six and quickly went to the bathroom to freshen up and relieve ourselves, and then returned to bed, hugging, kissing and caressing one another as if it was the very first time. I had never had as much pleasure and been so satisfied both with everyday life and sex until Victoria came into my life. She had said the same thing to me as we lay in bed holding one another. Every time we had sex it seemed different, and that having multiple orgasms now was a real surprise to her but understood she had never felt this way about anyone else before either and understood it must be true love. Told me that when I tied or restrained her it had made it just that much more intense for her and loved me for satisfying her submissive needs and it just drove her over the edge. Said she was getting hot just thinking about it and asked me to feel on her now. Before we knew it we were at it again as we made love and when we finished told her she was going with me today. We should eat first then come back and shower so we didn't smell like sex.

We fixed breakfast together again which was becoming routine as we prepared sausage, bacon, and eggs with a fried onion, toast and we again split a grapefruit, and having our morning coffee and coffee cake. We took our vitamins and soon cleaned up the kitchen together, as we sat back down and drank the last of the coffee as we just looked and smiled at one another. It was six thirty when we returned to the bedroom. Vicky made-up the bed while I shaved, and by the time I had finished she entered and we then showered together. When we finished we laid out a towel on top of the bed and applied a light coating of oil and lotion to ourselves. She asked what I wanted her to wear. I said what does my dear want to wear. She didn't want to wear any panties, and I looked at her as she spread her beautiful legs open for me. She said it isn't swollen anymore; but it needs some air and was more comfortable that way as she applied a light coating of petroleum jelly and the antiseptic cooling salve. I said do you have a dress that falls below your knees because you know it rises when you sit down, said she was well aware of that. She chose a solid tan colored skirt and wore her crotch less panty hose with designs, and a short sleeve pink blouse, with a jacket that matched the skirt with elbow length sleeves; she wore the gold necklace with matching earrings. She fixed her hair with a swirl in back, and wore her tan open toe high heel shoes with the matching purse, and her new perfume. I wore my bark blue pin stripped suit, a light blue shirt, and muted gold tie, and black shoes. I took a picture of her, and then she took one of me. We had taken our time getting ready and when we prepared to leave home it was almost eight, we went around checking the house before going to the garage. I opened the car door for Victoria.

We pulled out; and I made sure the garage door closed as I slowly pulled away as we headed for my office. We arrived and walked to the front door and placed my key in the lock, opened the door and punched in the code. It was about a quarter two nine when we pulled up. We were the first ones to arrive as we went upstairs to my office. I asked Vicky to have a seat, and then asked if she could walk around. I said of course and went to the lunchroom and made the coffee. She later returned to the lunch room where I was and said the building was just wonderful and very beautiful. I asked if she would like a cup of coffee, she said yes please. We then went to my office and I turned on my computer and the television, and asked if there was anything she wanted to see. No she replied, as I turned to a morning news show with the volume very low. I did my usual morning thing, checking listings, as my people began arriving. Joanne came in and was happy and surprised that Vicky was here, and said she would be right back. Joanne came back and said let me show you around. She took Victoria to her office, then to Fitz, and then introduced her to Ms. Jones. Then downstairs and introduced Ms. Washington to her, the new associates hadn't yet come in yet. Hippies came into my office and asked, are you ready for today. Yes, I replied as he sat down in front of my desk. We will have to go in separate cars, because I had a property to look at and was also going to the court house to get a marriage license. He said really. I said yes, and I brought her with me today and she's around here somewhere with Joanne. He wanted to be the first to congratulate me. He said it was a long time overdue. He asked what property as I handed him the sheet with the information, along with my offer and their counter offer. He asked what I was going to do. Said meet their offer and tear it down. Yes, it's less than a mile from the new complex, and asked him to check if he had any paper work to file and we could ride together. He came back and said no, he didn't, but we would use two cars, because he was bringing Ms. Jones. I said well a show of force. He said when we went the last time and we were talking, she had gone through every job they had ever performed for the past two years since they started. He said let me tell her to charge up her lap top and we will see you at ten. It wasn't long before Joanne and Victoria returned and was in Joanne's office sitting on the couch talking. I went to Joanne's office, and said sorry to interrupt, asked about the check, she said Hippies had it. I returned to my office and Hippies entered again and said he had all the paperwork we needed and also the check. Soon it was almost time, about a quarter two; he said he was waiting on Anne, as I went to get Victoria just as Anne walked up to me and said she was ready. We were all ready and prepared to leave, as we went downstairs and outside and I opened the car door for Victoria and we soon pulled out and Hippies and Anne followed.

We arrived and parked outside the club house just as Mr. Peters his secretary and one of his agents pulled up. We all shook hands and entered the club house as Hippies prepared to review the contract and handed Mr. Peters the nonperformance rider. We sat down at the table that had been set up the last time we were here and signed both contracts, the riders as we exchanged documents and we both had original copies. We discussed a start date, and we both agreed on tomorrow, to run concurrently for sixty days. Hippies then handed Mr. Peters the certified check, and we all shook hands again before departing. Our agent here would adjust his hours to those of the marketing company and would account for all keys. Both parties were in total agreement and I said to Mr. Peters I hope this goes well for both of us, because it could mean more business from me. He said he had a dozen employees and they were good at what they did. Peters and I shook hands again before departing. Hippies asked where the property that I was looking to purchase was located, and told him to just follow me. And several minutes later we pulled into a parking lot of a single story very dated office complex which covered several acers. We got out and Hippies walked up to me, and said for the land. Yes I replied, as we returned to our cars and departed. He and Anne were probably going to lunch. As Victoria and I headed for the county center and went to the recorder's office and filled out the necessary forms needed for a marriage license. Once we had that completed we returned it along with the necessary fee, one was handed to us but we would still have to wait three days before we could use it.

We departed happy and then drove to the Paris restaurant for lunch. We arrived and I used the valet parking. Entered we were promptly seated in a booth marked reserved. A waiter appeared and presented us with menus, and placed glasses of ice water on our table, he waited for us to order. Vicky said she would have whatever I had. I ordered the steak and lobster, with rice, and broccoli, and the house salad, with French dressing and two glasses of domestic red wine. He thanked us, went and placed our orders. While we waited for our food Victoria said to me, she was so very happy I wanted her to be my wife, she had dreamed of being with someone successful, but more than that, someone she could really love without any reservations. She loved me more than anything in the world and would always be by my side. We held hands; I kissed hers and said we needed to look at some wedding rings. I didn't want anything fancy, and she felt the same way, at least we both agreed on that. Our food soon arrived and it looked grand; the waiter asked if there was anything else. I said no, and thanked him. We ate our food and marveled at the flavors, and smells, it was all the more pleasant because we were together. We took our time eating, and savored every mouthful and when we finished, I ordered dessert, coconut pie with whipped cream on top and some coffee, and we were very satisfied. The waiter brought the bill and I placed the money in the folder. When he returned, I told him to keep the change. We finished drinking our coffee and soon departed, and waited for the valet to pull up our car, when he did I opened the door for Victoria. Tipped the valet and we headed for the Sweet Wood Mall and Howards Jewelry store.

We parked at the nearest entrance, I exited and opened the door for my soon to be wife. I was overjoyed and so was she, as we entered and went straight to the jewelry store. The same salesman greeted us from when I had purchased the necklace for Joanne and he waited on us again personally. We told him what we were looking for and Victoria showed him the ring she wore constantly, the gold engagement ring. He showed us several solid gold rings, and we chose a set that had two diamonds set in the center of the band, and they matched her engagement ring perfectly. I said we would take those, and he showed me a matching necklace, with earrings and bracelet. I said that's perfect. I used my credit card, and Vicky hugged me, and said I love you Charlie. We left with everything in a bag, then went and looked at some cute dresses. I suggested to Vicky that she pick something out for our wedding day. She found a skirt and jacket set, it was a lime green, the skirt was above the knee, and had a jacket with sleeves that ended just above the elbow with a matching vest, and said she wanted to try it on, and went to the fitting room. She came out and said she wasn't satisfied with the color, went back to the rack and picked out one that was light blue, and returned to the fitting room and tried it on; she modeled it for me and said she was much happier with the color, and it looked marvelous on her. She changed back and we looked at a few more and found a couple of summer dresses, and soon said she was satisfied and ready to go. The saleslady bagged the items, I paid and we left. I asked her if there was anything else she wanted, she said yes. I asked her what it was, and she said me.

We kissed right there in the middle of the mall, and then headed for the car. I placed the items in the trunk and we headed back to my office. It was close to three when we returned, and I went straight to my office and Victoria asked to use the washroom, and showed her where it was, as she headed that way. Hippies had made copies of all the agreements and they were in folders on my desk, and I filed them in my desk file drawer. I pulled out the info on the old office complex and submitted a bid, I offered $6,000,000.00 and filled out a fax cover sheet and sent it. So far

the day has been very productive, and was quite satisfied, when I
went downstairs and Phillips was at the front desk today. I spoke to
him and found my new associates at different stations. I sat and
spoke to Mrs. Hartman, asked how she was doing and if she was
satisfied working out of our office. She replied she was more than
happy, and thanked me for the invitation to the association dinner.
She stated that at the last office the associates would have to pay
their own way, and said it would be a privilege to come as a
member of Harcourt Reality. I thanked her for her enthusiasm and
spoke to Mrs. Newman. Asked her if she was satisfied working
here. She said yes and the environment was pleasant, wasn't
anyone breathing downs her back and she was starting to pick up
listing because it was just different, and more relaxed atmosphere
and thanked me for the invitation to the dinner, she also said the
same thing as Mrs. Hartman about having to pay and was very
thankful. And said she wouldn't disappoint and would be sure to
attend. I thanked her and went to find Samantha. She was busy, I
stepped in and said, just wanted to say hi, she said please come in.
I did and had a seat in front of her desk, and noticing she had
brought some plants in of her own, and I asked about them, she
said they were happy here and went on to explain they were
cuttings from a much larger plant and were easy to grow. And I
asked what about you. Said to me that was a silly question, she was
overjoyed, and had gotten seven applications accepted since being
here and we would soon receive the fees. I am glad you are happy
here and I am personally happy to have you as part of the
origination. Stated she had met Victoria, and she is very sweet and
personable. Thank you and told her we are going to be married, she
stood up and came around her desk and hugged me. I'm so happy
for you and you deserve to have someone who loves you. She said
it's so obvious that we were both in love. I stated we went to get
the license and rings today. When and where, she asked. I said the
courthouse, the when I didn't know yet, because I had to see about
selling the condo complex first. Said don't you worry about that,
we all have discussed it and Fitz has taken charge and we have
kind of worked out a plan. I will be making pop appearances also. I

thanked her, and exited her office as I looked in the waiting area and it was empty, and returned upstairs to my office.

I looked over before entering and Victoria and Joanne were sitting on her sofa talking. After I entered, noticed a fax, picked it up to read. It was from Beverly Heights Reality and it was an acceptance conformation on my offer for the dilapidated office complex I looked at today. It was from Mr. Hogan, the listing agent and broker, and he also sent me the occupancy rate sheet, with the rents and lengths, looks like they had other intentions for the site also; they hadn't renewed any leases in the past nine months, and this one I may try to develop. But first would have to come up with a plan, get permits and approvals, and search and check around for what would best work at that location. I had an architect and that was a plus. But first things first, let me acquire it, one thing at a time. I walked around to Pat and Anne's office and checked on them, they both were busy on their computers and decided not to disturb them. I knew we had a backlog of work, especially the apartment complexes, entering the rent reports and the information from the banks, the only reason no one got away with not paying rent was because the banks would red flag the non-payments. Then there was the taxes which were something we really had to stay on top of, at least I had gotten that under control. Joanne had done all of that in the past as I acquired more property and was one of the reasons renters sent there checks to the bank. It still was the way to go. I had continuously turned over my profits into assets. It was a better write off than just sitting on cash. Though I did have a couple offshore accounts that I pumped money into. I wasn't being slick, I was being smart. I used donations also to various originations, the hospitals and several schools. My assets were so well hidden I didn't come up on anybody's radar, and the amazing thing is, I did it in nine years. I amazed myself when I sat back and looked at it all. I would know this year for sure how much when we would do a self-audit. Then I will probably hand out some bonuses to my employees, and some pay raises.

It was five when Victoria returned to my office; she hugged me as I sat at my desk. I stood and walked over and we sat together on the sofa. Joanne came in and sat in one of the chairs. I told Samantha so it's no secret any longer. Joanne said she hoped we had many happy years together. I informed her about the office complex, and that they had accepted my offer. She said that was good and asked what I was going to do with it. I said have it demolished, because it was one of the first ones built in the area, and now the land is what's of value. And was seriously thinking of developing it myself and hiring Mr. Brown, and have him draw up some plans for something modern and energy efficient.

Joanne said we looked cute together, and could tell we were happy with each other. I said god sent her to me, it wasn't the way I would have imagined it, but it happened anyway and I have never loved anyone like I love her. Tears filled Victoria's eyes as she began crying and hugged me. Joanne brought her some tissue. I told Joanne she's a crier. Joanne said she's emotional, and said she would be to if she were as happy as she is. Vicky dried her eyes and in a halting voice, said I made her so very happy, she had a hard time controlling her emotions, she had never been this happy in her life before ever, and thanked God every day for me. I patted her on her back, and told her I loved her, as she turned and said I know you do, I feel so blessed. I looked at my watch and said it's almost time for us to go. Joanne said let me go clean up, as Vicky asked if she could go with her, and she said come on honey, as they walked out together. I went and straightened my desk and prepared for tomorrow when Mr. Washington would come and we closed our deal. Well everything was set for tomorrow when Vicky soon returned and I looked at her walk, the shape of her legs, and her face and truly saw the woman of my dreams. I stood and walked towards her and hugged her as we held each other, and then put my jacket on as we headed downstairs in the elevator. I said to her after we got off, when I get you home I am going to eat you. She said shame on you Mr. Charlie, as we sat in the waiting area as everyone slowly gathered, when everyone was accounted for, Joanne, Hippies, Fitz, Pat, Anne, Samantha, Phillips, Green, Brown, Hartman and Newman. I have an announcement to make, I asked Victoria to stand. Victoria and I are getting married, we haven't set a date yet, but it will be at the court house, and we probably will have a reception. Just wanted, you all to know. They congratulated us, and then we all walked out together. I punched the code and the doors closed.

We got in our cars and headed home. When we arrived I backed inside as usual. Vicky stepped out, as I opened the trunk and we carried her packages to the back door. I opened it and let her in and we went straight upstairs and undressed. Washed our hands and brushed our teeth and neither one of us was hungry. I said to her as we stood nude facing each other that I was hungry for her and thought of putting my face between your legs and licking you all day as a shiver went through her. Said she wanted to feed her man and laid on the bed, and spread her legs open for me as I laid down between them and smelled her sweetness and put my face in her pussy and began to lick and suck her as I held her with my arms under her thighs, and felt her breast squeezing her nipples. She moaned loudly and soon exploded as I held her and continued as she came again, reaching down, trembling and pulled me on top of her. We kissed as I slowly slid into her, stroking back and forth slowly as she screamed, then the both of us climaxed together as we just laid there holding one another until I rolled on my side as we looked at each other and continued to feeling on one another. We lay there a long time, and were so happy just being together. We decided to go wash up, fix a pizza and have some drinks before we showered and went to bed. After we washed up Vicky hung up her new clothes, and put the jewelry away, before we headed downstairs in our jogging suits. We took a pizza out of the freezer, turned on the oven, and I doctored it with olive oil, seasonings and extra cheese before placing it in the oven. We had an unfinished bottle of wine, and it was just enough for two glasses. It wasn't long before the pizza was done and we sat and ate and drank the wine as we looked at one another smiling the whole time. When we finished, we were very satisfied and cleaned up as usual. Then went to the basement and fixed some drinks and sat on the couch and hugged. We watched some television and decided to play some pool; we each won a game and enjoyed our activities together. When we tired, we closed up, shut everything down and went upstairs so we could bath each other, we weighed ourselves and found we were both ten pounds lighter. We enjoyed bathing and feeling each other and soon we both had climaxed again and were feeling the effects of and over active sex drive and alcohol, as we dried one another off. We hugged and kissed, told one another how much we loved the other before spreading out a towel and applying some oil to our tired bodies as we felt each other more. We were very tired now and by the time we finished, pulled the covers back and the only thing we could do was hold each other, and that's all I remember as we very soon went to sleep.

Thirty-five
Thursday: Day Thirty-five.

I woke up first, looked over at Victoria, she was sound asleep. I wasn't ready to get up yet, my bladder wasn't calling me home yet, and so I just laid and looked at the ceiling. It wasn't long before I had to get up and relieved myself. I felt better and washed my face, sat on the toilet and just held my head in my hands, and thought I hoped happiness didn't kill me, but what a way to go. I finished, cleaned myself up and returned to lie next to the love of my life. Even though she was sleeping hard, I would have to wake her or she would never forgive me. I touched her smooth skin, oh how she excited me so, I couldn't get over it. That first day, in the back of my mind, I knew inside we were going to have sex. But had never imagined it being so intense and appealing to what I felt was my dark side that I had suppressed and kept hidden only to myself for so long. I rubbed her back and she started to moan, and then slowly she rolled over and opened her big beautiful eyes. She smiled at me and reached for me as we embraced. She said in a low soft voice that she loved me, we kissed and I said the same. I ran my fingers thru her soft hair, rubbed her back down to her butt and then down to her thighs. Said to her, love it's time for us to get up and start another new day. She asked if I would hold her. I said always my love as we held each other; wasn't long before she had to pee. I released her as she arose and went into the bathroom, and then returned after she had freshened up and we laid and held each other again, feeling all over one another. I had one important meeting today, and had to attend. I said to Victoria we need to eat, she said yes sir, and asked me what I desired. I said what you usually prepare for breakfast.

We got out of bed and put on our robes and headed downstairs. We did our usual morning breakfast thing and soon we were eating and drinking coffee. We finished and cleaned up, and went back upstairs together. Vicky hugged me and asked me to hold her again. I said to her you looked ravishing yesterday and I am proud to be seen with you my dear. I held her with my left hand around her shoulders as I felt her chest with my right and slowly moving down between her legs as she opened them to let me feel her.

Asked her do you want me to touch you, yes please Mr. Charlie, I love you and please feel me. I felt her as she placed her head on my chest and climaxed, not once but twice. Looked at me and said, thank you, as she kissed me. I placed my leg between hers and held her tight as she humped my leg climaxing again several more times until I laid her on the bed exhausted. I covered her with her bathrobe and went to the closet and began dressing. I was wearing jeans today and dressing more casual. We were having photos taken today, but I had taken a suit and left it in the closet at work. I came over and sat on the bed next to her as she reached for my hand and put two of my fingers in her mouth as she turned toward me. I took my hand away from her mouth and pulled her up, placing her head in my chest as I petted her. I stood and she followed, putting her bathrobe on as we went downstairs and through the kitchen to the back door. I turned and pushed her gently against the wall looking into her eyes and kissed her as I held her hands at her side, then said, I love you Victoria and when I return I am going to make love to you again. I felt her again between her warm thighs, pinching her clit with two fingers as she shuttered again with another rousing climax, before placing the same hand in her open mouth as I said to her, you belong to me now and forever. She cried as she hugged me and said she couldn't get enough, kissed my neck and cried more, and said I love you so, so much Mr. Charlie. I kissed her lips one last time and walked out the door, as I turned to get in my car saw her standing there, her eyes filled with tears, of joy holding on to the door frame.

I got in, started the car, opened the door and pulled out, closing the garage door behind me as I headed to the office. I was the first to reach the office, opened the doors and punched the pin number in, walked to the elevator, and rode up to my office, hung my sports jacket up and went to the bathroom and washed my hands before going to the lunch room and making coffee. I sat and waited until the first pot brewed, then put the second on to brew, and poured a cup and headed back to my office. I sat at my desk and turned everything on, remembering that today was picture day, and had decided a few days earlier to bring one of my older suits and leave it here along with a pair of shoes. Mr. Washington was coming to hand over his half of the mortgage origination company to me and that wasn't until eleven. After that the day was open and I thought about having Chinese for lunch. I opened the security cabinet and moved the mouse, watched the screen come to life. It was eight forty-five, turned on the television and watched the morning news; this was something I couldn't do before we moved. The weather was the most important thing to me after watching the markets, and luckily it was still a bull market. Read the business section of the newspaper from yesterday, only one article caught my eye.

Huge complex to be marketed as condos after being sold to Harcourt Realty, and they had hired New Age Marketing to handle the sales, and expected sales to be brisk since there was a growing demand for quality housing in the area. The units were considered to be luxury and were extra-large in size and the amenities were top shelf and they were located in an exclusive residential area. Sales were to begin at the end of the week with daily open house showings. Well I see, Mr. Peters wasted no time, probably knew the reporters and tipped them off if he just didn't write the story himself.

I watched as Joanne pulled in and parked, oh she was dressed for the photos, and her appearance was very striking. She was a very beautiful woman and received compliments all the time. It was still early when she came into my office. She was dressed like she was a CEO, she wore a business suit with a skirt just above the knee, a solid dark blue color, high heels, stockings to match and had her hair was done. She wore her makeup well, as I stood and complimented her on her appearance. She looked at me and said I know you are not going to take photos dressed like that. I said no, but had a suit in the closet; she suggested I should change now. I said yes Mrs. Bradley, as she went to her office and I went to the closet, and took out my suit and trousers and headed to the washroom to change my pants. Returned and finished dressing. It was a plain black suit, white shirt, black socks and loafers, with a silver tie. As a matter of fact, it was the same suit I wore in the last photos I had taken and was ready now.

It was past nine and everyone was here, a little after nine thirty the photographer came to Joanne's office and then to mine. We shook hands and I explained what I wanted and we went down stairs, and he suggested for the portrait shots he use the back side of the elevator down stairs for a background, it was marble. He was concerned about reflections but had a flat colored back ground sheet he hung from the wall with masking tape. I paged everyone and we all went outside, he lined us up. Joanne and I center, with Hippies and Fitz flanking both of us, with Green and Phillips next to Fitz on Joanne's side, then Pat, Samantha, and Anne, with Ms. Brown and Mrs. Newman and Hartman behind. He took several shots, with me in front, with everyone turned slightly across, facing center, then with Joanne, Hippies, and Fitz, then with, Samantha, Anne, and Pat. He took several that way, then with Green and Phillips center, flanked by Brown, Newman and Hartman. We were finished outside and everyone lined up for their individual portrait photos, he took several of everyone. We were soon finished and he folded up his equipment and said we would have them tomorrow. I thanked him as I returned to my office to change.

Close to eleven Mr. and Mrs. Washington entered my office, I greeted them, and asked them to have a seat on the sofa or couch. I picked up the phone and called Hippies to my office and asked him to bring the paper work, called downstairs and asked Samantha to come to my office. Mr. Washington said he had gone to the old office and saw the sign before coming here. Said this was really beautiful. I thanked him as Hippies entered and took a seat. The Washington's were a lovely couple, but you could see the years of stress on their faces and were beginning to slowly recover from the daily grind of trying to make a living. I told Mr. Washington, I had thought about his first offer and was going to give him what he had originally asked for. Samantha entered and hugged her dad and kissed her mom and I asked her to sit with them. He was surprised by it, and thanked me. I said don't, I know it was a very stressful business to be in and after talking to Samantha, I made her and employee of my company to relieve her of that stress of working off of a percentage. Besides, I could use her elsewhere, if we needed too. Hippies presented him with the papers to sign, which he did and handed him a check, he looked at it and said its more than you said. Yes it was for $500,000.00. I said it was a retirement gift from me to you and your wife for all the years we had helped each other. I told him I had been blessed and had to pass it on. He hugged me and shook my hand; I wished him well and hugged Mrs. Washington as well. I asked Samantha if she would show her parents out and if they wanted to look around they were more than welcome. Hippies said to me ok, one more piece of business concluded. About twenty minutes later, Samantha entered my office; she grabbed my hand and hugged me and started to cry, and said that she wanted to thank me for what I had done for her parents. I hugged her and patted her on her back and said to her, God said to treat people like you want to be treated, she cried even more then as Joanne came and asked her what the matter is. I asked Joanne, take her to your office please, I'm going to lunch, and would return later. Samantha thanked me and left with Joanne.

I arrived at Wong's and was greeted by no other than Mrs. Wong, she said right this way, and presented me with the menu and sat down and asked, when you marry. I looked at her and smiled and said very soon. She said, girl love you very, very much. I said yes and I love her. She loves you hard, you not find ever again, Wong know ok. I said yes and she is sweet. I told her I was ready to order and would have the lunch box with chicken, fried rice, and miso soup. She took my order and disappeared to the kitchen. I sipped the tea Fawn had brought to the table as I waited for my food. Pulled out my phone and checked on Victoria, she was cleaning, and doing some wash, and then fixed herself some ramen noodles, then sat down to eat. I turned off when my food arrived, delivered by Fawn. I thanked her and thought, about what had happened today. I had more than enough money and my offer before today to Washington, was cut throat and I felt bad when I looked at the sum total of what I had accomplished. And it was through the hard work of people like him and his wife and it was time I paid the people who deserved it. I also felt better for having done it. I enjoyed my food and Fawn soon brought the bill, I paid and left, as Mrs. Wong caught me before I got to the door and said to me. You marry girl and be happy man. I said for sure, and thanked her and said I would be back soon. Before returning to the office I stopped at a furniture store. I was looking for one of those huge oversized wall clocks to place on my office wall, found what I was looking for and they had one in a box. I picked a couple of large pictures also but would have them delivered. Paid with my company credit card, loaded the box with the clock in the back of the car and continued on my way back. I arrived back at the office and removed the boxed clock and took it up to my office. Took it out the box and decided to place it where I could just glance up at it. Looked in my drawer where I kept some odds and ends found a hook and nail unopened and some batteries. Looked in a small box where we had kept some tools at the old office and pulled out the hammer. After placing the batteries in the clock and setting the time, I hung my clock. Put everything back and sat down and it was perfect. I preferred the wall clock over having to look at my watch which I didn't always wear, and was satisfied now.

Joanne saw me return and noticed my clock, and said she liked it, before telling me how nice it was of me what I had done for the Washington's. Said that she had never heard of anyone being so generous ever, and that Samantha will forever do whatever I wanted just because of that. I can't help myself, and told her I wanted to audit our assets soon. Said I was afraid we were much larger and more monetized than we thought, and it had been a while since we had done one. Said she would do it herself. You know you have weekends off, when you feel our people have things under control. She would monitor on weekends rather than working all day. I was going to do the same and she asked if I wanted her to look in on the condo sales. No, you watch over the office, that's enough and said Fitz has taken that over along with Pat, Anne, and Samantha, so I think that's pretty well covered. She asked what you are going to do now. I was thinking of leaving early. We have cleared up everything that was carried over from the old office. She said yes we have. I like that, you beat me to it. You mean the clock. Yes she replied. Told her where I had made the purchase and that they had many different styles, and if you do to use the corporate card. You look very lovely, and kissed her on the cheek as I left.

I headed home and it was just after two when I backed inside, and entered. I was calling for Victoria, and found her downstairs preparing to use a wet mop. Surprise I said, she didn't hear me because the radio was on. She came and hugged and kissed me. All she wore was her smock as I felt underneath and she started moaning. I told her to finish cleaning, she said ok. I went upstairs, undressed, and freshened up, putting on a pair of shorts and a long t-shirt, before going back downstairs to the basement and fixing myself a drink as Vicky was mopping. I turned the radio down, and told her to come here for a moment. I asked her to take the smock off and then continue, she did and continued mopping. I sat and sipped my drink and watched Victoria as she cleaned, this is what masters do. This excited me very much and I know it was exciting to her. I could tell by her movements. She finished mopping and then I noticed the vacuum cleaner, and then she went and unloosened the cord and plugged it in, and began vacuuming the carpeted area. I thought next time I would have her wear some hi-heels that would be even sexier. She finished, wound up the cord, and placed the vacuum in the closet. She came to where I was sitting, and told her to put her hands behind her back, as I felt between her legs. Asked her, if watching her clean in the nude was exciting to her. She said very, and she was about ready to explode. I felt her and squeezed as she climaxed. I pulled her to me and we hugged. Put your smock back on baby. She said why, I said so I can maintain some measure of self-control. I asked her what she had for lunch, and replied some ramen noodles. What's was for dinner. She hadn't thought about it. We weren't hungry and decided to wait, went to the bedroom, undressed and climbed onto the bed.

Tell me what I said when I left. She said you were going to make love to me, and I have been waiting all day for you Mr. Charlie. Please fuck me Mr. Charlie; I lay next to her pulling her to me and feeling her butt and between her legs, I said you are so wet. She replied when I came to the basement it excited her more, and every time I told her to do something it made her wetter, and said she was about to come right now. I said don't you come yet or I will spank you. She replied spank me because she had lost all self-control as she climaxed right then and screamed, and please make love to me, please. I climbed on top of her and I wasn't gentle this time and she screamed, fuck me, yes fuck your pussy Mr. Charlie. I was rough with her as she exploded and climaxed, over and over again. I came in her as she screamed. We lay breathless for several long minutes. We held each other and she said that she was so excited by everything I did and said to her. Then when I ordered her around she tingled inside, and couldn't get enough of me, and was excited now and asked me to feel her again now. I did and she held on to me. You have tired me out and we need to shower, because I want to get some sleep now, as I kissed her and said I am glad you are here. We dragged ourselves to the bathroom and it was a good thing there was a seat in the shower, we were both weak from all the sex as we bathed each other, which we both enjoyed doing. We felt each other as the warm water ran over our bodies. When we finished, and dried off, took a dry towel and spread on top of the bed, as we have done in the past, and rubbed oil on one another. I said to her I can't get enough of you, I love you so much. We removed the towels, pulled the covers back and climbed in bed. We were soon in each other's arms until I turned over and she held me placing an arm around me as we fell asleep.

Thirty-six
Friday: Day Thirty-six.

I opened my eyes, looked over at the illuminated clock, and it was two thirty am. I got up and went to the bathroom, what a relief, as I washed my face and hands, rinsed my mouth and returned to bed. Vicky had rolled over and was laying on her side with her back to me. She rolled over and reached out as I grabbed her hand. She rose up and went to the bathroom and I could hear her as she flushed the toilet and washed her hands and face also before returning to bed. We pulled the covers over us and began touching one another before I kissed her and turned over and felt her rubbing my back before I dosed off again. When I woke up again it was five thirty. I lay on my back and Vicky rolled over, and asked if I was awake. I said yes, and she came closer and hugged me. She rubbed my face as I turned to look at her. She said love of my life; I love you so much as she felt my body. I turned and felt her as she moaned and placed her head against mine. We had slept more than eight hours. We needed the rest more than anything, and now we needed some food. Vicky said we needed to get some groceries and was running out of everything. I said we will go today love. Told her not to ask me to rub or touch her, because I couldn't take anymore. Please, no more pussy please, I can't do this every day. I had to pee and went to the bathroom and weighed myself. I felt good and my jeans had more slack in the waist and when I looked, had lost thirteen and a half pounds. Was she trying to kill, me with pussy. I could just imagine the headlines (man dies from overdose of pussy); it was so funny I started to laugh out loud, (coroner determines death by nymphomaniac), and wondered if it had ever happened. I laughed so hard and long Vicky came in to see if I was all right. I said yes, and had a thought that was really funny to me. She asked what it was. Said I had just weighed myself and had lost thirteen pounds, and told her about what made me laugh, she said that wasn't very funny. I told her to weigh herself; she did and had lost fifteen pounds. I told her we must eat and keep our hands to ourselves. She said that was going to be difficult, but would try. I put on my jogging suit, and she dressed the same, now I can't see you and get aroused. We headed downstairs to the kitchen and scrounged up something to eat. We managed to fix a decent breakfast, eggs, bacon, sausage, toast with jelly with the last grapefruit.

The fridge was so empty I wiped it down on the inside after making some fresh dishwater; it hadn't looked this empty since it was new. We ate and drank coffee and we ate the last donut and the last piece of coffee cake. I looked in the freezer, in the cabinets; it looked like I was unemployed. I turned to her and said you could have gone to the grocery store anytime. She stood there, looking stupid and sad. I asked her what she had to say for herself since your job is to maintain the house. Sorry was all she said. I shook my head in discuss and said ok then, we are going to the grocery store today, and if you decide not to go in the future you let me know so I can, you understand me Victoria, she said yes sir. It was very early, and one of the bulk retailers would let you in with a corporate account at seven, otherwise you had to wait till ten. We would take the minivan I rarely used now and it had been a while since I needed to haul some large objects or a quantity of material. I used it more often in the past when I was scouting out property or needed to take clients around in the past. We went upstairs and dressed. I made sure I had my wallet and other trinkets, we both wore jeans and I could see the weight loss on Vicky. It's not that she looked bad, but didn't want her to disappear on me. I went around and made sure the house was secure before we headed to the garage.

We got in the minivan and I pulled it out and let it run a few minutes, letting the smoke clear out the garage since it had been a while since driving it last. After I closed all the garage doors we were off, and arrived at Dave's Discount ten minutes before they opened, several people were outside the front doors waiting as we sat in the van. I got out and opened the side doors and folded the rear seats down, I knew we were going to have quite a load; I really didn't need a list because we didn't have anything left as I checked all the cabinets, the laundry room and the basement fridge. I had asked Vicky about the laundry, and cleaning supplies. She had no answer, so I checked and found we were down to the last bottle of everything.

The doors opened and I told her to get a cart and I took a flat bed, showed my membership and we entered, most people who shopped at this hour were people who had small shops and this is how they stocked up. The cleaning supplies were in the first section we came to, so I just placed cases on the flat bed, detergent, bleach, dish washing liquid, softener, disinfectant spray, toilet paper, and paper towels as we headed to the meat coolers, this is when I started placing stuff in Vicky's cart. Placing, three double packets of bacon, a variety of cheeses, then to the walk in coolers and placed a couple dozen eggs in her cart, then two boxes of three pizzas each. Vicky said where are you going to put all of this? I said you never saw the freezer and fridge in the basement. I said guess you were too busy cleaning. I reached and filled her cart with cases of assorted can goods, and then the bathroom supplies, toothpaste, mouthwash, soap, bath washes, and other assorted supplies and asked her if I had forgotten anything. She didn't think so, as we then headed for the checkout, the total came to $665.34, as we then pushed it to the loading dock. I left her with the supplies with her and got the van and pulled it over. I opened the doors and placed the large bulky and heavy cases in first and then Vicky started to load the other stuff from her cart. With that completed we headed home. It took us about an hour to haul in and put everything away where it belonged. Then I said come, as we headed back out to the regular grocery store and I having Vicky push the cart as, I filled it with veggies, and donuts and everything I thought we would need. Then turned to her and asked her was there anything I missed or she wanted. She couldn't think of anything. I walked up to her, looked her in her face and said are you sure. She was looking down and acting coy. I placed my hand under her chin and raised her head up and looked in her eyes, and said, are you positive. She wanted some lipstick and fingernail polish. I said ok. She went and got herself some douche, deodorant and other feminine items before we headed for the checkout. After we packed this load in the van, I drove to the health food store to get a resupply of vitamins.

Then we headed home. Joanne called me on my cell phone and asked me if I was coming in today, I said no, and asked her if everything was ok, said everything was fine. Ok. Joanne said enjoy your day, I thanked her and hung up. We arrived home and put the purchases away, and it was near eleven as I rechecked to make sure I hadn't missed anything. I told Vicky to come with me as we got back in the van and headed for Super Burger, went inside and had hamburgers with French fries, and some soda. Vicky looked happier now and I could tell she was hungry. After we ate I drove to the forest preserve and we went for a walk, we walked a little more than an hour, before returning to the van and heading home. I had tired Victoria out, and suggested we have a bottle of wine, so we went to the basement and opened a bottle of white wine, I don't care for white, but women do. I sipped on a glass and Vicky really liked the taste. She had several glasses and it wasn't long before she was laid out on the couch asleep.

I had accomplished what I intended to do, since I was a little pissed at her letting us run out of groceries and this was her punishment. I left her there and returned upstairs to the kitchen to straighten things out, arranged the food in the fridge better and in the freezer also, and returned back downstairs to do the same. I took her shoes off and covered her with a light blanket I kept in the basement, before returning back upstairs. I set out some ground beef to thaw and went to the bedroom and put on some more comfortable clothes. It was about six o'clock when I finished cooking and had everything prepared, we were having tacos. It was after six when I went downstairs to wake her; she sat up slowly as she began to wake. I told her to wash her hands and come upstairs to eat. I left her sitting on the couch and returned to the kitchen and began preparing our plates. She appeared after several minutes and told her to have a seat. I placed a plate in front of her and a glass of soda. Then returned for mine, we said grace and sat and ate in silence, she eventually said the food was wonderful, finished and asked if she could have another. She helped herself to more before cleaning her plate. I cleared the table and washed the dishes and put away what we hadn't eaten. She approached me, and said you are mad at me, aren't you. I'm not mad, just very disappointed with you. She was sorry I felt that way, and asked what she could do to make it up to me. I told her not to let us run out of food or anything else again without telling me, or going to the store and taking care of things. To start making out a list and she would have to start going to the grocery store. She sat down and sipped her soda. I went to the office and turned on my computer and checked the data from work. She came into the room and sat down. I hadn't hugged her or kissed her since we left to go shopping, and told her to go find something to do, clean the house or something. She got up and left the room. I sat back and checked my files, everything at work was ok. I went through the internal house cameras and she was upstairs vacuuming, she had tears in her eyes, she stopped and sat against the wall in the hall with her head between her knees crying. I didn't feel sorry for her and anticipated her next move. I bet she was going to come to me and offer herself, probably nude with a whip in her hands. I watched her as she stood and continued vacuuming. The house was clean and I knew this was hard on her to find something to clean or to do. I went downstairs to the basement and fixed a drink. I waited to see what she would eventually do. I went back upstairs to my office and sat at my desk and looked at the cameras. Vicky was cleaning the bathroom, good she got over it. I turned it off and went back to the basement to freshen my drink, turned on the radio, and decided to shoot some pool.

I had been playing about half an hour, when I saw in the corner of my eye Victoria. She came over, waited a few minutes, and said Charlie. I was surprised; she was still wearing the shorts and t-shirt. I said yes Victoria. Said she wanted to talk to me. Ok, as I placed the pool stick back in the rack and went and sat in the chair by the couch. She sat on the couch, said she was very sorry that she had let the food and supplies run out, and wanted me to forgive her. She said please forgive her. I said ok, you are forgiven, and then refreshed my drink. I asked her if she wanted one. Yes please. I fixed her one and she sat at the bar. She sipped her drink. And Vicky asked if I still loved her. I told her yes. She said I hadn't held her or kissed her, and felt I didn't want her any longer. I said because we aren't all over each other doesn't mean I stopped loving you. We were acting like children who had a chance to eat all the candy they wanted, and like children, just because it's there doesn't mean you have to over indulge. That's all that's happening. Said she understood, and sipped her drink. She asked if I was going to hug her anytime today. Yes I reassured her. She asked if I would hug her now. Sure, and she came behind the bar and we hugged, and I kissed her. Said again she was sorry that I was pissed off at her and wouldn't let it happen again, as she returned to her stool and sat down, and sipped more of her drink. I enjoyed the dinner very much and would cook tomorrow. I looked at the clock; it was almost nine. I finished my drink and Vicky had finished hers, as I cleaned up the bar and took our glasses upstairs, washed them in the kitchen and left them in the dish rack. I then went upstairs and undressed and went to the bathroom. Vicky followed, as I entered the shower and began to bathe. Vicky came in and we showered and bathed each other. We dried off and oiled up. I pulled the covers back on the bed and got in. I kissed her and said I do love you. She kissed me back and I rolled over and laid in the bed waiting to go to sleep, and felt her hand rubbing on me. She started speaking to me, saying please Charlie don't treat me like this, please Charlie, I love you. I turned over and held her and rubbed her as she cried and said I am so sorry Charlie I let you down, I love you, and you scared me. I don't want to be alone, you are all I have now, I know you love me, please tell me. I love you Victoria and you won't be alone as I held her and she fell asleep in my arms. I slowly released her, and turned on my side, turned the remaining lights out, and I went to sleep.

Thirty-seven

Saturday: Day Thirty-seven.

I woke up and again it was early. I rolled over and looked at her, beautiful, fragile, and mine now. I was all she had and would take care of her, knowing what it meant to be alone. Yes I knew, and that's how I had thrown myself into what I have created, in this material world. I tried to bring happiness to the people that crossed my path in life that needed help and that was small compared to all the pain in the world. I had given to charities, hospitals, churches, and individuals; and it brought them happiness. But it didn't do away with the loneliness of being by you self, night after night, and there weren't enough blankets to remove the chill of an empty bed. I removed myself and went to the bathroom. When I returned it was almost six as I got back in bed, pulled the covers back over me, turned and rubbed Victoria's back. I moved closer to her so our bodies were touching, reaching over her with my arm and rubbed her stomach, kissed her back, and ran my fingers through her hair as she started to waken. She reached for my hand and held it to her chest as she started to whimper and then she turned over and wrapped her arm around me. She snuggled as close to me as she could get. And I said in a soft voice, I love you Victoria and always will as she held me tighter and was crying quietly, and pressed her body next to mine. I held her tight and rubbed her back as shivers went through her. She said in a soft voice she had to pee, rose and went to the bathroom and returned shortly, getting back in bed, and began kissing me and said she loved me. Said she wanted me all the time, would be good, loyal and love me. She was crying because she was happy as I held her tight. I might be upset with what you do sometimes, but it doesn't mean I don't love you, you understand. Yes Charlie my love, she replied, and wanted to feel me, asking if it was ok, and said she needed me so much. Please Mr. Charlie make love to me, please, please. She begged until I relented and felt her in all her intimate places, as she kissed me with a passion that was true. I felt her with gentle hands as she held me for dear life, and when she climaxed I held her even tighter, as she begged me to never stop touching her as she was rocked with multiple organisms. I held her

and she began crying, she held on and said never let her go, please
Master Charlie, as I held her head with one hand as I rubbed her all
over. Slowly she began to calm down. She climbed on top of me
with my legs between hers and looked me in my eyes, and slid
down so I was inside of her, she made love to me, and she felt
good, her warmth and wetness. I told her I would never leave her;
we would be together forever as man and wife. Said she loved the
way I felt inside of her, and all she wanted was me, nothing else,
not money, jewels, furs, or anything else, said she was in heaven
now with me inside of her. She lay on top of me just barely
moving, not wanting me to come. After a while she moved around
enough to make me have a climax, and then she didn't move, said
she felt the love inside of her, in her mouth or ass as long as it was
me in her. Finally she rolled over to the side and we just looked at
one another and touched until, I asked are you ok now. She kissed
me again, oh Charlie I love you so much. We rose and cleaned
ourselves and took a quick rinse.

We donned our bathrobes and went downstairs to prepare
something to eat, as always I did the coffee as she prepared the
breakfast food, as we had done before, we sat down and ate
together, and she was alright now. She asked me what I wanted her
to do today. I looked at her and said you are coming with me; a
smile came over her face as we finished eating our food. We
cleaned up the dishes, pots and pans, and sat and finished the
coffee before returning upstairs. I told her she could wear whatever
she wanted, we took our robes off and I asked her to come here. I
held her, feeling, and kissed her. I said that we would be happy
together as she looked at me and smiled, I said that's my girl. I
released her, and put on a pair of underwear and a clean pair of
jeans, t- shirt, and white socks and would change into my athletic
shoes, setting them by the door, finding one of my old sports
jackets, and filling my pockets with my necessities. I shaved and
brushed my teeth, placed some lotion on my hands and came back
to see what Vicky was going to wear. It was going to be a warm
day, and she decided on wearing a short dress, she oiled her body
and put on a pair of soft cotton panties, and a summer blouse,
sandals with a matching purse. She fixed her hair looking elegant

and simple, and had her sun glasses and a sun hat. I closed the windows and turned the air-conditioning on; it was to be near eighty degrees and humid today. We were ready and it was close to nine, when we walked out of the house. I decided to take the BGT, and opened the door for Vicky and soon pulled out. I then said to her when you go grocery shopping take the van. She said yes sir Mr. Charlie, as we headed to the gas station, filling the gas tank before going inside and bought several of the local newspapers and picked up the free real estate sales and rental books. I had so many the clerk placed them in a poly bag.

Got back in the car and we drove to the office, pulled up and parked and was surprised at all the cars in the reserved spaces. We went inside and it looked like a week day. Green and Phillips were both in, along with Brown, Hartman and Newman. Vicky and I took the elevator upstairs and when we walked out found everyone but Hippies. Joanne, Pat, Anne and Samantha were all in her office. I stopped and said good morning and asked what was going on. They saw I had a bag of newspapers and Victoria was with me. Said they were going to see the condos, when in walked Fitz with some coffee. I had these newspapers to check on the advertisements, and would be in the conference room. I asked Vicky to come with me. I took everything out of the bag and laid the newspapers out, and pulled the real-estate sections from each paper looking for the ads. Found full page ads for the condos in the first, before Pat and Anne came in and helped out finding the ads in every newspaper. Fitz walked in and asked what we had found. We found full page ads in every paper, Fitz looked through the weekly's and found ads for several of our complexes and none for the condos in the rental one, but found one in the sales. He said sometimes it takes more than a week for ads to appear in these. I asked what's the plan is, and Samantha, walked in, and had just overheard what I said. Her and Anne were planning to go today with their lap tops and had made a sign on some poster board that said Harcourt Realty, Mortgage Dept., applications accepted here. Based on what Mr. Peters had said about the loan officers working on commission meant they could enhance our reputation and make some money also. They could now work as loan officers since we were fully licensed. I asked are both of you going. And both said yes, since they had weekends off. Fitz said he was going just to see and then do some checking during the week. I asked Fitz to find an independent manager to set up the condo board. I don't want any involvement after we sell, and we are obligated for a year on every sale anyway. Ok boss. Pat said she was going as an assistant if she was needed. They had three lap tops, a portable fax, and combination printer. Fitz had called the resident agent and had him put a table and chairs away just for them. He found out there were a dozen tables and about eighty or more folding chairs there already. They said that they would handle this. Ok. I took one of the ads and the real estate sections and placed them in my office. I wished them well and told them to have a good day. I led Victoria out after she had spoken to Joanne. Joanne said everything was going well, and was dressed in jeans today and looked much more relaxed. The agents had showings today and wouldn't be here very long. I might stop back on my way from the condo sales event.

Victoria and I left and got in the car and headed for the condo sale. We drove about fifty five minutes. I circled around the entire complex, and saw that there were banners near the sign that had the name of the complex. Highwood Hills Estates, they were located at the main entrance and at the back entrance also, and after circling we entered the parking lot to the club house and there were over a dozen autos in the lot. I parked further away from the entrance door, and for sat several minutes observing. There were signs on the lawn directing people to the sales office which had been set up in the club house. And groups of people were walking the paths back and forth to several of the closest buildings. The club house would attract sales with its amenities. I stepped out and came around opening the door for Vicky. She had beautiful legs and the dress fell just above her knees and shapely butt, she smiled at me, she wore no makeup except for some lipstick and her skin glowed and was flawless.

We walked toward the club house and entered. After stepping inside, an agent approached us offering to help. I asked for Mr. Peters, he looked around and said he was probably out showing some of the units and would return shortly. I thanked him and said

I was Charlie Harcourt; he didn't know who we were, and I stated we didn't need any help and thanked him anyway. We looked around and there were several tables with cardboard signs advertising bank loans from several banks and mortgage originators. We walked around fifteen minutes or so before I spotted Mr. Peters with a couple as he returned and directed them to a table, where one of his agents started to write up a sales contract. He looked around and spotted us and walked over and shook my hand as he greeted us. He said the turnout was more than he ever expected on the first day and said the signs and the ads in the papers helped. I mentioned to him the article in the business section from a few days earlier. Yes, he pulled out all the stops for this one. I also mentioned my loan department people were coming and were going to set up a table also. He welcomed it because of the truly overwhelming response. Just then Samantha, Anne and Pat came in with their lap tops, and I said to Mr. Peters they are here now. He excused himself and helped them set up which only took a of couple minutes. He returned and said he had to call in several extra agents he wasn't going to use until later next week, but then things became hectic, and when it looked like his staff would be overwhelmed he needed the extra help. Told him I was just here to observe and would not interfere with his operation. He said that was alright and to come anytime. He said he hoped this turned out very beneficial for both of us, and said the units were really very nice for the price. He also stated, I probably could price them higher but they wouldn't sell as fast. Told him I wasn't trying to hold on to them, and had other projects in the works, and stated my leasing department head was looking for an independent agent to set up the condo board here. Peterson recommended an agency as he handed me their business card, and I thanked him. He said he had to help out, as we shook hands again and he stepped away to assist his agents. I walked over to where Samantha and Anne were assisting people with loan applications, and I caught Pat while she was free, and handed her the card and asked her to photograph it with their phone number and send it to Fitz with the notation from me that it was recommended by Peters for the condo board. She did it immediately, and handed the card back to me, I thanked her.

Victoria noticed people walking around looking at the club house and all the amenities. Vicky said its very busy Charlie and that's good for you. I took her hand and we left, and even though I had parked away from the main entrance, there were even more vehicles than when we arrived. We got in the car and left the complex. Victoria asked how much money I would make selling the complex. I said several million, she gasped. She had no idea that I was going to make all that. She put her hands together and her eyes were moist when I glanced over at her, and asked her if she was hungry, she said yes. What you would like? She said in a halting voice, some sea food. Ok sweetie.

Soon we pulled up to the Red Fin Inn, I parked and came around and opened the door for Victoria as she stood and looked me in the eyes, and said she was praying on the way here because it never occurred to her how really fortunate she was until now of being with me. She prayed we always stayed safe and out of harm's way as she hugged and kissed me. I said don't cry ok, it's all good. We entered and since it was before noon, it wasn't crowded yet, and we were seated at a small booth and the menus placed on the table. I ordered a couple glasses of beer, the waiter departed and returned, and asked if we were ready. Vicky was still deciding what she wanted, as I placed my order and when he was finished with me, she had finally decided what she wanted and the waiter took her order and departed. Vicky said to me, that she had no idea about property or what it cost, and asked me how I got started. I explained how, and when and my lucky stock and how it changed things. Joanne coming to work for me and what we had accomplished together, my wife's death, the tragic death of Joanne husband, and how with her being in the office, she handled that end of things, and as I reinvesting my money into more properties and was able to build my business. How I stayed out of the lime light by diversifying my assets and operating under different names. She said that I was smart, and very thankful we were together, and said all that didn't matter to her as long we were together. Our food arrived and we dug in as she ate and had a smile on her face and didn't say much. Only that the food was good and she loved me. I looked at her and thought how lucky I was. We ate

all our food and when the waiter returned and asked if we wanted
dessert, we declined and he brought the bill. I placed a $100.00, on
the tray and said keep the change, he thanked me and we departed.

I asked Vicky if she wanted to stop and shop and if she wanted
anything. She looked at me and said no Charlie, I have what I want
most of all. I headed back to the office, we walked in and checked
on things. Mr. Phillips was at the desk and we spoke and shortly
Ms. Brown entered with a couple and they went to a cube and sat
down and she began to write up a contract. Vicky and I went
upstairs, Joanne had left and so had Fitz. Hippies had the day off
and we were the only people upstairs. I told her I had to use the
facilities and stepped out; she followed and used the women's,
washrooms. They smelled fresh and had been cleaned earlier in the
day. I returned to my office and soon Vicky returned, she said we
are all alone as she asked me to hug her. She kissed me and said
she felt good being in my arms. I looked at the newspapers and
found the theater section, and decided we would go see a movie; I
hadn't been in quite a while. So we decided on one and prepared to
depart. Before I left, asked Phillips to check the washrooms after
closing and before he left and tell Green to do the same thing when
he was on duty. Yes sir he replied. We walked to the car and drove
to the theater.

We arrived and decided on an action movie, the theater was
modern with reclining seats and we bought some popcorn and sat
back and enjoyed the show. After a couple hours we left. The
theater was across a large parking lot from an exclusive department
store and I drove over. I let Vicky out as she said please Charlie; I
know what you want to do. I said what; she replied that I wanted to
shower her with more gifts. I said yes Mrs. Harcourt has to look
like I love her, and because I do you are subject to my whims to
shower you with whatever I want to do for you. Don't you cry we
are just going to look, ok sweetie. She relented because she had no
other choice. We entered and I said to her you need some lingerie,
you only have one set. She found several more and I purchased
them, and she said Charlie please can we go home now. I said yes
baby. She said thank you for treating me so well and that she felt

so very special. I looked her in her eyes and said you are special, to me.

We arrived back at the car and I opened the door for her; I wasn't finished yet, and drove to the Vincent dealership. I had always liked Vincent's, and my wife would soon need a car. We got out and walked in and were greeted by a salesman, Mr. Hanks. We were just looking; I asked Victoria if she saw one that appealed to her. She said they were very beautiful automobiles as we walked around and looked before asking her what colors do you like. She said the dark blue with the tan interior; I waved the salesman over and inquired if they had an automobile with the colors Vicky had described, he said just a minute sir. He returned and I asked if it had all the options. I asked Vicky to go sit in the one that was on the floor; he double checked, returned and said yes sir. I asked if he had a demo that we could drive. Stated he did indeed. I went over and asked Victoria to come with me. We followed and the salesman as he led us to a demo by the front door outside. I asked Vicky to drive, she looked at me a little strange, but got behind the wheel anyway, as the salesman showed her how to adjust the seat, the steering column, and brake pedals, and with the salesman in the front seat and I in back. He showed her how to adjust the mirrors. He asked her if she was comfortable, she replied yes, and then directed her towards the street. She is a very good driver and after a while observed how well she was getting use to how the car handled, as she drove for several miles, before directing her back to the dealership. We got out and she said that was fun, and asked me was I going to trade the BGT in for that one. I stalled with my answer as we went back inside. He said he had the one I asked about, fully loaded. I will take it as he directed us to his small office, he then asked about financing. I replied cash.

And what name on the sales contract. I said Mrs. Victoria Harcourt. It took a several long seconds before Victoria realized what I had just said. It was good she was sitting down. She stood up and loudly almost screaming said no, Charlie, please no Charlie and began crying. I stood and said, Victoria my dear. She held me, and said that I was too good to her and she didn't deserve and wouldn't accept it. The dealership staff had heard her, and peered around corners to look at this very beautiful woman, holding on to me full of tears, as she said no please don't. I asked the salesman to please give us a moment as he stepped out of his small office. I sat her down and said look at me, she looked up at me crying, her beautiful big brown eyes filled with tears as they ran down her face like rain. She tried to dry them with her handkerchief, as I explained to her that she was going to be my wife, and there isn't anything I won't do for you. You need to understand this now, life is short and I want the best for you. I know in your heart you are happy being with me, and I love you for that, but I want you safe all the time, and that means I will look out for you even when I'm not around. I told you the other day you would have to shop. I want you safe when you do, you do understand that don't you, and I only want the best for you ok. I explained to her it was her wedding gift from me, she cried and said that she couldn't give me anything back. I said the greatest gift you have given me is yourself and your love for me, you understand that, you in my arms and in my life is the greatest gift of all. With tears in her eyes she thanked me, and held me tight, kissing me all over my face. I said dry your tears my love. She tried to compose herself as the salesman returned. Mr. Hanks filled out the sales contract. I went to the cashier's window with him and presented my corporate card, and a few minutes later they handed me the paperwork and we returned to the office where I had left Victoria. She had regained some of her composure somewhat, but you could tell she had been crying before asking where the washroom was, and Mr. Hanks showed her where. He returned and said to me she is so very beautiful. I thanked him and said we were getting married in a couple of days, he congratulated me, and I thanked him. He said the vehicle would be ready shortly; they were washing it and asked if I wanted any of the optional services performed. He went through the list and I chose several. Asked if we wanted to leave it here until they were complete, and would deliver it when done, and also informed me that they will pick the auto up when it needed servicing, and bring it back. He informed me they would apply for the license plates and he said if we waited until next week they would have them and all the extra services performed. I said keep it and when it was ready we would pick it up. Victoria returned from the washroom, and I shook hands with Mr. Hanks, and he complimented Victoria and congratulated us on our upcoming marriage.

I walked Vicky outside and opened the door for her and before she got in she looked at me. I kissed her and told her I loved her more than anything in the world as she grabbed me, pulling me to her and holding me tight. She released me and got in, and after I closed the door and looked toward the dealership, everyone inside was looking out. I drove away and headed home. I backed inside and removed the bags for Vicky and walked her to the door and unlocked it and said I had to do something first, I opened the door where the van was, got in and pulled it outside and parked it on the outside where there was space for two other vehicles. Locked it and brought in the remote for the garage door, pulled the BGT back out and parked it where the van had been. Closed both doors and went inside the house. Vicky hadn't gone upstairs yet, she was waiting on me when I entered, and flew into my arms. She asked me to hold her while she got her cry out, and after a few minutes we headed upstairs with the bags in hand. I started to undress and she removed her shoes and knelt at the foot of the bed, with her hands folded, she was praying, she remained like that for several minutes making the sign of the cross before she rose and came to me and said, she prayed for us. That she hadn't gotten down on her knees and prayed since the day she first saw me. She asked God to forgive her sins and promised him she would be honest and faithful to me, and asked for a long and happy life together. She looked at me crying, as I held her for a long time.

We finally undressed; saying today has been one of the most wonderful days in her life ever. We put on some shorts and t- shirts and went downstairs and fixed a light snack and sat in the nook and ate. I said to her when I was a child growing up, we didn't have much, but we ate every day. There were things any child would want but my parents couldn't and wouldn't give them to me. I didn't ask for anything either. I told her about sitting and looking and reading the large mail order catalogs they had back then, and realizing all the things you could have if you had money. How my mother was strict and I didn't get away with anything, and was the youngest of five children, was the baby and only child, and all my brothers and sisters were half relations, was the only child to her current marriage and the other siblings were fifteen or more years older and some were even married and had children my age. How I couldn't wait to leave home and after I finished high school, enlisted for three years in the army. Crossed both oceans and saw quite a bit from my military adventure and was in a combat environment my very last year. Then for the first time in my young life saw people eating from trash dumps, it affected me, the same way as when I was a child and saw dead animals and would cry. Later, after working a job when I returned they had a buyout of employees as they wanted to downsize. I was fortunate to have a monthly pension even thought I was far from retirement age, and then took the real estate course, passed the associates exam and eventually the brokers, and shortly thereafter struck out on my own. Had some money saved up and eventually bought a building, then bought another, and another and saved my money, and saw a stock that was cheap and in an emerging technology, and eventually invested more as it appeared it might be good for a long term investment. It went through a price explosion, and before I knew it turned out to be a windfall. I cashed some of it in and had close to twenty million dollars, took that and continued to buy more real estate, and moving from individual building to buying my first apartment complex, and continued with the same strategy all the way up until now. Joanne came in looking for a job; she had just gotten her real estate license. I said to her that I really needed someone in the office, since I was in the street. Really needed someone to manage my holdings and offered her a modest salary, and told her to go for the brokers, she did and was successful; I said to her I grow, you grow, and she has been with me ever since that day.

She is a very attractive woman, and had a child and her husband had passed. Don't think many times I thought about asking her for a date, but I wanted more, and she had come after my wife passed away and I was still grieving. But I had set my sights on making money and had never forgotten those hungry people overseas.

Then the country elected the great communicator here as president and then the economy became harder for working people. Then I started to see homeless people, as the whole economy changed, from everyone benefiting, to only a few. I remember you saying when you, Joanne and Pat went to lunch at Martha's you all talked about the things I had done for them. Well it goes back to those poor souls eating out the garbage. I helped them because there is a difference between need and greed. I can't spend all the money I have so diligently worked to accumulate, so I give some away in the hope it helps someone. When I see a needy person, you know what goes through my mind, there by the grace of God go I. I am very thankful for what I have been able to achieve, and even more thankful God blessed me with you to be in my life now. So you see, you and I are the same, I can give to you because you ask for nothing more than my love, you have that and all I can give to you. I don't give to you to make you happy, but to make myself happy, and doing it because I love you more than anything else. Marriage is sharing, you are going to be my better half, and together we will be one. I have never felt for anyone what I feel for you, no matter what you think of yourself, or what you have done before we met. You are who you are and I accept that. We finished with our snack and cleaned up. The day had been a very good one, and we hugged again.

I asked Victoria if she would have a drink with me. She said of course as long as I didn't try to put her to sleep. I looked at her and laughed as we went downstairs to the bar and fixed ourselves a drink and we sat and talked more. I told her not that it makes much difference, but I couldn't wait to put that ring on her finger. She looked at the engagement ring on her finger and asked me to kiss it, and I did and she kissed it also. We had a couple more drinks before heading up stairs to bathe. We undressed and showered together. We enjoyed each other all the time and came out and dried off, again spreading a towel on the bed as we oiled one another, when we finished, pulled the covers back, got in and just held one another. I said to her you just don't know how happy you make me feel, I have prayed also. I didn't know how it would turn out, just kept at it, and prayed every day and to say thanks for you,

and all I have been able to accomplish. And I will do even better
with you at my side, we fell asleep holding one another.

Thirty-eight

Sunday: Day Thirty-eight.

It was four in the morning when we were awaken by loud claps of thunder and a very heavy down pour of rain. I hadn't looked at any news since Friday and especially the weather, as Vicky held on to me in a frightening panic, it had really scared her. And knew how she felt about severe weather as she clung onto me and cried. We laid back down as I held her and reassured her it would soon pass. Shortly it seemed it had and the few lights that were on flickered, and then I could see the outside lights as they came on. I knew what that meant, the power was out and we had switched over to generator power. I and a couple of my neighbors had backup generators. Power to the house was underground and the entire neighborhood, but before it reached our neighborhood it was all above ground. I said go back to sleep as we lay back down and eventually went back to sleep.

It was seven when I awoke again and Vicky was right behind me and I could only move one way to get out of bed. I moved so I could sit up and climbed out of bed, and pulled the covers back up over her, and went to the bathroom. When I returned her eyes were open as she sat up and kissed me on her way to the bathroom. When she returned we got back in bed and held each other. I kissed her and she said a since of calm had come over her during the night after the storm had passed and she no longer felt scared of being alone. Victoria said her prayers had been answered, and felt that God had spoken to her. She couldn't explain it, but felt a real sense of relief, and of true healing and a release of all the anguish and fear she had felt before in her heart. She kissed me and said it was time for her to be my wife and help mate. She got out of bed and came around to my side, took my hand and pulled me up. I stood and she kissed me. She brought my robe to me and returned to put hers on. She hugged me again as I looked in her eyes and saw a sparkle that wasn't there before. I bent forward and kissed her, it was a warm kiss as our lips touched. I felt a spark as a new feeling came over both of us. We held each other and said to one another that we loved each other. Then we went downstairs and found out what had happened during the storm as we turned the radio on and heard there were some flooding and power outages. I put the coffee on and turned the television on in the living room to the morning news. The weather soon came on and they said it hadn't been as severe as predicted. I returned to the kitchen and reported to Vicky what had happened during the night. How there was some flooding and power outages. I went and checked the monitoring station in the laundry room and we were still on generator, the outside lights had gone out when the sun came up.

I returned as Vicky was placing our food on the plates as I grabbed some paper towels and the silver ware and placed them on the table. I went back and poured our coffee before we sat down to eat. Vicky blessed the table and we ate. She had a smile on her face that I had never seen before. Sure she had smiled off and on before, but nothing like the one that she had now. I could see true happiness in her eyes. I thought it was about time but everyone has their own trials and tribulations to go through and was happy that she felt happy, and that was all that mattered to me. We ate, and the food even seemed to taste better. We finished and helped each other clean up, as we sat back down and drank more coffee until the pot was empty. I held her hand and felt the smoothness and just looked at her glowing face. We finished as I washed the coffee cups, and then we went to the living room where I had left the television on and we sat next to one another as I placed my arm around her shoulder, and she held my other hand. She turned to me and said in the softest voice, I love you so much Charlie.

We looked at the news until the talking heads appeared, then turned it off and went upstairs. We brushed our teeth and took off our robes and got back in bed and held each other and felt on one another, and Vicky said that never had she ever felt like she felt now, like a new woman. I felt her warm body, and told her I wanted to go back and check on the condo sales again, and that we could do anything she wanted after that. Charlie she said, I want you to buy yourself something, like what I asked her. I feel like you do, I don't need anything as long as I have you. She said how about a new suit, when was the last time you bought one. I said several months ago. Told her if I get a suit, you have to get something also. She reluctantly said ok. I said you may want some comfortable shoes to drive in. Yes she replied that sounded good, but that was all she would agree to. I felt her body and her breast and she said to me that she was all mine as I felt her warmth she took me in her hand, and said make love to me Charlie. We made love and it was, or it seemed so very different, more genteel and caring as we came together and kissed and said forever. We laid with our arms and legs on one another as we kissed and felt each other; it seemed all the tension had left her. I sat up and pulled her to me, and we showered together. After we dried off and applied oils to one another, she said she felt very sexy, and wanted to redo her nails, I said we are in no rush. She went and began removing the old polish from her toes and finger nails, as I sat and watched her. I put on my underwear, then went and shaved. When I returned she was applying the new polish, it was a peach color and was very pretty on her. I asked her what she was going to wear, and said she hadn't decided. I said that since it was going to be a nice day, but humid because of the rain, I was going to wear some shorts and a t-shirt. I brought out a bottle of natural insect repellant and applied it to my whole body and once Vicky's nails had dried, I applied it all over her also, as we did one another's backs. She wore some shorts also and a cute top. She wore her small gold chain and earrings. We both wore our sandals. She went to the bathroom and fixed her hair and when she reappeared was looking sexy and very beautiful, picked up her small purse and said she was ready. We didn't wear any cologne or perfume the natural bug repellant had a pleasant smell. We kissed and held hands as we went downstairs and checked the house, the air had been on so all the windows were already closed and locked. I checked the power panel and the outside power had been restored and the backup generator had automatically shut down.

I decided to drive the Cambo this time, after pulling out and closing the garage door, I stopped and looked at Vicky in the sun light as it streamed in through the sun roof, she looked at me and smiled and leaned over and kissed me. I almost wanted to cry, she was so very beautiful to me. I pulled out onto the street and went to the gas station to fill up, and repeated the process I had done the day before with the newspapers, returning to the car and driving to the office. We were the only car there as we entered and I punched in the pin. We headed to the conference room and pulled the home and real estate sections from each paper, lining them up in order. The conference table was large enough to do it on as we found the full page ads again, that told you were to go, and the times. The coverage was very good, and wondered how well my girls had made out yesterday. I pulled the ads and placed them in a stack and took them to my office and Vicky was right behind me. When I was through she said Charlie, I turned to look at her and said yes Victoria. Hold me please, I held her as she said the most wonderful feeling had just come over her, and loved being here with me. I asked her if she was ready. She said yes, as we rode down on the elevator. I punched in the pin and we walked out and I locked the door. As I opened the car door for her, I kissed her and said I can never get enough of you and love having you with me.

We drove to the condo complex, circled like we had the day before, and then pulled into the parking lot. I had to park further away from the club house because of the large number of cars in the parking lot. We got out and I stood and looked around at the grounds. There were small groups of people, and they were walking to some of the far buildings. The whole site was almost forty acers if I remembered correctly. It seemed to be organized a little differently today than yesterday. I took Vicky by the hand and we walked to the club house and entered. It was much better organized, there were at least forty or fifty people, mostly all were couples and some had small children. I could see people who had pre approvals and were taking numbers sitting in chairs that had been arranged in one section and in another section, a group waiting to be shown units. I looked at the loan officers and observed there were many more here today than yesterday and there amongst them were Samantha and Anne. They were busy and had several people filling out applications, and they were busy on their lap tops. I turned too Victoria and said we are going to leave now, just as Mr. Peters stopped us, he asked us to step to the side out of the way of the people walking around. He spoke to us, saying he was glad I came because; he really wanted to thank me for this great opportunity. Said it was the largest complex he had been employed to sell since starting his company and the turnout was far more than he ever expected. He stated the people were surprised at the quality of the construction, and even said one man who had worked on the original construction had purchased a unit because, he said they had been built the right way which made him feel good about selling them. He wouldn't want to be associated with any shoddy construction if he could help it. He said you don't mind me asking, why are you selling instead of renting. I said we did a cost analysis, and the long term operating cost didn't meet with our long term profit expectations, and beside it was designed to be a condo. He said he understood. Besides it would be better with owners, based on the layout of the property. And stated with the interest generated and the overwhelming turnout more than half should be sold in the first thirty days. He thanked me for sending my loan people to help out. Said he needed to go as he shook my hand again, turned and left to help out his agents.

Anne saw us and waved, she was waving us over, and Vicky and I headed over to where they were seated. Anne greeted us both and hugged Vicky and just wanted to say things were going well and should soon add to our bottom line, and thanked me for providing the car because she wouldn't have made it with her old one. Told her that I appreciated her and Samantha's enthusiasm and it would be rewarded. I said don't let me stop you; we were on our way out. Samantha stood and hugged Vicky and then me and thanked me, and said she would report during the week how well they had faired, ok. Vicky and I exited the premises and headed for our car. Vicky said your employees are loyal to you and some haven't even been with you very long, and said she truly understood why. Because I was fair, generous and honest and that was the reason she loved me so much and had heard what Anne said, and only a fair and decent person would do that. Just like what you did for me and the things you have said to me, and why I love you so, so much Charlie.

We got in the car and, I said to Vicky, you wanted me to get a new suit. I know the one I want, I have one but its kind of old and besides it's time for a new one. She asked what it was exactly, and said it was a white linen suit and maybe they might even have a panama hat to go with it. We headed to Sweet Wood Mall to the exclusive store we had shopped at several times before. We arrived and entered and went directly to the men's suit section, where we were greeted by a salesman. I explained what I was looking for and he directed us to a section he said contained the summer suits. They had several and he measured me and picked one in my size. I tried on the jacket, he handed me the trousers and directed me to the fitting room, I tried them on and came out, they had a little slack in the waist but that was fine I didn't like my pants tight in that area. The trousers were a little long, and he cuffed them and marked them and said they could take them up, he checked the waist and said they should, take an inch up there also. I said ok, and asked if I could try the hat on. He retrieved the hat from the hat display tree and brought it over and I tried it on. I walked over to the mirror and admired myself. Vicky said, oh Charlie you look fantastic, like in the old movies. I told the salesman I would take the suit. He had another one in beige, and I tried it on also and liked the way it fit. The pants fitted the same as the first one and I decided on taking both, along with the hat and returned to the dressing room, came out and handed him the suit. He took my name and said they would be ready tomorrow afternoon. I paid so all I would have to do would be to pick them up. I thanked him and Vicky hugged me and we headed to the shoe department. She found a pair of flats with and open toe, they were similar to sandals, the shoe salesman approached and she showed him the shoes, he returned with a couple boxes, as she tried them on, and said they were comfortable. I saw a pair with a low heel, that I thought were cute, and asked if he had them in her size, he left and returned with a couple more boxes, she tried on two pairs and picked the ones she said fitted her best. We purchased the ones she liked and then we walked around some more.

Vicky said she was hungry, and I asked what she wanted. Chinese was her answer. I said to her, you really like the food, as we headed to Wong's. We entered and Mrs. Wong was all smiles as I asked for a table. She looked at me, you special she said, and led us to a quiet table, she saw the ring on Vicky's finger, pointed and said, when you marry. I looked at her and smiled, and said

very soon. She placed the menus on the table, left and came back
with a pot of green tea and two cups. She left and soon Fawn came
and asked if we were ready to order. I let Vicky order first and she
ordered the chicken and broccoli with brown rice, and I ordered the
Hunan shrimp and vegetables also with brown rice, and a seaweed
salad, she then left to place our order. Vicky reached out and held
my hand, and said thank you so much Charlie. I appreciate all you
have done for me, and I am more than grateful, and was sorry she
had upset me, and it wouldn't ever happen again. Told me she
loved me and would tell me all the time how she felt. She kissed
my hand and held it until our food arrived. We sat back as Fawn
placed the food before us. I thanked her as she departed to serve
the other patrons. We dug in, and as always the food was fantastic,
or rather we really loved eating here, and it had turned out to be
Victoria's favorite restaurant also. We ate and savored the flavors
and drank the tea, and when we finished, Fawn returned and
cleared the table, asking if we wanted any desert, we declined. She
then returned with the bill and the cookies. I looked at Vicky and
held the cookie up as I opened the wrapper, and breaking it in half,
and removing the folded paper inside, and reading, (life is short,
don't waste any more time) and asked Vicky what did hers say, she
opened it, as I ate the remainder of my cookie, she read the small
slip of paper (you are with the love of your life now) and she
smiled this time, she handed me the paper and I read it. I said to
her at least you have stopped crying. She smiled at me, took my
hand and kissed it again. I paid the bill and we left, and Mrs. Wong
gave me thumbs up. We would soon be working on her restaurant
expansion and it wouldn't take long and Fitz could handle it if I
didn't. Vicky and I returned to the car and she said to me that she
was ready to go home. I said ok and that I was a little tired and
wanted to take a nap and she agreed with me. The temperature was
rising and because of the rain the humidity was also making it
more uncomfortable.

We arrived home and it never looked so good, as I backed
inside. We entered, closing the door behind us, took our shoes off
and headed upstairs to undress and washing our hands and
brushing our teeth. I climbed in the bed nude and Vicky joined me.

I just wanted to relax, even though it was early evening we have had a full day for a Sunday. We pulled the covers over us, kissed and soon went to sleep. When we woke it was around seven. I laid and looked over at Victoria. She woke also and I asked her what she wanted to do. Said she wanted me to tie her up, and make love to her.

I said really, really she replied, as I looked in her eyes. She said please Charlie; I need to serve you master. I hugged and kissed her and told her to get what you want me to use on you as she got out of bed and went and removed from the closet several items. Rope, hand cuffs, whips, and the blindfold and told me to use whatever else I wanted to use and said she felt like being my slave and wanted to submit to whatever I wanted to do. I instructed her to get the collar and leash, she did and returned. I stood and she went and got my leather pants and vest and asked me to please wear them. I put them on and then placed the collar around her neck, and as I did she asked me to talk to her in a degrading and derogatory manner and not to hold back on my treatment of her. I placed the leather cuffs on her wrist, ankles and the wide leather waist belt on, and hooked the leash to the collar. I looked her in her pretty eyes, and said to her, this is what you really want me to do to you. She said yes Charlie; please treat me like a bitch. I want to be your slave, and it would make me very happy to serve the man she loved. I will only do this because you asked me to, and because I love you. She said that is what she wanted. I kissed her and said, I love you, she kissed me back. I said on the floor on all fours you stinking bitch. She complied as I took the end of the leash and the whip and told her to crawl and led her into the large empty bed room down the hall as I whipped her butt as she crawled.

I looked at her and said you piece of shit whore. And asked her, what are you? She replied she was my bitch. Told her not to move as I returned to the bedroom and retrieved the other items we kept in a bag. I placed everything in the bag and returned to where I had left her. I decided to insert the dildo and butt plug with a narrow one inch strap that hooked to the waist belt inside of her. I proceeded to spread lubricant on the butt plug and some on her rectum, and then inserted it slowly into her ass, working it in and out as she moaned until it popped into place and gave her ass a couple of good hard smacks with my hand. Then as she moaned and panted, took the dildo with its five inches of soft ribbed latex and inserted it into her now very moist pussy. And then taking the narrow strap and attaching it to the waist belt, first to the rear and running it across the butt plug and dildo to the front keeping them in place and securing it to the belt in front, as she moaned. I grabbed the leash and told her to start crawling bitch as I led her around in circles and flogged her back, butt, thighs, and her breast. After several minutes told her to stop, as she was starting to sweat. Had her stand and attached her wrist to the sides of the waist belt. Then taking the blindfold and placing it over her eyes. I then looked in the bag, and brought out two big oversized clothes pins, and slowly placed one on each hard aroused nipple, clamping it to the areola as she gritted her teeth and flinched. I said, you are my slut bitch, and I will do with you what I please, do you understand me slave. She replied yes sir master. I reached in the bag and removed two more clothes pins and kneeling before her, placed them on her pussy lips as she squirmed. Then I grabbed the wide leather paddle, held the leash and smacked her round ass, as her whole body quivered as she was having multiple explosive orgasms. I paddled her ass as I made her walk around the large room. I looked at her swollen nipples and twisted and played with them. I removed a mouth gag that was shaped like a short thick penis about three inches long, placing it in her mouth and fastening it behind her head. I said you are my cunt, and you will serve me bitch. I looked at her body, now moist with perspiration, as I played with her nipples and twisting and pulling removed the clothes pins slowly before removing them as she flinched

Then I placed the very aroused and swollen nipple in my mouth, biting and teasing them with my tongue, pulling and biting them softly. She was drooling as I removed the gag, and asked her if she was going to be a good little slave bitch, she replied yes sir master. I kissed her and she kissed me back as her anxious tongue entered my mouth. I then stood back, and whipped her all over her body and not sparing any part of her, as her knees began to buckle; I held the leash and forcing her to remain standing. Then I felt her all over with my hands and asking her do you want me to fuck your stinking ass bitch. In a halting voice she said yes sir master; please fuck your worthless slave bitch. I rubbed her ass, it had turned a little red, and her juices were running down her thighs as I asked if the dirty slut had enough. She was hesitant, then I lightly slapped her face, and said answer me bitch. No sir master she replied. I told her to kneel, and helped her down on her knees. I placed two fingers in her mouth and she greedily sucked them before I pulled my hard dick out and teased her mouth with it. I said only good bitches get dick. I unhooked her hands from the belt and told her to bend over. I hooked her wrist to her ankles, causing her to become very exposed to me. I removed the clothes pins from her pussy lips and looked at how they had swollen, before I released the strap that held the butt plug and dildo in place, playing with the butt plug, pushing it in and out, before removing it completely along with the dildo.

I reached for a belt that was three inches wide and smacked her ass and watched as she tried to move, using it on her inner thighs and pussy, causing her to have another enormous organism. I pulled my dick out and stuck it in her very hot and wet pussy. It felt good as I reached around and played with her clit, and just let it stay in as she climaxed continuously. I pulled out and stuck it in her hot ass, sliding in and out while feeling her clit the whole time as she continued to climax. I pulled out, and unhooked her wrist from her ankles, removed the blind fold, and pulled her leash and told her to crawl as I whipped her using a riding crop, and made her crawl back to the bedroom where I told her to stay put.

I washed myself after having stuck it in her ass and returned. Grabbed the leash and told her to stand with her hands behind her. She had her head down, I said look at me bitch, she raised her head, she looking like a scolded child. I asked her what she was; she said she was my nasty little slave bitch master. Asked her if she was ready to serve, and she said yes sir master. Then asked what you want bitch. She replied she wanted master to fuck her worthless pussy and ass, and to stick it in her mouth. She was covered in perspiration as pussy juice ran down her thighs; I removed the collar, and all the cuffs. I kissed her and she cried and held me and said thank you master Charlie and I told her to get on her knees as I removed the vest and leather pants and she took me in her mouth and sucked me for several minutes before I told her to stand. I held her and rubbed her as she kissed me all over and told her to get in the bed where I climbed on top of her and inserted my hard penis in her again as she moaned and fingered her ass at the same time as she exploded below me and said yes, yes master, fuck your bitch master and then I came and slowly rolled off of her and then she climbed on top of me kissing me and telling me she loved me. Then she just laid there as I held her, rubbing her sweaty body. When we recovered, we got up and went to the bathroom and showered a long time as we washed each other and had more sex and gave her a golden shower. When we finally came out, we were exhausted; we oiled one another and said we would clean everything up later. We crawled into the bed. Told me she felt better now. She needed that and wanted to please me. She loved me as we held each other until not long after we were asleep.

Thirty-nine
Monday: Day Thirty-nine.

It seemed like the weekend passed fairly quickly, as I woke and lay in bed. One thing for sure it had a surprise ending for me as I rolled over and looked at Vicky. My love was still asleep, as I removed myself from bed and went to the bathroom and shaved and refreshed myself. We had a good rest prior to our tryst, but we had just worn ourselves out again. I enjoyed it, but found it mentally difficult to physically hurt and demean her. She wanted it, if that's what it took every now and then to keep her happy, I would do it. I reached over and touched her, she was still sleeping. When I looked at the clock it was a little after six and decided to go downstairs and put the coffee on. Man I was hungry as I got up and went to the bathroom before returning, putting my bathrobe on and proceeded downstairs to the kitchen. I started the coffee and then returned to the bedroom. I looked at my sleeping beauty and sat on her side of the bed and felt her and looked at her as I whispered in her ear, baby, time to get up. I love you Victoria and kissed the side of her face and she moaned as I felt her head and ran my fingers through her hair. I covered her up, and went back downstairs to indulge myself with some food, hell I had done it all these years and in only the past month had anyone else prepared breakfast for me. First I poured myself some coffee and took the donuts out, sat and ate one and drank some coffee, and now I felt like proceeding. I took out some sausage, three eggs and an onion, taking the bread out, turned on the oven and placing the bread in an aluminum pan and placing it in the oven. Slicing up the onion and seasoned the sausage before making patties and placing them in the frying pan on a low fire after adding a little olive oil. I covered it, and sipped some coffee and ate another donut. After a while when the sausage and onions were done, I cooked my eggs. I had turned over my bread, adding cheese and soon everything was complete. I sat down and began to eat, as I drank more coffee, sat back and belched, then knew I was good to go. Took my vitamins, and took a couple extra, as I cleaned everything up and headed back upstairs. I brushed my teeth, and rinsed my mouth, applied some natural insect repellant, since it had such a pleasant smell and it was spring and summer was just a week or two away.

I entered the bed room looking at the clock, it was seven, got back in the bed and rubbed on Victoria, as she rolled over and slowly opened her eyes, and smiled at me. I kissed her and she yawned and stretched. I said are you ready to start the day; she was still recovering from yesterday. I said to her, you want me to talk dirty now, she said no Charlie. Well beautiful time to get up. Told her I had fixed breakfast and had already eaten. She finally rose and got up and came around and hugged me, before going to the bathroom. I put my underwear on and hung my robe up, and was placing what I was going to wear on the couch, when she returned. She came over and we sat on the bed, she thanked me for last night. Knew I really didn't want to hurt her, couldn't explain it, said she needed it now and then, and asked me to cater to her needs and fantasy. I told her I would do it just for her. And I want you to be the woman of my dreams, said she would be whatever I wanted, whenever I wanted. Ok then.

This was our very personal bargain between us as we hugged and kissed. I said we didn't clean up from last night. Said she would take care of everything. And we have to pick up your car, and I would have to pick up my suits. And sometime tomorrow we are going to the court house, ok. She said ok Charlie. So clean up, eat and look beautiful, bring the shoes you want to drive in and just leave them in your car, you can always change them. That sounds good, but you are going to work aren't you. Yes I replied. I said come here, she came and I held her and kissed her. Told her I wanted to get dressed because I liked starting early, and said it would probably be around eleven when I would head back home but would call first. And we have to also get you a phone. She said why. So I can talk to you anywhere you are, and you can call me if you're out, and also for emergency's, she said ok Charlie, just for you. I dressed in my jeans and t- shirt, gym socks and athletic shoes, and grabbed one of my sport coats. I was ready to go, as Victoria went downstairs with me and I reminded her to take her vitamins. When we reached the back door, I took her and pressed her against the wall, kissed her as she kissed me back and felt between her legs, making her moan and bring her to a rousing climax. She wrapped both arms around my neck and held on as I whispered in her ear, you belong to me now. She said yes I do. I kissed her lips and slowly released her. She said I love you Charlie. And I love you to Victoria, as I walked out she stood in the doorway as I got in the car. I pulled out and closed the garage door and headed for the office.

Driving to the office seemed even more pleasant now and the air smelled fresh and clean, and most of all I was very happy. I stopped at the donut shop and bought a couple dozen assorted donuts and continued on my way. As usual I was the first one there; it was a few minutes after eight. I looked around and it was a little cloudy as I got out of the car and carried the donuts and walked to the door, put my key in and entered, the door closed and entered the pin. Walked around the ground floor, checking the washrooms, conference room, lunch room and loading dock doors and then took the freight elevator up, checked the washrooms and walked around and left the donuts in the lunch room as I went up the stairs to the roof, made sure I set the door so I wouldn't be locked out even though I had the keys, and walked around the perimeter and saw the roof mounted cameras, before returning and locking the door. Went downstairs and put the coffee on, after the first pot finished, put the second one on. Poured a cup, grabbed a paper towel and a donut and sat and ate one. When I finished, washed my hands and went to my office and turned on the television, computer and opened the cabinet for the security cameras.

I took some of the ads for the condos to the conference room and pinned them to the bulletin board. I had very little to do, except wait for a closing date on the office complex, and the next closing for the last Kashia condo which was later this week, and final confirmation on the demolition of the mall down the street, and what would happen with my offer on the golf course. Once the Kashia condo closed I wouldn't have any more small deals, they would all be handled by my associates downstairs. The only thing of importance then would be my net and gross profits and an audit of my assets. I pulled out my phone and checked on Vicky, saw she had stripped down the beds and cleaned up the empty bed room and had started a load of wash. I thought I would turn the empty bedroom into our play room, she would really like that, it shouldn't be difficult to do, all we really needed was a place for our toys, the closet or a cabinet, or put a shelving unit in the closet, and some hooks in the ceiling. When I built the house it was built to more ridged specks than most homes. We could even ad some furniture and I had seen a couch without a back; they call it a day bed which would be fine and it came with a matching couch and that should do it. I turned off the app. as Joanne and some of my employees started pulling into the parking lot.

Joanne came in first at her usual time and ducked in and said good morning as she went to get a cup of coffee after stopping by her office. She returned to mine and sat down and asked about the weekend. Told her it appeared that we might not have the condos much longer as sales were very brisk to say the least and Anne and Samantha spent the weekend there and would really be the ones to talk to. I didn't know if one of them would be there all week or if they were going to switch up. Fitz had said he would check during the week. Said I posted one of the full page adds in the conference room. I asked how far she had gotten with the audit. She stated that she started by listing all of the complexes, and based them being under the different management companies names, would have to list each one separately. She decided to hire two appraisers to check each property, and it would take about a month. The cash reserves weren't going to be hard and would start on them today, and the expenses of moving was close two $2,000,000.00. She hoped Anne would come in to help her with some of the audit. It was after nine and called, and Anne was in and asked her to come to my office. We asked her to have a seat as we quizzed her about the weekend. Samantha was down stairs processing about thirty-two applications they had taken and would be here until she cleared those up. Joanne asked her to help with our internal audit, and asked how much had Hippies added to her work load. Said she had about half a day's worth of things he needed done and she should have those cleared up by noon. Ok and asked her if she would get Pat, she left and they both returned. I asked Pat how much she had left to do. Stated she should be caught up around noon also. I said to Joanne take your pick of whom you want to help you. Pat could assist Samantha and get some idea about the loan processing operations.

I would be leaving around eleven and would be out all day and tomorrow. I would have to be here for the Kashia closing. Oh Joanne said they bumped it to Thursday and Green had called Mrs. Kashia and informed her of the change. Green said, she asked if you were going to be there and he said as far as he knew. I said this is Ms. Brown's sale so she will have to go. Joanne dismissed Anne and Pat, and said there was something strange about this Mrs. Kashia, because when she called, she had answered and being a woman detected something in her voice. Said she owned the condo we closed on last week; the one Victoria use to live in. I said she hit on me after the last closing when Phillips went with me, it was his sale. Joanne said now I get it. I said nothing to her about Vicky, only that I had found her a place when she asked, and nothing else. Told Joanne she came on very strong. Joanne said you found her a place, didn't you, in your heart Charlie, and that's very good and a warm place to be. I said tomorrow we are going to the court house. I love her so very much, like I never loved anyone before. I bought her a car Saturday and she was very upset that I had done that, she jumped up and said no and began crying. I have to get her to accept things, and every time she says all she wants is me. Joanne said she had never seen a person so in love before as she is and she loves you with all her heart and soul. I know you, so I don't have to worry about you not loving and caring for her. You make sure you bring her back, whenever, so I can see the new Mrs. Charles Harcourt. You know I will, I told her she would need a phone, you know what she said, why Charlie, and explained to her for emergencies, and so I can talk to you. Joanne said she's so sweet and innocent, and said she had work to do. You know Charlie; you aren't small time anymore and when I finish with this audit, you may have to really try hard to maintain a low profile. I said we will see won't we. Joanne said yes we will and headed to her office. It was ten when Hippies came in. I saw him walk by and he soon returned to my office with a cup of coffee, and sat down, he said the Kashia closing had changed days but was still at eleven, and the sellers had accepted my offer for the office complex, and he had applied for a tax reduction for the mall site down the street. Said the heirs of the golf course were willing to accept my bid, if the court ruled in their favor. And he would work with Joanne on the audit, and thought it was good that I had decided to do it now. Harold said I guess Joanne told you about hiring the appraisers. I replied yes, and told him that I had a funny feeling that our net worth was going to be much more than we thought, and said he agreed with me. I should expect to start looking at charities for possible large donations to lower our tax burden, and investments other than real estate, said it could still be the core, but said I needed more diversification. I asked would you look into it for me. I am tying the knot tomorrow, and my concentration was spread a little thin right now.

I told him about the condo sales, and it was seeming to go well, and Samantha, Anne and Pats participation over the weekend and my going two days in a row to check in on it. He said it must have been something, because he stopped by Samantha's on his way up and she was very busy, and he told her to come up and get some coffee. He said he would check on where to best invest, and knew I wanted to still keep a low profile. Told him I may if no offers come in after I demolish the office complex, build a state of the art building, but that will be when Fitz can give me an idea if it would be worth it, and what the vacancy rates were on office space out there. He said that sounds like a winner as he got up to leave. Have a great day because I didn't look like I would be here all day and would see him again Wednesday for sure. He said congratulations and be sure to bring Mrs. Harcourt in, and said you need a new will now. I said yes, and would give it some thought. It was close to eleven now and pulled out my phone and looked in on Victoria, she must have taken a shower and was oiling herself, and was deciding on what to wear. I closed the app and, no sooner than I had, the store called and said I could pick up my suits. I thanked them and would pick them up first before heading home. I closed up and shut down my office and headed out and waved to Joanne, since she was on the phone as I departed.

I got in my car and headed to the Mall to pick up my new suits. It took about thirty minutes to arrive and went directly to the men's section. Gave my name and five minutes later the salesman came out with them both and asked if I would like to try them on. I decided to and he checked the fit and length, and he was satisfied, and I was to. I returned and put my jeans back on and he had placed them in a travel bag and handed me the hat box with the Panama hat inside and I departed. After getting in the car, called home, and after I said her name she answered. I said sweetheart I have just picked up my suits and I am on my way home. Vicky said come home safe and she would be ready, and I love you, I said the same and hung up.

It didn't take but about half an hour to get home since traffic was light and left the car in the driveway and went in the front door. The mailman had just left and I took the mail to the office before going upstairs. I entered the bedroom with my new suits and found Victoria wearing stockings with the attached garter and nothing else, she hugged me as I entered the room. I hung my suits up. Said she was undecided what dress to wear, and asked me to pick one out. I said the white one, then said she changed her mind about wearing the stocking and sat on the couch and took them off, she stood nude facing me and said Charlie do you see anything different about me. I looked close and said you're getting more beautiful every day, she said look close, I did. She said her breast had gotten larger, and had heard it happens when you are truly in love. I came over and cupped them in my hand and kissed each one. Said if she wore the white dress, I should wear the white suit, I said ok. We dressed, and I wore a pair of sandals, and she wore some also. It was a warm day and almost eighty degrees. I transferred my keys and wallet to my new suit, and my phone. Brushed my teeth and hair, came out and put my jacket on. She had applied the bug repellent and it smelled good and we were soon ready. Asked if she had her sun glasses, and she replied yes, she took her tan purse, and said to her we have to get you a white one.

We went out the front door, as I locked it behind us, I opened the door for her, and before she got in she said Charlie, hold me please, I need you to hold me. I held her as she said I was too good to her. I said Victoria, we are happy with one another, and there isn't anything that is too good for you, because you belong to me, you accept that don't you, she said yes, you love me, again yes, I love you and there isn't anything I won't do for you. Now get in the car, Victoria, wife to be. She kissed me and got in. I got in and she reached for my hand, pulled it to her lips and kissed it. I started the car and pulled off, and we headed to the dealer, but first she would need a cell phone, and took a detour and went to my local Talkie store and we went inside and purchased a cell phone and she picked the color and a case, this took about fifty minutes, and now she had a phone and a number and I placed her number in my contacts, and placed my number in her phone along with Joanne, Hippies and Fitz just in case.

We finished and it took about forty-five minutes before we pulled into the automobile dealership. Parked in the guess spot and I came around and opened the door for Victoria. I said to her as she stood, you know you are very beautiful to me, you are elegant, poised, and tomorrow you will be my wife, so be my wife now, sweetheart. I will Charlie because you love me, and will be whatever you want me to be, but at home is our world ok Charlie, yes Vicky, forever. She kissed me and with poise and grace together we entered the showroom. Mr. Hanks greeted us at the door, and welcomed us inside. Asked us to his office as he handed me the final paper work and I looked through it and found the VIN number, pulled out my phone and called my insurance man, gave him the necessary information and we were now covered. Mr. Hanks led us to the auto reception room. It was a room with a ballroom feeling, a red carpet led up to the car; it was sitting there waiting for Vicky. Looking like a Hollywood star, the salesman opened the door for her and then slid into the passenger side and gave her a brief explanation of some of the key features. He asked her if she had a phone and she handed him her new phone and he paired it with the vehicle, and showed her how to use it. The girl was making progress and entering the 21st century. I knew it would take her a few days to get adjusted, but anyway she had to regain some independence, and start doing more things on her own. After half an hour, the salesman and I felt she was ready; she had entered our home address into the navigation and set home as her destination. I kissed her and said to her I would be behind her on her maiden trip. She looked good, and truly deserved it.

Victoria could drive really well, noticed on a section where the speed limit was fifty she didn't hesitate giving it some gas. When we arrived home, I parked on the side and came over as she got out and hugged me. Charlie you are so wonderful and I am so thankful, as she hugged me again. I said wait here if you don't have to use the bathroom or want to change clothes. Said she wanted to change and so did I, as we entered the front door and telling her that I had to pair the garage door to her car and give her a set of keys to the house. But first we went upstairs and changed clothes. I put on my jeans and t-shirt from earlier but I would keep my sandals, and retrieved my sports coat, and made sure I had transferred my wallet and keys. I went to the closet and pulled out the drawer where I kept the extra sets of house keys, took the new key fob of Vicky's, and placed it on the same ring. She had put on a pair on leggings and her short skirt, with a pretty blouse, and kept her sandals and purse. I turned to her and said, what do you say to this idea, she said yes Charlie what is it; I said how about we make the empty bed room our play room. She looked at me and smiled. Would you Charlie, you would do that for me, I said yes. She hugged me and kissed me and said that would be the most wonderful thing ever. I want to put a couple of pieces of furniture in it for us to play on and a cabinet for all our stuff. She said that sounds really great. I said but first I have to show you the locks to the house. We went downstairs and I opened one of the kitchen drawers and removed the remote for the van. We went back to the front door and showed her how not to get locked out without her keys and how to lock both locks, she understood. Had her lock the door and we went to her car and I paired her auto to the garage door where she would park, and after several minutes, that had been accomplished, tested it several times and had her sit in the driver's seat and do it. Told her to back down the drive, as I turned around and backed my car inside; she pulled up and pressed the button and closed the door. I

got in the passenger side, buckled up and gave her directions to
where we were going.

Since I had shopped for the office several times recently I knew
just where to go and the furniture I had in mind. We arrived and
Victoria parked and we got out and she locked the doors with her
remote and said that was great. We went inside and a saleslady
approached and asked to help. I explained that there was a couch I
had seen on one of my previous visits and she led us upstairs. I
showed Victoria the couch and matching day bed, and asked if it
came in leather. She stepped away, returned and said it did, and
gave me a selection of the different colors. I asked Victoria what
color, we got it down to either brown or black, we decided on
black leather. I also saw a large wooden cabinet, it was about six
and a half feet tall and five foot wide, with double doors, was solid
wood and had adjustable, shelves that were set back from the door,
and had two drawers at the bottom. The space from the door was
important because I wanted to hang stuff on the inside of the doors.
We said we would take the items and she placed the orders and
checked to see if they were in stock and said they were and would
be delivered the following week. I took care of the paperwork and
paid, as Vicky walked around looking, then she came back to
where I was standing and held my hand. We concluded our
business and we looked some more before exiting the store.

Vicky said she was hungry, and I asked her if she had eaten
anything this morning. Said she had coffee, donut and poached
eggs with toast and had taken her vitamins as I instructed. I asked
her what she wanted to eat. She said the sea food restaurant the
Red Fin Inn, and yes she replied because she was really hungry.
We got in the car and I directed her to the Red Fin Inn and she
pulled in and parked. I felt comfortable with her driving, which I
wasn't with quite a few people. We got out and entered as she held
my hand. It wasn't crowded, probably because it was a Monday.
We were seated and soon placed our order. Vicky said to me that
she was glad I decided to have ourselves a play room, because now
she felt she was truly at home, and only I could make her happy,
and was looking forward to tomorrow. She wouldn't wear white,
because that was the color you wear for your first marriage, and

was sorry that I wasn't the first. Then to my surprise she asked me if I had sold the condos for Mrs. Kashia. I said the one she used to reside in, and Thursday the last one she was selling. Asked if she had asked about her, and please tell her the truth about anything she said. I said she described you as undesirable and asked if I had found you a place, said I had and left it at that. Vicky asked did she try to seduce you. I said yes and told her all of the things she had did and what she had said to me. Vicky said Charlie, I love you, and you did find me a place to live didn't you, in your heart and she started crying. I said don't, please don't, we said we weren't going to go there anymore, remember and she dried her moist eyes and smiled at me, and said yes Charlie, that's behind us.

Our food arrived and Vicky smiled at me. I said eat up you little cutie. She must have been starving, the girl ate again like the first time I fed her, we finished and when the waiter asked if we wanted desert, she said yes, and ordered some cheese cake, and I had lemon meringue pie, and coffee. I paid and tipped the waiter and we soon left. Vicky kissed me before I got in the car and she drove us home using the navigation system. Said she wanted to go home and be with me, and that she never got enough of being with me. She pulled up the driveway and turned around, pressed the button and the garage door went up, and she carefully backed inside. She turned the engine off and asked me for the owner's manual in the glove box and said she was going to read it and get to know her car better. I took it out and handed it to her. We got out went inside, and then she asked what I was going to do now.

Told her I had to look and see if I had the hooks I needed for our play room. She went inside and I went to a bin on the garage wall where I kept a variety of different things to maintain the house and found what I was looking for. They were heavy duty hooks about ten inches long and would support two hundred pounds or more. I took four and looked in my work bench and found my stud finder and my battery powered drill and a pair of large slip joint pliers, there was a step stool upstairs in the hall closet as I placed everything in my canvas work bag I used for carrying tools in when working around the house. While I still had my clothes on I would mount these in the ceiling. I entered and went upstairs and took everything to the spare room. Went to the bed room and hung my jacket up. Vicky had undressed and put on her house clothes and was sitting on the bedroom couch reading her owner's manual. I removed the tall step stool and went in the spare bedroom and proceeded to install the hooks and after finding the ceiling joist and drilling a small pilot hold and hitting the joist dead center, and spacing them about four feet apart to form a square. I used a larger bit and drilled a couple inches before screwing the hooks in. It took about an hour before I soon finished. Bagged up my tools and set them in the hallway, placed the stool back in the hall closet before taking out the vacuum cleaner and cleaning up the dust from the plaster and vacuuming myself off. Put everything back and returned my tools to the garage and put the drill batteries on charge. Took off my shoes and went upstairs. Victoria was almost through reading her manual. When she finished, said now she knew more about her car and said she wanted to put the manual back, and grabbed her keys and went downstairs and put it back inside her car. When she returned I had undressed and was preparing to shower the dust off of myself. She said wait for her as she undressed and we went and showered together, we didn't stay long and soon dried off. It was about six when I put on some clean shorts and t-shirt and picked up all my dirty clothes and placed them in the hamper.

I took Vicky by the hand and we went downstairs and had a drink. I came from behind the bar and reached around her and felt her breast. They had grown and she pulled up her shirt and said, do you see the stretch marks, and took a bar stirrer and placed underneath one and it stayed in place. Then said she couldn't do that before. I said you have been eating more regular and taking vitamins which you badly needed, you skin has a glow and the dark spots have cleared up. I said remember the first time I took you to the Red Fin Inn; you couldn't eat all your food, now you clean the plate the last couple times we have been, at least your stomach isn't sticking out. Said she did sit-ups during the day when she wasn't too tired, from working or making love to me. I said very well you want to keep it all in proportion. Said she wasn't going to be a fat girl. I told her in a few weeks we would take a short trip, it would be our honeymoon. Charlie she said, that isn't necessary because she was happy with me and if we went, it would be ok, but said as long as we were together she was beyond happy.

We played some pool and had several drinks. She was excited about getting married and had decided what she was going to wear. I said that's good and she asked me what I was going to wear, and just to mess with her, said some jeans and a dirty t-shirt. She said I know you wouldn't, I said you are right, we will look like royalty, and then take you to lunch, where ever you want. She wasn't hungry now and would wait until tomorrow to decide. It had gotten late and we decided to go to bed, she wanted to hold me and feel on me, and said today was exciting, and she was happy and wanted to feel me next to her. We went upstairs and oiled ourselves before we climbed in bed. Said I hoped she didn't want to use our new play room until after the furniture had arrived, and said when you want to play, I would like you to put on the black dress with the spaghetti straps, and if you want to you could get some stiletto shoes to go along with the dress. She asked if we could go back to the store where we bought some of the toys, I said sure anytime you want baby. We laid and felt on each other and rubbed one another asleep again.

Forty

Tuesday: Day Forty.

It was going to be a very sunny day; the sun was just coming up when I opened my eyes. I looked at the clock and it was five thirty. Turned over and looked at Vicky before getting up, and going to the bathroom. I spent several minutes in the bathroom, shaving and brushing my teeth before returning. Vicky's eyes were open as she got up and ran pass me and kissed me on her way. She took her time and almost ten minutes had passed before she returned. I sat on the side of the bed as she came and stood in front of me and pushed me onto my back, leaned over me, then straddled me and put her breast in my face, they were warm and she smelled good, then she kissed me sticking her tongue down my throat and raised her head and said that's what is going to happen to me for the rest of my life, as I held her waist. She climbed over and we lay in bed holding one another. She asked me if I was ready to eat breakfast, yes was my reply, as we decided to get up now even though it was earlier than usual, we put on our bathrobes and went downstairs. Said we should have some poached eggs and sausage, with cheese toast. She then asked if there was anything else. Yes I replied. She asked what that would be. I said you in my life forever. She said oh Charlie that is something I can do. Said she had a question, what would she use as money when she went shopping. I said use your debit-credit card. Said she didn't know how much money she had in her account. I said you don't have to worry about that. I haven't done it yet, but you have been promoted from housekeeper, to wife and a pay raise comes with that. She asked how I could do that. Told her in order to keep your health insurance, she would always be an employee. I am an employee, it was that way for several reasons, but you don't have any more money worries that would be taken care of, also you will also have to go to the DMV again soon, for the name change on your driver's license, and to social security also . Do you have any more questions Victoria? What time are we going to the court house, said she didn't want to rush but wanted to savor the day, and had to polish her nails for me. I asked her what time she wanted to go, she said as early as possible. I said ok love, that's good because it was going to be before noon. Said she was the happiest and luckiest girl in the world today as she came over and kissed me and said let's eat. I have noticed a change in her, a new warmth, more sure of herself, and acting more like a normal person, her insecurities are gone along with the uncertainties she might have had with every passing day and especially after today. We cleaned up the kitchen together, sitting back down and finishing our morning coffee, we held hands and looked at each other and soon finished washing the cups and heading back upstairs.

I knew what I was going to wearing, the beige suit I just purchased and a summer knit with sandals, as I turned to Vicky and told her. She would wear the blue dress, and beige shoes, with matching purse, no stockings, and the matching jewelry to the rings. I asked what color lipstick and polish, brownish red, for both she replied. We both headed for the bathroom. I brushed my teeth, and Vicky did other things, before we entered the shower together and bathed one another, coming out and drying off, then oiled ourselves and applied the bug repellant. We wanted to be covered; it was almost eight o'clock now. Vicky did her finger nails and toes and I had my underwear on as I sat on the couch opposite her, watching her. She was so very beautiful to me, and really would have done this sooner, but it's still quick considering it's only been a little more than a month. After about half an hour she was finished and the polish had dried. I noticed she had shaved herself and had that clean appearance besides being clean for real. She put on a pair of soft cotton panties, the dress, taking her shoes and purse out, and checking the contents before adding some additional items. I put on my trousers, belt and my usual assortment of stuff and placed my phone in my jacket pocket. The license was in the office as I put my sandals on. She was wearing sandals also with a solid heel and open toes. She came out of the bathroom and her hair had waves and was just short of her shoulders. I had the rings, my sun glasses and would get the license on our way out as I asked her if she was ready. She said yes sir Mr. Charlie, as we walked downstairs together. I went to the office to retrieve the marriage license, and then we went out to the garage. Vicky asked which one, as I opened the door to the BGT for her. I got in, and opened the garage door and pulled out. I waited for the door to close before pulling away and off we went.

We headed for the county center and arrived almost twenty minutes later and were able to get a parking spot close to the entrance just as another car was pulling out. We stepped out and walked heading for the court house. Entered and after having gone through security and passing through the metal detectors we were then directed to the place where the judge was preforming the wedding ceremonies. I passed the license to the clerk and the judge asked us if we were ready, we said yes together, and he said those words magical words, do you take Charles, and then my turn, do you take Victoria, and we kissed and exchanged rings. Held hands and asked another couple to take our picture with our phones, and we also did the same for them, then we happily departed. We were told the license would be mailed after it was recorded. It was still early, around noon and I asked Victoria where she wanted to go for lunch, she told me to choose.

I drove to the Paris restaurant; we used the valet parking, and then entered, and were immediately taken to a reserved booth. Victoria had the most beautiful smile on her face as we ordered steak and lobster, asparagus, with a baked potato and a salad with Italian dressing, and two glass of Shiraz. We toasted one another, finally we were married. And I said you know I really fell in love with you when we met, you help turn me around for the better, and I have even prospered more since you came into my life in this very short amount of time. She said we will be happy together, I told her yes, very, very happy. Our food arrived and we enjoyed every mouthful, and each other. When we finished eating, I paid the bill and we decided to see a movie. It was about two people who survived a plane crash, were complete strangers, and in the end, fell in love. We enjoyed the movie and I said Joanne and everyone want to meet the new Mrs. Charles Harcourt.

We drove to the office and entered, Mr. Phillips congratulated us when we entered, as we rode up and went to Joanne's office where she was holding court with Hippies and Fitz. They all stood and gave us there congratulations. I just wanted to let you all meet the new Mrs. Charlie Harcourt. Joanne told her how happy she was for her. They took pictures of us with their phones and Joanne said if I don't see you, she would know why. Reminded her I would have to be here Thursday. Victoria and I started to leave, but before we could Pat and Anne came in also. Pat hugged me and had tears in her eyes and said she was happy for me. Then Samantha came, she hugged us both, and was happy for us also. We thanked everyone, said good bye and we headed home. I opened the car door for Mrs. Harcourt, she kissed me and we departed. We arrived home and once we were inside, went directly to the bedroom and undressed, washed or hands and brushed our teeth, and jumped in bed and made wild passionate love, until we were totally exhausted, we held each other until we fell asleep. When we woke it was late afternoon, we both used the bathroom and returned to bed, we smelled each other's sweat from our love making and started again before we decided to shower as we enjoyed being in the warm water, we dried off, oiled ourselves and put on our bathrobes and went downstairs and had a drink and some snacks before we returned to the bedroom, where we climbed into bed and holding each other, rubbing and touching as Victoria started to cry and said she was so very happy. I held her and told her I loved her and nothing would ever come between us. Charlie she said, I feel the same way, as she wrapped herself around me and we fell into a beautiful and most restful sleep.

Forty-one

Wednesday: Day Forty-one.

We woke to a beautiful sun filled day, we stayed at home. I asked Victoria her opinion of things, asking her if there was anything in the house she would like to change, like the colors of the rooms or the decor. She replied that there was no rush and she would probably want to over time, but said to me that proved to her that I really loved her and said it was sweet of me to even ask. I said this is your home now also and we will do everything together from now on and whatever you say has meaning to me. We hugged and kissed and decided to barbeque, Vicky said she would make some potato salad, as we sat outside and I grilled some sausages, chicken and burgers, we had our drinks and it just felt good not being alone any longer and just having her companionship put my mind at ease. Said I would soon be changing my work schedule in a few short weeks and would have shorter hours so we would be together more often. The day passed with us lounging around and she asked about the sauna in the basement. She said I hadn't used it since she was here. Said I had used it, but only twice since I had the house built. I just didn't have the time and sitting in it by yourself, wasn't very much fun. She said she had a personal question to ask me. I said yes. All the years between your wife's death and now you didn't have any relationships with any women. She said didn't you get lonely. Yes was my reply. Then she asked about sex and what did I do. I masturbated quite a bit and watched the videos, some with you in them. She came over and said my poor Charlie, you can have me whenever you want, just take me ok baby, as she placed my hand between her warm thighs, and said I belong to you now and we belong to each other. She licked my ear and placed her hand on my groin and rubbed it as we hugged. I told her how much she made me happy and was now spending a very enjoyable day with my wife. Evening came and I lit the fire pit and we had our drinks. We ate more and enjoyed being home and being with each other. Finally, it was almost midnight when we closed up shop and went inside, we smelled like smoke and meat. We went to the bedroom and made love, we enjoyed the lust that overtook us every time and we came together and decided to sleep and shower in the morning as we fell asleep in one another's arms, again.

Forty-two
Thursday: Day Forty-two.

I awoke, turned and looked at the clock; it was seven as I sat up, and then went to use the bathroom. I came back, looked at Vicky as she was starting to wake. I lay back down next to her and pulled her to me and kissed her, we were both very musty but the smell of us was all good. I said come sweetie, we must bathe and helped her up as we stood and felt each other. She said last night was so beautiful to her. I said it's always beautiful with you as we used the facilities before we showered together. We began to shower and as I bathed her I became very highly aroused for some reason all of a sudden, I reached out and held her and told her I wanted her now, I applied a generous amount of soap and lathered her vagina and anus as I held her arms behind her and bent her over and entered her, my penis seemed so very hard and very soon she climaxed several times before I then entered her anus before I climaxed, exhausted I released her as she turned around and grabbed my penis and washed me. Vicky said oh Charlie, I love you so much as we kissed and bathed each other. It felt good to be clean again as we dried each other off before applying the light body oil to one another. I always looked forward to oiling her, rubbing my hands all over her beautiful body and she felt the same about me. We finished and she said Charlie, I know you are going in today, but I just want to tell you how happy you make me feel and how much I love you. God bless you as she hugged me tight and I did the same. We finally released one another as I put on my briefs and then shaved.

When I returned Vicky had stripped the bed down and even the mattress cover, it was all pilled on the floor. She had a full load and said it wasn't even a problem with the twin washers and dryers. I had a closing today, and would still wear my jeans, and the knit from the day before, some white socks and my athletic shoes and sports jacket. I finished dressing and told Vicky that today would be the last closing on a house or condo and that after this; it would be only for larger properties, and said today's closing was for Mrs. Kashia. She said I trust you Charlie, and please don't say anything about me ok, which was in the past and said she held no grudges against her. I said thank you Vicky, love of my life. I helped her take the dirty linen downstairs. She asked since I was dressed if I wanted her to make breakfast. I asked her if she felt like it. Yes husband of mine. Ok my sweet wife. We did our breakfast thing, I finished the coffee and sat and watched her. It wasn't long before we were sitting in the nook eating and looking at one another as we soon finished and said that she would clean up. We really needed the nourishment after this morning's sex as we took out vitamins. Vicky said I didn't have to help her clean up. I told her maybe not this time but next time for sure. We kissed and she walked me to the door. Charlie when do I go to the DMV? When we get the marriage license back then we and can also go to the bank and change your name on all the necessary documents. I pushed her against the wall, and she opened her robe and said, feel me my husband. I did and watched the excitement rise in her again as she climaxed and fell into my arms, and I sucked her neck and nipped at her ear, before she stuck her tongue in my mouth. I said you are the love of my life, and stay sweet till I return. I turned and walked out the door, got into my car as she stood and watched me until I closed the garage door.

I enjoyed my drive to the office, my stomach was full, and so was my heart. It was a little after nine when I arrived. I wasn't the first one there today. I walked in, said good morning to Mr. Green and went upstairs to the lunch room and poured myself a cup of coffee before going to my office. The closing documents were on my desk as I scanned through them and everything was in order. I called downstairs to Mr. Green and asked if Ms. Brown had come in yet. He said she just walked in. I asked him to send her up please; yes sir and he hung up. A few minutes later Ms. Caren Brown walked in and I said, good morning, your closing is today. Yes she knew. You will ride with me and we will leave around ten thirty, yes sir she replied, and asked if there wasn't anything else. I asked how you have been doing deal wise. Said she had brought in a listing and found two buyers for homes, and was waiting for one contract to be accepted, and a closing date on the other. I said very well and I will see you in a very little while, and before she departed, said congratulations on your marriage and wished me well. I thanked her as she departed.

Shortly after I received a phone call from Mr. Rogers, he explained they were finished demolishing the mall buildings and were in the process of removing all the debris and wanted to know if I wanted to continue having the property fenced off when they were finished. I said no that wouldn't even be necessary. He was just checking to see what I might want to do, and told him I would soon have another property for him, but I was waiting to close first. He said that I could give him the address now and he could look then be better able to give me a cost estimate. I said ok then, and gave him the information and said he would be in contact and would fax the estimate to me and then we would talk again once I had acquired it. I said sure thing and gave him my fax number, thanked him and hung up. Then I received the call from Mr. Hogan of Beverly Heights Reality, and said a closing date had been set for the office complex, would be in two weeks. There were only six tenants left and four would be gone by closing and the remaining two would be moved out by the end of the month. He said he would see me at the closing, and then hung up.

I then called Mrs. Kashia and asked if she wanted me to pick her up again. Yes please she replied and said to her we would be there shortly. Said she would wait downstairs for me. I said the selling agent and I were preparing to leave and should see her in about ten or fifteen minutes. I looked at the clock and Ms. Brown entered and sat down, it was ten twenty, and told her I was just getting ready to page her. I asked how her brother was doing. She said after he finished working for me he picked up a job designing a couple of homes. I said that is very good, and might want him to design and office tower for me, and possibly design the entire complex. She said that would be wonderful, and said how generous I had been with him. I stood and complimented her on her dress. Said she understood that I liked the women to look their best and professional. She was wearing a, dark brown business suit, white blouse, stockings with hi-heels, gold earrings and her lipstick and nail polish matched and were ruby red, her hair was braided in a pony tail that went down her back, and was tied with a ribbon the same color as her business suit. I placed the papers needed in my briefcase and said; you are an asset to my business, as we walked out together. I opened the car door for her and she got in.

We reached Mrs. Kashia building in about ten minutes, she was waiting outside. I got out and opened the back door for her, she got in and I introduced her to Ms. Brown an informed her she was the selling agent for the unit and had found the buyers even though they had met before. We headed for the closing office. I parked and opened the car door for Mrs. Kashia; Ms. Brown came around as I reached in and grabbed my briefcase. I held the door for the ladies as we entered and were asked to have a seat in the waiting room, the buyer hadn't arrived yet. Mrs. Kashia made sure that she sat across from me again, she was impeccably dressed, a business suit with an extremely short skirt, a very sheer blouse, pantyhose, hi-heels, gold bracelet, necklace, and matching earring, her makeup was perfect, with peach lipstick and matching polish. As she sat down, made sure I could see before she crossed her legs, that her panty hose was crotch less, the ones with the very large openings with no panties, she kept her jacked buttoned, she wasn't going to stop flirting with me. I sat with my hands folded on my brief case, it was on my lap and maybe she would see the ring that hadn't been there before. The buyers soon arrived and we were shown to the room for the closing. It began and the papers were passed around, signatures gathered, the checks passed, more checks, and the deed transferred, and the deal was over and done quickly. We all rose and shook hands, and since we were the listing and buying agents it went very quickly. I asked Mrs. Kashia if she wanted to deposit her check, again she said yes please, and thank you. We exited and Ms. Brown sat in back this time as I opened the front passenger door for Mrs. Kashia. She got in, and we drove to the same bank as before. When she sat down in the car her short skirt exposed her sexy thighs and she even pulled it up slightly so I could get a good look before she sat with her purse in her lap for the ride to the bank. I escorted her inside, and waited as she deposited her check. Walked with her back outside to the car, opened the door for her and drove her home.

I got out and opened the door for her again and walked her to the entrance. She asked me to come up with her since she wanted to talk to me in private. I went in with her and up to her apartment, we entered her unit. She asked me to please have a seat, and stated that I had performed very well and in a professional manner and thanked me for doing it in such a timely fashion. Said she wanted to be very honest with me, that she wanted to have a close personal relationship with me. I stated that wouldn't be possible now as I showed her my wedding ring and said I had just married the girl of my dreams. Told her she was a very attractive and a very beautiful woman and would soon find someone. I had to end this as I then stood and thanked her for her business and headed toward the door. She followed closely and said please wouldn't I consider having an affair with her. I said that was out of the question as she removed her jacket, and I could see she was very aroused as her nipples were hard and very visible through her very sheer blouse, it was so sheer it was like a nitty, then it struck me, it was. I shook her hand and thanked her for her business as I reached for the door and opened it, she said please, and as I turned around she removed her skirt as I stepped into the hallway and headed for the elevator. Just as I turned around and looked back, she had one hand between her legs and the other on the door jamb as she jerked herself off and climaxed just as the elevator doors opened and I stepped inside. When I turned to press the down button she just stood there looking at me and hoping I would return. The elevator doors closed slowly and she stepped back inside her unit and closed the door. I had my pocket voice activated recorder with me this time, just to be on the safe side, you never know.

I went downstairs and got into the car and Ms. Brown had moved to the front seat during my brief visit. Ms. Brown looked at me, and asked if I was all right. Said I am now, it that obvious. She said that woman wants you really bad, and looked like she would do anything to entice you and she had even noticed her very over obvious gestures. I said you are so right about that and this was her second time trying, but it's the last time for sure. We returned to the office and I let Ms. Brown out, and before we went in she stopped me and said, Mr. Harcourt you are an attractive man, you treat women with respect and you admire them also. There aren't many men like you and said I have heard so many good things about you. I admire and am proud to work for you, and just want to thank you for giving me this opportunity to be part of your company. I said thank you so very much, and it's a real pleasure, like I said before to have you working for me. You stick with me and you will do very well.

We went inside and I went to my office, I hadn't spoken to Joanne today and stopped by her office. She said come in and please sit down. Told me she hoped to finish a rough audit by tomorrow, but the official one wouldn't be until the appraisers were finished. I said that sounds great, and informed her they were almost finished down the street, and that a closing on the office complex was also set, and things were looking up. Samantha was going out to the condo complex sales office later and Anne was going tomorrow, and both were going again this weekend. I would skip this weekend and maybe go the following. Asked how our new brokers were doing, she said very well and she was taking this Saturday off and would only stop buy if she left the house, I said that sounds great. Well I'm going to end my day now and will see you tomorrow. Said she was glad I was slowing down some, that I needed to relax more. I said that does why we moved remember. Go home to your wife; she is probably waiting on you. Your right, you know you don't have to stay until closings either. Her reply was only if she wanted to. See you tomorrow Joanne as I walked to my office and surprisingly had never turned anything on. Went to see Hippies but he was gone and Pat and Anne were busy, so I just left. I got in my car and thought, it has finally come to this, come and goes whenever I please, it's been like this the whole time only now it wasn't because I was chasing a deal or a property.

I headed home but stopped at the hardware store and bought sixteen feet of a nice metal chain and had it cut into four foot lengths, they also had a plastic chain, same size as the metal and had it cut the same. Paid for it and headed home. It was a little after one when I backed inside and would take this to our new play room. I entered and didn't see Victoria, removed my shoes and went upstairs, took the chain to the soon to be play room, and took out a length of each to see if I had guessed correctly the approximate length. I was right on the money; put the bag in the closet after checking the length. Went to our bedroom and washed my hands, took off my clothes and slipped on some shorts and a t-shirt and headed down stairs to the basement, where I found Victoria reading the owner's manual for the sauna as she stood and came over and hugged me. She wanted us to start using it, and needed to know how to operate it. I asked if she had eaten, and answered no not yet. Vicky said it was easy because it was really a steam bath, but she would clean it first before we would begin using it.

Ok, but I am hungry as we went upstairs and heated some of what we had barbequed yesterday along with some of the corn on the Cobb. I made some coleslaw, and shortly we were sitting down eating. I cleaned up the kitchen and the food processor while she went and finished with the laundry. She had made up the beds, so when I finished I helped her fold the king size sheets and place them in the basket. I asked her if she was done. Said she needed to vacuum and that would be it for today, and said she did different things on different days and that way at least once a week everything was cleaned. I said ok baby as we hugged, and told her I would be in my office for a short spell. She said ok and went upstairs. I went to my office and turned on my computer and checked for any needed updates and it had been a while since I had turned it on there must have been fifteen or so. That didn't stop me from using it but after half an hour it asked for a re-start and I did. I re-entered my pass word and continued where I left off, searching commercial properties, found several that were of interest, and it was more the surrounding areas that would dictate what would be the most suitable. I was thinking of the potential and a place for some tax write-offs. Soon Vicky was vacuuming downstairs and I looked around at the stair case and thought of adding a pneumatic elevator. I had more than enough room for one, and it could go to the basement. I had looked at several sights while looking for other stuff and had ran across some site and read up on them and decided to call and made an appointment for a representative to come out and see about an instillation. I was ready to spent more time at home and enjoy life with my new wife.

When she finished and came to the office we decided to go for a walk. We put some bug repellant on and I changed into my dressier shorts so I would have more pockets for my phone, keys and wallet and she put on a pair of matching shorts and a blouse and her running shoes. We decided to walk around in the neighborhood. There were sidewalks and walking and bicycle trails and I asked her if she could ride a bike. Yes she could and asked her if she wanted a bike, and we could then go together, she said why not but stated, she had heard walking was the best exercise. While we walked through the neighborhood several of my neighbors waved at us, and after we had made it to the end of our very long street where there was a large circle with a hundred foot in diameter grassy area with a large tree in the center and the street ended, we headed back the way we came.

On the way back several of my neighbors had gathered at the end of their driveways and greeted us, they hadn't seen me since the last neighborhood meeting almost two months ago when we gathered to decide on how to and when to have the trees trimmed. I introduced them to my new wife Victoria, and several said it was about time I had gotten married and asked if I was now going to slow down now. All the houses were large and so were the lots, the smallest was on two acers, mine was on four and one of only six that large and anyone who lived here had a net worth of at least a million dollars or more. My closest neighbors Mr. and Mrs. Henderson invited us to sit on their patio; they had been out talking to Mr. Woo and his wife, the Knights, Donovan's, along with the Richards, they lived across the street and on both sides of my house, and were usually gathered together to play cards, poker, or grill and the women spent time together also. The Henderson's had a large patio, canopied with a fire pit and a very large grill, outdoor couches and chairs and there was room for at least twenty people easy, most were our age or older and were always eager to speak to me when they or I had a chance. Mr. Henderson brought out some drinks, a wine cooler he made by the pitcher full, filled some glasses and passed them around.

Since I hadn't been seen in a while, Mr. Woo said he noticed I had moved my office and had passed the new one and said it was very impressive. I said we had outgrown our old space and since moving business had also picked up. They all said they were all very surprised I had gotten married and asked when we had tied the knot. I said just the day before yesterday. They said this calls for a celebration. Mrs. Henderson asked her husband to fire up the grill and that led to another one of their spontaneous get together which they were known for. Vicky was overcome by the friendliness of my neighbors as she held my hand, the women began going inside to help prepare some food and they invited Victoria to come join them. The fellows wanted to know now that Woo had told them all about my new office, what I had been up to lately.

Richards said he had seen the ad for the condo sales and saw my company name at the bottom of the page and asked how it was going. I said from early indications and since it had only been a week, it was looking very good for sales. The Woo's owned a chain of dry cleaners, and did very well; Donovan had been a stock trader, retired and still dabbled in investments. Henderson, and Knight, were retired and had been involved in various industries, and Richards was a physician and the administrator of the local hospital. Mr. Henderson fired up his massive gas grill as his wife rolled out a cart with various meats on it and returned inside, and he soon began cooking. Soon we were joined by the Brogans, another couple from the neighborhood. Mr. Brogan joined our circle and his wife, went inside with the other women. Soon they all came out and Vicky sat next to me again as she held my hand and drank some cooler and said she was having fun and several of the women asked if she would join them some time when they went shopping. She said they had put their numbers in her phone. Said I was surprised you brought it. She wanted to get used to carrying it because I said she needed to. I said that's very good baby. How do you like them, said they were friendly, and nosy like most women, some more than others. The food was soon ready and I fixed Vicky a plate and then returned and fixed myself one.

Everyone had a plate and enjoyed the food, conversation and company.

Mr. Henderson proposed a toast to us and congratulated us on our marriage, as it started getting dark and the sun went down, the fire pit was lit, as Vicky sat close and I had my arm around her. Everyone was enjoying themselves, and later Dr. Richards and his wife said they had to go, and we all said good night. About an hour or so later I said to Vicky it was time for us to go also as we thanked everyone, shaking hands and after many hugs, Victoria and I walked back home. We walked down there drive way and down the street and around and up our seemingly long expansive drive, as the driveway lights were on as we walked, and a hundred feet from the house it was like day light as the motion detectors turned the outside lights on. We entered and Vicky said she had a very good time, and that she thought I had some great neighbors. She said they are all well to do, and was surprised by the conversations, and said I guess if you never have had to go without, then you look at things differently. Said they were really nice neighbors and was glad she had met them, but most of all she was happy to be home with me. Well we had eaten enough for today and she wanted us to shower together and go to bed. We went upstairs and bathed and after we dried ourselves and oiled we climbed into bed and we held each other kissed and felt on one another before falling asleep.

Forty-three

Friday: Day Forty-three.

When we woke, it was seven. I went to the bathroom right away and sat on the toilet and thought about all that barbeque. What a refreshing feeling when I finished, washed my face and then shaved. I turned around as Vicky came in and couldn't kiss her since I was brushing my teeth, I soon finished and departed. I felt better now and when Vicky finally came out and said it must have been the barbeque. We hugged and kissed, and then went downstairs and fixed breakfast together. Soon we were eating and looking at one another. I said you have really calmed down. She said how. I said we just held each other and went to sleep, have we grown old already. She told me that her feelings for me were the same but felt secure and loved and that I had even told her we were overdoing it, and now she had more self-control and felt so much better. We finished eating and cleaned up the kitchen together.

After we went back upstairs and I told her about the elevator I was going to see about having installed in the house. Really Charlie, yes Vicky and also said it was time to redecorate the house, and my spending more time here and I can work from home just as well as being at work. But I just like the thrill of going and connecting with my employees. I dressed in my usual attire jeans and athletic shoes and a t-shirt plus sports coat. I said the second set of keys to all the cars are in the key box by the back door. Said yes she knew, and said I could drive her car if I wanted to. I could set the seat position, said hers was number one. Told her it was the same for the Cambo and she could use it or the BGT, which ever one held her fancy, just make sure there is gas in it before you decide to go anywhere. She said yes sir Master Charlie. I said come here as she came and looked me in the eyes and said she couldn't wait for us to finish the play room. It was after eight and her phone rang. I said if it was a call from anyone not in her contacts not to answer it. If they are in your contacts there name will appear, and there picture if you take one of them and move it to the contact list. I said you are very good at comprehending things. She looked at her phone and answered, it was Mrs. Henderson. Vicky walked away and spoke for several minutes before hanging up. She said it was Mrs. Henderson and wanted to know if she was available for lunch. She and Mrs. Woo wanted to take her out. What did you say? Said she would call them back because she wanted to check with me first. I said it's up to you what you do, and when you do it, you may be my wife but you're not my prisoner. Just make sure you ask how they are going to dress so you can fit in sweetie. I am going in so feel free and you can always call or text me. I showed her how and she said that is great. Said that I am leaving now and she went downstairs with me. I said if they pick you up go out the front door; if you drive you know what to do. I pressed her against the wall and felt her, teasing and kissing her as I left, as she watched me until I closed the garage door.

By the time I arrived at work it was after nine again and walked inside and said good morning to Mr. Phillips and walked around to Samantha's office, she was in, and had a seat since she was on the phone before she shortly finished the call. I asked about the department, she laughed at that one, and said the department is doing fine and said all the loans she processed had been approved and was going to spend Saturday and Sunday at the sale again. Said Anne had assisted her, and was such a big help. When you feel you need a full time assistant let me know, said she wouldn't hesitate if it came to that but after this condo sale ended things should calm down to a leisurely pace. I said well you have a great day, oh and just because your office is down here don't hesitate to come upstairs for coffee or donuts, you are part of the inner circle. She said thank you, and would remember that. I departed and went upstairs and waved at Joanne on my way to the coffee pot. I poured a cup and came back to Joanne's office. Good morning Joanne, as I entered. Good morning Charles, and said please have a seat. She said Mr. Charlie; you are worth about a half a billion dollars. I said what. She said her rough estimates were based on some actual accounts and the most accurate figures would be in after the appraisals were completed, then she would take the highest and lowest and come up with an average for each asset. We may have to give out a bonus to get where we want to be with taxes. I don't have a problem with that. I said Hippies was looking into diversifying our portfolio to lower our taxes also. Yes and he mentioned some municipal bonds, tax free you know. Yes I know and that's one possibility just as Hippies walked in. Then we all sat on the sofa and chairs. He said young man we needed to add another member to the board, and that he found some municipal bonds we could invest in and he assumed Joanne had told me that I was worth over half a billion. He stated that's no small feat son, and since Victoria was already and employee and my wife, he had assigned her to the vacant position on the board and she now held a position, and also would soon draw up a new will for me and that there were some fine points in it that I would have to decide on. Other than that, the only other thing was there was approximately six million dollars roughly that I had to dispose of, and wanted to know what to do with it. I said a million apiece to each board member, that leaves one million left, one hundred grand to Anne, Samantha, Pat, Phillips and Green and twenty-five to each associate, then donate the rest to charity. Let everyone come up with a list of the most deserving and that's it. Hippies said you are kidding aren't you. If what you said is correct, then that's it.

Hippies said let me hug you. I stood and he hugged me, and said I was the best boss ever. Joanne came around and hugged me also as tears were in her eyes. I said you all helped me make it, so it's only fair you help me spend it. Oh I said but wait until we have the hard figures, and please don't tell the others yet. Fitz yes, but no one else, anything of importance beside that. They looked at one another, and said no. I said these are to be considered fiscal year-end bonus correct. He said correct. Ok good. How much in the corporate account, Joanne looked, and said nine million. Great I was going shopping. I asked Hippies what details. He said to come with him as we went to his office. He said have a seat. He said if something were to happen to you, who would be your beneficiary, for the cash and for the business. I said split it equally between Joanne and Victoria. If something was to happen to you and your wife. I said then it would be Joanne, Fitz, and yourself. He said you like to keep it simple, don't you. Yes I replied. He said he would draw it up and have it ready by next week. I said have a great week end, as I departed, and waved at Joanne as I left. Just as

I got in the car, Vicky called me and said lover, I'm going out with Mrs. Henderson and Mrs. Woo. I said ok baby and if you happen to go to the Paris just give them my business card ok. She said yes sweet heart, I love you, love you back.

I headed home and decided I would trade in the BGT; it was time for a new one since I had this one for about three years. Wasn't any sense of me being cheap with myself and after arriving home I backed inside the garage. I observed that Victoria was riding with our neighbors because her new car was still here. I went inside and headed to my office and looked in my file cabinet and removed the title to the BGT, then on my way out removed the second set of keys to it from the key box. Then I went to the garage, opened the trunk and searched around for any personal items before pulling out and after closing the garage door drove to the dealership. It took me about forty minutes before I arrived, parked and walked inside. A salesman walked up and asked if he could help. I told him I wanted to do a trade-in; and probably because of how I was dressed he seemed too hesitate and didn't seem to take me serious until I asked for Mr. Haskins. He proceeded to get Mr. Haskins and they returned together to the showroom. Mr. Haskins said Mr. Harcourt what can I do for you, as he shook my hand. I explained that I wanted to trade the BGT in for the FSX99, and asked if he had any in stock. He showed me the three he had in stock. I looked at all three and told him I wanted all the options. One of them happened to be in the color I had chosen when I was looking at their web site, and was fully loaded and the interior was what I also preferred. I asked about a trade-in, he said that his appraiser would have to look at it. The appraiser looked and returned and he would give me $70,000.00 credit toward the purchase with a trade-in. It's a deal, as I handed him the keys and title to the BGT and he had the FSX99 pulled out and cleaned, and prepped. We then went to fill out the paperwork, he gave me the VIN number, and I called my insurance man and changed cars. Once that was taken care of, I used my corporate charge card, and soon the car was brought around and he showed me some of the new features, as we synced my phone to the car. Mr. Haskins shook my hand and said it was always a pleasure doing business with me, and I drove away. I had only spent an hour there at the dealership. I drove home, went in the front door, and through the house to the work shop and opened the drawer with the garage door remotes and opened the door where the BGT had been parked, went out and synced the car to the garage door. When that was complete, walked back inside putting the remote back before going and turning the FSX99 around, leaving it outside and closed the garage door. Went inside the house and filed my sales receipts and other paperwork away. I received a text from Vicky that they had been shopping and were going to lunch at the Paris, I texted her back. Ok great baby. She texted me back, I love you Charlie.

Decided I would have the elevator installed, and then have the entire house painted, the carpets cleaned or replaced, and then I would be finished with any major changes to the house. I went and looked at the deck; it was thirty by fifty feet. I would leave it but have the stain reapplied and add an above ground pool next to it. I walked out the front door and walked around. Didn't have any trees close to the house, which I liked, but the drive way needed a recoat and could use some enhancements. It was time to take care of the house. Then we, Victoria and I could redecorate the house, adding some new pictures and accents wouldn't hurt. Have the heating and air conditioning systems serviced also. I went back inside and fixed myself some lunch. Decided to fix a ham sandwich and have a salad. After I fixed everything I poured myself a glass of wine and sat down and indulged myself. While eating, decided that after I finished, would marinade some meats for a barbeque. I wasn't planning on going anywhere this weekend. Soon finished and washed my dishes and removed some meats from the freezer, some ribs, chops and chicken, setting them in the kitchen sink to thaw, and washed my hands and decided to look on the RELS again. Went to my office and turned on my computer and checked for updates, there were only two, and while they were downloading went upstairs and put on the shorts I wore yesterday when Vicky and I went for our walk. After changing, came back downstairs and searched for different properties. Saw several apartment buildings that looked like they had some potential; with a gut rehab could possibly be profitable. I printed them out and when they were finished printing, had about a dozen that I would look into later and give some serious consideration. I would get more involved with property rehabs and conversions like I had done in the past; it had paid off then and was how I had gotten a firm start in the market place.

I decided to check on the meats I had taken out. The chicken had thawed and I began cleaning the four chicken breasts, removed my kitchen shears and trimmed the fat off and washed them, placed them in a bowl and let them sit and drain. I washed my hands and removed the seasonings, sauces and liquid smoke from the cabinet. Sprinkled the seasoning generously on them and made sure it was all over, and placed them in a smaller stainless steel bowl and poured some of the liquids over them, stuck them with a steak knife, and washed my hands again before covering them with the lid and placing them in the fridge. The thick chops were almost fully thawed and placed them on the cutting board and split them almost in half, making a butterfly, and soon finished that, rinsed them and placed them in another bowl, and did them the same as with the chicken. Well those were ready now, but would have to wait a little longer for the ribs to thaw.

Took the utensils and cutting board and washed them thoroughly and left the in the rack to dry. I decided to go to the basement and after looking around, found the place where the elevator would be after being installed. Then looked at the half of the basement that was walled off and decided, it should be opened up completely and have the walls painted, expand the bar, and add maybe another pool table and ping pong and more furniture. Since the ceiling was high, ten feet, I could have seats on a platform by the pool tables. My house was on a hill, and the entire neighborhoods elevation was the highest in the area and flooding wasn't a problem even when there were very heavy rains. If there was flooding you might not be able to get out the neighborhood once you left, but your house would be dry. I decided to fix myself a drink, and after I had, sat and was thinking, when I received a text from Vicky, she was now on her way home.

When Vicky arrived back home; I was downstairs shooting pool, Mrs. Henderson and Mrs. Woo came inside with her. She called my name and I went upstairs. Greeted the ladies and Victoria had several bags and had set them by the stairs. She hugged and kissed me and said she had a wonderful time and enjoyed herself. I said that's very good. I asked the ladies if they wanted anything, water, tea, soda or a drink. They said they would have water and I took out three bottles of water and handed it to each as they sat in the kitchen. Victoria asked whose car was that in the driveway. I said it was ours that I traded in the BGT on the FSX99. She said it's so very beautiful. I left it there so you would see it. She asked how soon before we will go for a ride. Soon I replied. Told her I had decided we would redo the house after I had the elevator installed, and that she would have to help choose colors for several of the rooms. Dorothy, Mrs. Henderson said the house looks lovely now, why would you want to change anything. Stated I had been concentrating on work these past few years and hadn't really made any improvements since I had it built, and since Vicky is now in my life now I want her to feel more at home and am willing to decorate more to her liking, and anyway it's time for a change. She said that was a very generous gesture and very open minded. June, Mrs. Woo said that was good of me to let Vicky change things, most men wouldn't do that and would resist. They prepared to leave and I said good bye to them, as Vicky showed them to the door and thanked them for inviting her.

She returned and hugged me, and asked are you really going to redecorate the house. I sure am, and you are going to help me. She kissed me and started crying as I held her. She looked up at me and said never had anyone ever been as kind and generous to her ever in life and she loved me so very much. Told her the man was coming next week to see where I wanted the elevator, and after that, I would have my friend Hector who did my office come and paint the whole house and I would open the basement completely up, and have the driveway recoated. Come let me show you the car, we went to the garage, and said get in, she got in and said, this is so nice Charlie. It's for when we go out together. I backed inside, I decided to treat myself and when we do the house, it will be a treat for both of us. We went inside the house and when we entered the kitchen she saw the ribs in the sink, asked what are you planning on doing. I am marinating some meats for the weekend. Hadn't planned on going anywhere, but that doesn't mean we won't, but anyway had also seasoned some chicken and chops and were waiting for these to thaw so I could clean them. I have to pull the skin off the back first before I do. She said let her change clothes and she would help. I asked her what she bought while she was out. Just a dress and some shorts and a pair of heels. Too bad we don't have a swimming pool. I asked her do you want one. Are you serious? Yes I told her it would be an above ground pool and just off the deck and had already considered it.

She wanted to put her new clothes away first and said she would come back and help me clean the ribs. I took a beer from the fridge, and poured it in a glass and stepped out onto the deck. It was about four and the sun was still bright with a few clouds. It sure felt good being at home but I really missed being around the action at work. Vicky returned while I was on the deck and had started cleaning the ribs and when I returned to the kitchen; she was pulling the skin off the back. When she finished, I rubbed them with the several seasonings and brown sugar and then cut the slabs in half and added my secret liquid ingredients. I placed them in a large stainless-steel bowl and placed the plastic cover on the bowl before setting them inside the fridge with the other meats. I cleaned up and washed down the counter top and washed my hands. I asked Vicky if she was hungry. No she replied and felt she had eaten enough for today, but might have something light later. She poured herself a beer and said lets go sit outside. We sat out on the deck under the umbrella, and she asked why I had traded the car in. I told her it was time and I had it for three years, but the real reason was I had the money and that if I didn't spend it would be taxed. I asked her about her new friends. She said they were very nice and like most women talked a lot, but were fun and funny, and they loved to shop. Said that June Woo was more like her though, didn't just spend on unnecessary stuff, and was more down to earth. Dorothy was more of a home body, and really liked things for the house. She enjoyed there company very much, and thanked me for not trying to keep her all to myself. Told her I was glad that

she had gone out with them and that I loved her and you have been
alone in the house long enough.

Asked what made me want to redo the house. I told you earlier
that it needs your touch; it has been this way since it was built.
Painting and improving the space will give you and I both
something else to do. Besides I have put in place my organization
so Joanne and I could spend more time away from the job. And as
a matter of fact, do you know anything about how companies
operate. She had some idea, that they had presidents, and boards of
directors, and then there were others, supervisors or directors and
then the people who did the real work. I said you do understand,
well you are now a member of the board of Harcourt Real Estate
Corp. which means your salary just increased. You are no longer
my housekeeper but my wife, and that automatically makes you a
member of the board because we had a spot to fill. Charlie, what
does it all mean? I just want you, nothing else, and I love you and
want to be with you ok. I said you will, it just means, you aren't
the scared desperate woman I met that fateful evening a little over
a month ago and fell in love with, you are now Mrs. Victoria
Harcourt. I asked her when you went to the restaurant what
happened. She said when they got there, Dorothy parked and they
walked inside and to where the maître was, they were passing out
numbers and people were waiting. Dorothy asked for a table for
three and he started to hand us a number, and I handed him your
card, he handed it back and told us to follow him, and he seated us
in the reserved booth we sat at the last time we went there together.
Dorothy and June wanted to know how I did that. I just said
Charlie said show them his card, that was all he said and we had
very prompt service. June and Dorothy both commented about the
excellent service, and how the other patrons were looking at us.

She asked Charlie, please explain what happened and why. I
said you know I have helped a lot of people and that includes the
people that own and run the restaurant. I helped them also, and it's
kind of how they show their appreciation, besides having a
business interest. The booth you sat at is my personal booth. I
never have to wait, it part of the deal I have with them, plus I own
part of the business also, it's real discreet, but it works for me since

they are one of the top rated restaurants and are always busy. Charlie you are so very amazing and I love you so much. We sat and talked a long time, and after the sun went down Vicky said she wanted us to shower and go to bed so she could hold me. We closed and locked up the house before going upstairs and undressing. We showered and had fun and came out and dried off, she wanted to give me a massage, said I needed it and she was the one to give it to me. I complied and spread a large beach size towel on the bed, and laid on my back, as Vicky started with my feet and told me to relax, she continued as she slowly made her way to my neck, she kissed me and I turned over, and started at my feet again and I almost went to sleep again when she reached my neck. I turned back over and she told me to do her back, she had applied oil to herself all ready and just needed her back done, she felt good as I applied the oil and wrapped my arms around her, playing with her breast and felling between her legs. We removed the towel and pulled the covers back, we climbed in bed and I felt her as we lay there together. I held her and smacked her butt, and she said that she would be good as I climbed on top of her and slowly inserted myself into her as she moaned and said that I was her man. I bit her neck and licked her ear as I held her down, and talked dirty to her, soon she erupted with her first climax, and I squeezed her hard nipples as she moaned and came again. She said fuck me Charlie, fuck your dirty bitch, and she came again and then we came together, as I lay on top of her and she held me, and then I rolled over and we held one another and fell asleep, holding each other once again.

Forty-four
The Following, Weeks.

We woke that Saturday morning, made love and were so very satisfied and so fulfilled as we continued feeling on one another before we soon went to the bathroom together to wash up. We returned and got back in bed and made love again. I said Mrs. Harcourt you are one beautiful and so very hot and exotic woman, and I love you so very much. Yes Mr. Harcourt I belong to you and give my whole being to you, I am here for you always, as we kissed and we both agreed it was time for us to start another beautiful day together. We showered and washed the love juices off from the night before and this morning and made love again in the shower, as we were enjoying ourselves and each other. We finished and dried each other off before oiling and applying the bug repellant to one another again. We decided to wear some summer dress clothes because; we were undecided about what we were going to do today. We fixed breakfast, ate and cleaned up the kitchen, and I said to Vicky, lets brush our teeth and take a ride. I wanted to stop by the office and maybe pass by the condo sale just because it was my operation. Said she wouldn't mind and would go anywhere anytime with me. We wore almost the same clothes we were wearing when we married, I wore the white linen suit and Vicky her white summer dress.

We checked the house and closed the upstairs windows and locked up. Victoria was looking fantastic and elegant as usual. I opened the door to the FSX99, and she stepped inside. After getting in, I buckled up and pulled out the garage. I asked if she had her phone, Yes it was in her purse as we pulled away. We departed our neighborhood, as we headed for the office. We arrived in style, and together we walked inside and were greeted by Mr. Phillips. We returned the greeting as I walked around to see who was there. Then Phillips informed me that Hartman had met a couple and then they departed, Brown had come and gone, Newman had left and said she would be back, and Green had a showing and would return later. He also said Joanne had come in for a short time before Anne and Samantha came in and then departed, and said they just needed some loan application forms before they headed to the condo sales event. I said thank you for the update. Vicky and I went upstairs to my office and I checked to see if anyone had left any notes. There was only one, it was from Hippies, and said my new will was ready and all I had to do was sign, and that the corporate board had been officially set up and gave a date of two days prior and that had made everything official. I turned to Victoria and said; time to go my dear and we went down stairs and departed and walked out to the car.

I opened the door for her and we drove away. About forty minutes later we circled the condo complex and, the parking lot was completely full, there were even more vehicles than before. We headed home and said to Victoria that I had seen enough. When we reached home, Vicky asked me to drive down our street; we had walked down it the other day and said she just wanted to see it all again before we drove up our driveway. I turned around and backed inside. She said to me that was a nice little drive. And then she suggested we start cooking before we became really hungry. We went inside and had changed into our house clothes and were comfortable as I lit the grill and we soon started cooking. We had an enjoyable day together, and we enjoyed sitting on the deck. That evening while sitting on the deck eating and drinking, we talked about our childhood and life experiences before we went inside holding hands. We held each other again, then undressed and made wild passionate love again, before going to sleep.

We had a very enjoyable week end, and when it ended and I returned to work coming in later and leaving earlier. Soon the mall was completely demolished and we had a sign posted saying the site was for sale and who to contact. The elevator man came, and after looking around, said that they could install the elevator without any problems since I had chosen the perfect location and there weren't any obstructions, it could be done rather quickly. I was home when they cut holes in the floors, and being concrete they had to make sure the dust was contained, they did a fine job, and the project was completed in less than a week and on time. Next I contacted Hector and he gave me an estimate. I showed him what I wanted done, and Vicky and I chose new colors for each room. Hectors crew completed the entire house in less than a week.

The house smelled like paint and we had every window open for a couple days, he opened up the basement, laid tile on the floor as I had decided to have all the carpet removed from the basement floor. We would use large area rugs instead.

I closed on the small office complex, contacted Mr. Rodgers again for the demolition, his charges were $16,000.00 to remove and haul away everything. I asked Mr. Brown to come up with some concepts for the space available and paid him for them. Gave him some of my ideas, and put him in contact with Fitz as to what was needed or what would be feasible in the area. The court finally came to rule on the golf course, it reverted back to the heirs, with no provisions. They sold it to me and I soon closed on the property and met with the board of the golf course. We sat down and I explained that I would keep it as a golf course, the name would change to the Evermore Golf Course and Club, the club house would be completely remodeled and up graded and membership would be open to the public. The mayor of the town was very happy; and the course would see major upgrades. I commissioned Mr. Brown to design condos at the southern end where the mall had once stood, with a combination of mixed use. Before he could complete his designs and concepts, we were approached by a major store operator who didn't have any store locations in the area, and who wanted to bring in there Market and Original stores. They only wanted half of the property, but not the half I was willing to sell to them. I wanted thirty of the sixty acers bordering the golf course and one main arterial street; they weren't satisfied with my division and offered me $16,000,000.00 for the entire sixty acres of property. I accepted their offer, because my original price was $4,000,000.00, after I had demolished the old mall. The mayor was happy with both the golf course decision and my sale of the old mall property. I had thought of a new restaurant there and went back to the original thought of having it at the golf course, but then decided to just let it operate as a golf course after rehabbing the club house. Soon club membership exploded and was operating in the black and I operated that as another separate enterprise, and what a money maker it was especially after upgrades to the course and a redesign, with an improved tunnel under the large six lane east-west street. What a few improvements won't do?

Then the real estate association dinner was a real total surprise; I had the three extra places at the two tables, Hippies and Fitz decided not to bring anyone, so I offered them to Mr. Peters, he accepted and attended accompanied by his secretary which turned out to be his girlfriend, and his head assistant. I wore my black pinstripe suit, dark blue shirt, and gold tie, Victoria wore the evening dress, I loved so much, the black trimmed in silver, her stocking and hi-heels, with her pearls, and her hair in a swirl. Of course we went in the FSX99. Joanne was dressed to kill, she wore a black dress also, and the diamond set I had given her.

All my people attended and were dressed really well, like they were paid well, which they really were. The condos had almost completely sold out and Mr. Peters and I enjoyed a good working relationship. It was time for the awards, and the most number of sales for one office went to, Harcourt Real Estate, everyone applauded, and they asked that I come forward to accept the award. I was asked to say a few words. Even though I was caught completely by surprise I said that it wouldn't have happened or even have been possible without the support of my loyal staff and thanked them all for their hard work and asked them to stand because they were the one who made it all possible. I left the podium and was about to sit down when they announced the award for largest amount of sales based on the monetary amount. It went again to Harcourt Realty.

I asked Joanne to accept the award, she stood and went forward and graciously accepted the award. She was asked to say a few words. She said that we had worked long and hard, not to win any awards, but to just be the best, and just as Charles Harcourt had said, it was from having a loyal and hardworking staff and thank you as she gracefully departed the podium. We all stood and applauded as she returned to our table, as she and I hugged.

The announcer said this was the award for the best full service office. Said it was a very difficult decision, and it was almost a tie. But the deciding factors were the number of and types of loans and above all the number of highly satisfied customers which were interviewed. The best full service award goes to, Harcourt Realty, and we all stood. I asked Samantha to accept the award. She accepted the award. She was asked to say a few words, as a very teary eyed Samantha accepted the award. Samantha said she worked at the best office, for the best boss, and was surrounded by the best people she had ever worked with and thanked everyone again. She turned and returned to our table and she hugged me, then Joanne with tears in her eyes.

The president asked everyone to stand and congratulate us because no office in his ten years as association president had won all three awards, at the same time in the same year. He said it was proof of hard work and dedication to the real estate profession. The applause lasted almost five minutes, before we were able to all sit down, and begin eating. I went to the washroom before the food was served and was approached by a beautiful woman; she introduced herself as Mrs. Joan Foresight. Yes I remember speaking with you, and said Mr. Peters is at my table, she accompanied me to our table, Mr. Peters stood and shook her hand, and I introduced her to my people and the associates at the second. She said it was a real pleasure. I sat down and Vicky said she was very happy for me and my company. We sat and enjoyed the food, and after wards, everyone mingled about. I asked Joanne and Samantha to hold onto the awards and we would place them where they would be seen with our pictures. There were plenty of hugs to go around and some networking also. The dinner finally concluded and we all finally departed. On the way out Joanne said to me, Charlie, you can't hide any longer now. I said you might be right about that. She hugged Victoria and I and said she loved us both.

Hector had completed dividing the store for the Wong's expansion, and added an emergency exit door, had the wall up and the door installed, and had placed the heavy plastic sheeting and a canvas barrier as they removed the wall dividing the old space and the new, he had started before the Wong's new lease began, and removed and cleaned and painted the space before removing the plastic sheets. We signed the new lease at the restaurant on a Monday, the day they are closed, and I had Victoria with me. They fed Fitz, Victoria and me as we all sat and ate with her son and daughter and their wives and husbands. We had a very good time and Mrs. Wong hugged all of us and said they were very happy and so were we.

Back at the office we mounted the photos we had taken on a wall down stairs, the group photo on top, with Joanne and I side by side, then the one where we were flanked by Hippies and Fitz, with our titles below each, then Pat, Anne, and Samantha, with their titles, then Green and Philips, and then Brown, Newman, and Hartman. And we placed the awards on a wide narrow shelf below the pictures. When I went into the office after the awards dinner Victoria was with me, it was around nine and we were greeted by handshakes and hugs from everyone. If they were happy so was I. The audit had been completed, and we all sat in the upstairs conference room. All were in attendance, Vicky, and I along with Joanne, Hippies, Fitz, Samantha, Anne and Pat.

Joanne gave the opening presentation. Addressed all of us and listed all the members of the board of directors and the chairman on the board behind her. Also listed were all the properties, listed by the different names I had created over the years as I built my company. The number of complexes under each name, there value based on the appraisals, and then the total value of all the listed properties, she continued with the investments in treasury bills, the cash accounts, the diversifications that Hippies had instigated, investments in municipal bonds, corporate bonds and several stocks, then our operating expenses, taxes, payroll, maintenance, depreciation, of assets, and the net worth of the Harcourt Real-Estate Corporation exceeded $500,000,000.00 dollars. After Joanne had spoken, Anne took the podium, and explained our tax liability, it was close to what Joanne had told me several weeks back, we needed to donate $10,000,000.00 to arrive at a near zero tax burden for the year, and she had narrowed down the list of charities we had to decide on. As a board we all decided on just one and that would be the local hospital. Buy a unanimous vote that was passed by the board. And then she passed the podium over to me. I thanked her and Joanne as I began to announce the yearend bonuses; there was $6,000,000.00 dollars left. Each board member would receive one million dollars apiece, and the remaining five employees, Pat, Anne, Samantha, Green and Phillips would divide the last remaining $1,000,000.00 dollars, after the three current associates received $50,000.00 each from it. This was also passed by unanimous vote. And then the meeting was officially adjourned and that concluded the first official for the record of Harcourt Realty Corporation. Everyone shook hands and hugged. We started out our new physical year on a really very upbeat note.

The condo complex almost sold completely out, and when Mr. Peters contract ended, we only had six unsold units left from the original 192, that was a tremendous amount of sales and the number of loans Samantha and Anne originated added a little over a $4,500,000.00 to our bottom line. They deserved the bonus they had received. The unsold units were to be handled by Hartman, since she lived closest to them, and they sold in less than a month and all the renters ended up being buyers.

Our home had been completely painted, the driveway recoated coated and some landscape improvements made, and the above ground pool installed next to the deck, the basement had a custom bar large enough to be in a pub, and I added another pool table and we brought down the old furniture that had been displaced from upstairs, improved the basement washroom, by having it made into two, and one with a shower next to the sauna. Vicky and I had purchased all new furniture for the living room and the old went downstairs and filled the large space. We added a new and complete living room set in our very large bed room with the addition of a large wall mounted flat screen television; and made the room more comfortable than ever before.

I was sitting one evening in my office with my feet up on the desk thinking about the past several months, now after Victoria came downstairs with the black dress on with the spaghetti straps, collar, stockings and stiletto hi-heels, and had the leash in her hand. She handed me the leash and ran her hands thru my hair, she had on perfume as I sat up and she then sat in my lap. She said Master Charlie, I've been really bad, I asked her what she had done, and she said that she had felt on herself and had played with her pussy and it was aching and she needed to be punished for being disobedient. I said well you know what's going to happen now, don't you. Yes sir master, she replied. I hooked the leash to her collar and led her up to our new play room. We entered into the room; it had been painted a dark blue. Vicky had chosen the color and it included the closet. And she had found this large wooden chair, like something from the middle ages a king would sit in. When we had seen it in the store, Victoria was elated and said we should purchase it. Said she could imagine her master sitting in it and watching his slave as she agonized while he decided what he was going to do to her stinking slut ass.

And so we purchased it which made her very happy. I opened the door and we entered, told her to stand, with her hands behind her back, as I sat in the large oversized chair and thought how I was going to make this a more titillating experience for her. I said to her you have been really bad, I stood and opened the cabinet; all our equipment or toys were located now inside of it. I took out the leather wrist cuffs and told her hold her hands out in front of her as I fastened them on to her wrist, she smiled at me, and I said is there anything funny slave. She said no sir master, so get that smirk off you face then, as she began looking more serious. I finished securing the cuffs to her wrist. The metal chains were hanging from the hooks in the ceiling as I returned to the cabinet for the clamps to secure her wrist to the chains. I told her to first remove her dress; she complied after placing it on the couch. I attached each wrist to a chain link, and as high up as was permissible, then I kissed her. I said it pains me to have to punish you, but since the slut in you is oozing out again, you leave me no choice, do you understand me slave, yes sir master she replied.

I kissed her and then licked her face and her ear sending shivers through her, she was facing the chair and the mirrored closet doors were behind her so I had an excellent view of her entire body, front and back. I let the anticipation rise in her as I returned to the cabinet and removed the spreader bar and attached it to her ankles, they were almost as far apart as her wrists. And with her hi-heels on gave her legs real definition. I stood in front of her and asked her what she had to say for herself. She said master I am sorry for being a nasty slut. I felt between her legs, she was soaking wet, and she shuttered at my light touch. I asked what are you now, said she was a dirty and nasty bitch, and wanted me to fuck her. I said you will take what I give you and when I decide, understand. Yes sir master was her reply. She looked so sexy, spread out and hanging there, it was hard not to just jerk off just looking at her, her ample breast with her hard nipples standing up. I was determined to make this last as long as possible as I took out the nipple clamps, walked over to Vicky and looked her in the face, it was filled with anticipation, as I applied them to her erect nipples, and pulled the small chain that ran between them, she squirmed, and was about ready to climax. She was a touch away when I asked her, you want to come don't you bitch. Yes sir master she replied, and begged for me to touch her.

I went to the cabinet and removed the riding crop, stood before her and slowly felt her body all over with it, rubbing the back of her thighs, between her legs, breast, and arms and back before I lightly touch her clit, causing her to scream as she was rocked with a massive climax. She was panting and was starting now to perspire, her skin started to glisten wet with sweat, I sat down and just looked at her, and she begged me to touch her. I waited a few very long minutes before I went and stood in front of her and pulled the chain attached to the nipple clamps, she winched as I tugged on them before they slipped off her now very moist body. I grabbed her hair from behind and kissed her lips, told her I loved her and that was why she was being punished. I returned to the cabinet and brought out the whip, and returned and began to use it lightly on her, before whipping her harder as she entered the zone where her total submissiveness came out to its fullest. I whipped her, not hard or to soft, but so she could feel it, enjoying every stroke as the whip made contact with her soft smooth skin before I then asked her what she had you to say for herself. She said thank you master. I then used it on her inner thighs as she erupted in another massive climax. I stopped, came closer and rubbed her body all over as she desperately tried to reach for me, as she begged for me to take and use her. I kissed her long and hard as she kissed me like never before as I felt her moist sweat drenched body. I knelt down before her and felt her vagina, playing with her pussy lips pulling them, as she shook. Taking her protruding clit and licking it before sucking it in my mouth and using my tongue on it as she shook with more multiple orgasms as I fingered her and pussy juice ran down her thighs before I stood before her as I rubbed the palm of my hand against her hot quivering pussy to make her climax again even more. I asked her who do you belong to bitch, and in a halting voice, she said you Master Charlie. I went to the cabinet and hung the whip up and removed the paddle and went and sat in the chair and just looked at her. I looked at her for several minutes before getting in her face, and asked her what do you want slave. She wanted her master to fuck her as I took the paddle and smacked each ass cheek several times. I removed the spreader bar, attached the leash before I released her wrist, and told her to get down on her hands and knees.

Took the leash and led her around the large room, while I smacked her ass with the paddle stopping before the chair. I sat down and pulled out my very hard and moist with excitement dick. I said, slut do you want this, she replied yes please master, I pulled her forward using the leash, and told her to please her master, she went down on me and I disappeared inside her mouth, as I felt her tongue performing her oral magic on me. I soon came and she sucked every drop, and then she wiped her face with me holding it in her soft hands. It took several minutes as she licked me until I was hard again and I led her over to the day bed, as she knelt, bent over it, with her ass up and out as I entered her from the rear and she moaned and climaxed again and again, before I came again also. I then sat next to her exhausted, moving to sit at her side, sitting on the floor next to her, as she placed her head on my shoulder. We sat there until we both recovered our breath, then she laid with her back on my lap looking up at me, said she had never been so satisfied until now and place her arms around my neck. We kissed and felt each other again, she said thank you Charlie, I love you forever. We eventually got up putting everything away and went to our bed room to shower. That was the first time we used our completed play room. We were both very satisfied.

We were very happy with each other and we never looked back, and we went everywhere together. Since Victoria was now a board member she came to the office more often than ever before. We were never there long when she did accompany me. She soon developed more friendships with our neighbor's wives and became a little more outgoing. We were very happy and loved each other more with each passing day. We entertained, and had our neighbors over for get-togethers and I even made some deals. Mr. Woo ended up renting my old office space for one of his cleaning locations and I also upgraded the strip mall where it was located.

Forty-five
One Year Later.

I didn't feel we were rich, because we always considered where we had come from and we loved each other more with each passing day. We didn't use the play room very often, maybe five times since we redid the house. Victoria and I went to Hawaii for two weeks on our delayed honeymoon, and Canada on a shorter trip where we drove. I went to my office maybe three or four days a week. Joanne had started taking a more relaxed approach to work also, we used the phone more. Fitz liked coming everyday but had shortened his hours and so had Hippies. Pat, Anne and Samantha really ran the office and handled things. After the bonuses were handed out everyone was more than happy. Mary Newman went for the broker's exam and passed and I made her and employee. Green and Phillips worked with her and they all rotated, and they had more time to make deals. We hired four more associates after Ms. Brown became Mrs. Green, then became pregnant and said she was sad to leave, but had always wanted to have children. They made me cry when they named there baby boy Charles. Her brother actually designed my first office building built from the ground up where the old office complex had stood. Instead of twelve stories, it ended up being eighteen with ample parking, and was a state of the art affair and ended up winning several design awards. Victoria and I even had a couple of parties for most of our closet neighbors. I am glad I have been able to tell you my story, of having found the love of my life; I am fully satisfied with life more now than ever before. And truly hope everyone finds a satisfying relationship filled with a lifetimes of love. I know I am.

Sincerely: Charles Harcourt